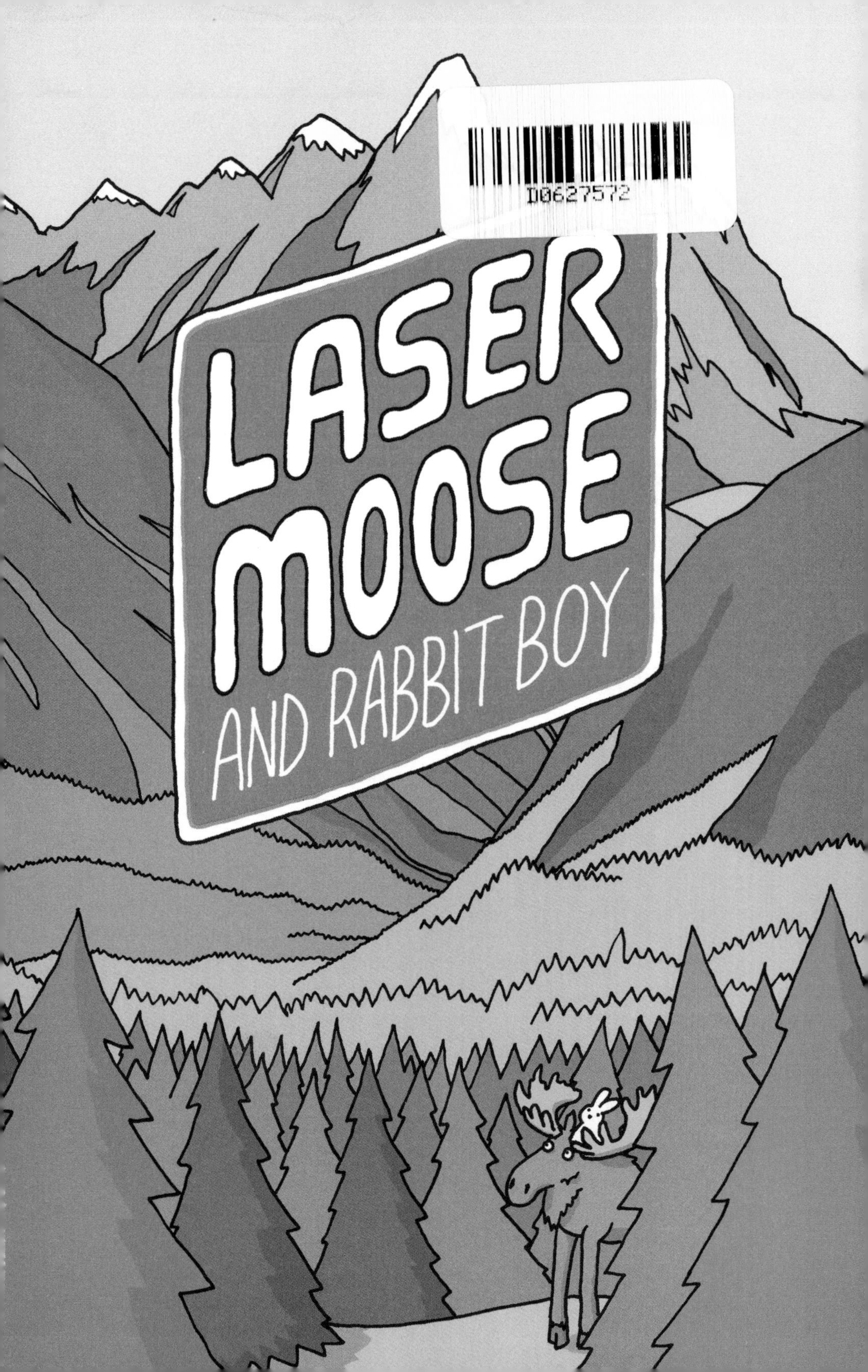
LASER
MOOSE
AND RABBIT BOY

LASER MOOSE AND RABBIT BOY

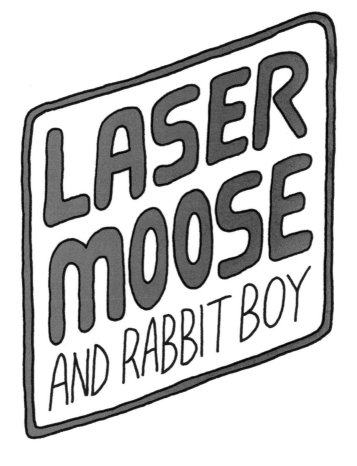

DOUG SAVAGE

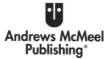

Andrews McMeel Publishing®
a division of Andrews McMeel Universal

for Georgeanna

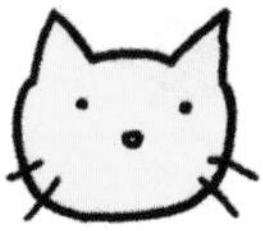

thank you for
believing in me

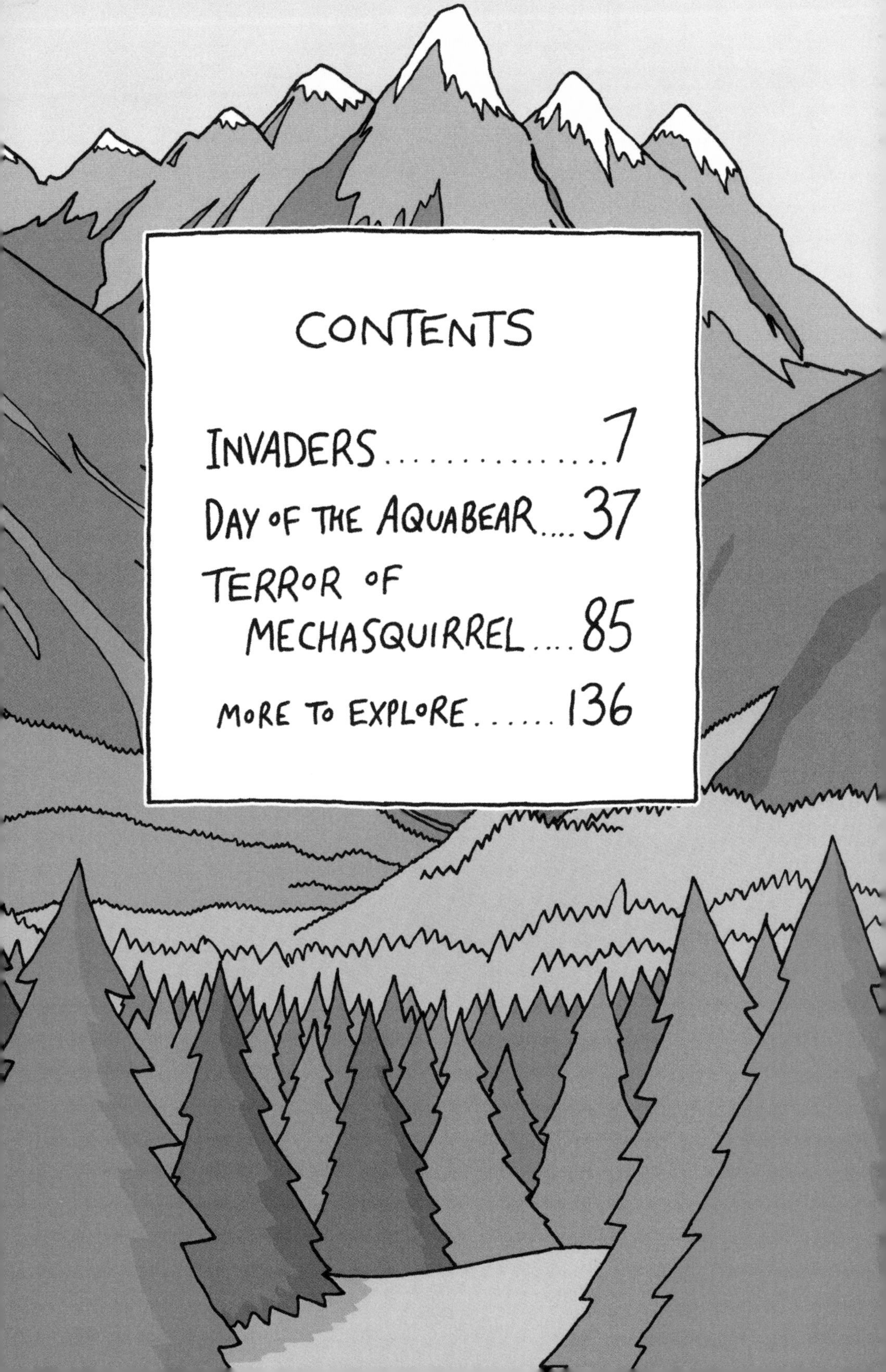

CONTENTS

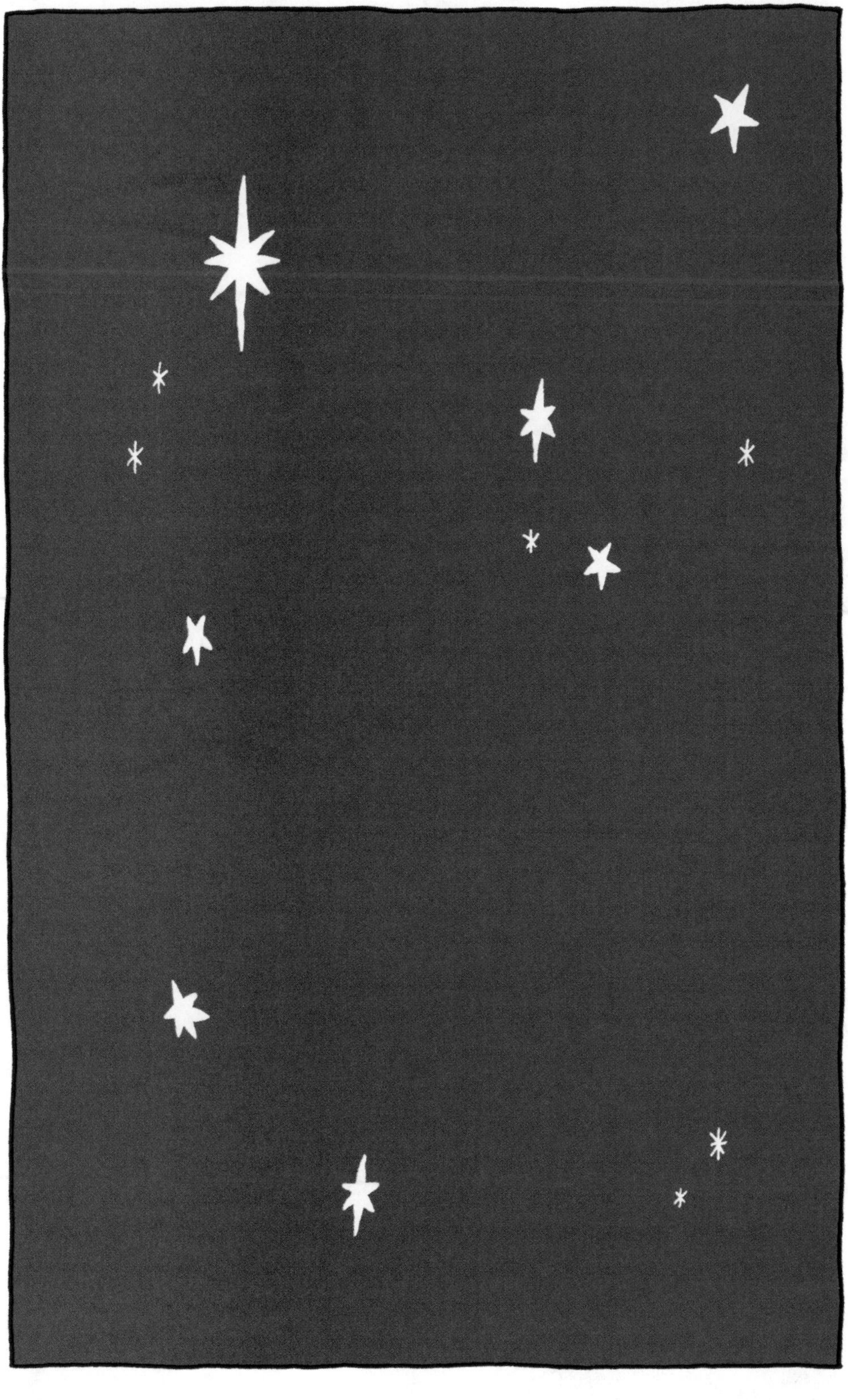

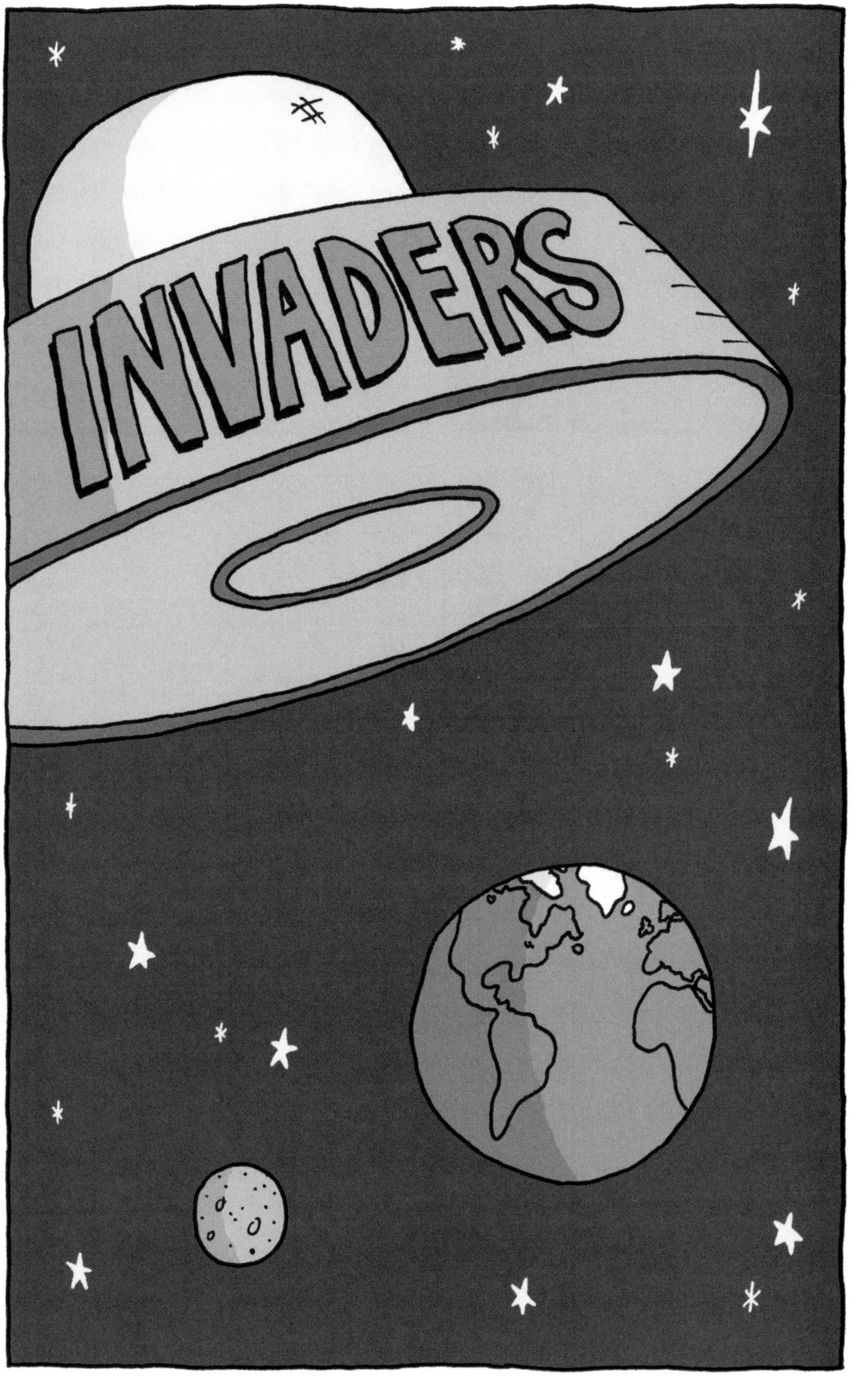
INVADERS

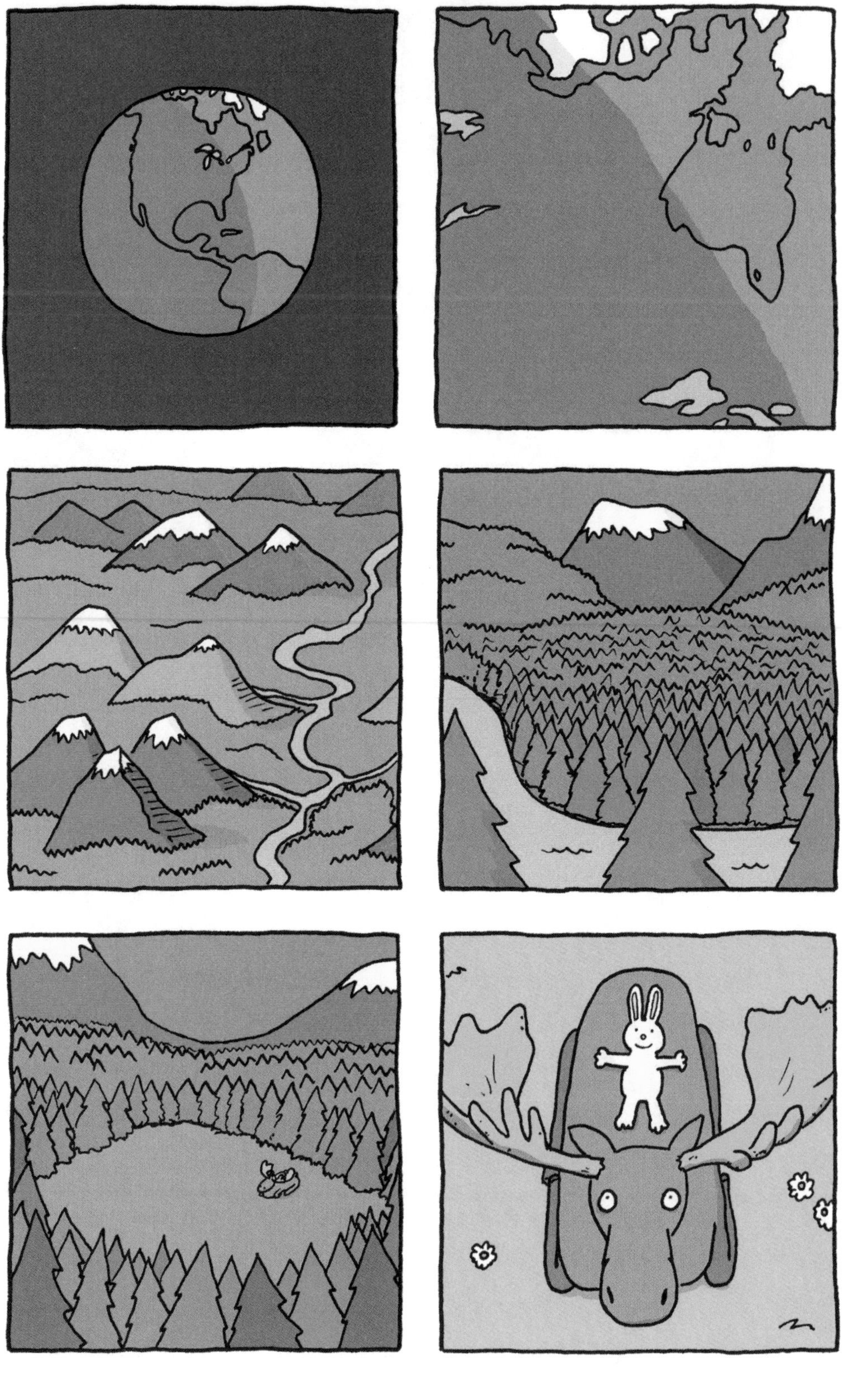

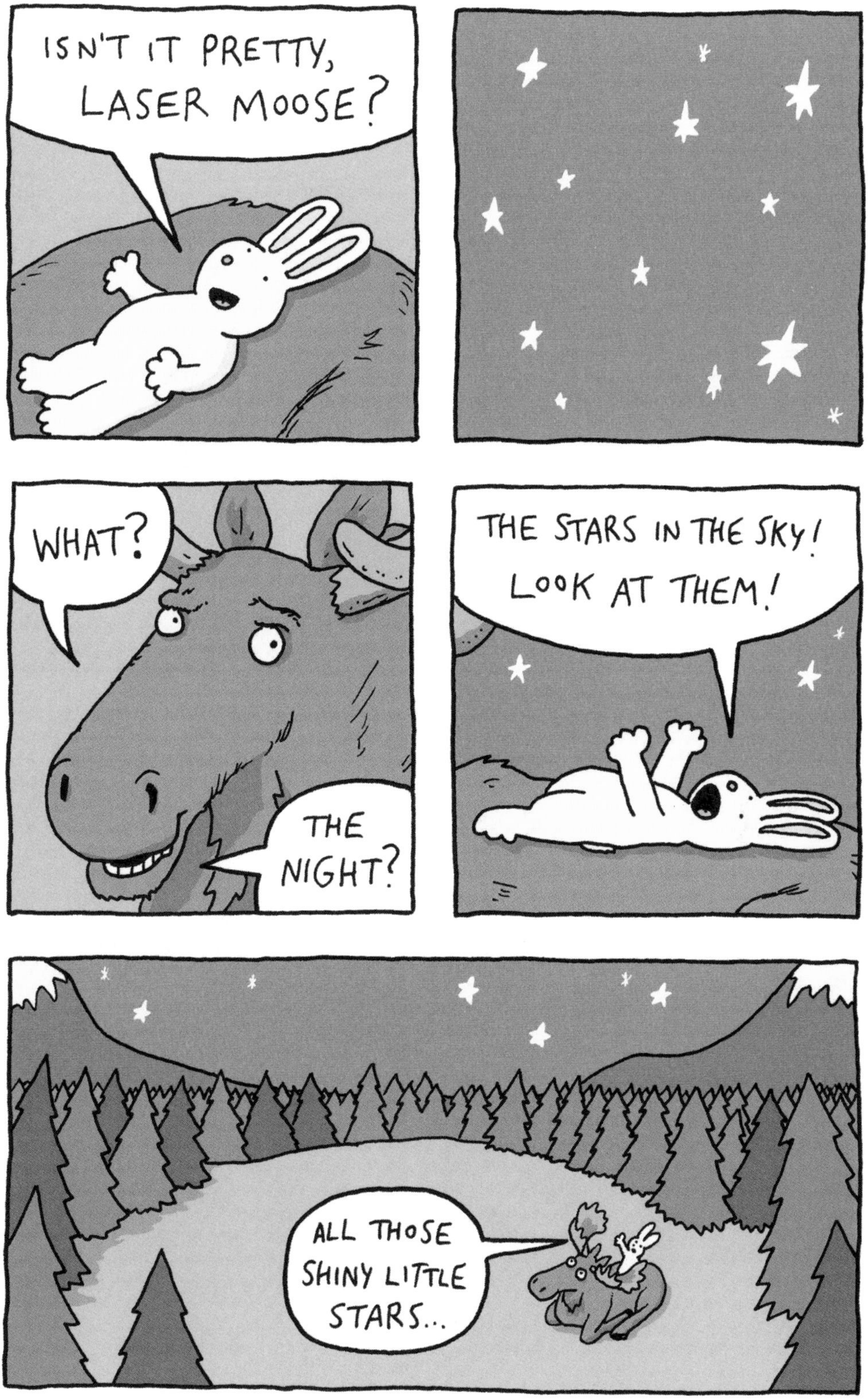
ISN'T IT PRETTY, LASER MOOSE?
WHAT?
THE NIGHT?
THE STARS IN THE SKY! LOOK AT THEM!
ALL THOSE SHINY LITTLE STARS...

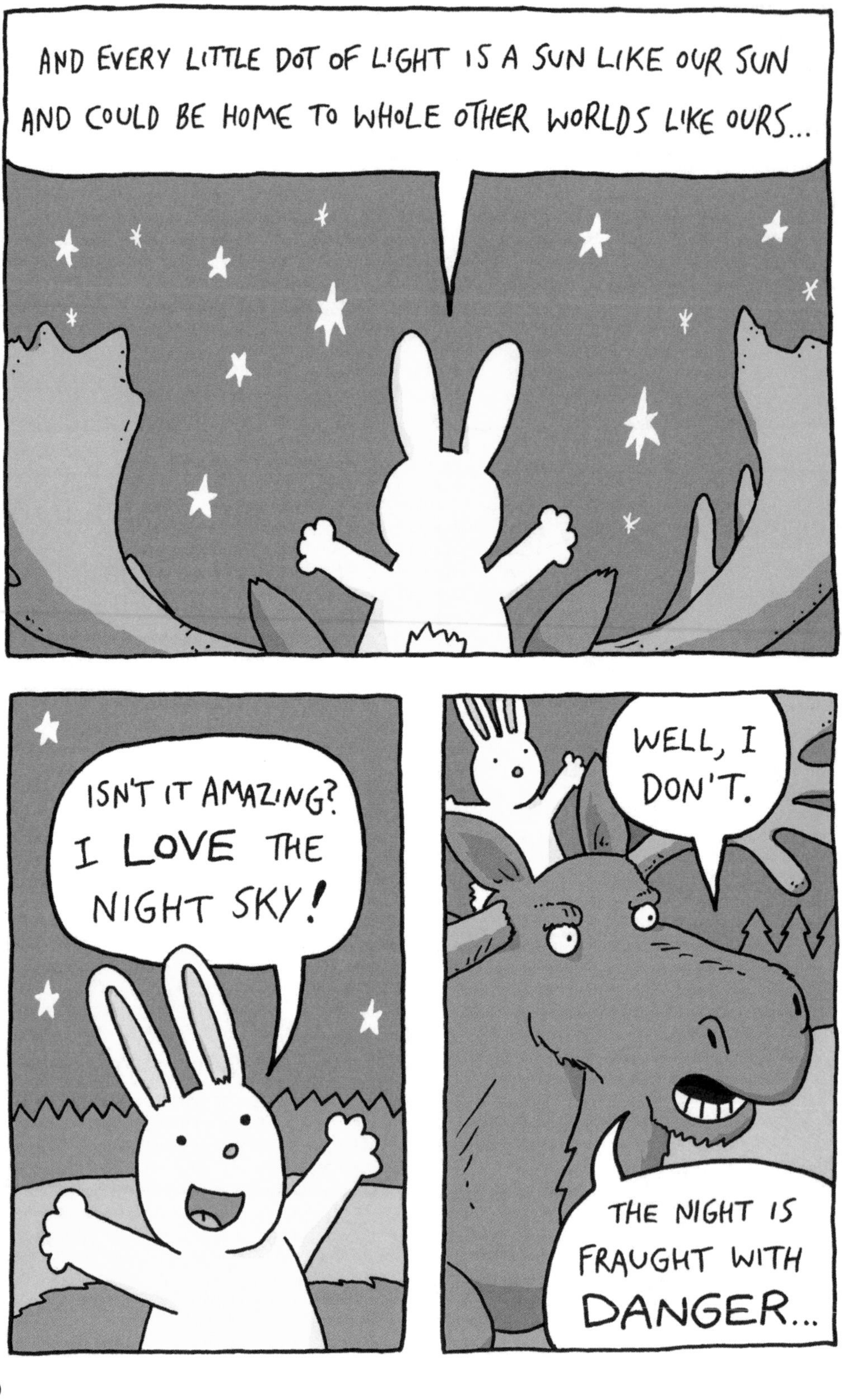

AND EVERY LITTLE DOT OF LIGHT IS A SUN LIKE OUR SUN AND COULD BE HOME TO WHOLE OTHER WORLDS LIKE OURS...
ISN'T IT AMAZING? I LOVE THE NIGHT SKY!
WELL, I DON'T.
THE NIGHT IS FRAUGHT WITH DANGER...

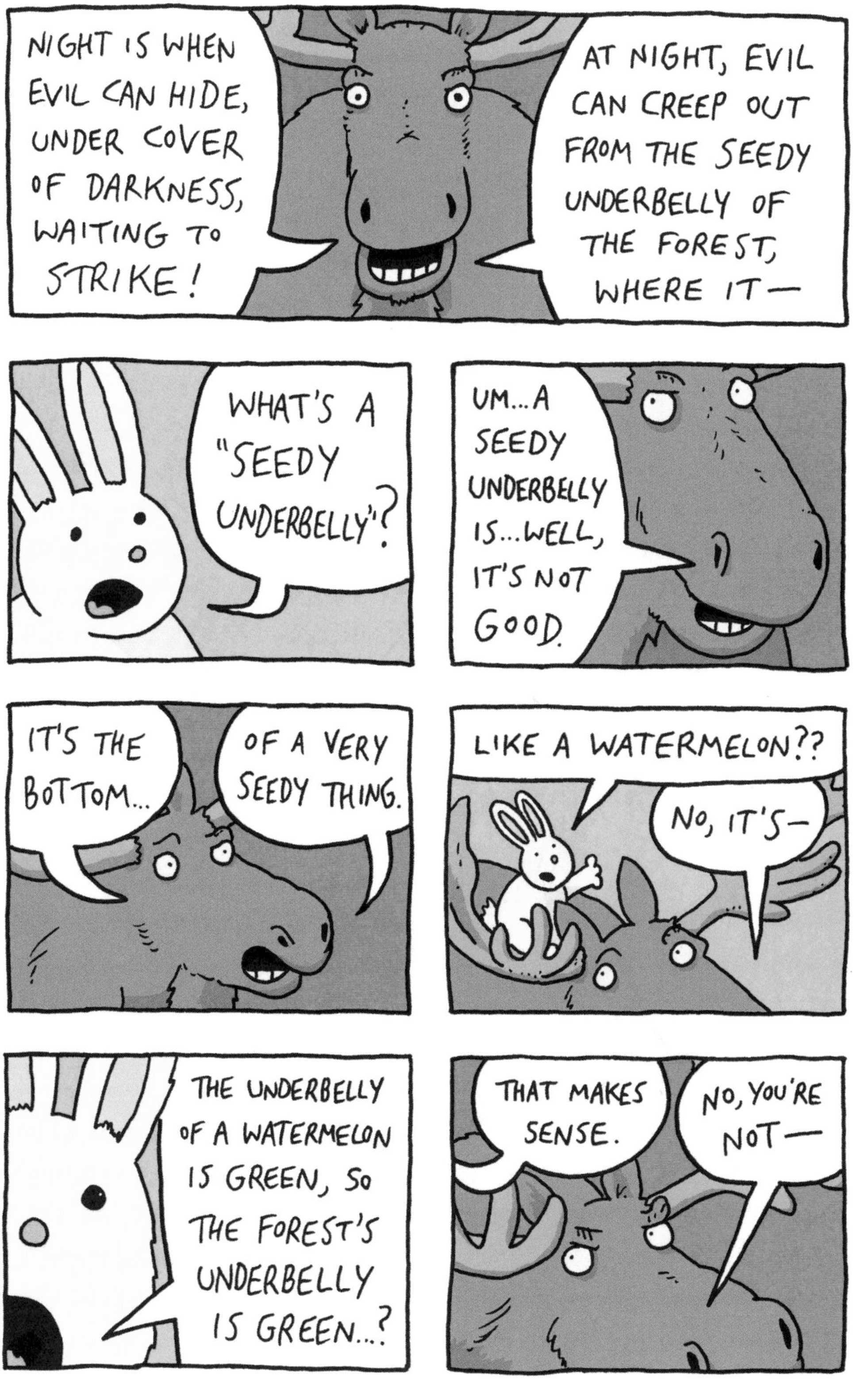
NIGHT IS WHEN EVIL CAN HIDE, UNDER COVER OF DARKNESS, WAITING TO STRIKE!
AT NIGHT, EVIL CAN CREEP OUT FROM THE SEEDY UNDERBELLY OF THE FOREST, WHERE IT—
WHAT'S A "SEEDY UNDERBELLY"?
UM...A SEEDY UNDERBELLY IS...WELL, IT'S NOT GOOD.
IT'S THE BOTTOM...
OF A VERY SEEDY THING.
LIKE A WATERMELON??
NO, IT'S—
THE UNDERBELLY OF A WATERMELON IS GREEN, SO THE FOREST'S UNDERBELLY IS GREEN...?
THAT MAKES SENSE.
NO, YOU'RE NOT—

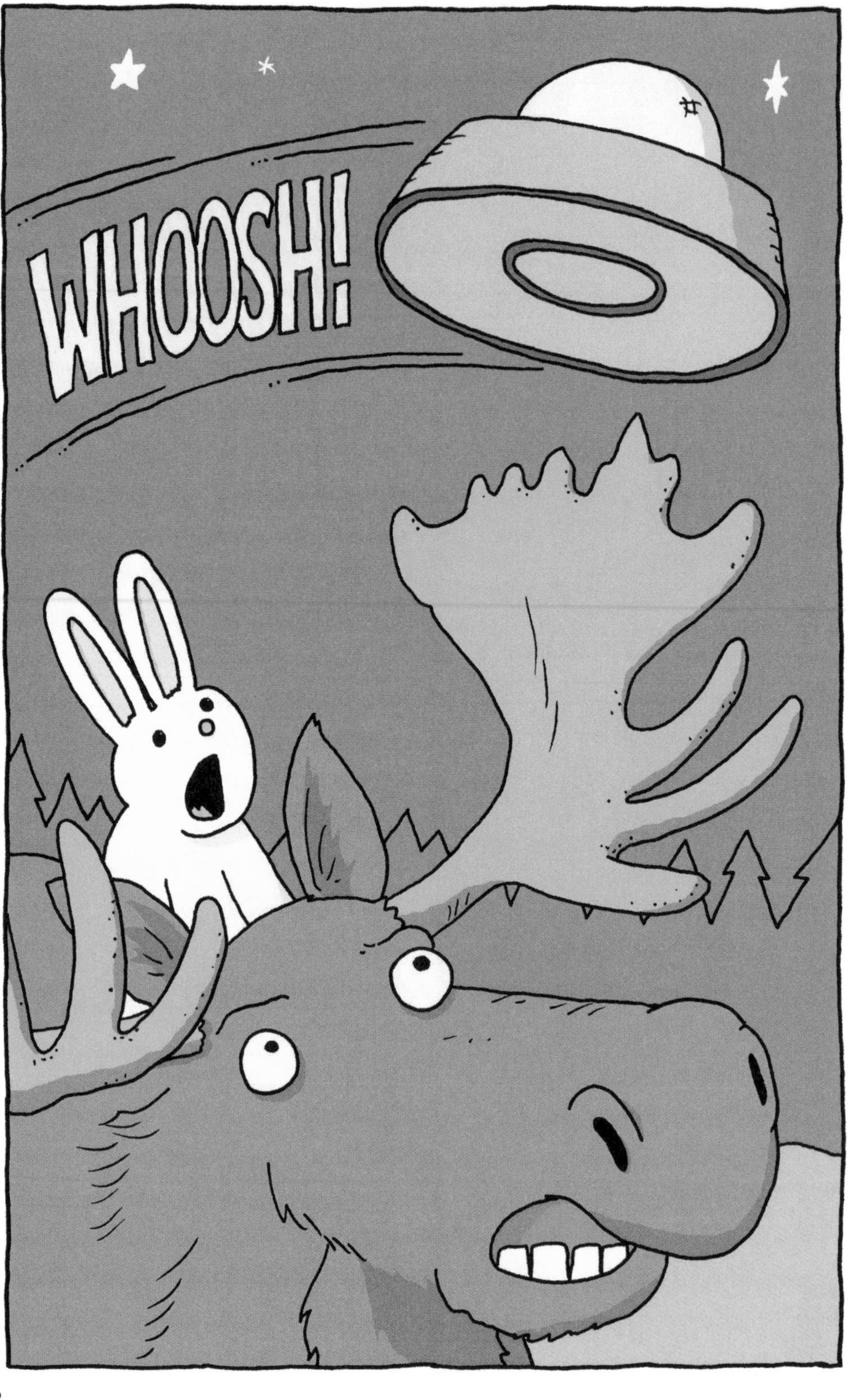
WHOOSH!

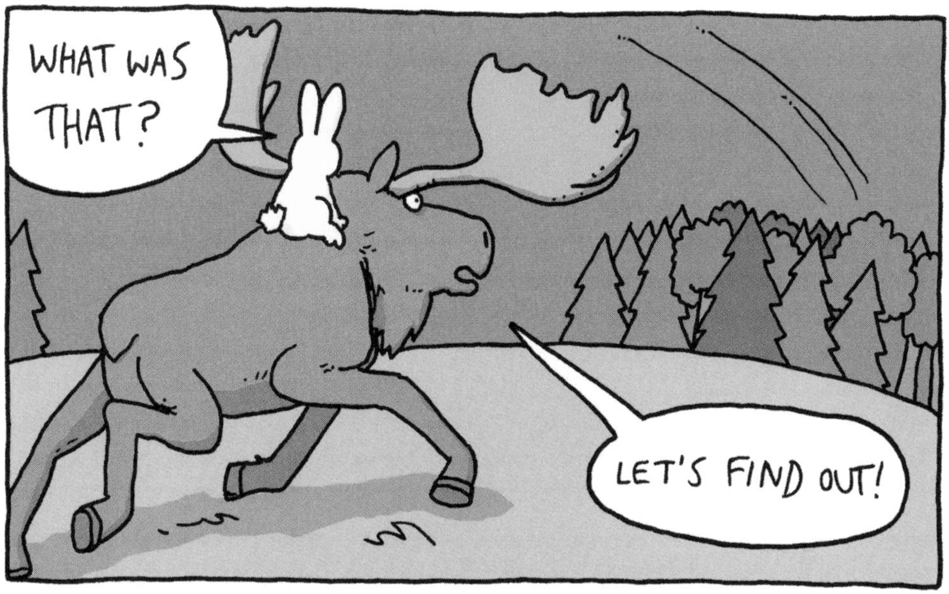
WHAT WAS THAT?
LET'S FIND OUT!

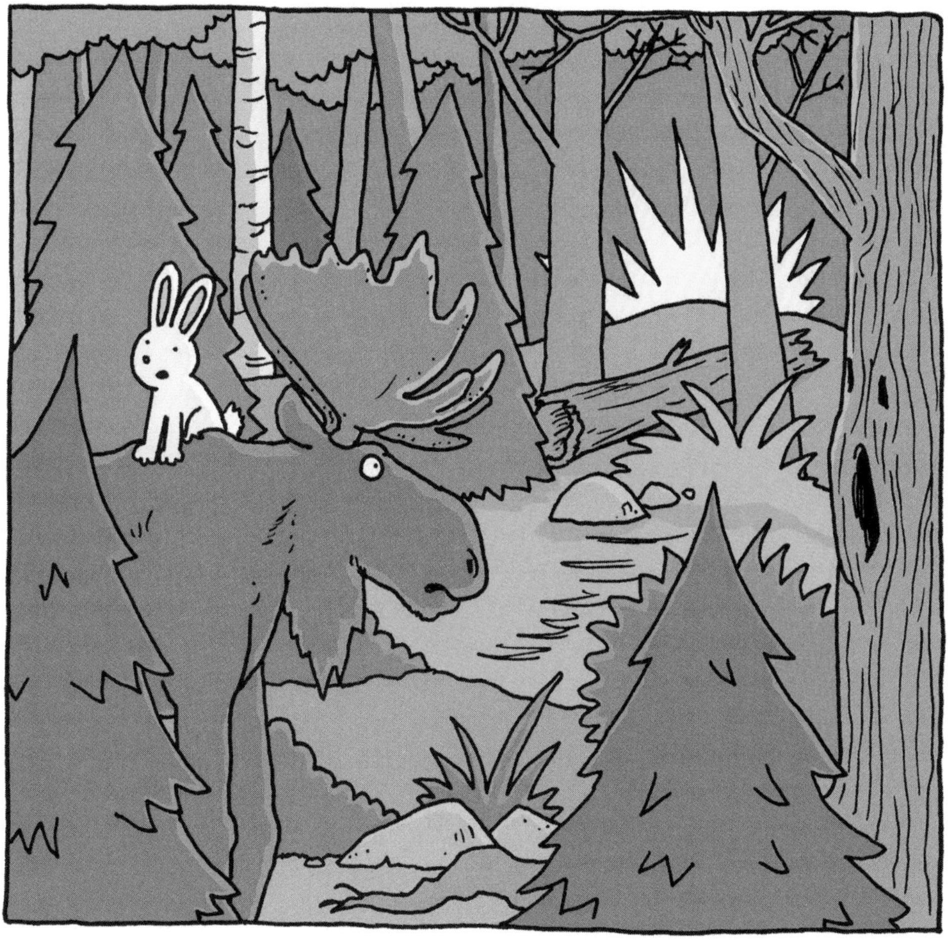

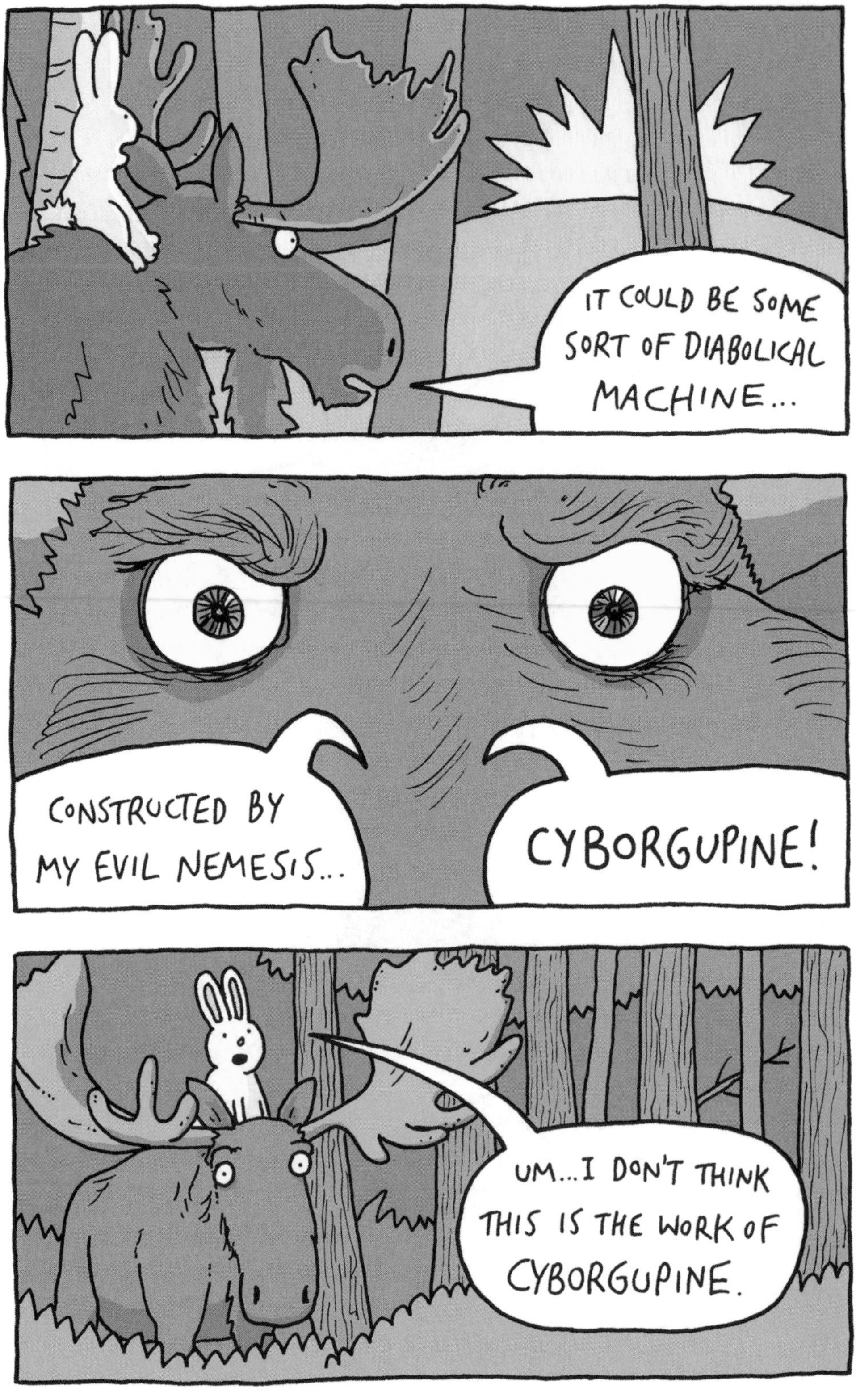
IT COULD BE SOME SORT OF DIABOLICAL MACHINE...
CONSTRUCTED BY MY EVIL NEMESIS...
CYBORGUPINE!
UM...I DON'T THINK THIS IS THE WORK OF CYBORGUPINE.

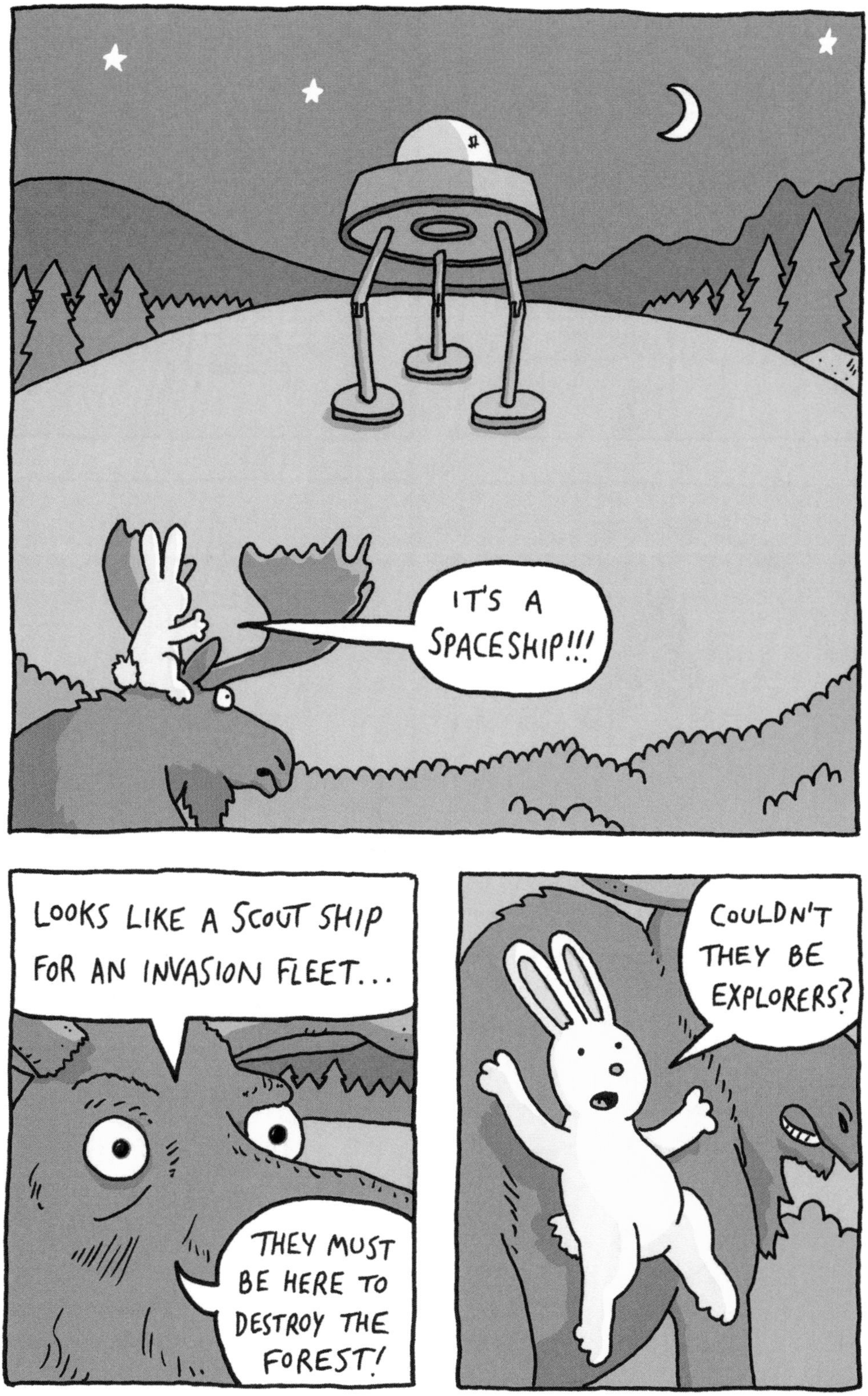
IT'S A SPACESHIP!!!
LOOKS LIKE A SCOUT SHIP FOR AN INVASION FLEET...
THEY MUST BE HERE TO DESTROY THE FOREST!
COULDN'T THEY BE EXPLORERS?

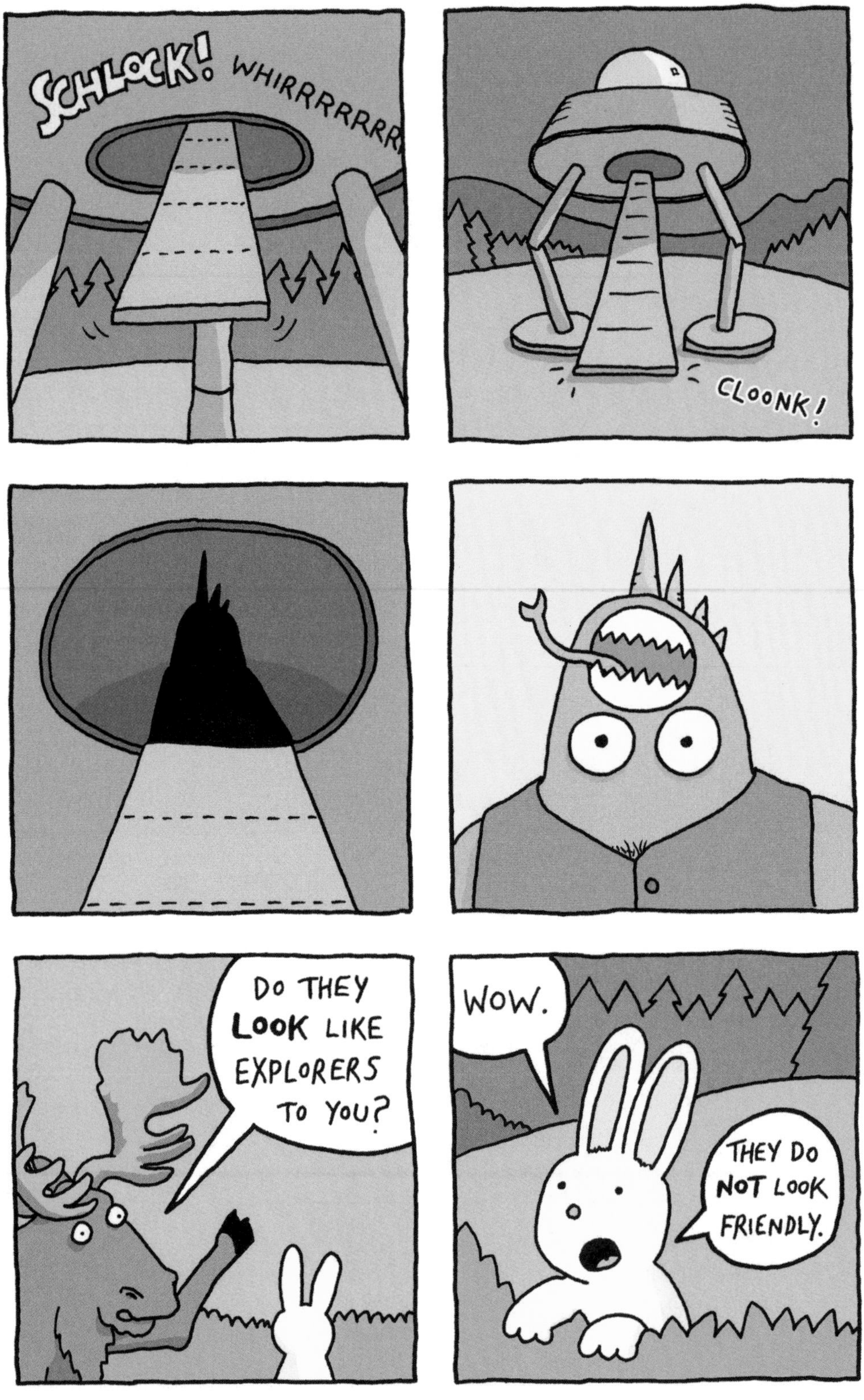
SCHLOCK!
WHIRRRRRRRR
CLOONK!
DO THEY **LOOK** LIKE EXPLORERS TO YOU?
WOW.
THEY DO **NOT** LOOK FRIENDLY.

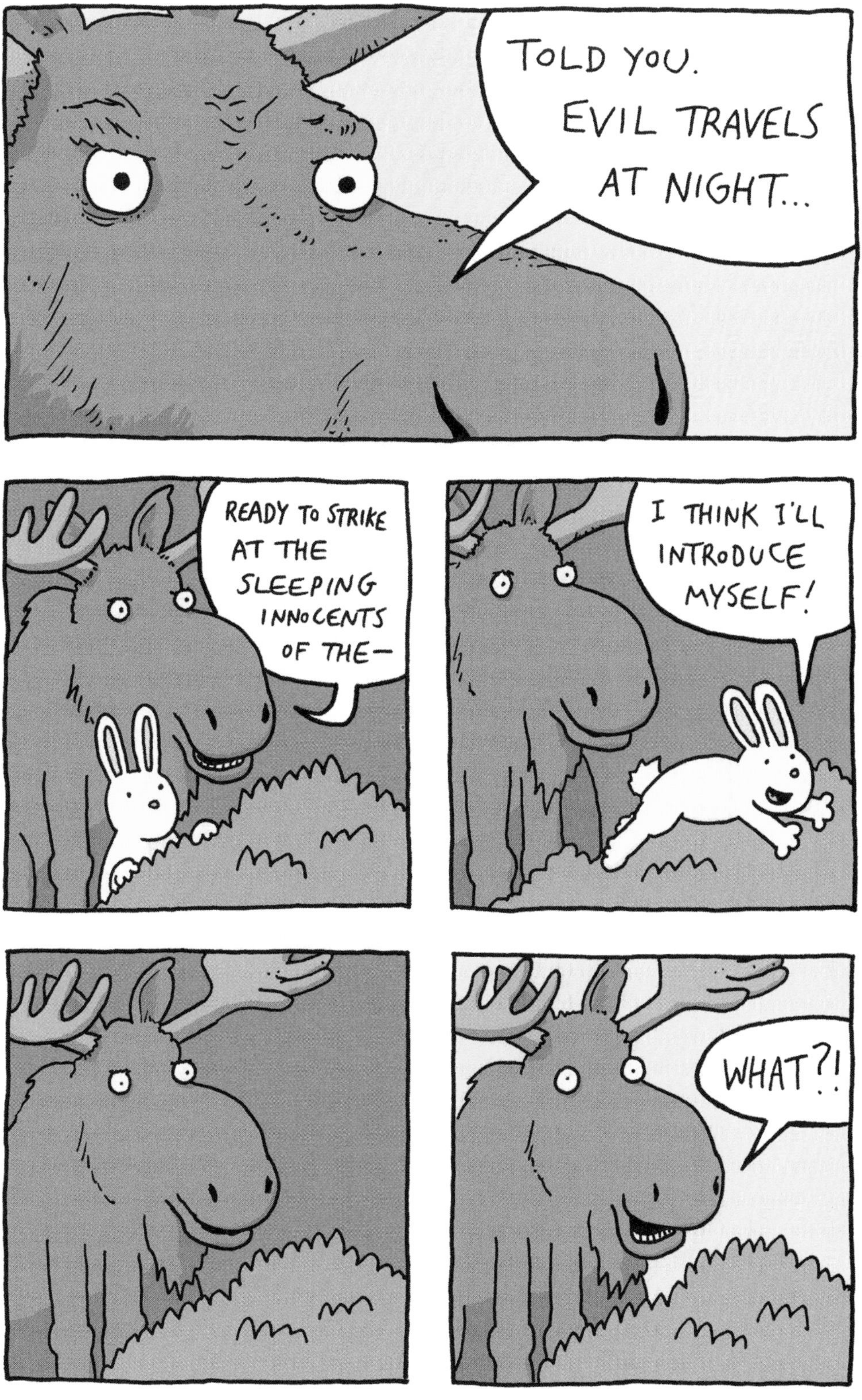
TOLD YOU. EVIL TRAVELS AT NIGHT...
READY TO STRIKE AT THE SLEEPING INNOCENTS OF THE—
I THINK I'LL INTRODUCE MYSELF!
WHAT?!

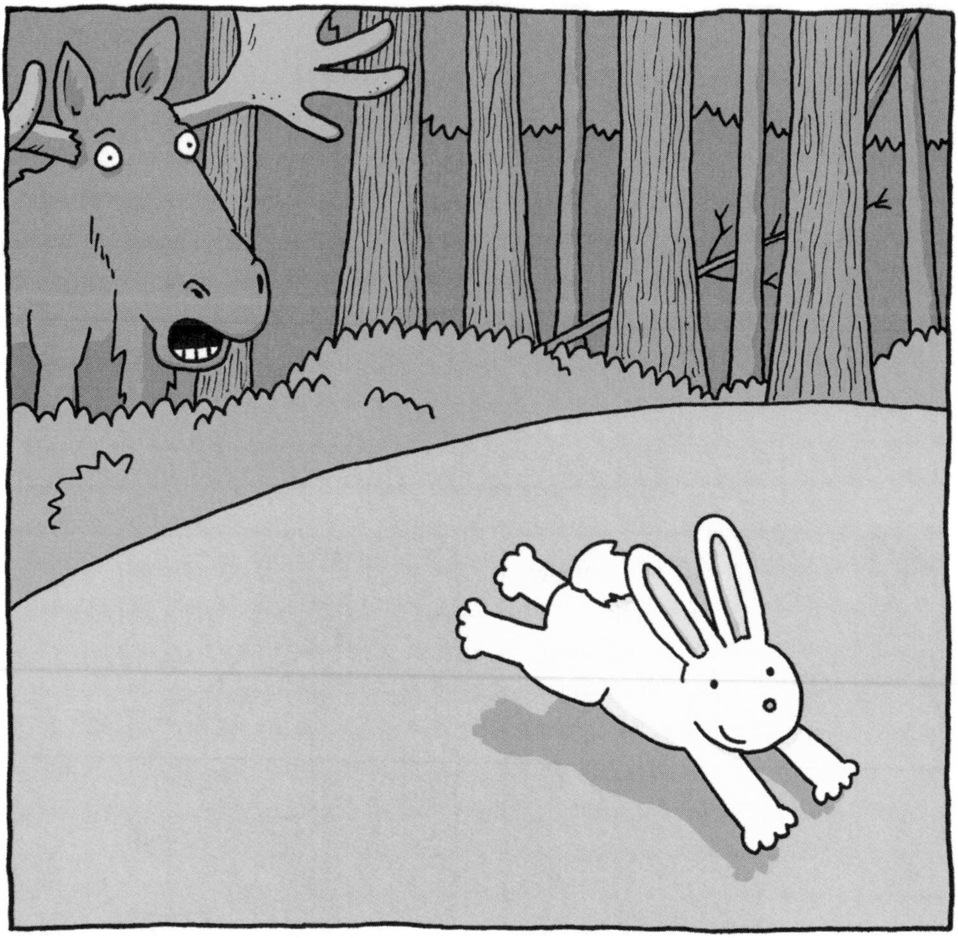

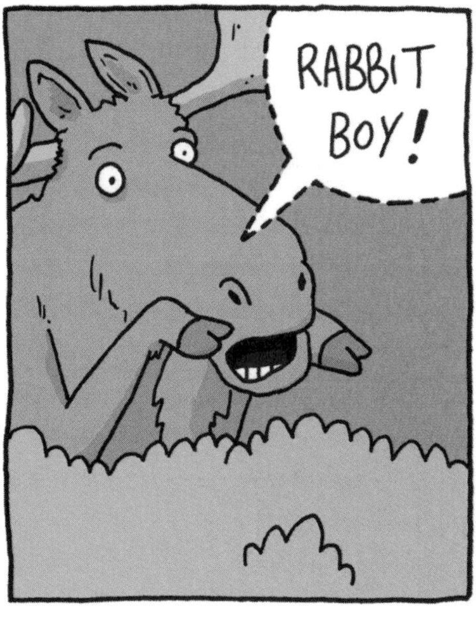
RABBIT BOY!

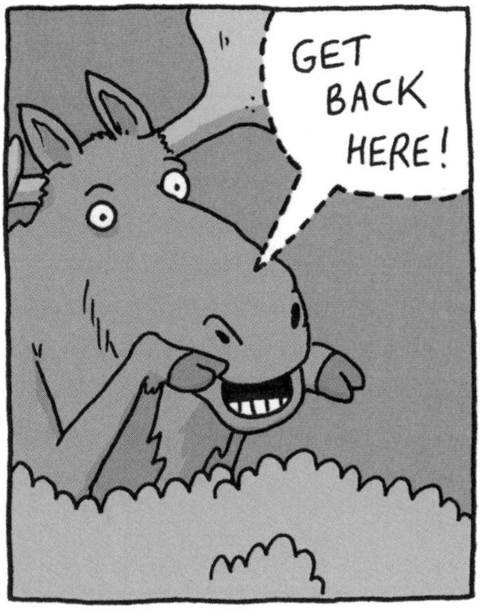
GET BACK HERE!

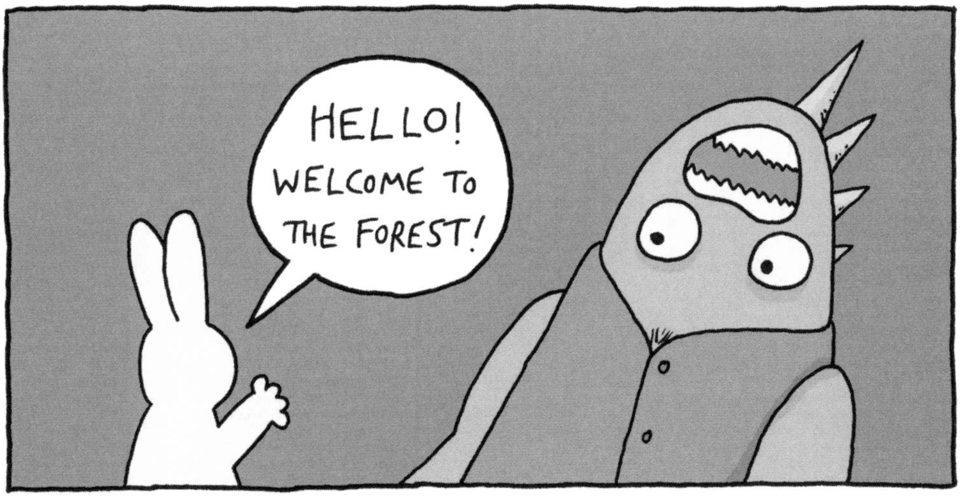
HELLO! WELCOME TO THE FOREST!

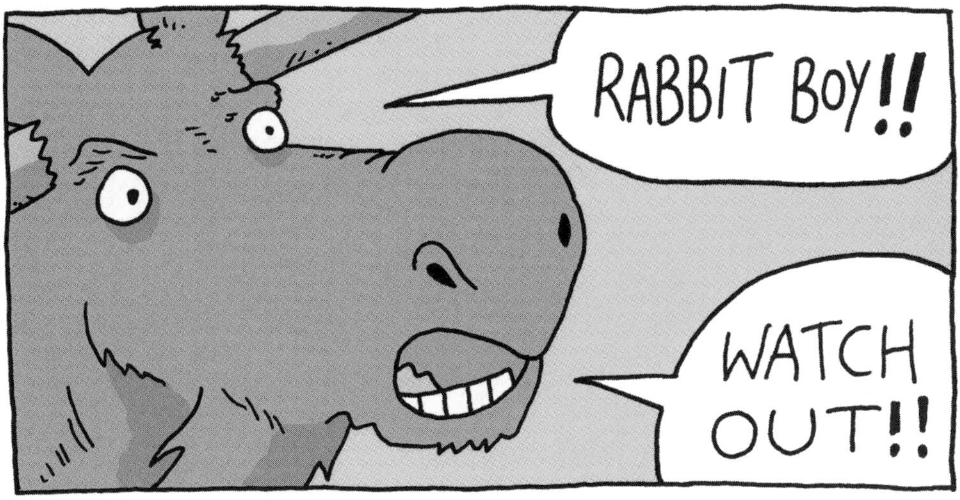
RABBIT BOY!!
WATCH OUT!!

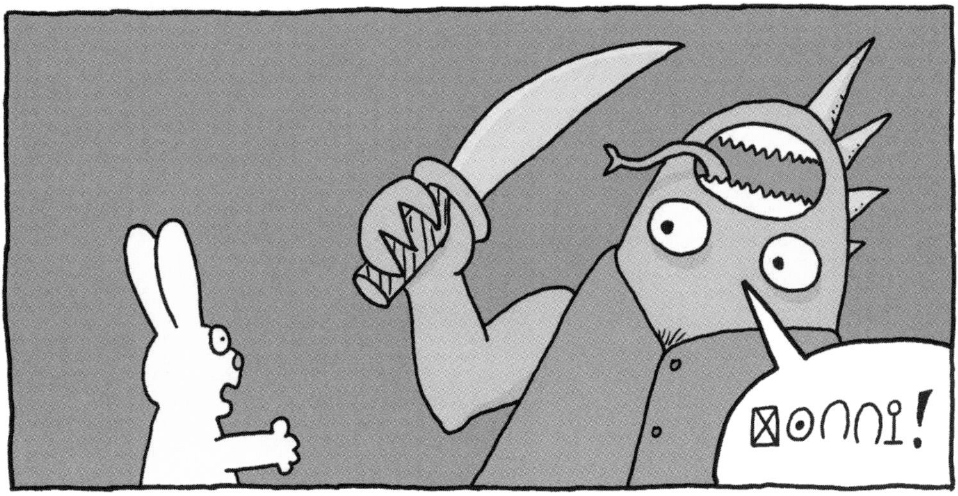

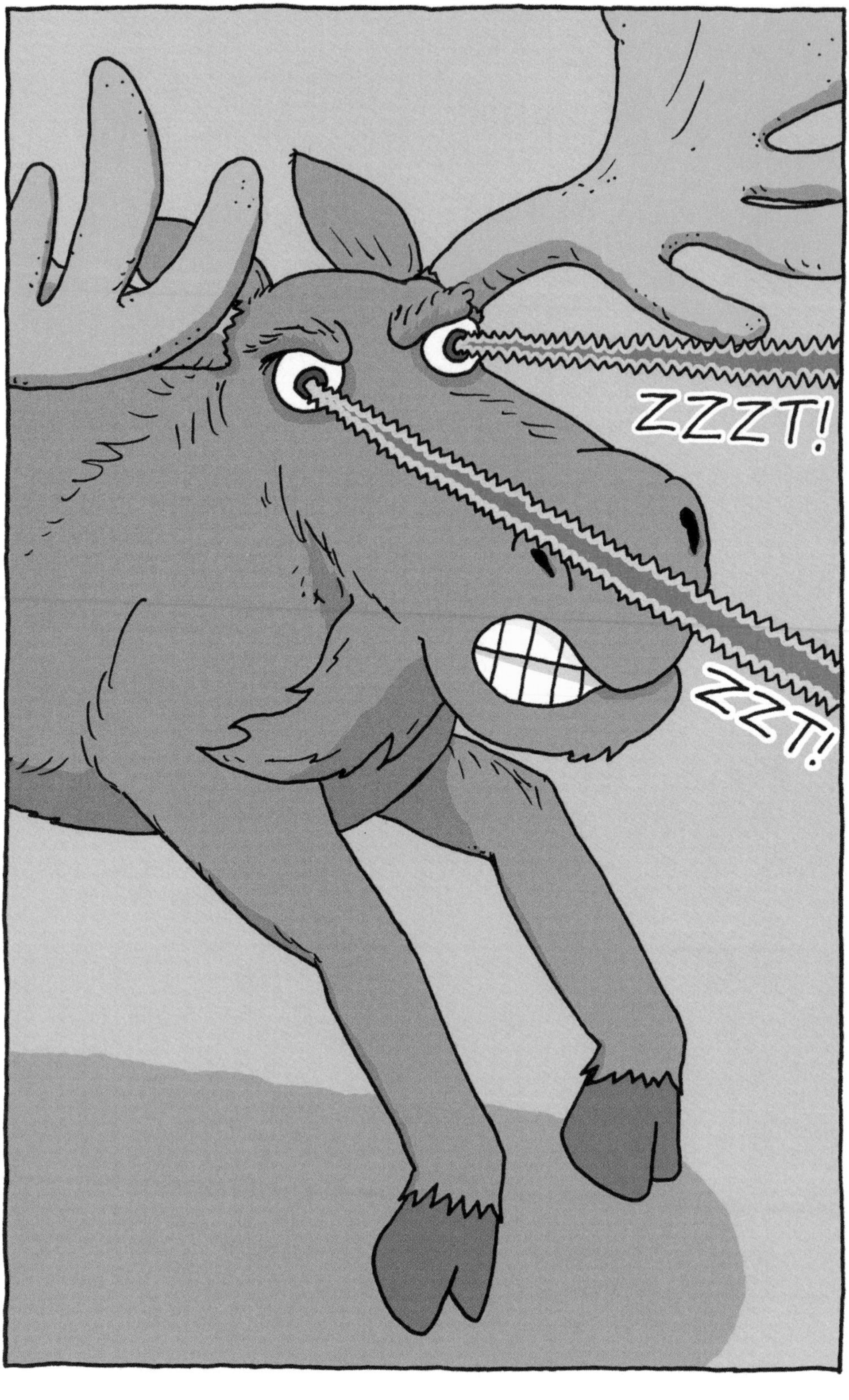
ZZZT!
ZZT!

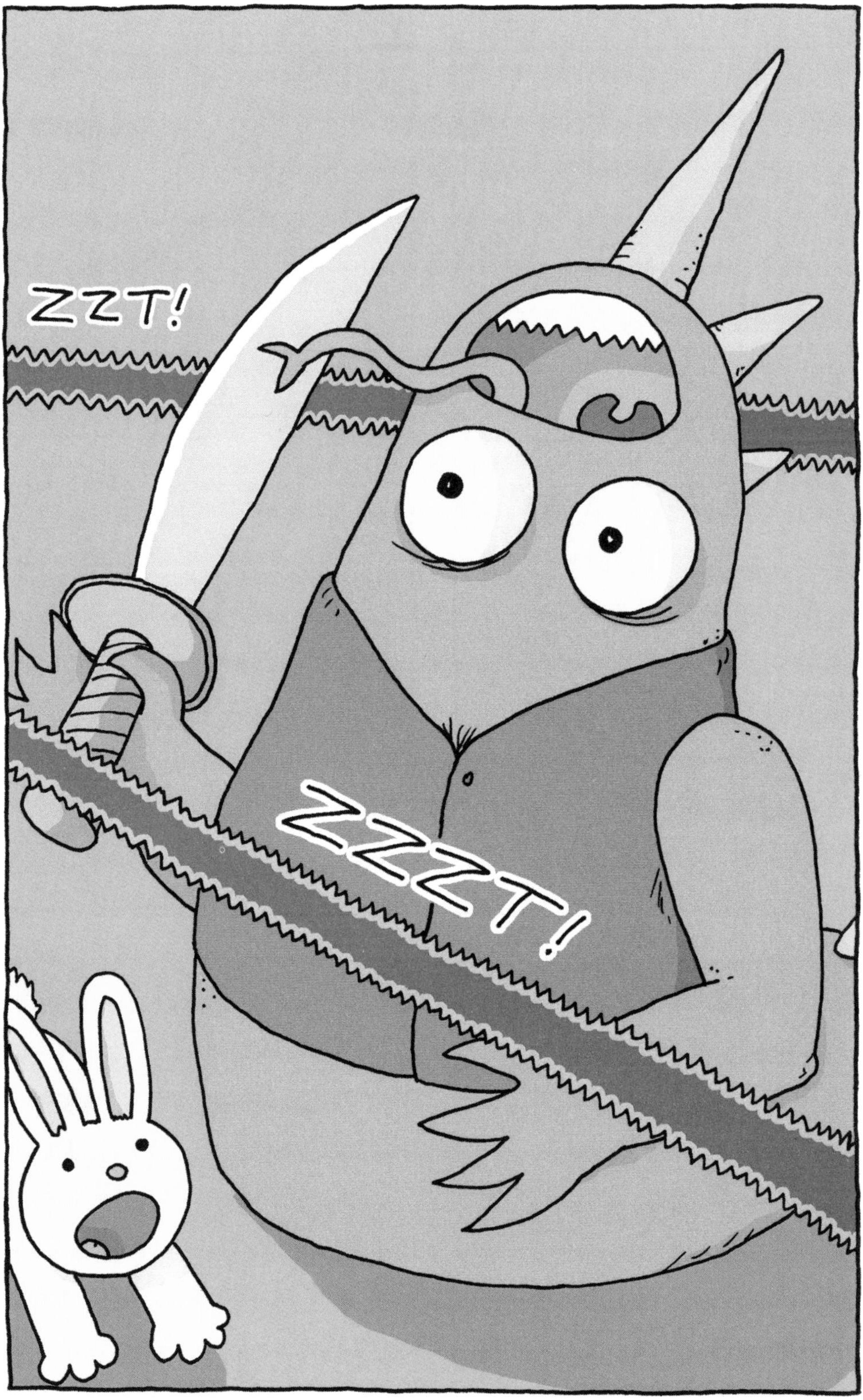
ZZT!
ZZZZT!

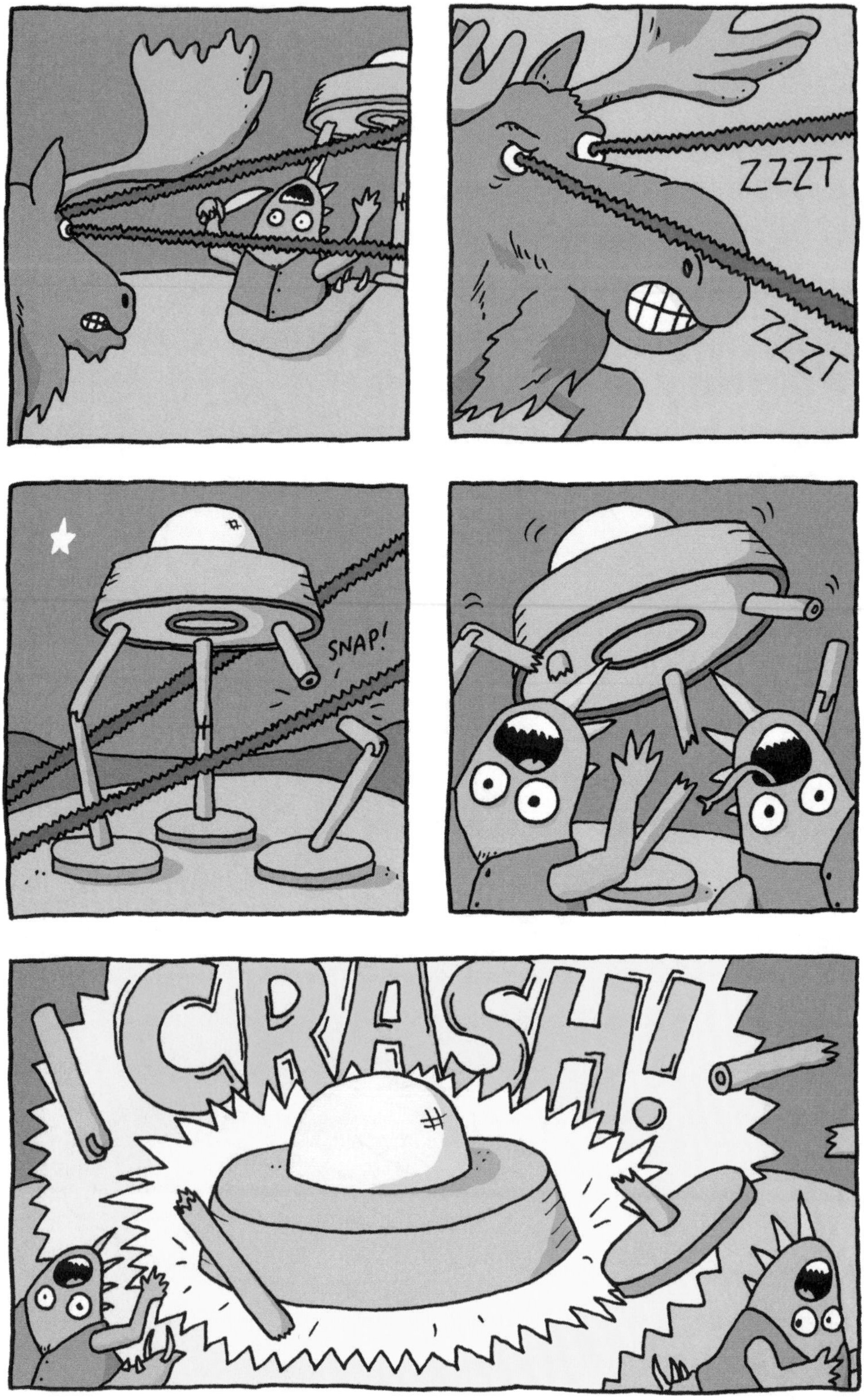
ZZZT
ZZZT
SNAP!
CRASH!

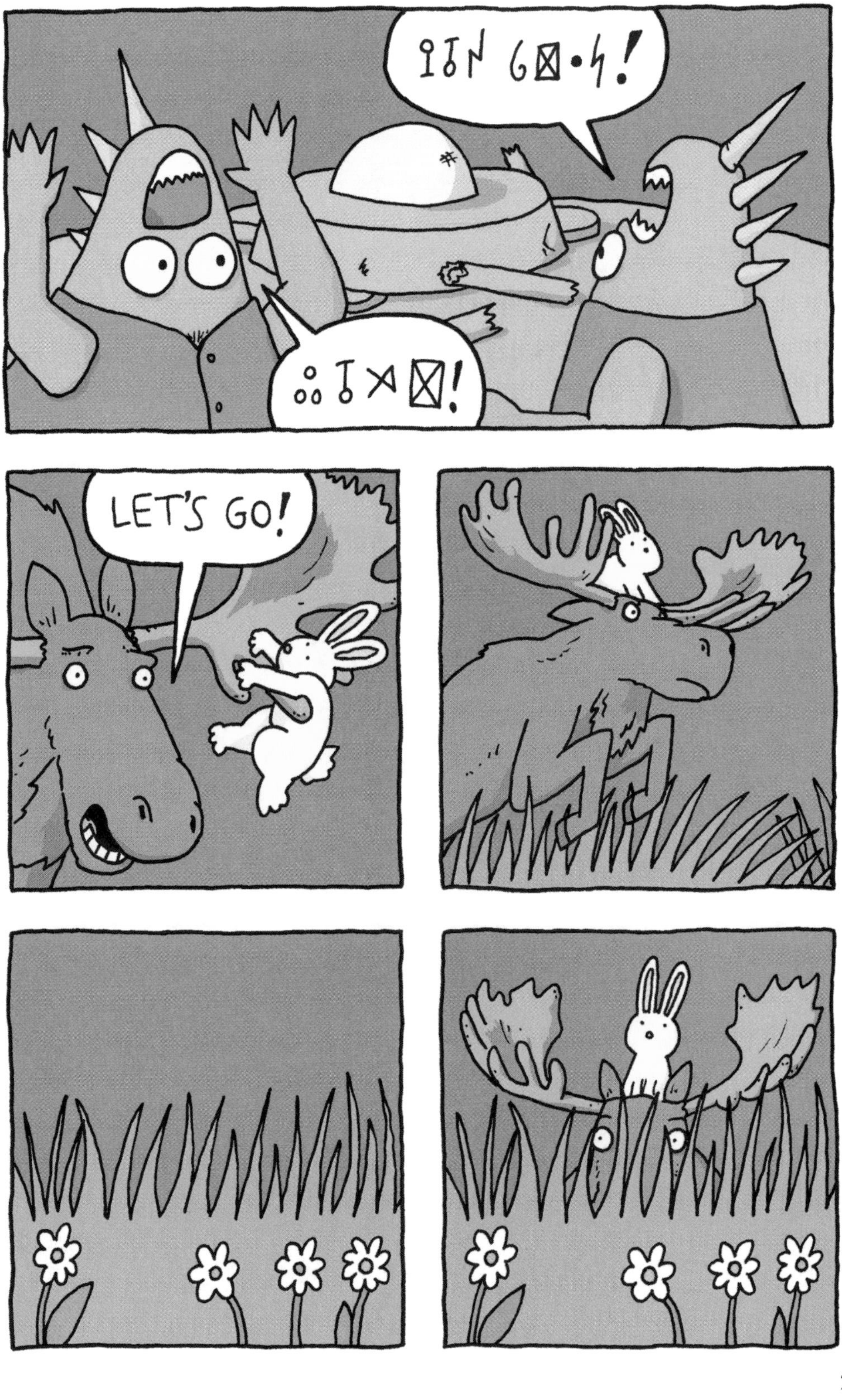
LET'S GO!

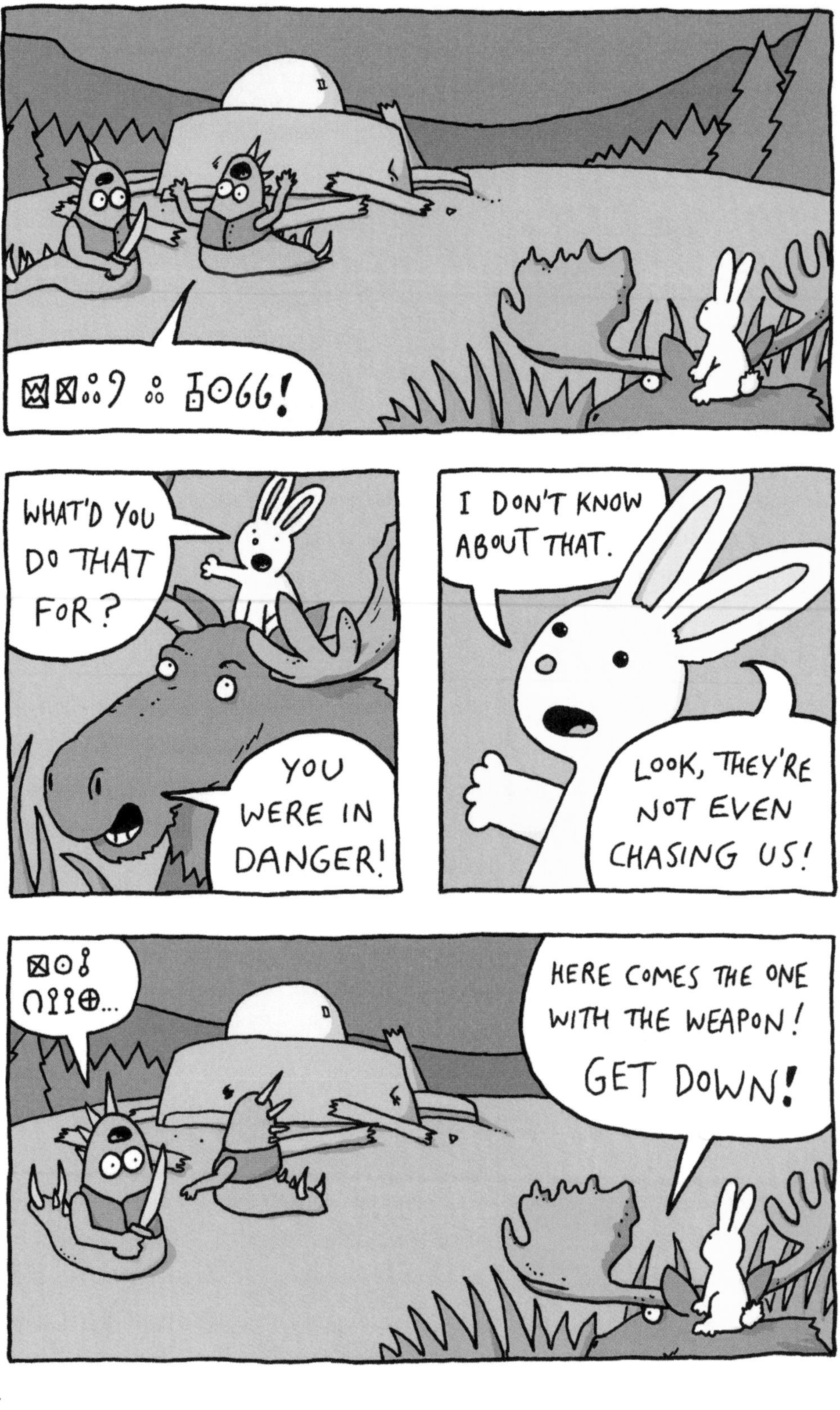
WHAT'D YOU DO THAT FOR?
YOU WERE IN DANGER!
I DON'T KNOW ABOUT THAT.
LOOK, THEY'RE NOT EVEN CHASING US!
HERE COMES THE ONE WITH THE WEAPON! GET DOWN!

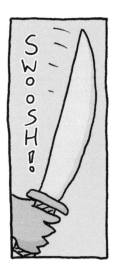

SWOOSH!!

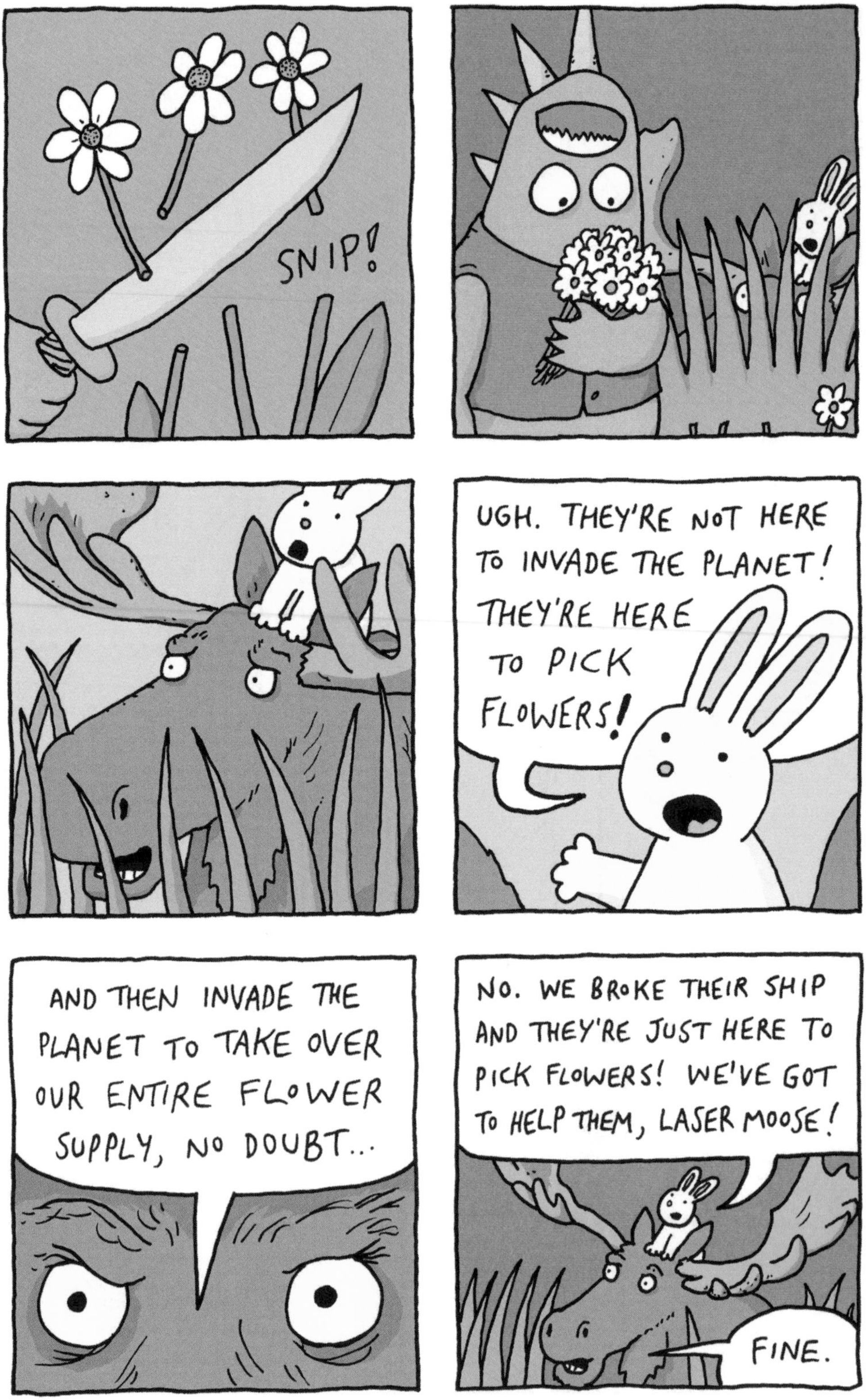
SNIP!
UGH. THEY'RE NOT HERE TO INVADE THE PLANET! THEY'RE HERE TO PICK FLOWERS!
AND THEN INVADE THE PLANET TO TAKE OVER OUR ENTIRE FLOWER SUPPLY, NO DOUBT...
NO. WE BROKE THEIR SHIP AND THEY'RE JUST HERE TO PICK FLOWERS! WE'VE GOT TO HELP THEM, LASER MOOSE!
FINE.

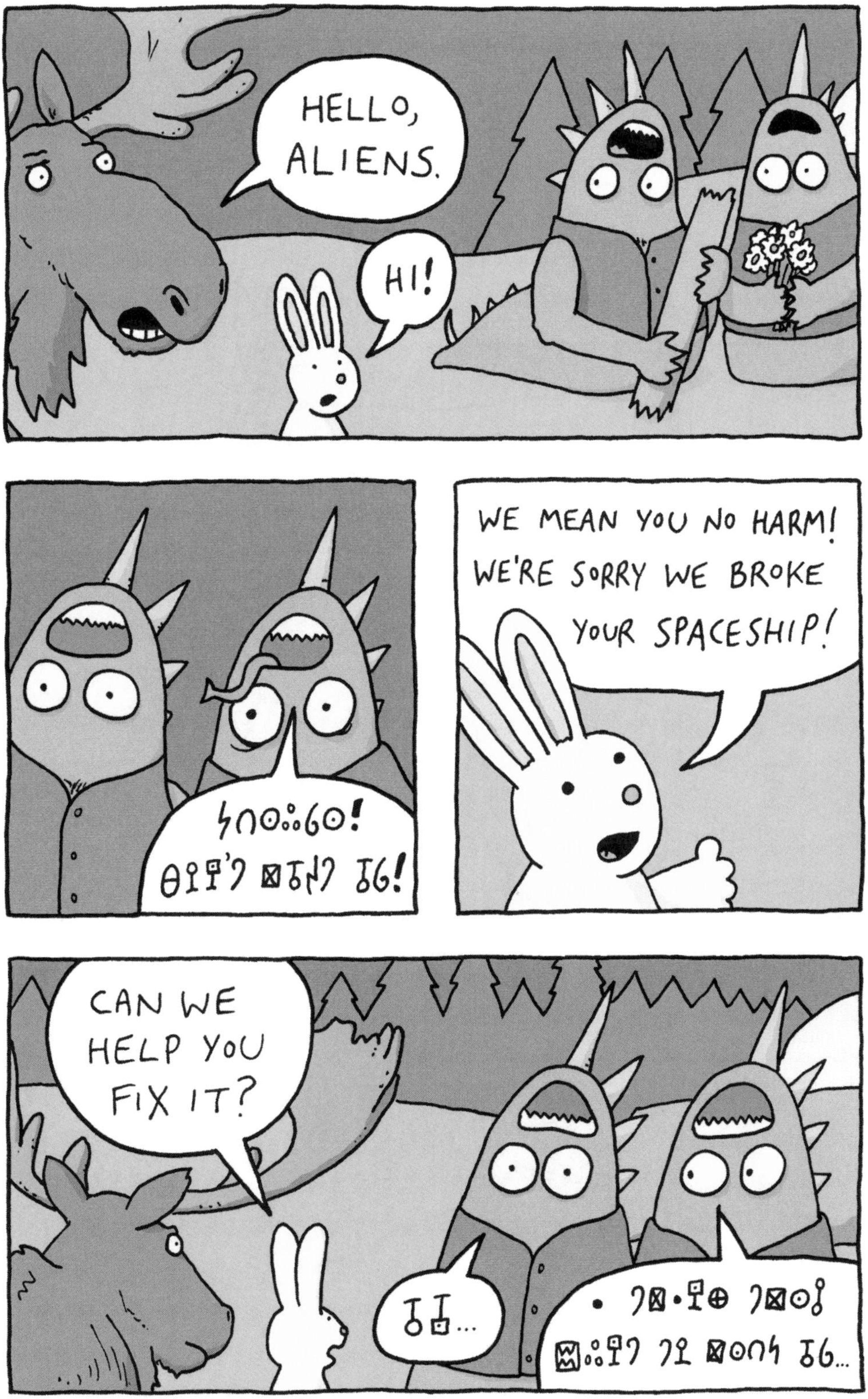
HELLO, ALIENS.
HI!
WE MEAN YOU NO HARM! WE'RE SORRY WE BROKE YOUR SPACESHIP!
CAN WE HELP YOU FIX IT?

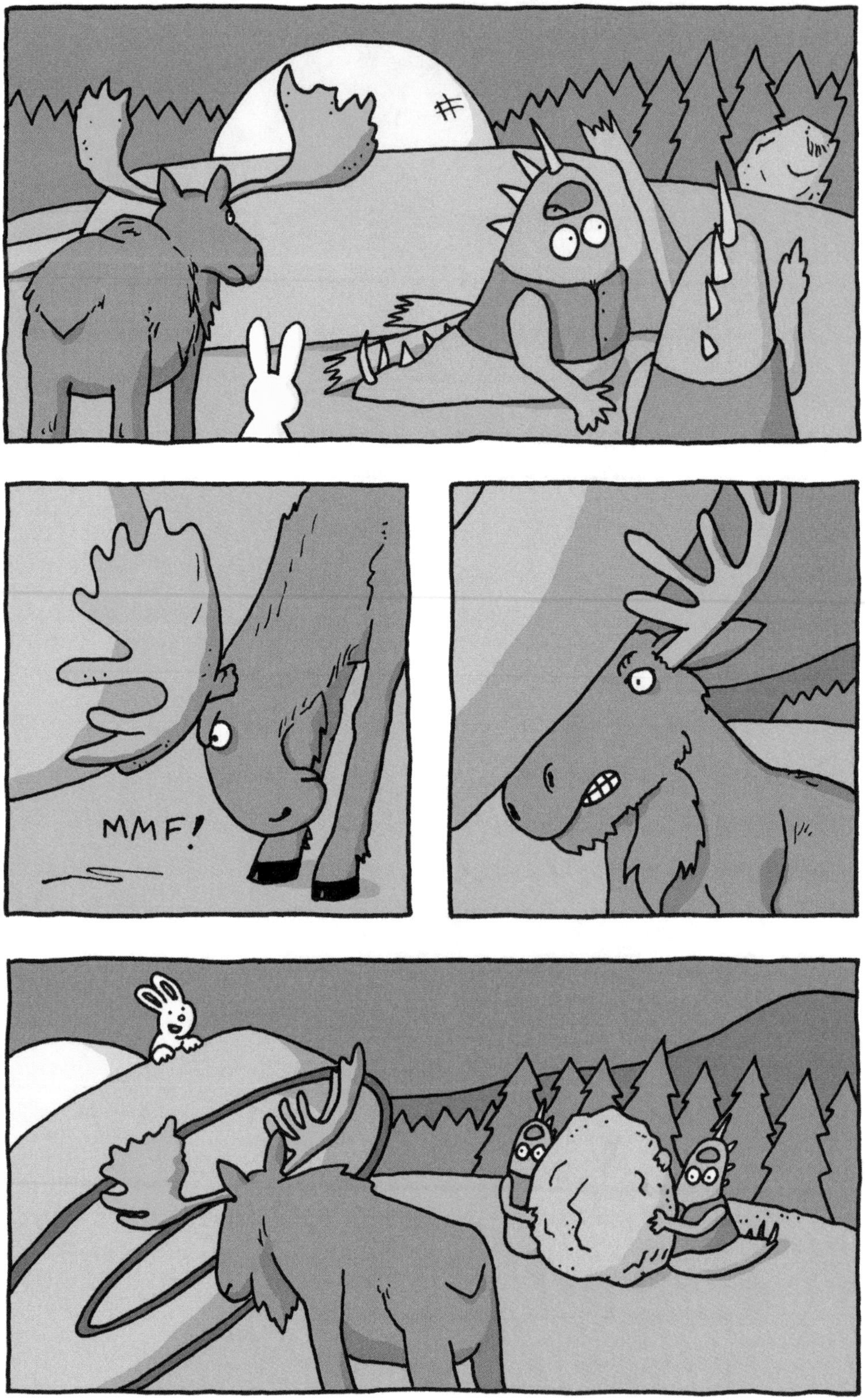
MMF!

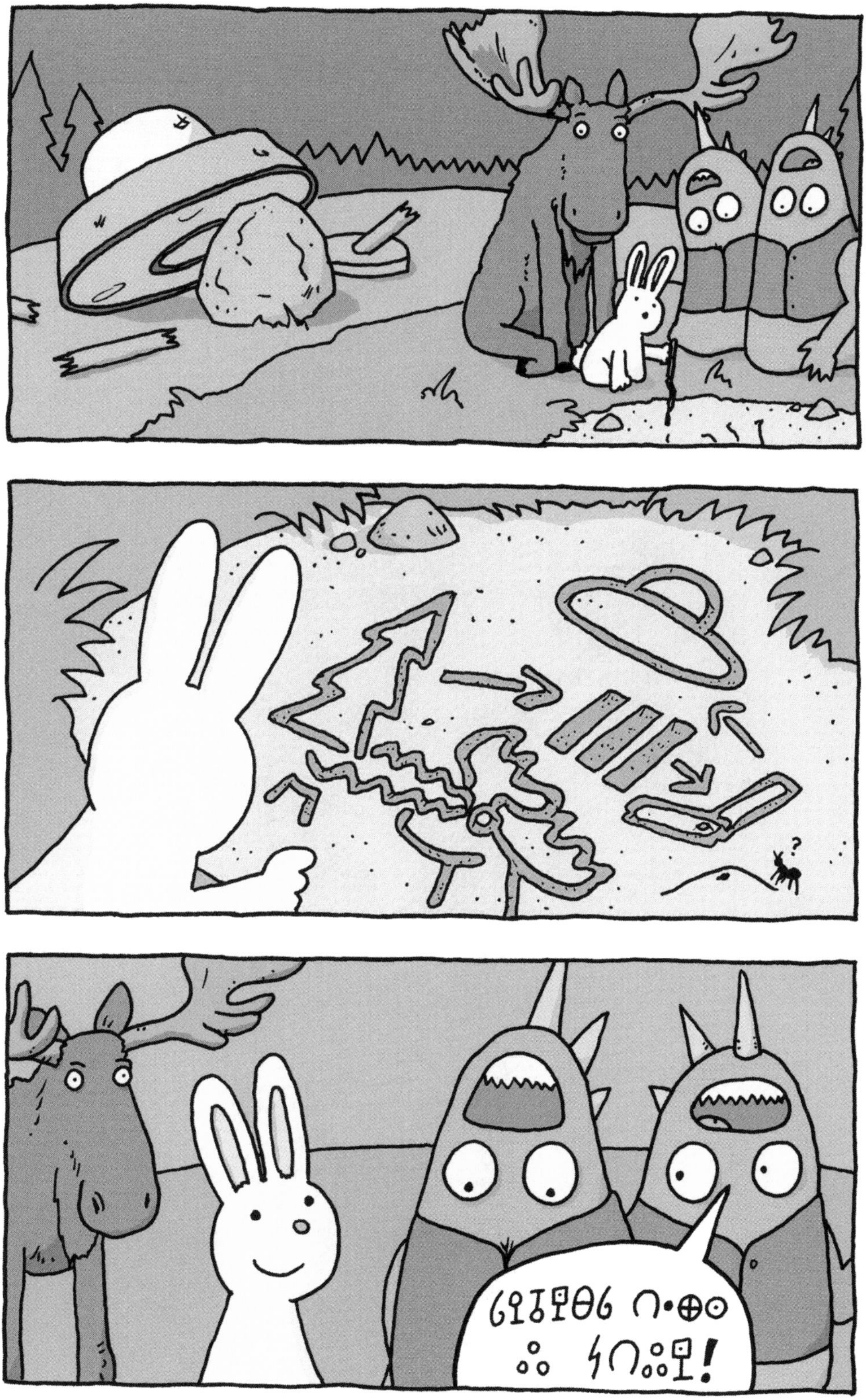

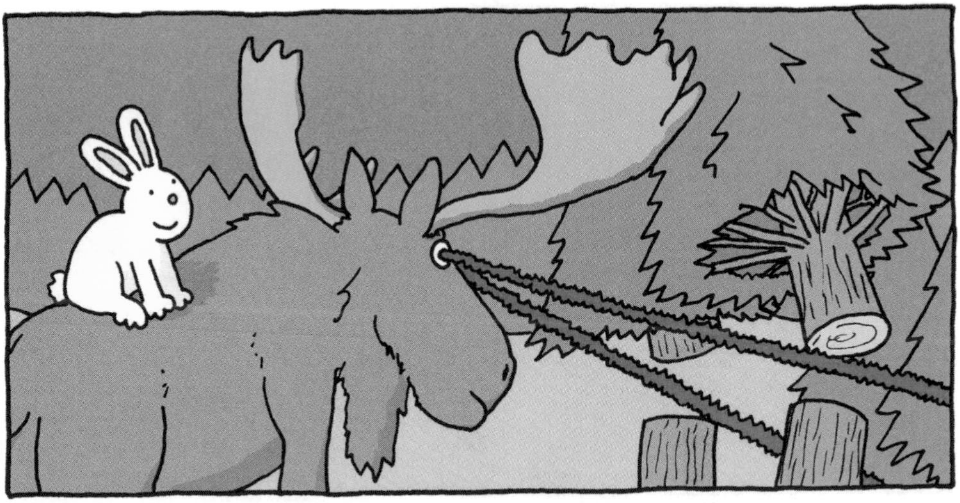

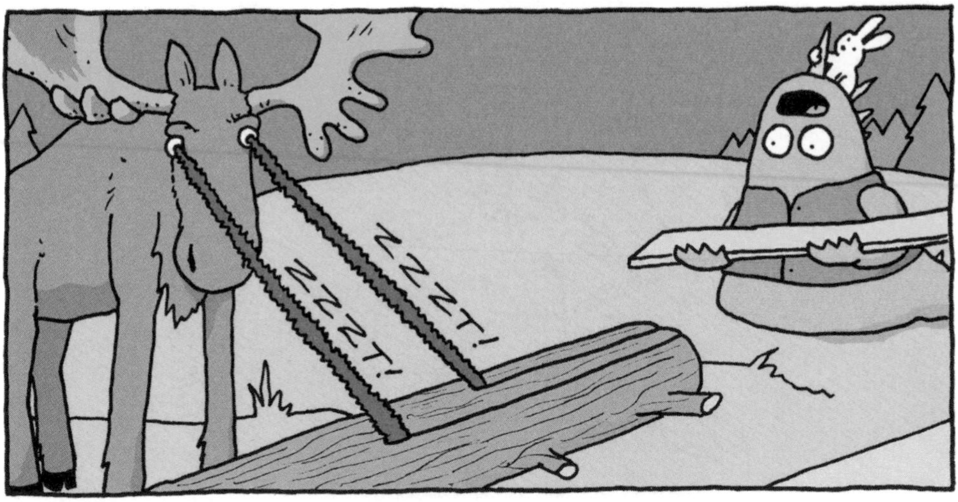
ZZZZT!
ZZZZT!

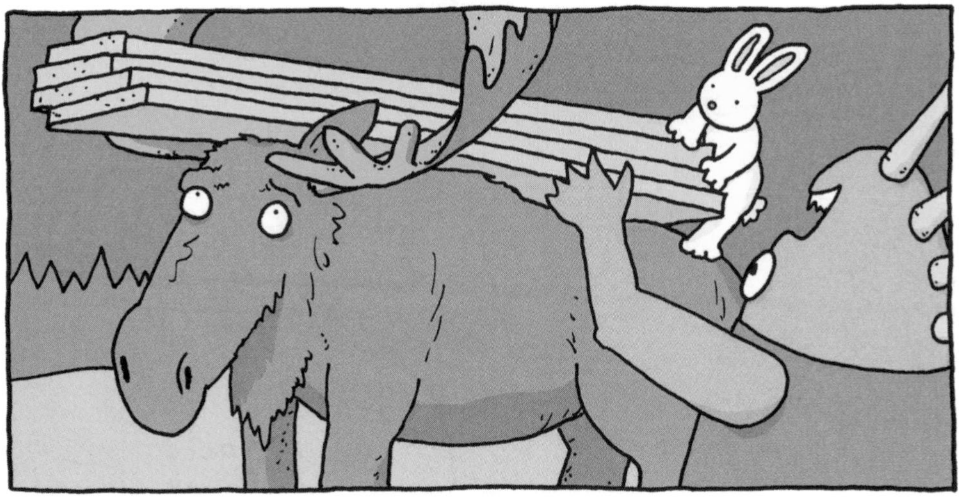

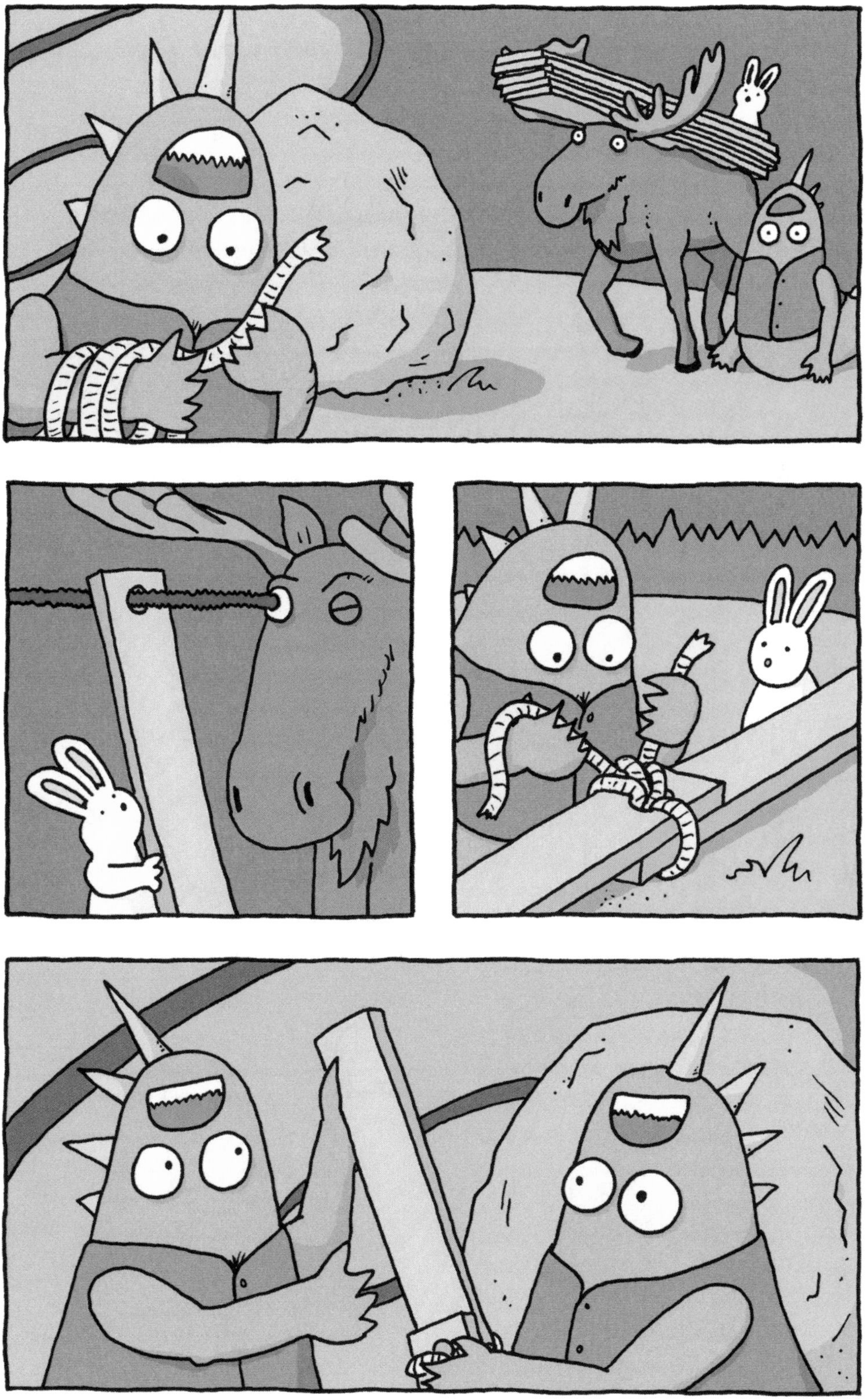

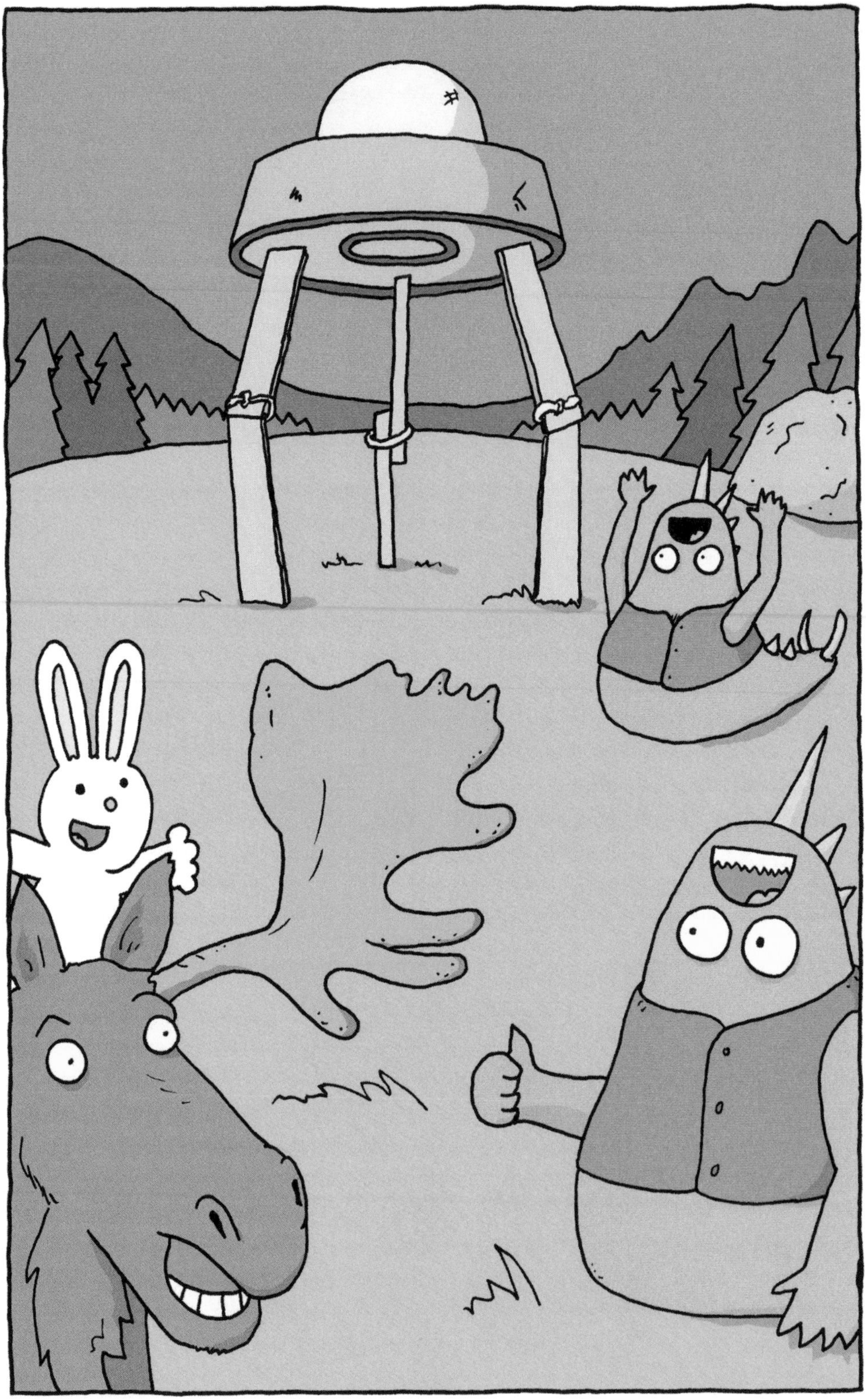

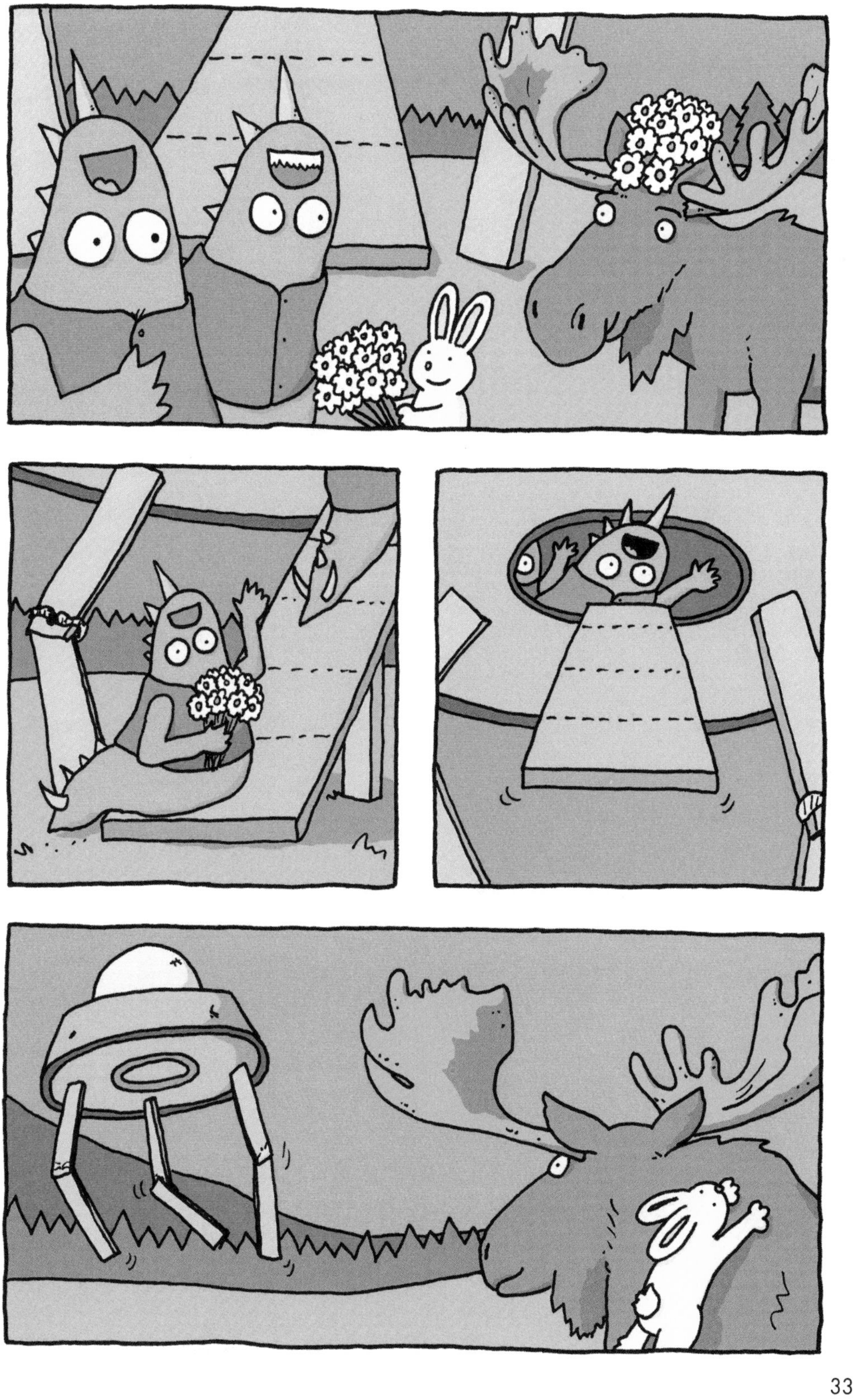

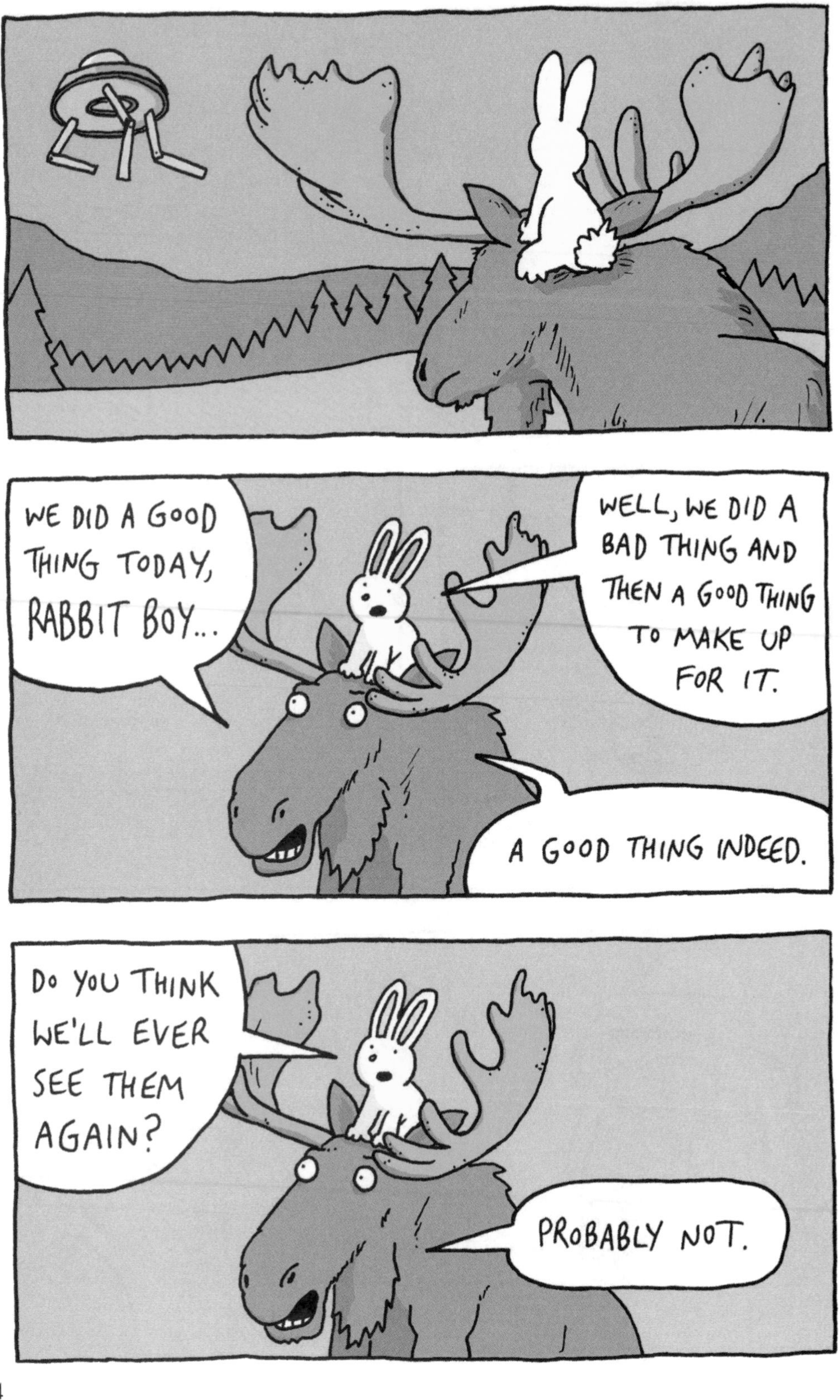
WE DID A GOOD THING TODAY, RABBIT BOY...
WELL, WE DID A BAD THING AND THEN A GOOD THING TO MAKE UP FOR IT.
A GOOD THING INDEED.
DO YOU THINK WE'LL EVER SEE THEM AGAIN?
PROBABLY NOT.

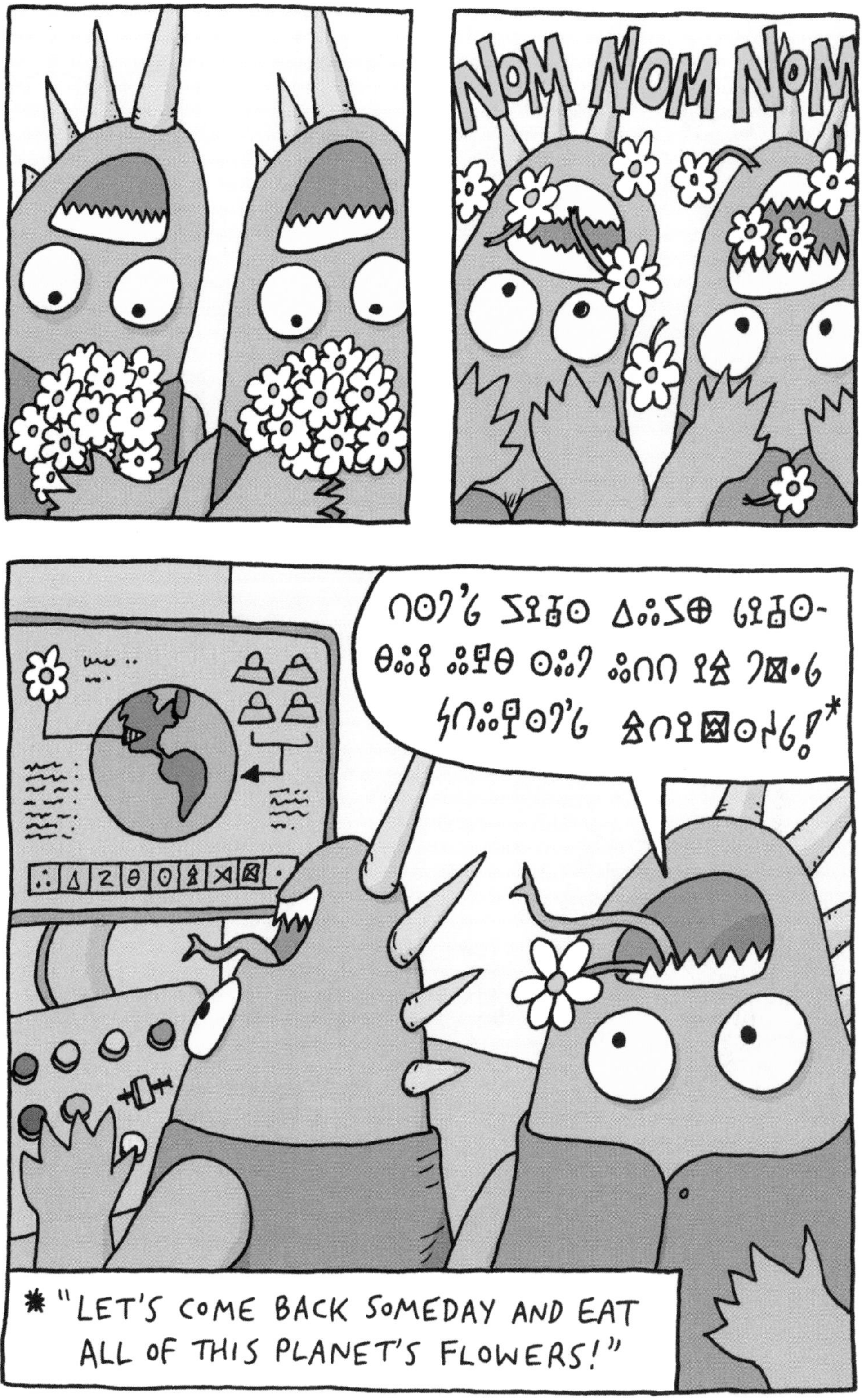
NOM NOM NOM
* "LET'S COME BACK SOMEDAY AND EAT ALL OF THIS PLANET'S FLOWERS!"

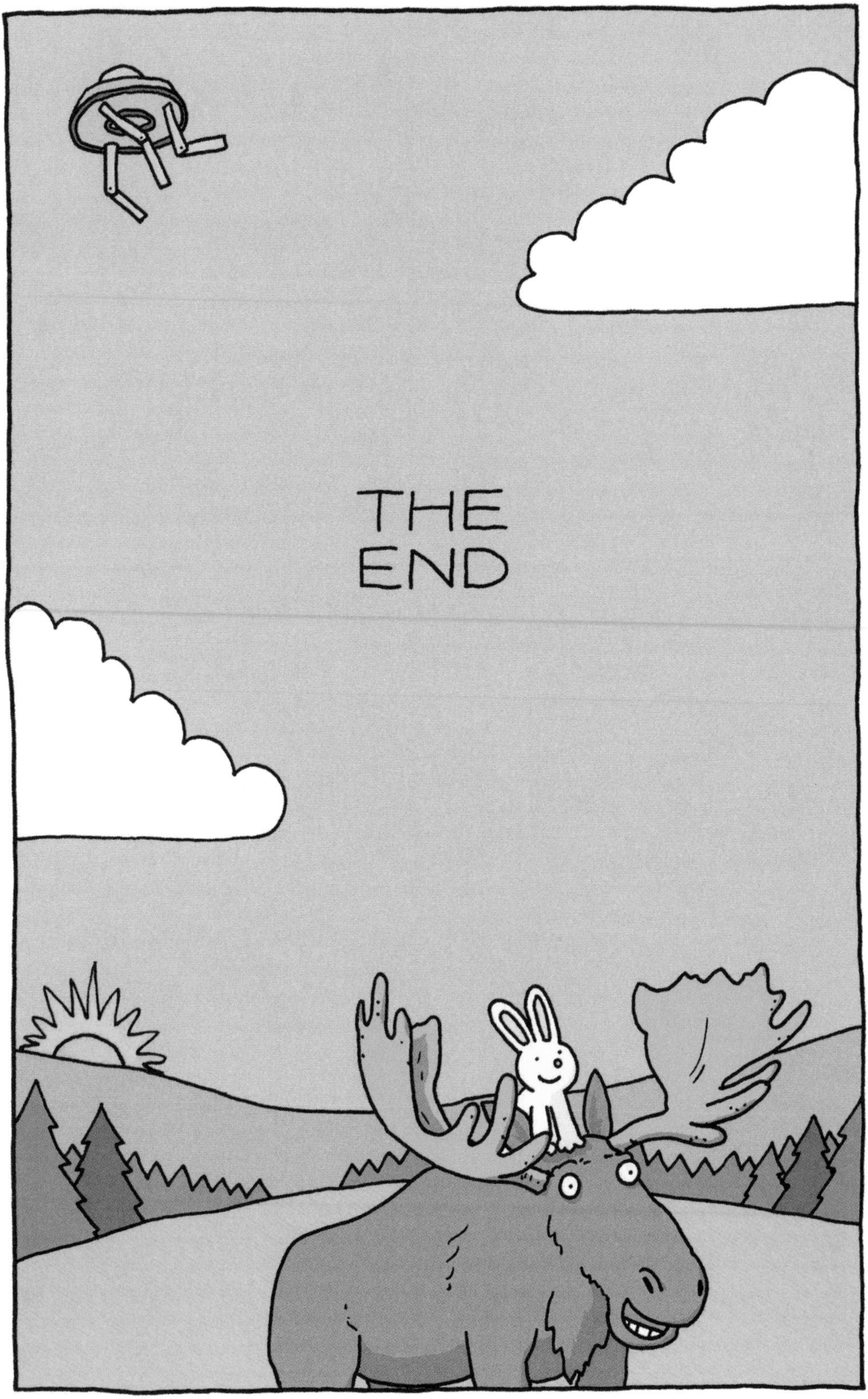
THE END

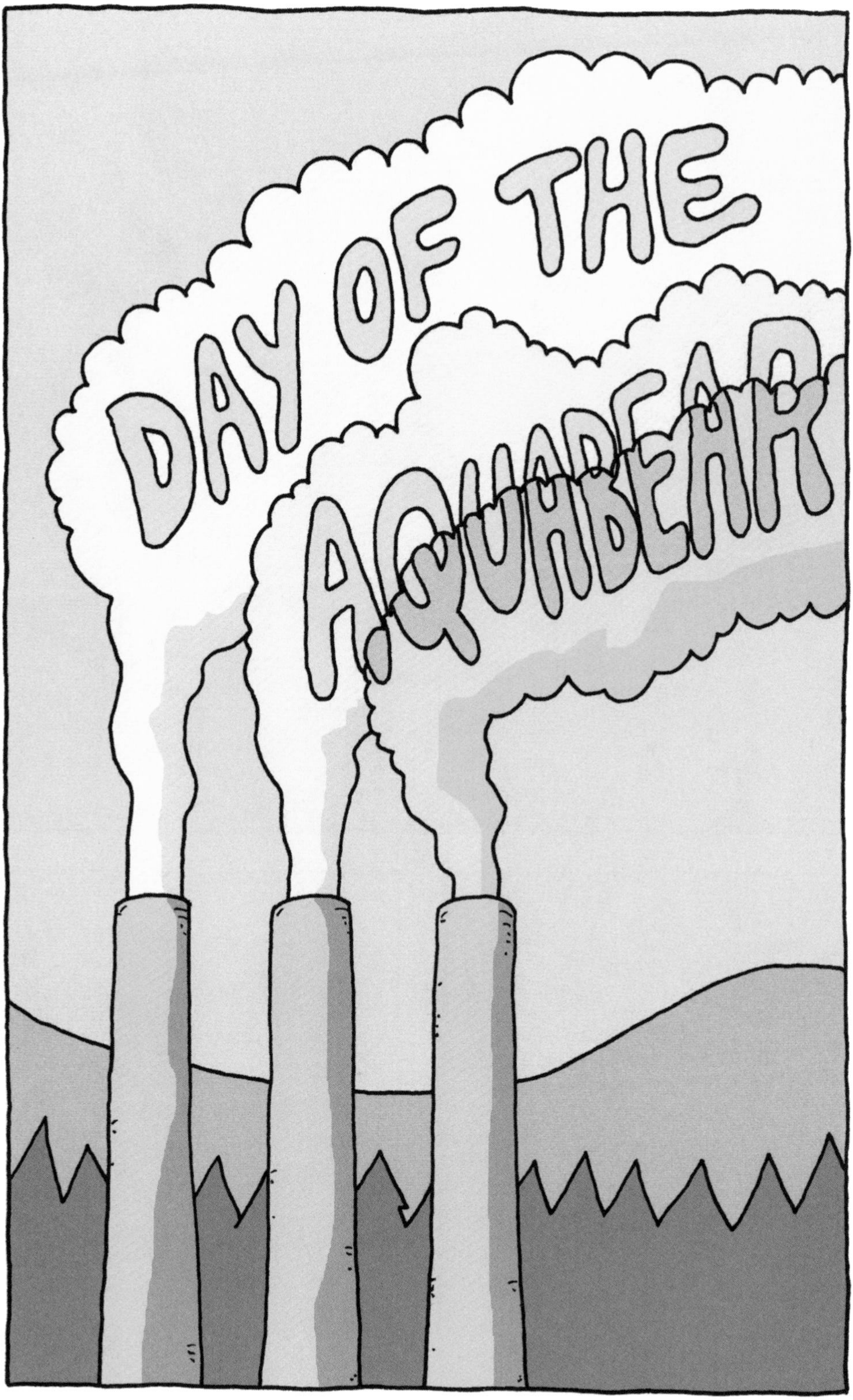
DAY OF THE
AQUABEAR

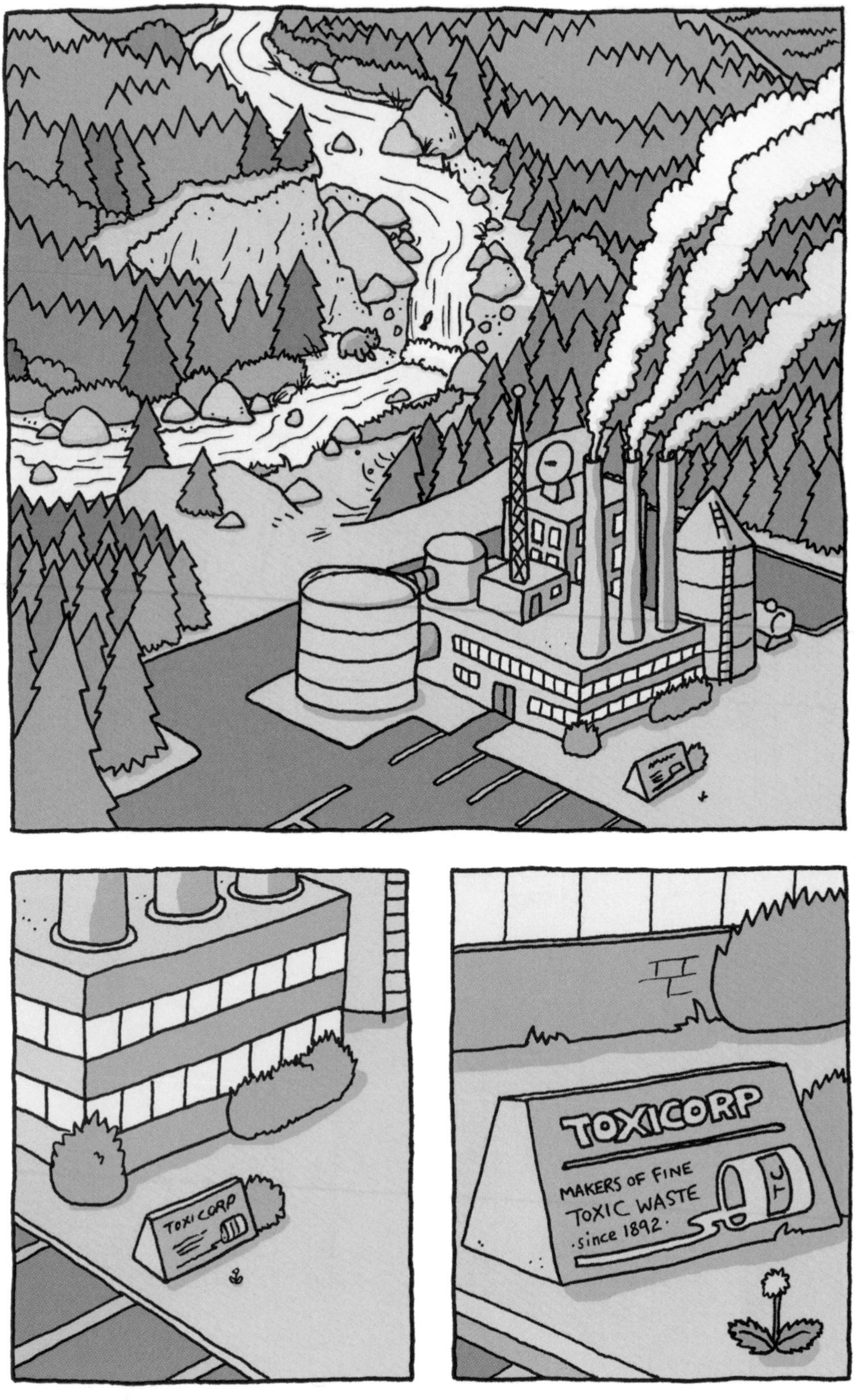
TOXICORP
TOXICORP
MAKERS OF FINE
TOXIC WASTE
·since 1892·

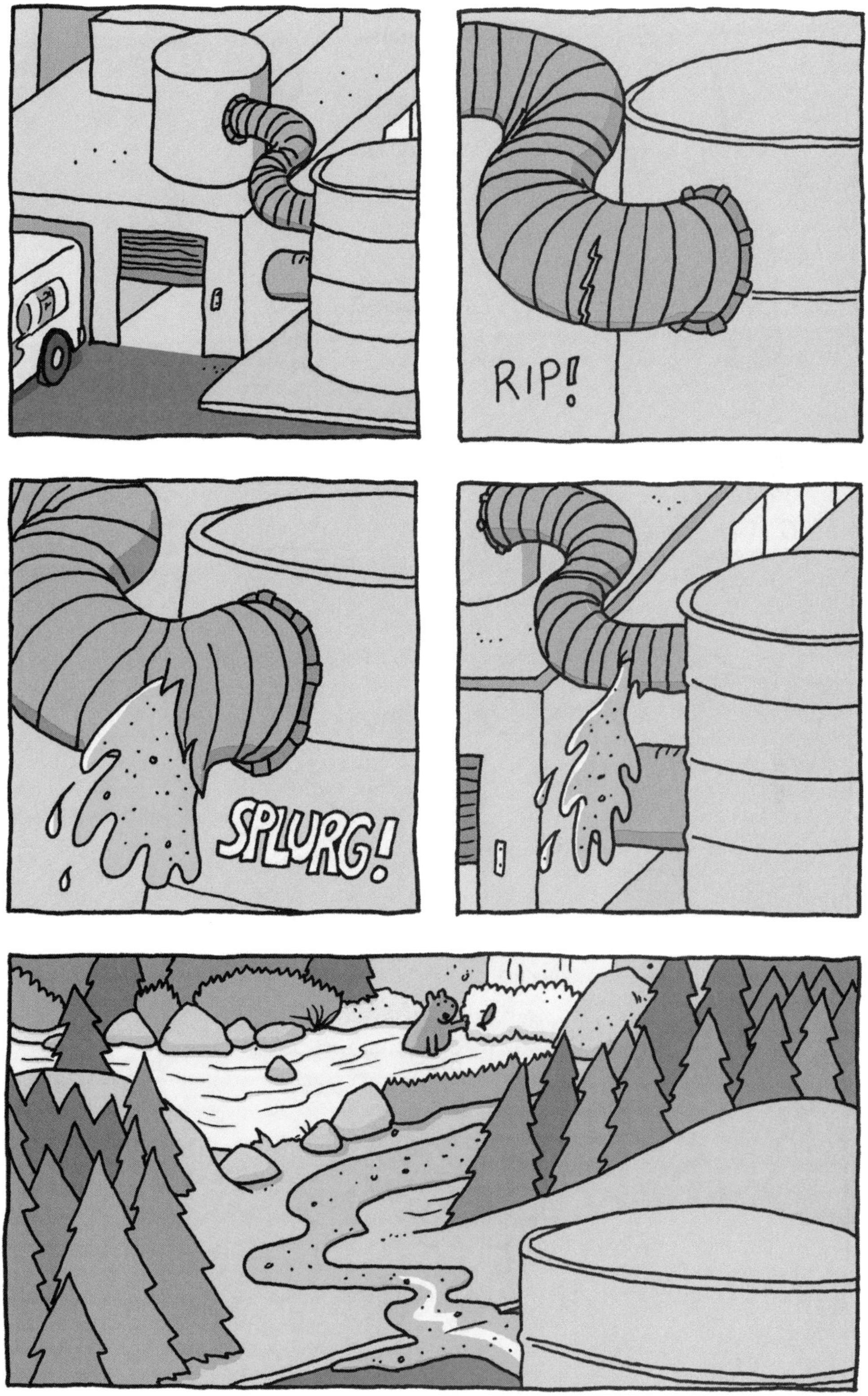
RIP!
SPLURG!

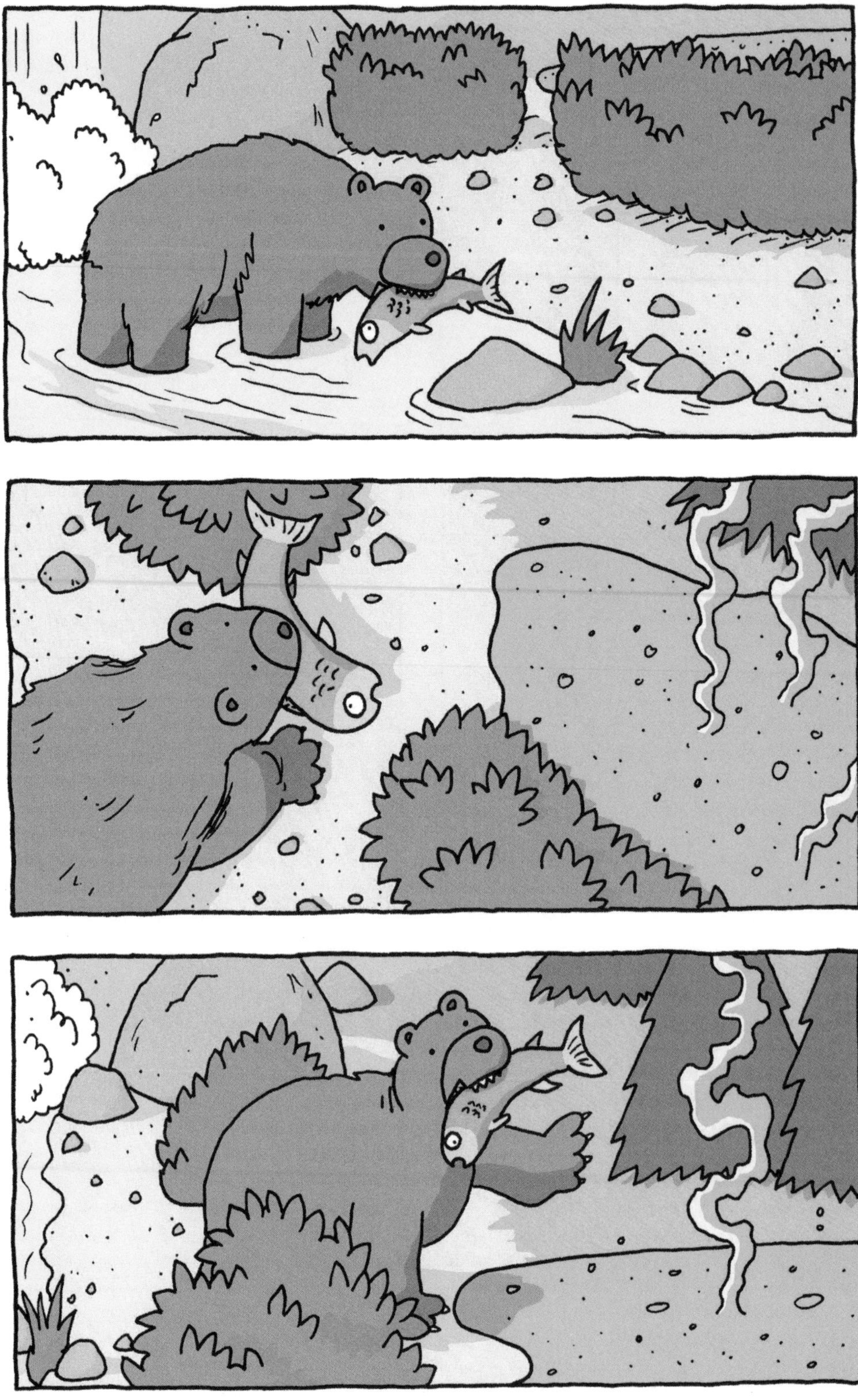

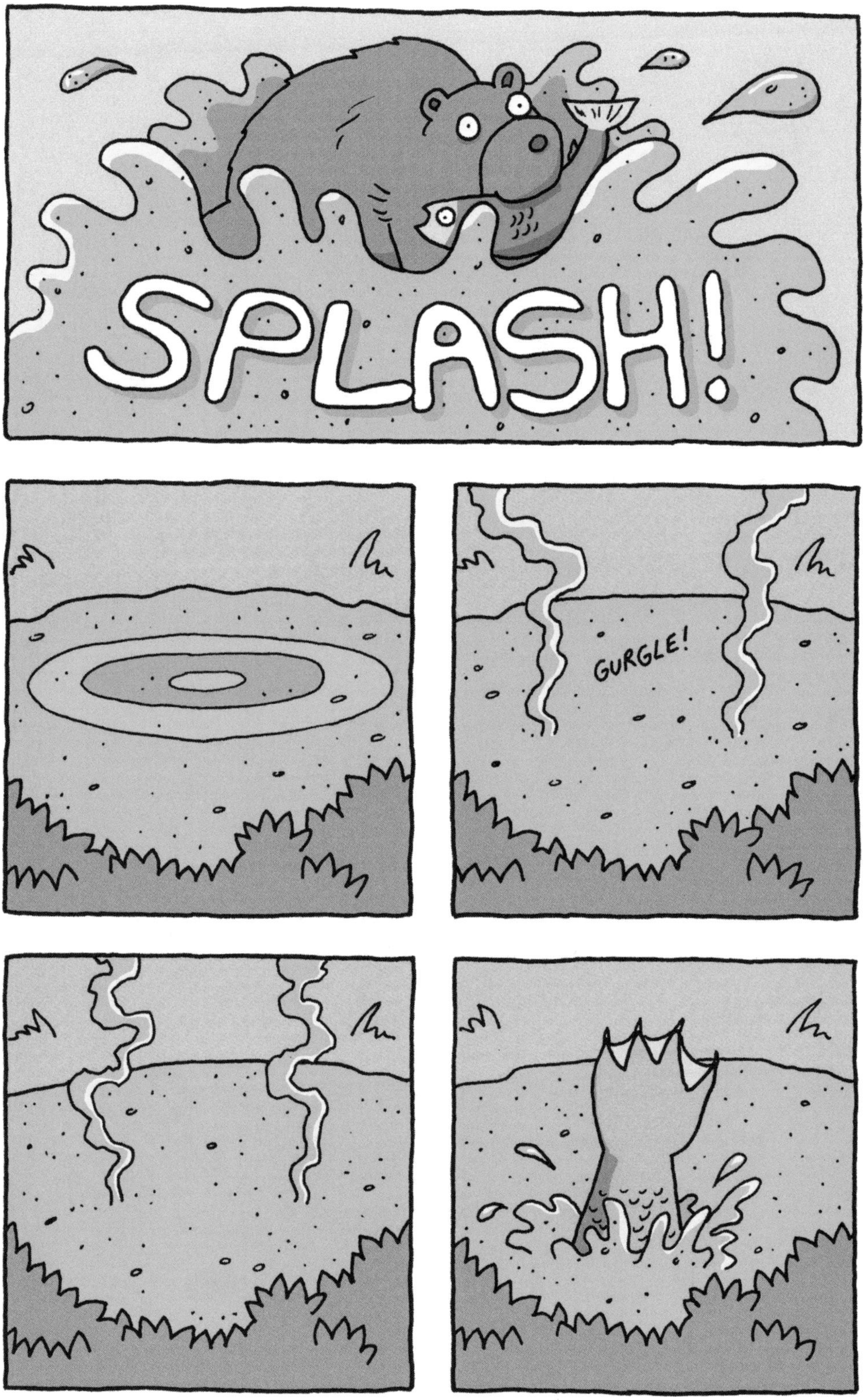
SPLASH!
GURGLE!

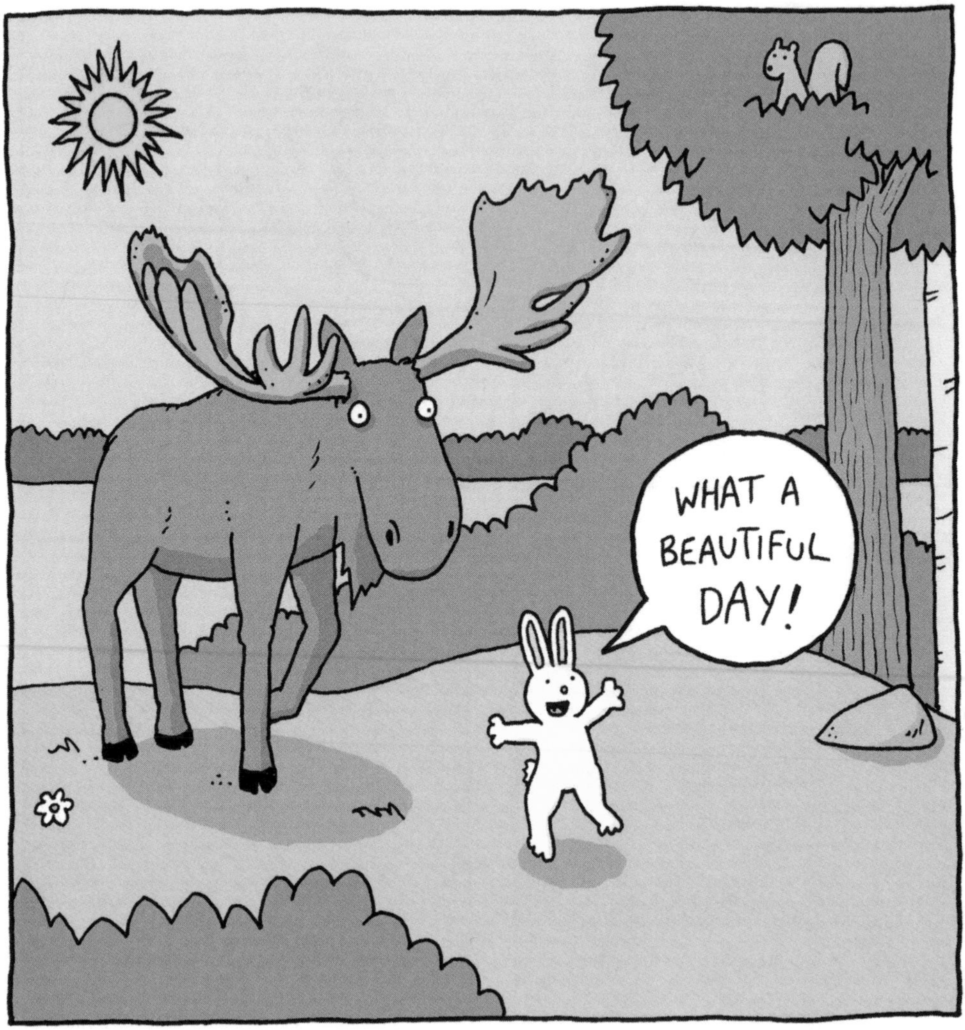
WHAT A BEAUTIFUL DAY!

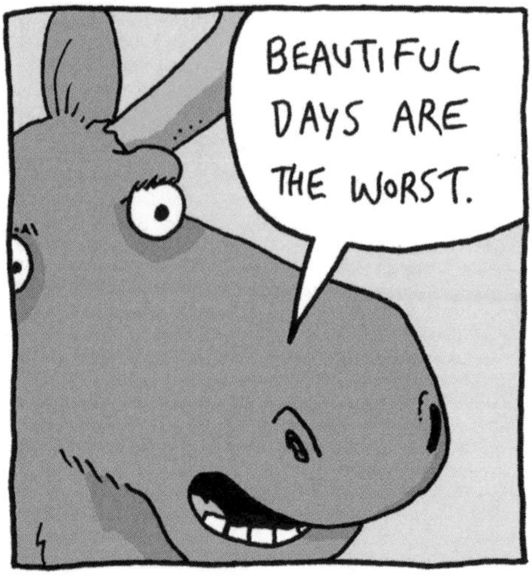
BEAUTIFUL DAYS ARE THE WORST.

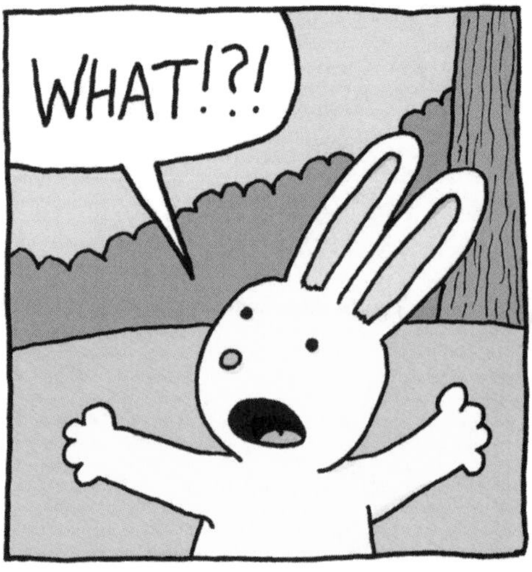
WHAT!?!

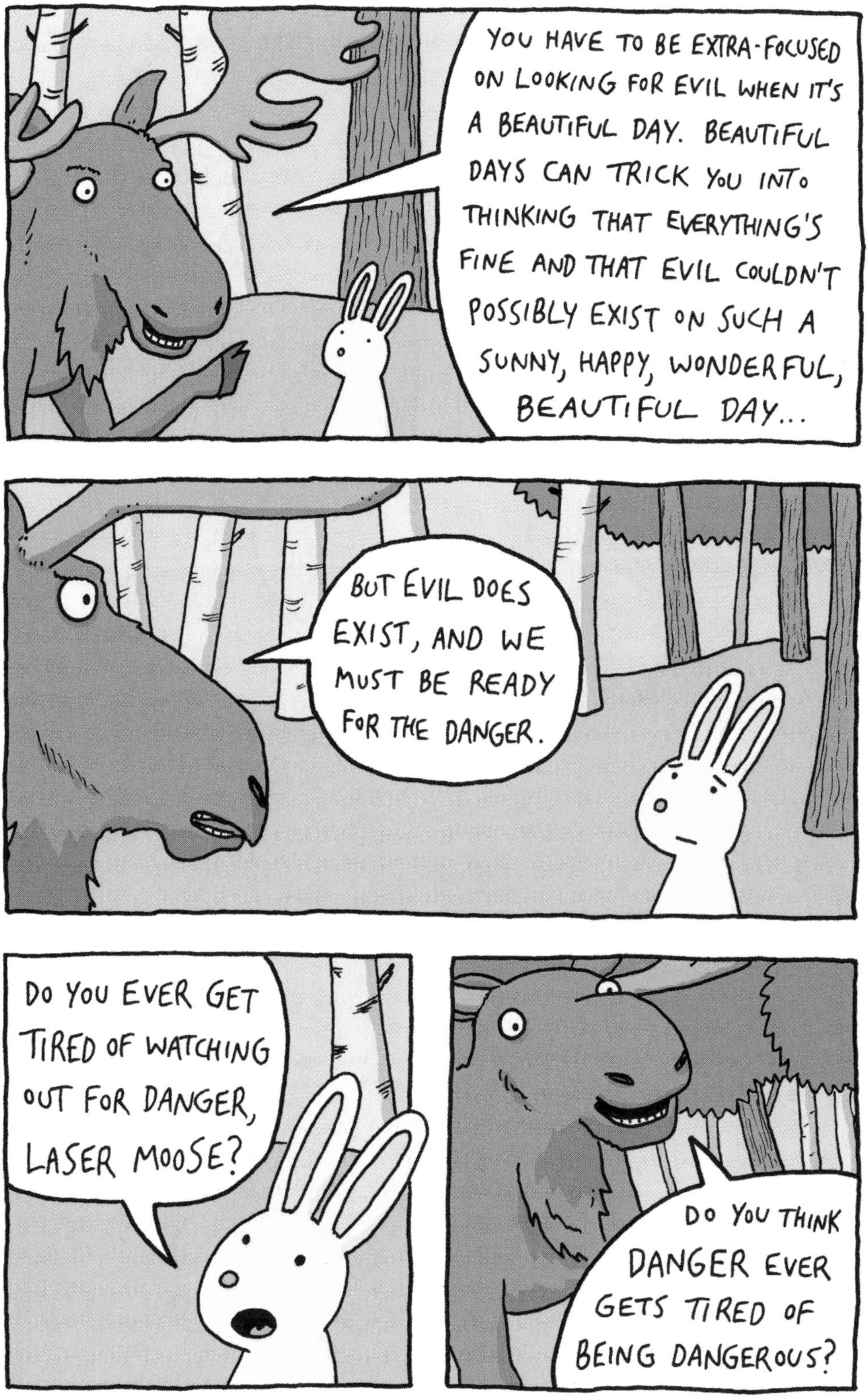
YOU HAVE TO BE EXTRA-FOCUSED ON LOOKING FOR EVIL WHEN IT'S A BEAUTIFUL DAY. BEAUTIFUL DAYS CAN TRICK YOU INTO THINKING THAT EVERYTHING'S FINE AND THAT EVIL COULDN'T POSSIBLY EXIST ON SUCH A SUNNY, HAPPY, WONDERFUL, BEAUTIFUL DAY...
BUT EVIL DOES EXIST, AND WE MUST BE READY FOR THE DANGER.
DO YOU EVER GET TIRED OF WATCHING OUT FOR DANGER, LASER MOOSE?
DO YOU THINK DANGER EVER GETS TIRED OF BEING DANGEROUS?

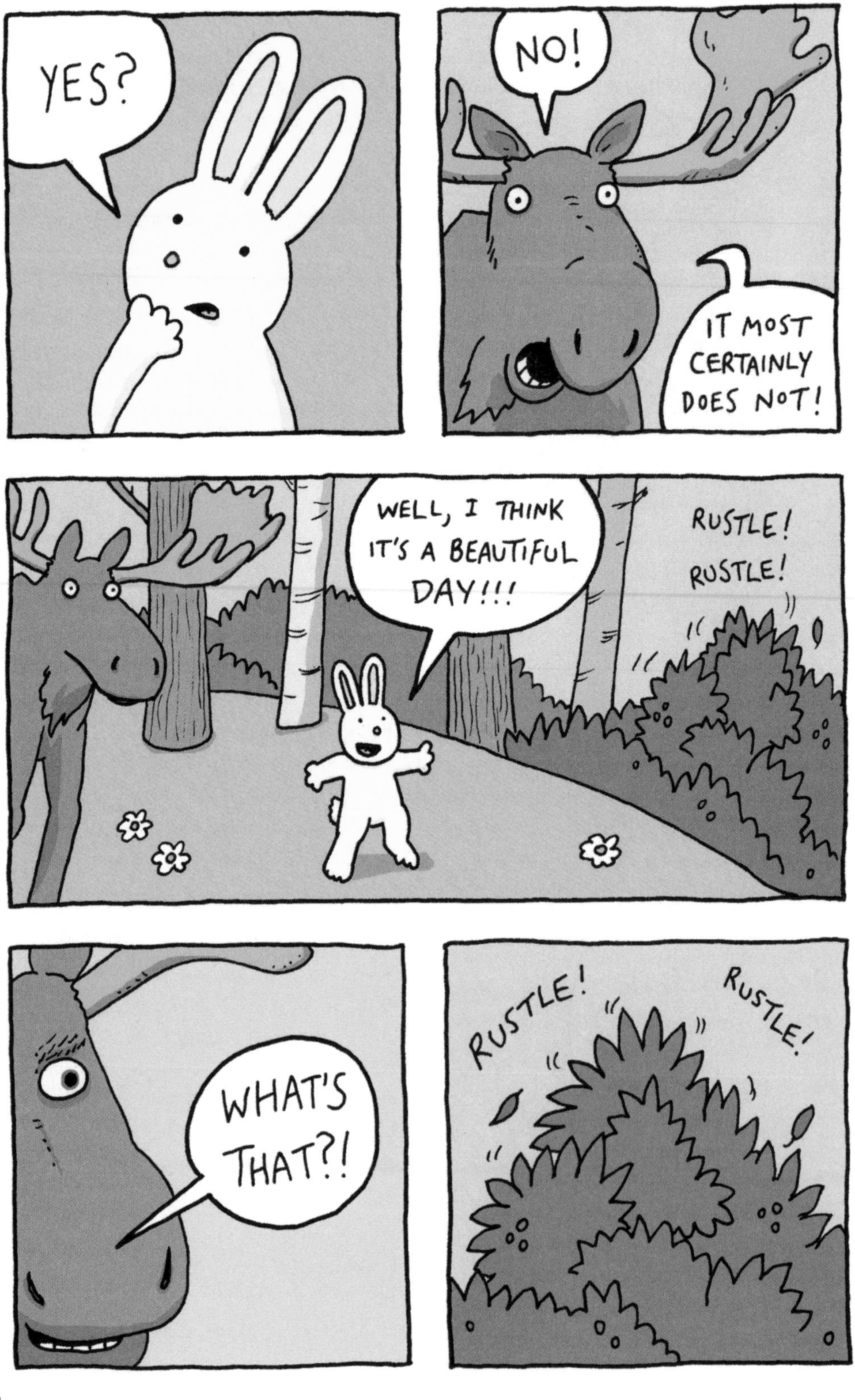
YES?
NO!
IT MOST CERTAINLY DOES NOT!
WELL, I THINK IT'S A BEAUTIFUL DAY!!!
RUSTLE! RUSTLE!
WHAT'S THAT?!
RUSTLE!
RUSTLE!

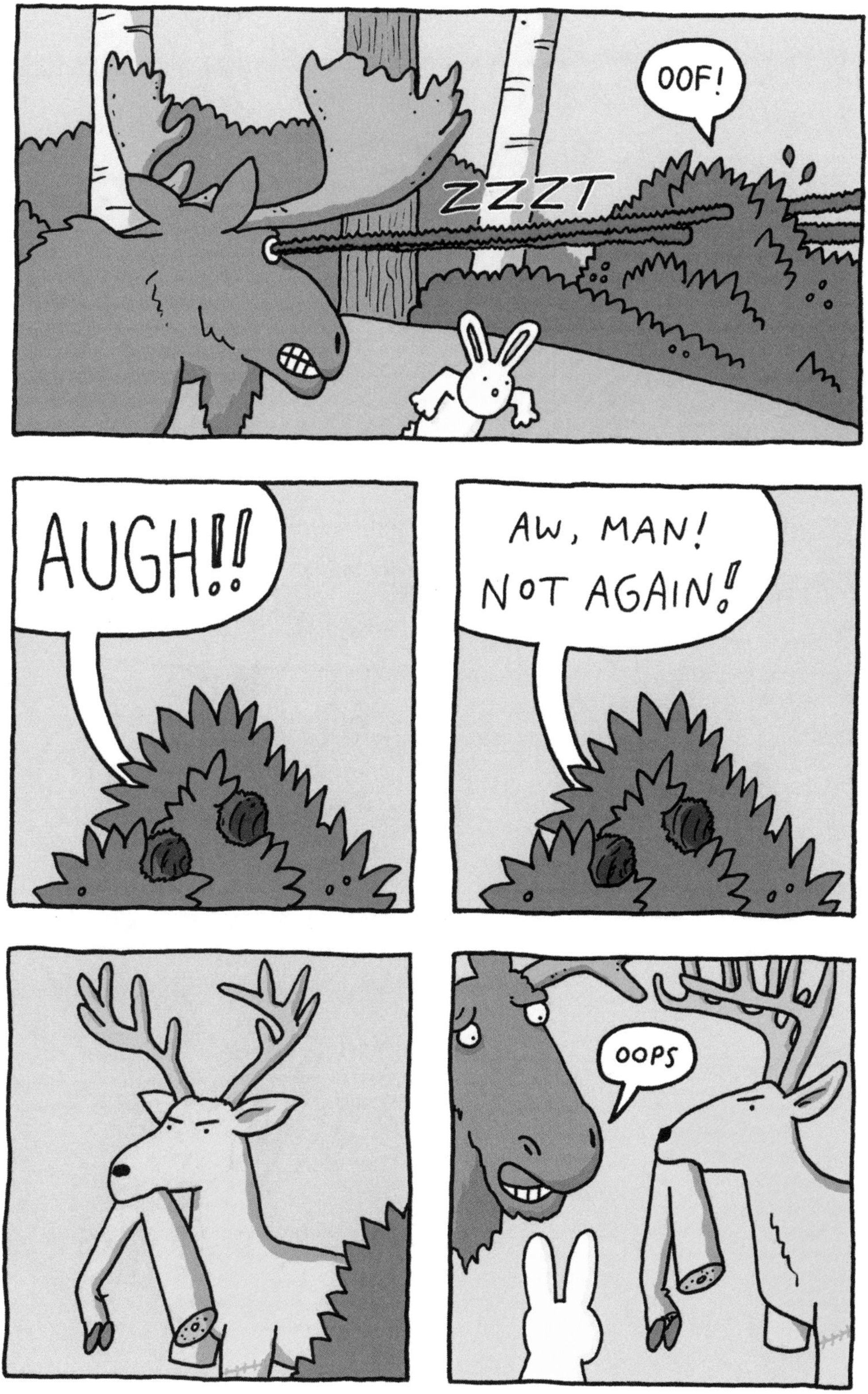
OOF!
ZZZT
AUGH!!
AW, MAN! NOT AGAIN!
OOPS

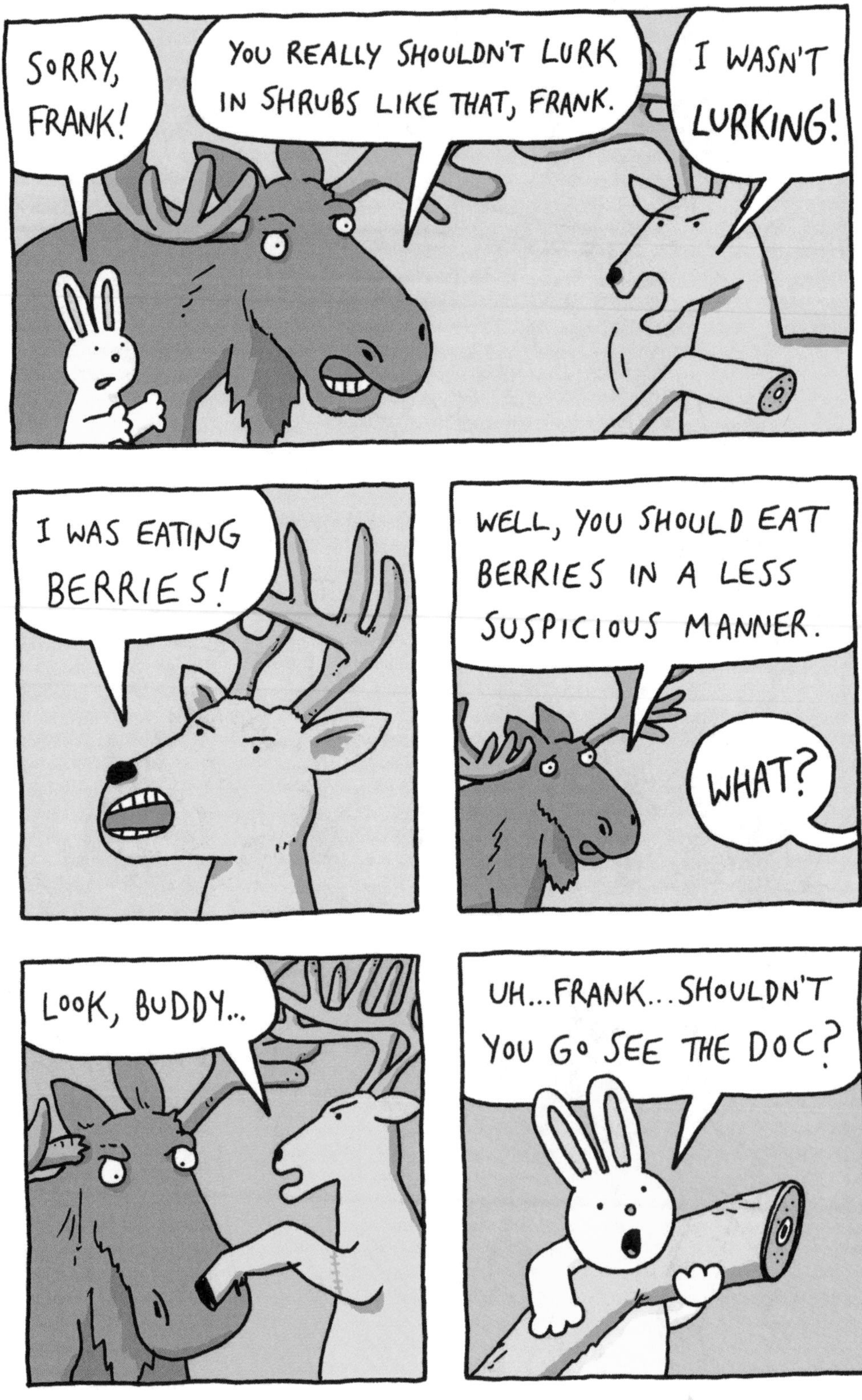
SORRY, FRANK!
YOU REALLY SHOULDN'T LURK IN SHRUBS LIKE THAT, FRANK.
I WASN'T LURKING!
I WAS EATING BERRIES!
WELL, YOU SHOULD EAT BERRIES IN A LESS SUSPICIOUS MANNER.
WHAT?
LOOK, BUDDY...
UH...FRANK...SHOULDN'T YOU GO SEE THE DOC?

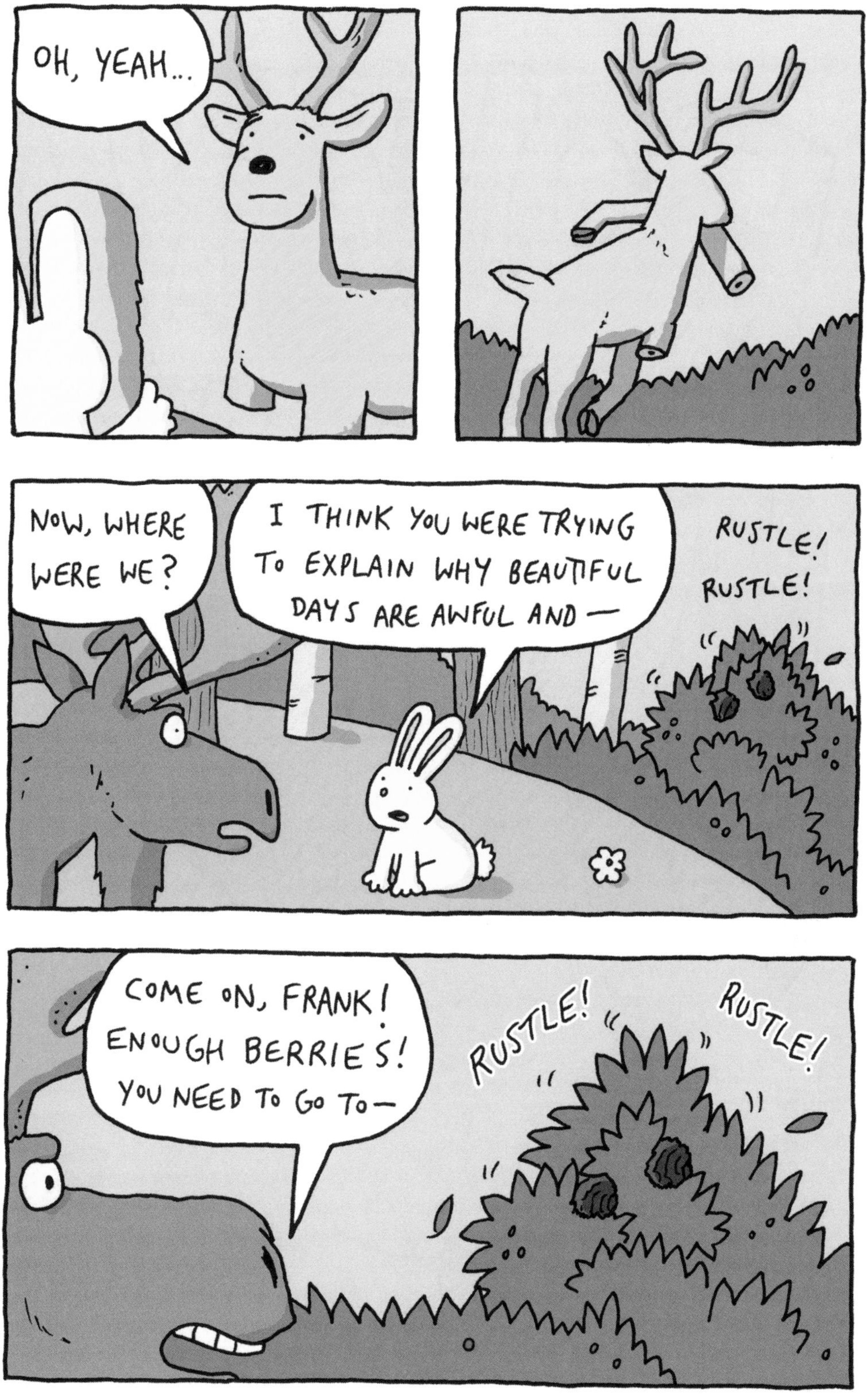
OH, YEAH...
NOW, WHERE WERE WE?
I THINK YOU WERE TRYING TO EXPLAIN WHY BEAUTIFUL DAYS ARE AWFUL AND—
RUSTLE! RUSTLE!
COME ON, FRANK! ENOUGH BERRIES! YOU NEED TO GO TO—
RUSTLE! RUSTLE!

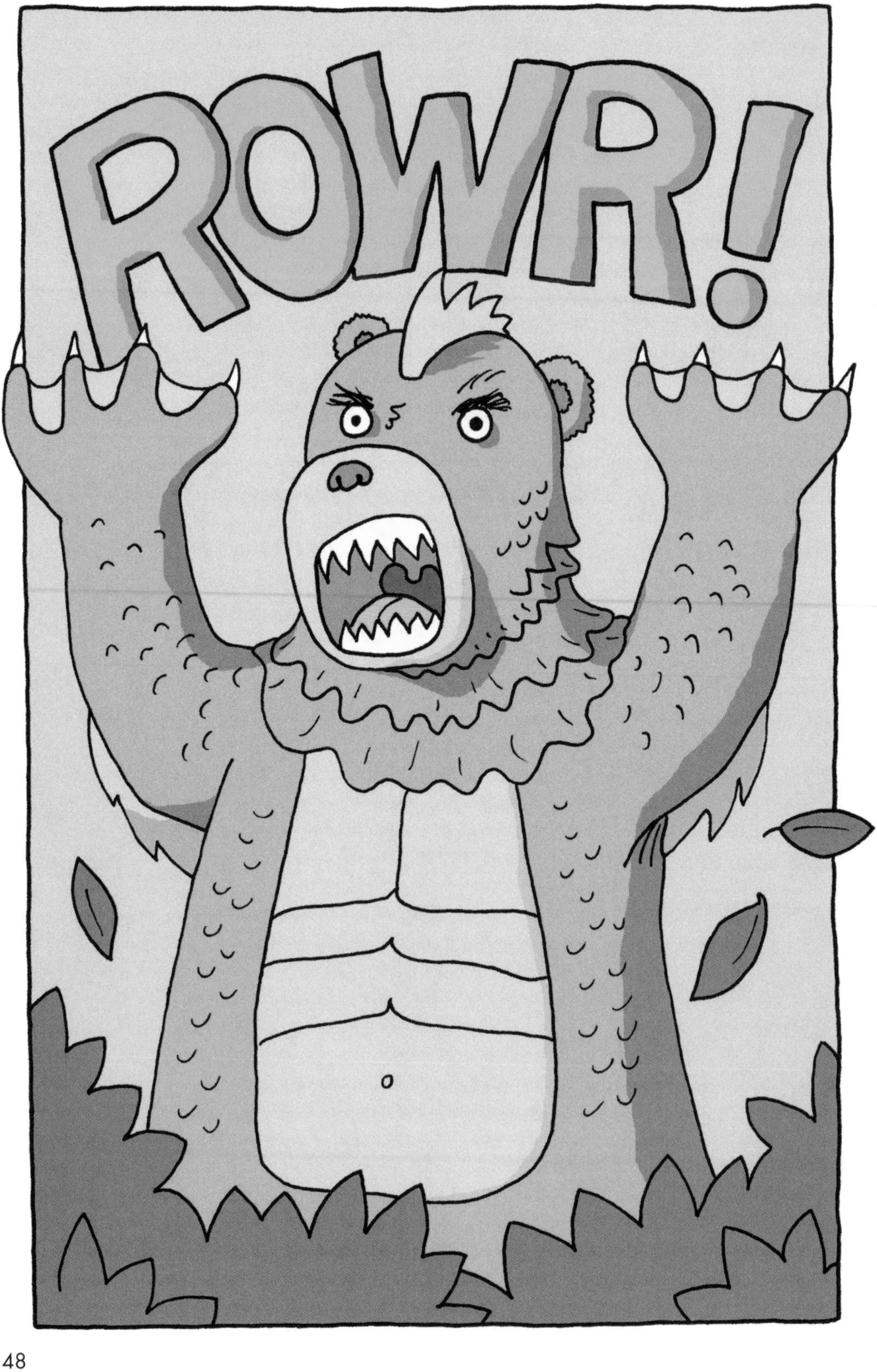
ROWR!

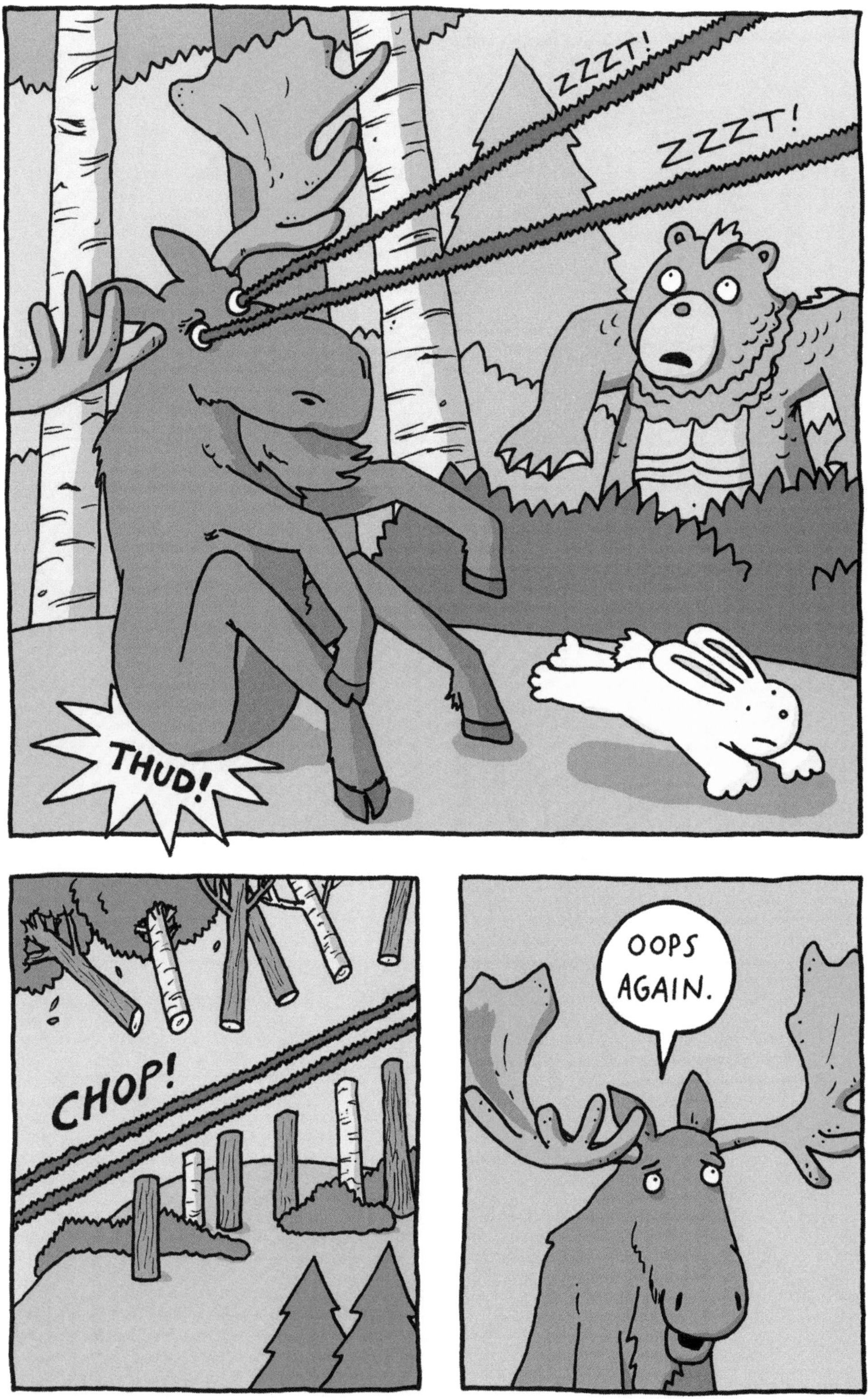
ZZZT!
ZZZT!
THUD!
CHOP!
OOPS AGAIN.

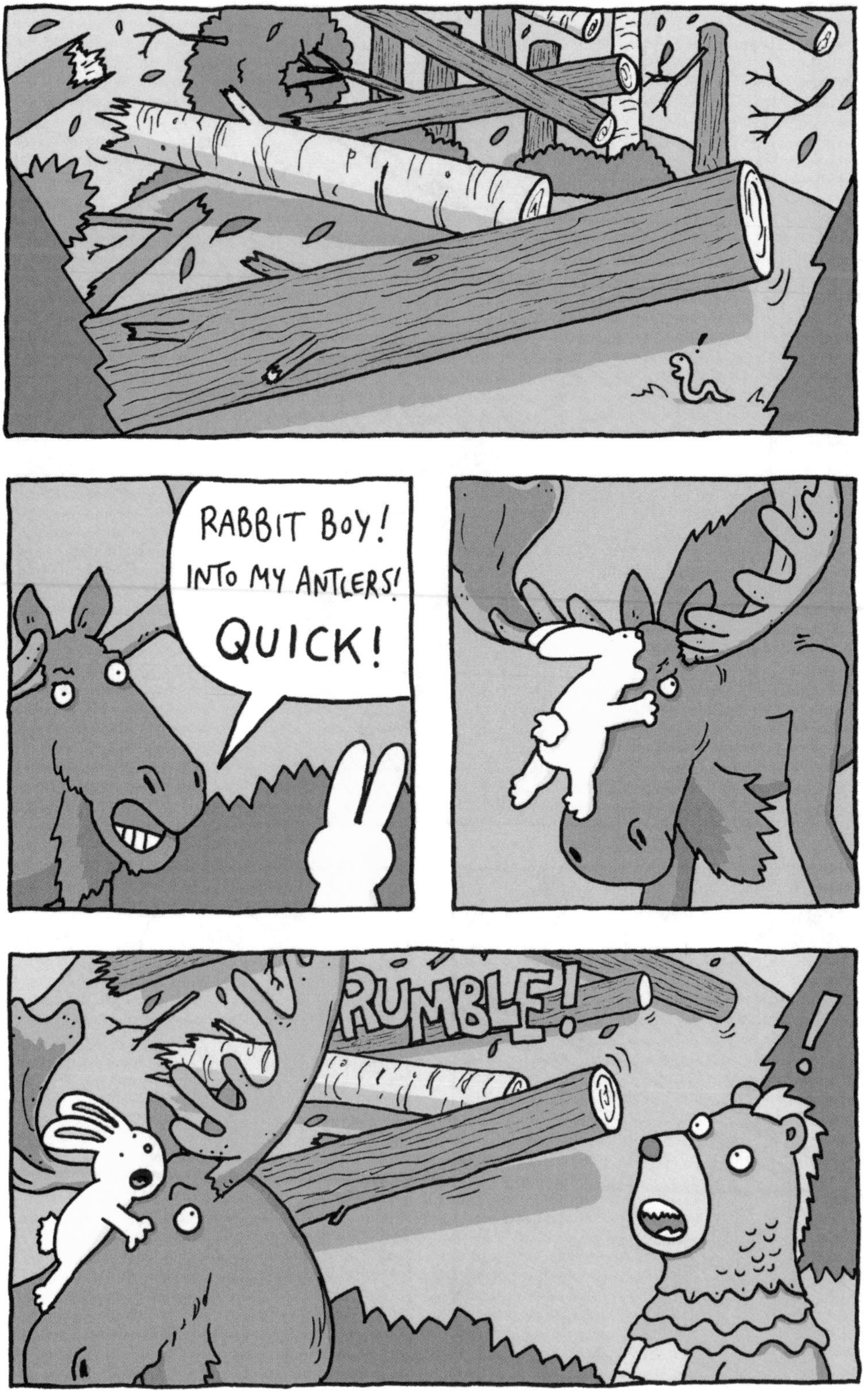
RABBIT BOY!
INTO MY ANTLERS!
QUICK!
RUMBLE!
!

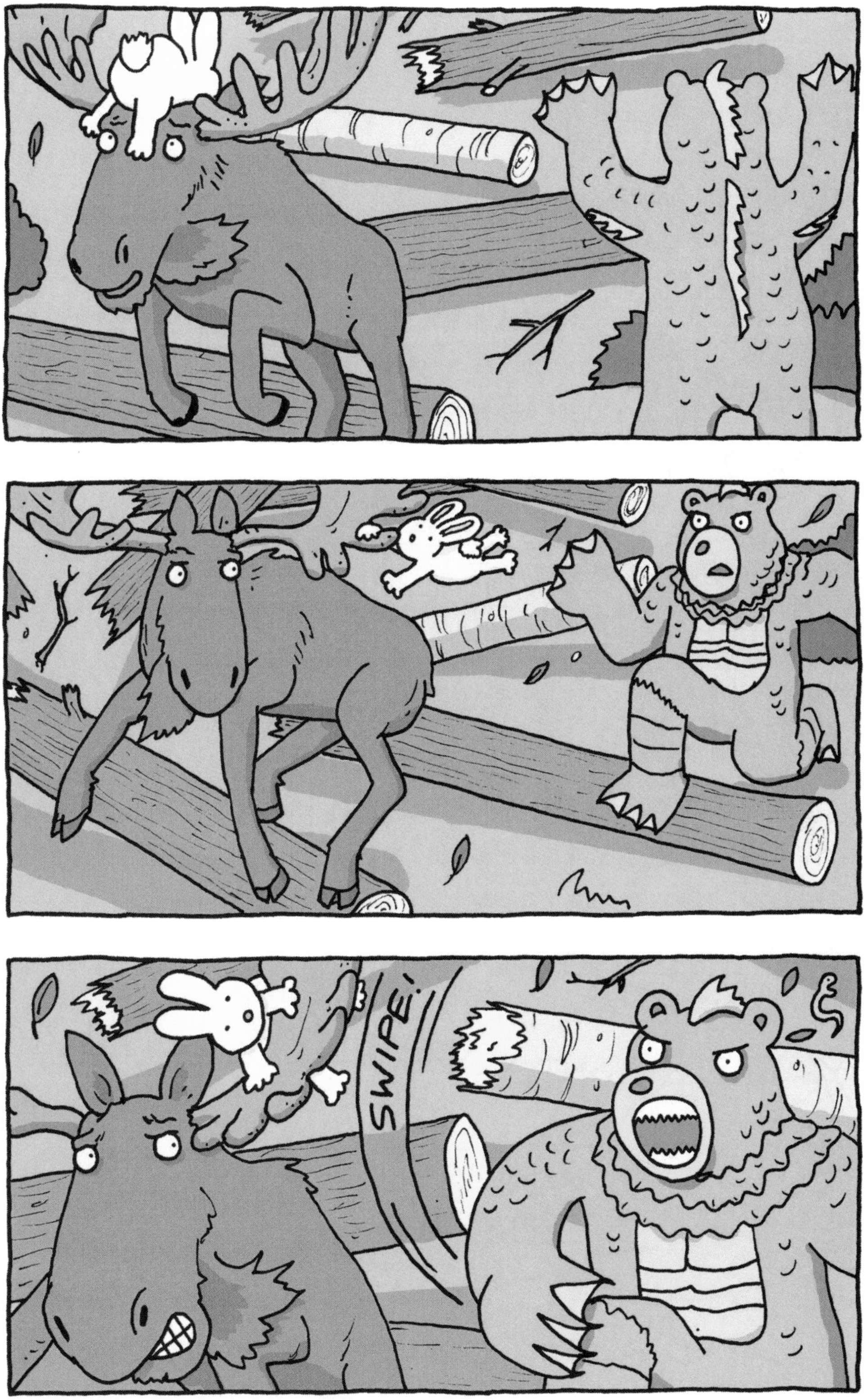
SWIPE!

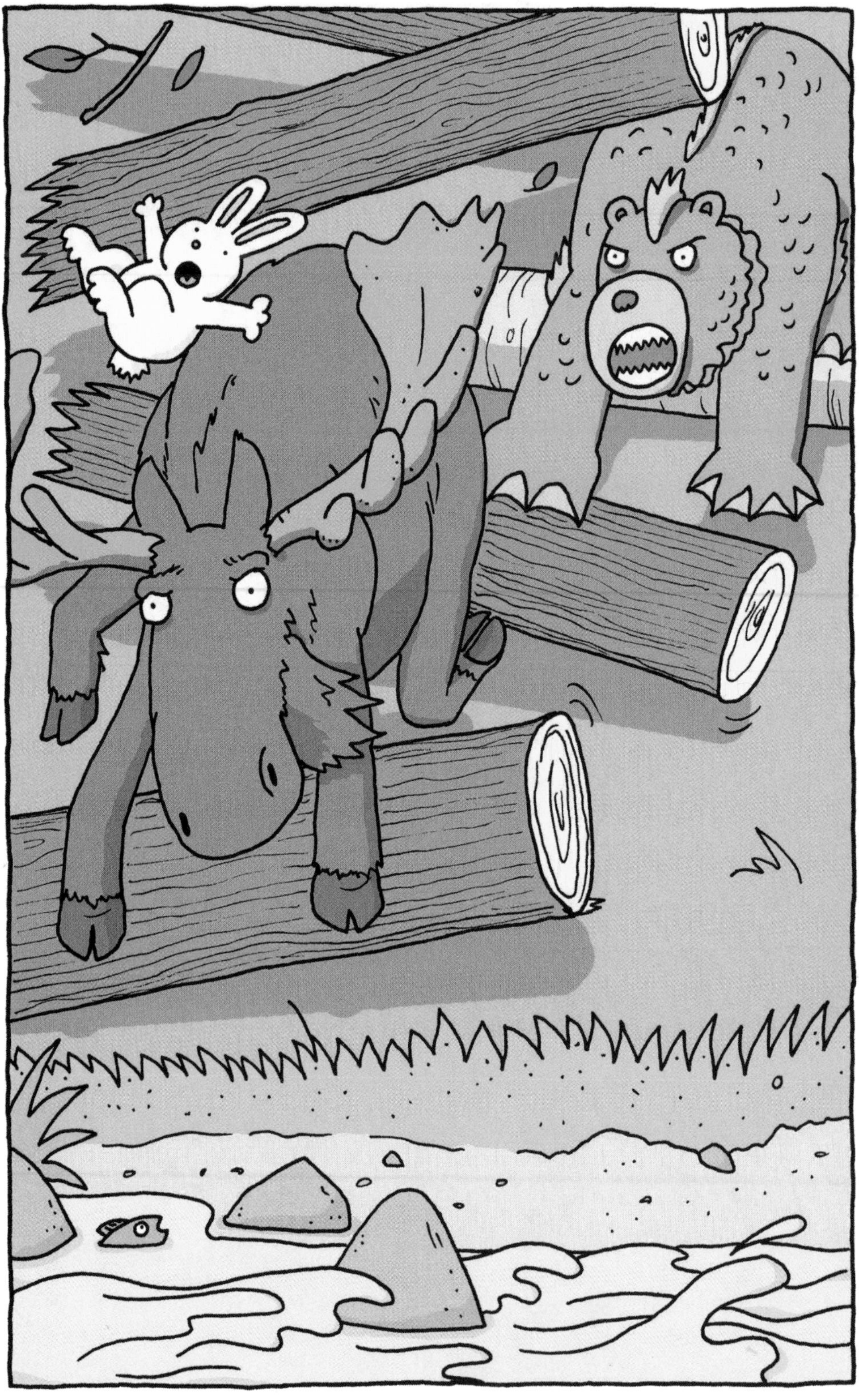

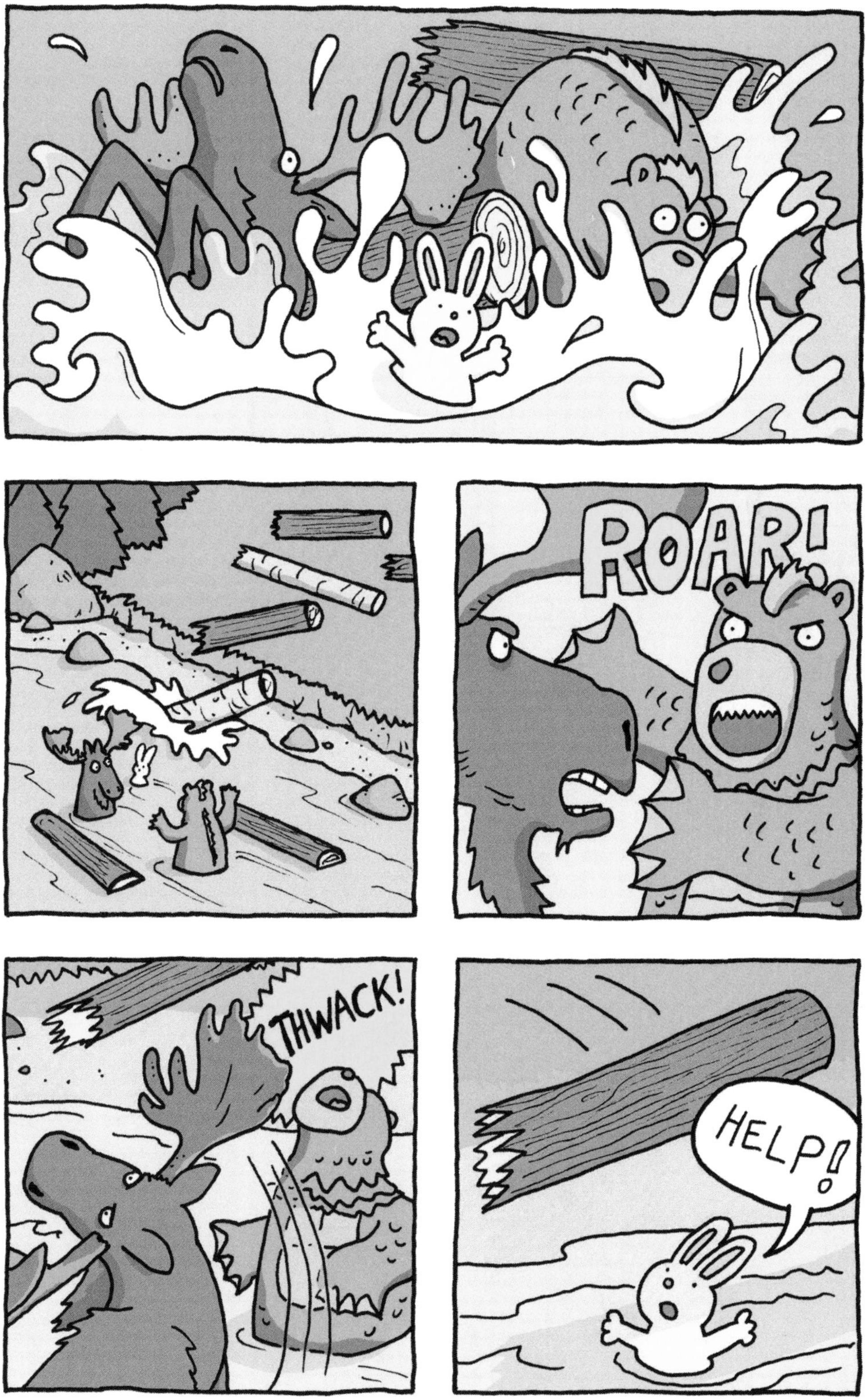
ROAR!
THWACK!
HELP!

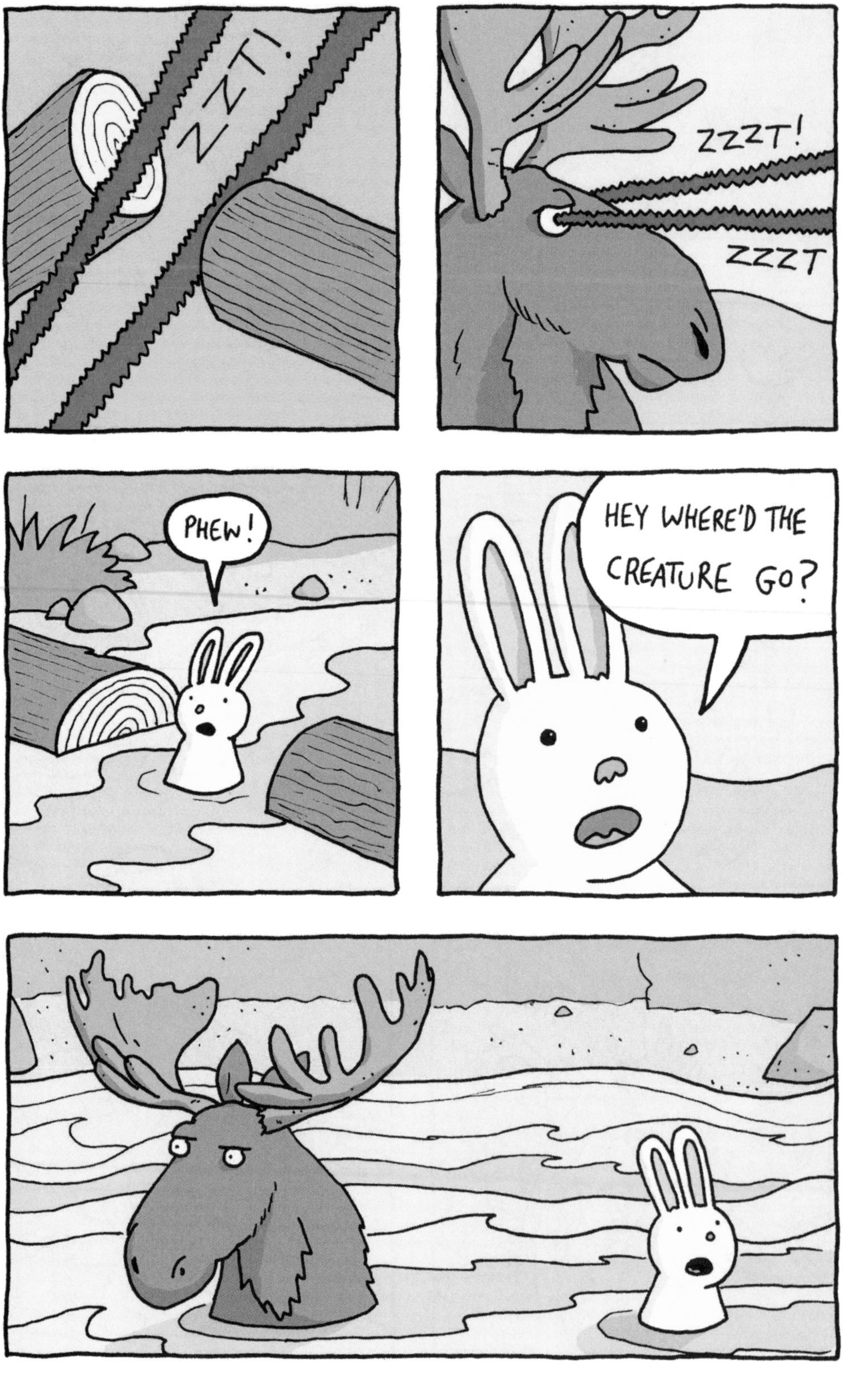

ZZZT!
ZZZT!
ZZZT
PHEW!
HEY WHERE'D THE CREATURE GO?

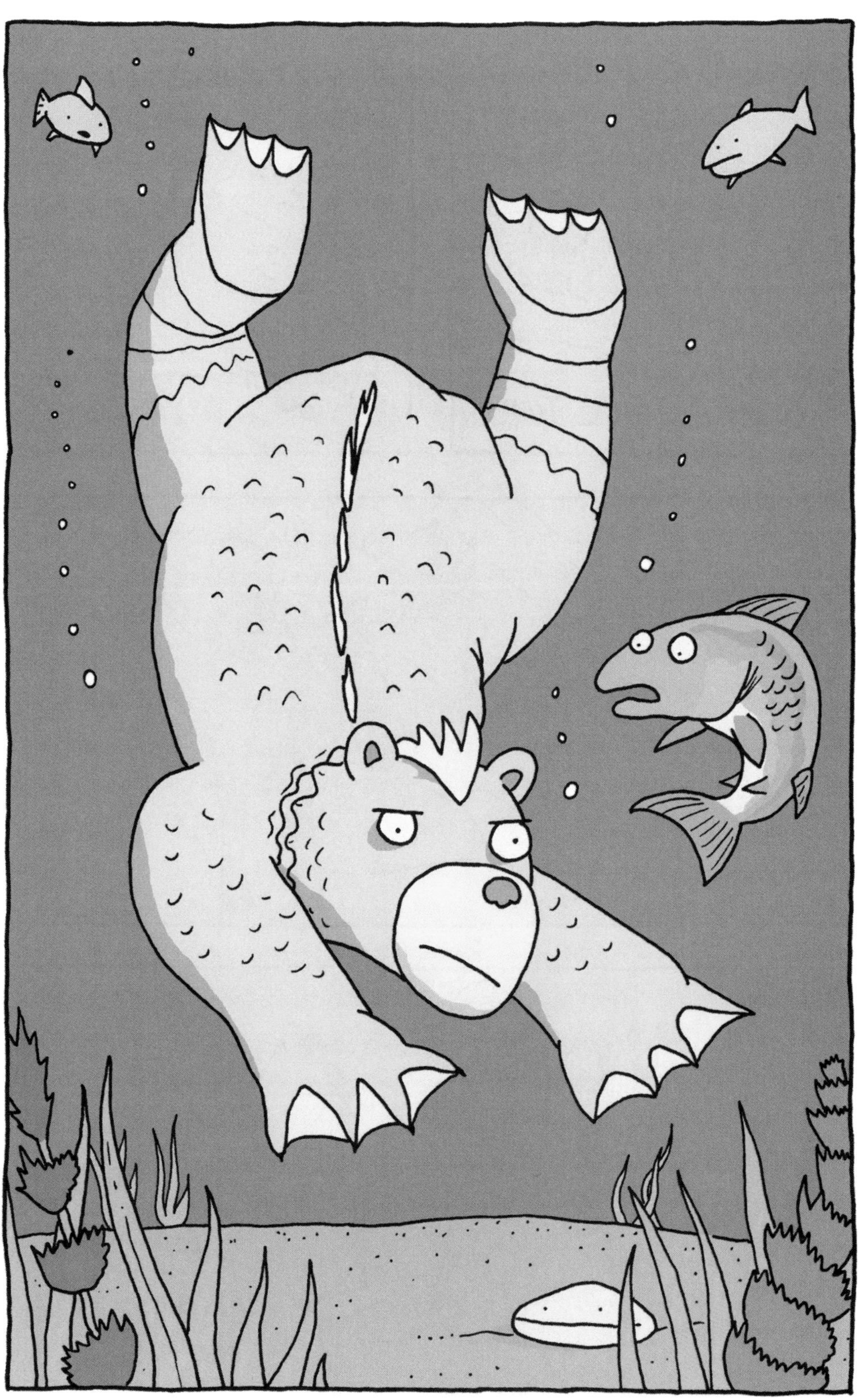

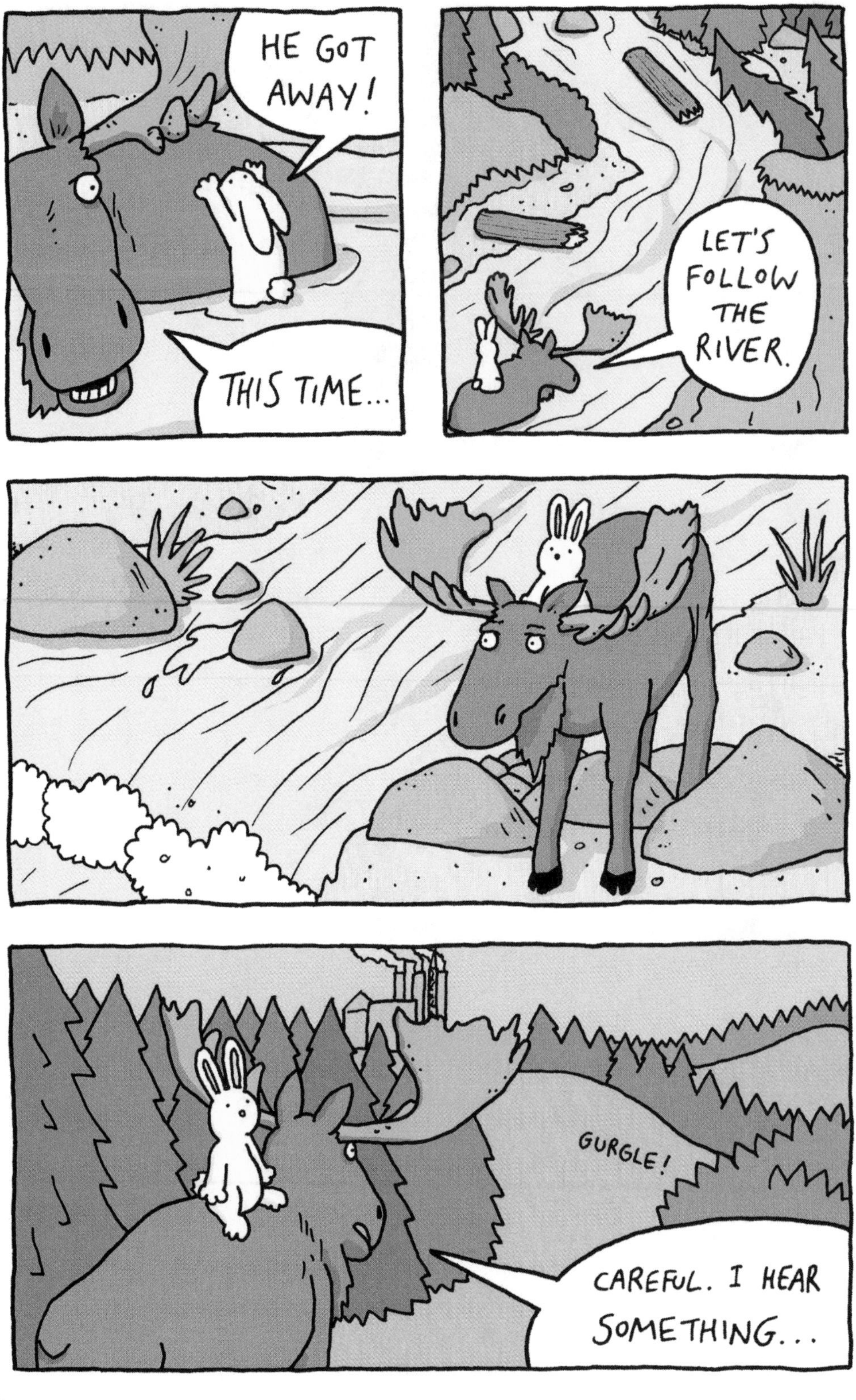
HE GOT AWAY!
THIS TIME...
LET'S FOLLOW THE RIVER.
GURGLE!
CAREFUL. I HEAR SOMETHING...

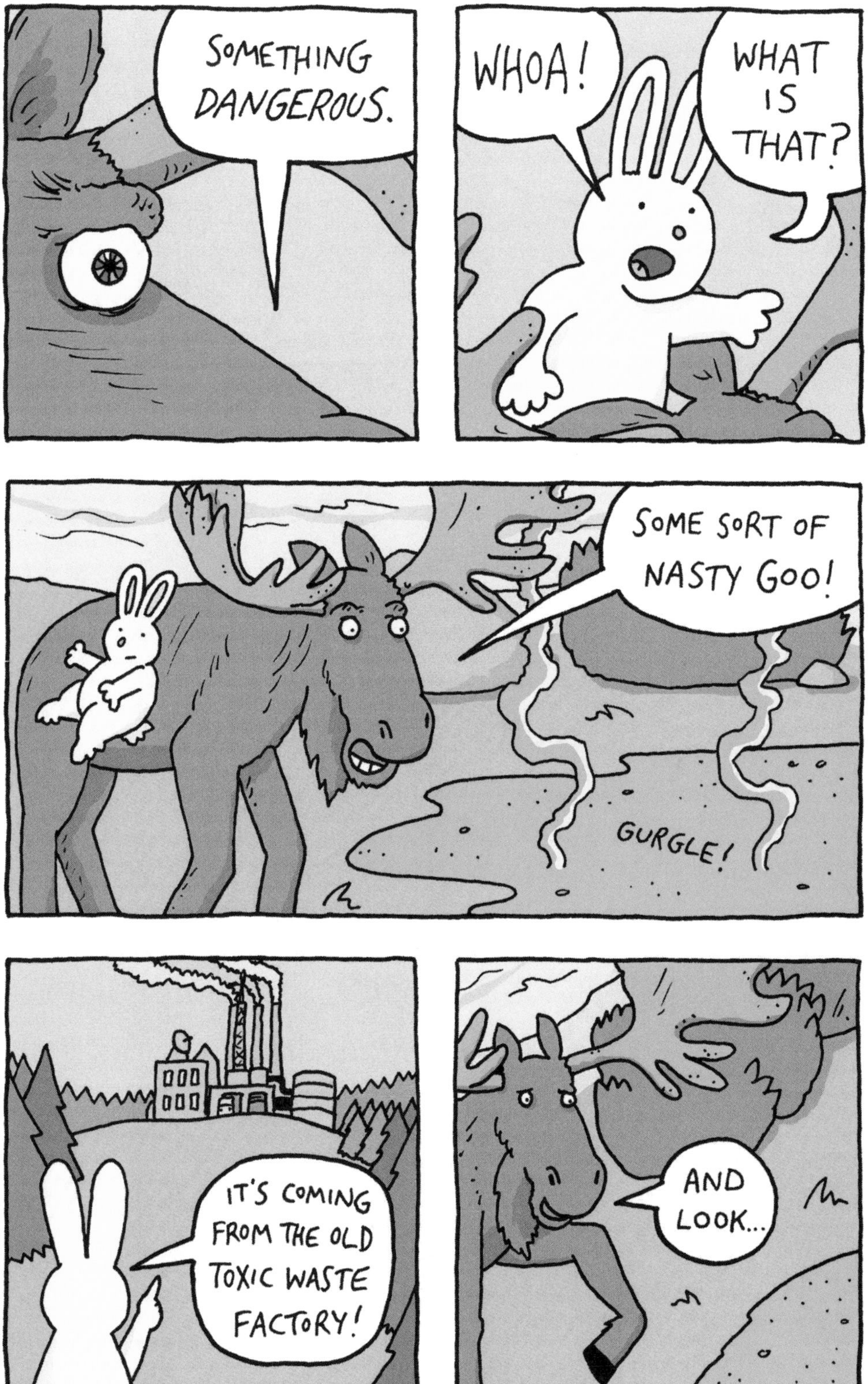
SOMETHING DANGEROUS.
WHOA!
WHAT IS THAT?
SOME SORT OF NASTY GOO!
GURGLE!
IT'S COMING FROM THE OLD TOXIC WASTE FACTORY!
AND LOOK...

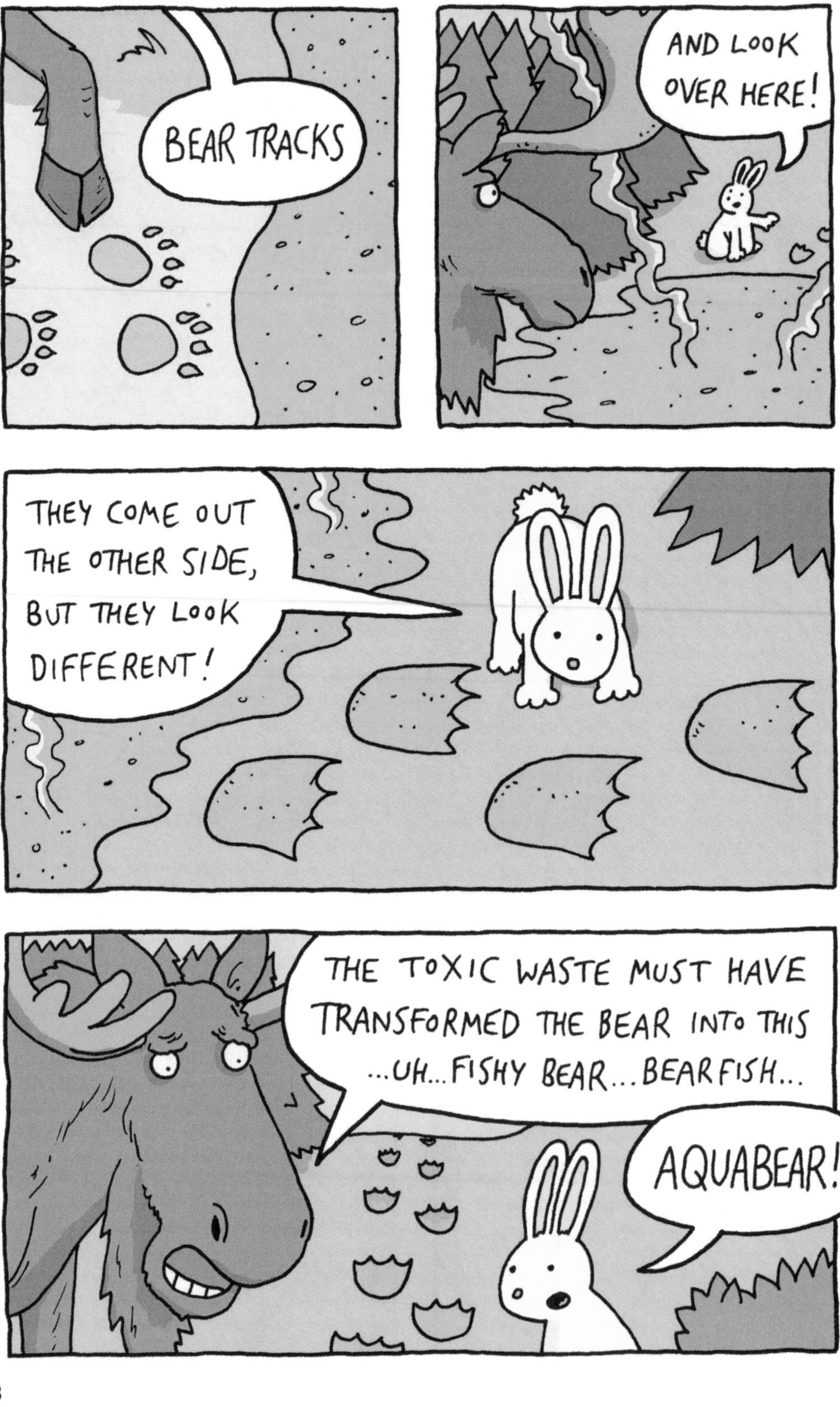
BEAR TRACKS
AND LOOK OVER HERE!
THEY COME OUT THE OTHER SIDE, BUT THEY LOOK DIFFERENT!
THE TOXIC WASTE MUST HAVE TRANSFORMED THE BEAR INTO THIS ...UH...FISHY BEAR...BEARFISH...
AQUABEAR!

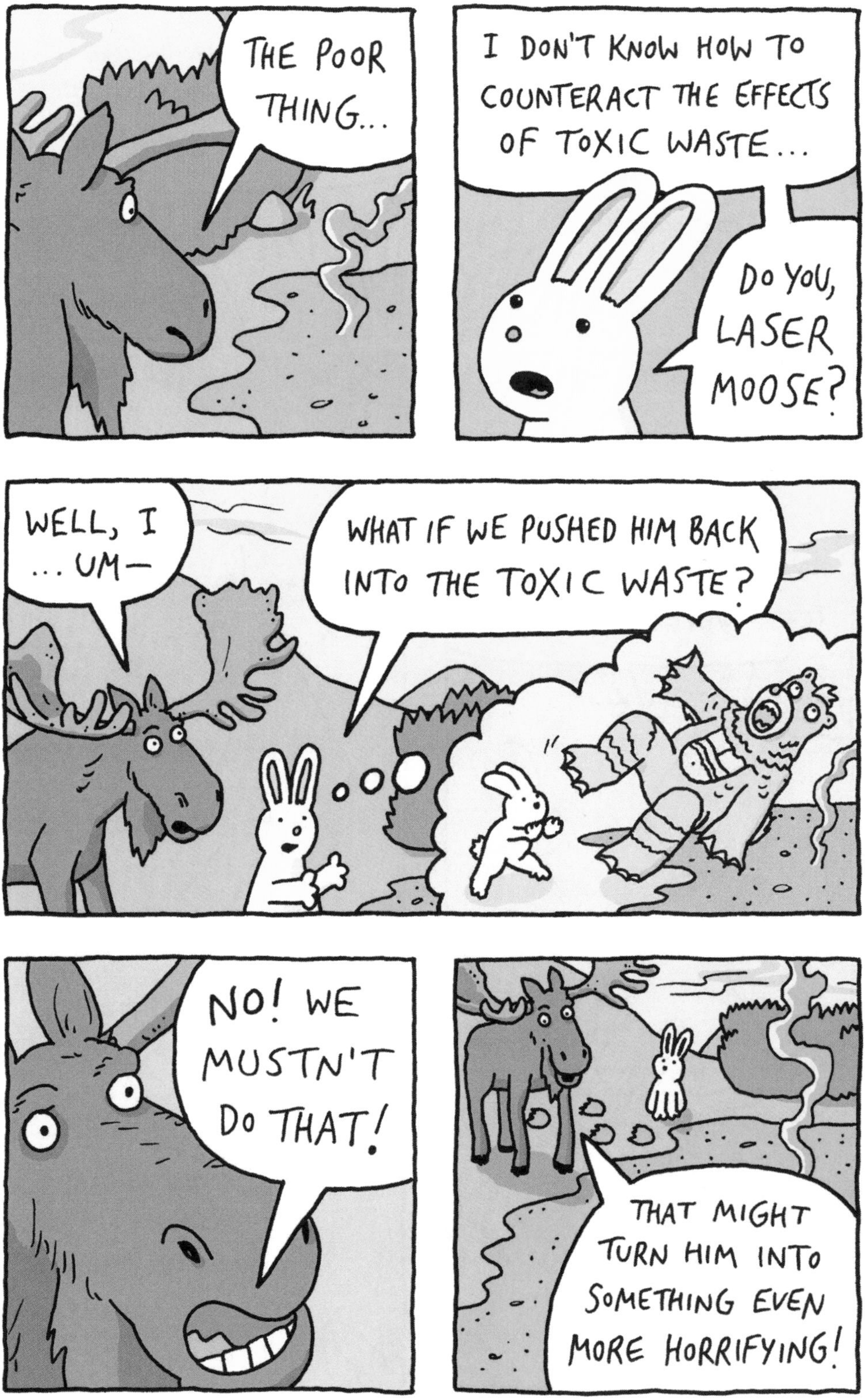
THE POOR THING...
I DON'T KNOW HOW TO COUNTERACT THE EFFECTS OF TOXIC WASTE...
DO YOU, LASER MOOSE?
WELL, I ...UM—
WHAT IF WE PUSHED HIM BACK INTO THE TOXIC WASTE?
NO! WE MUSTN'T DO THAT!
THAT MIGHT TURN HIM INTO SOMETHING EVEN MORE HORRIFYING!

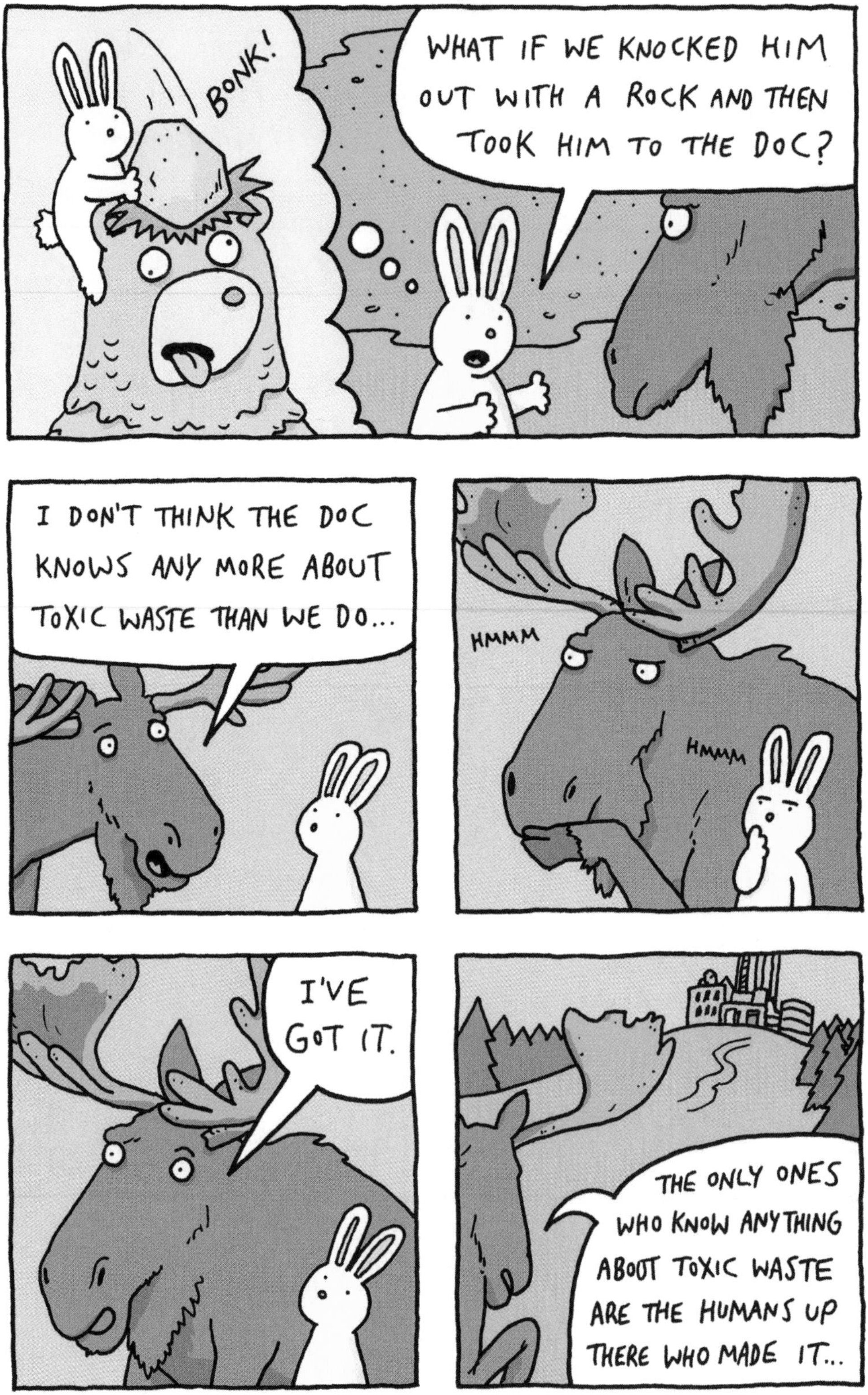
BONK!
WHAT IF WE KNOCKED HIM OUT WITH A ROCK AND THEN TOOK HIM TO THE DOC?
I DON'T THINK THE DOC KNOWS ANY MORE ABOUT TOXIC WASTE THAN WE DO...
HMMM
HMMM
I'VE GOT IT.
THE ONLY ONES WHO KNOW ANYTHING ABOUT TOXIC WASTE ARE THE HUMANS UP THERE WHO MADE IT...

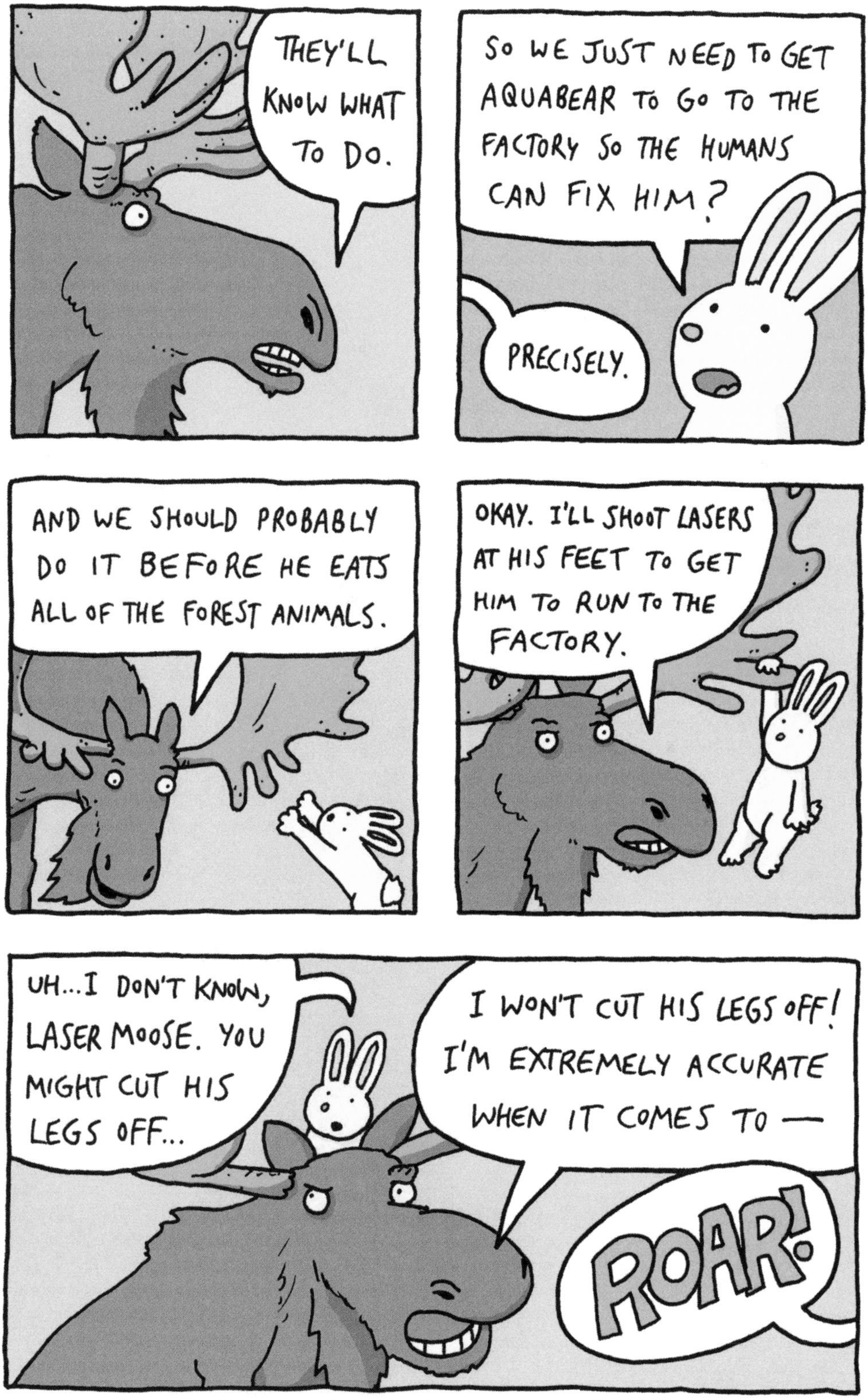
THEY'LL KNOW WHAT TO DO.
SO WE JUST NEED TO GET AQUABEAR TO GO TO THE FACTORY SO THE HUMANS CAN FIX HIM?
PRECISELY.
AND WE SHOULD PROBABLY DO IT BEFORE HE EATS ALL OF THE FOREST ANIMALS.
OKAY. I'LL SHOOT LASERS AT HIS FEET TO GET HIM TO RUN TO THE FACTORY.
UH...I DON'T KNOW, LASER MOOSE. YOU MIGHT CUT HIS LEGS OFF...
I WON'T CUT HIS LEGS OFF! I'M EXTREMELY ACCURATE WHEN IT COMES TO—
ROAR!

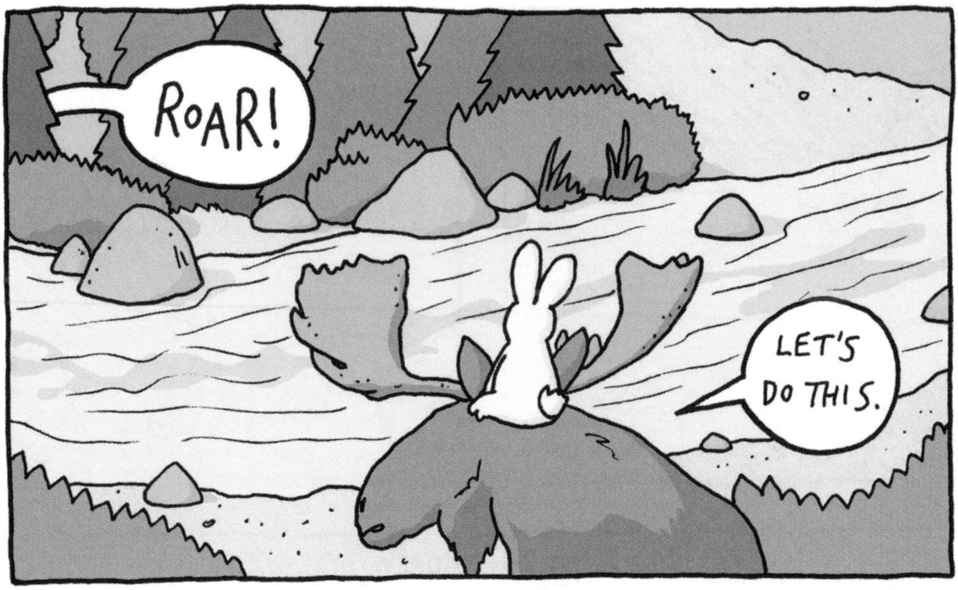
ROAR!
LET'S DO THIS.

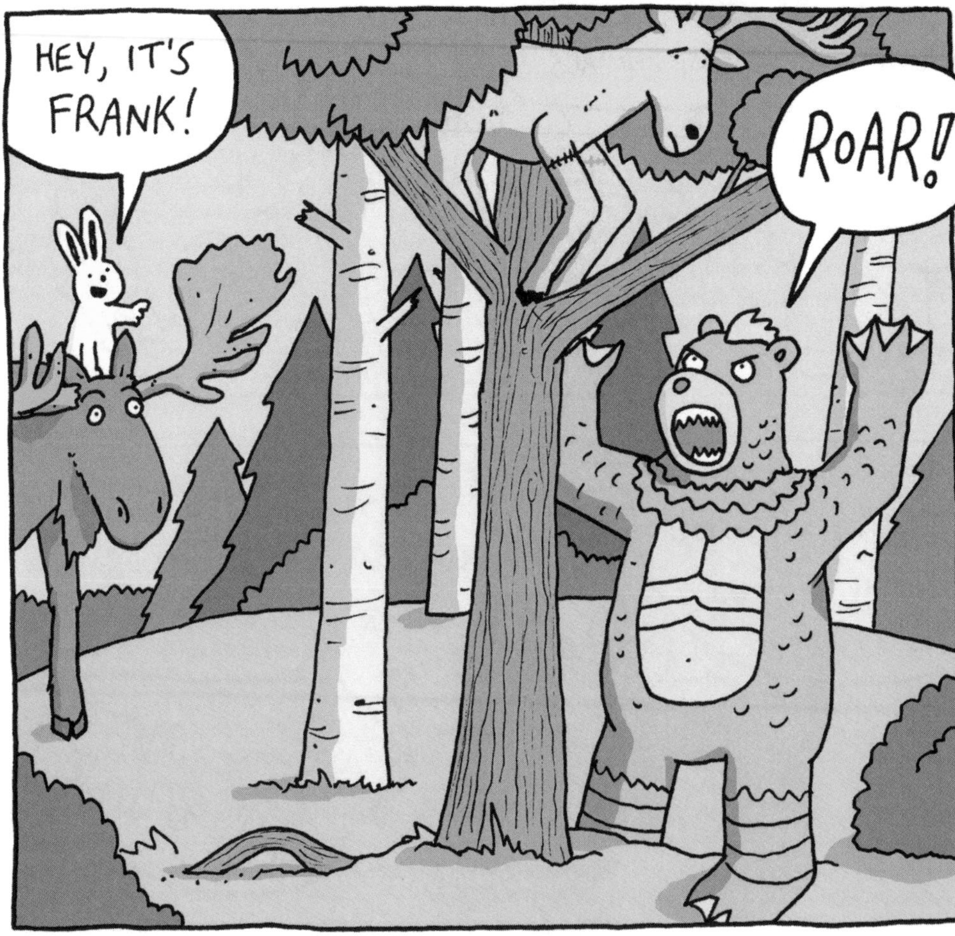
HEY, IT'S FRANK!
ROAR!

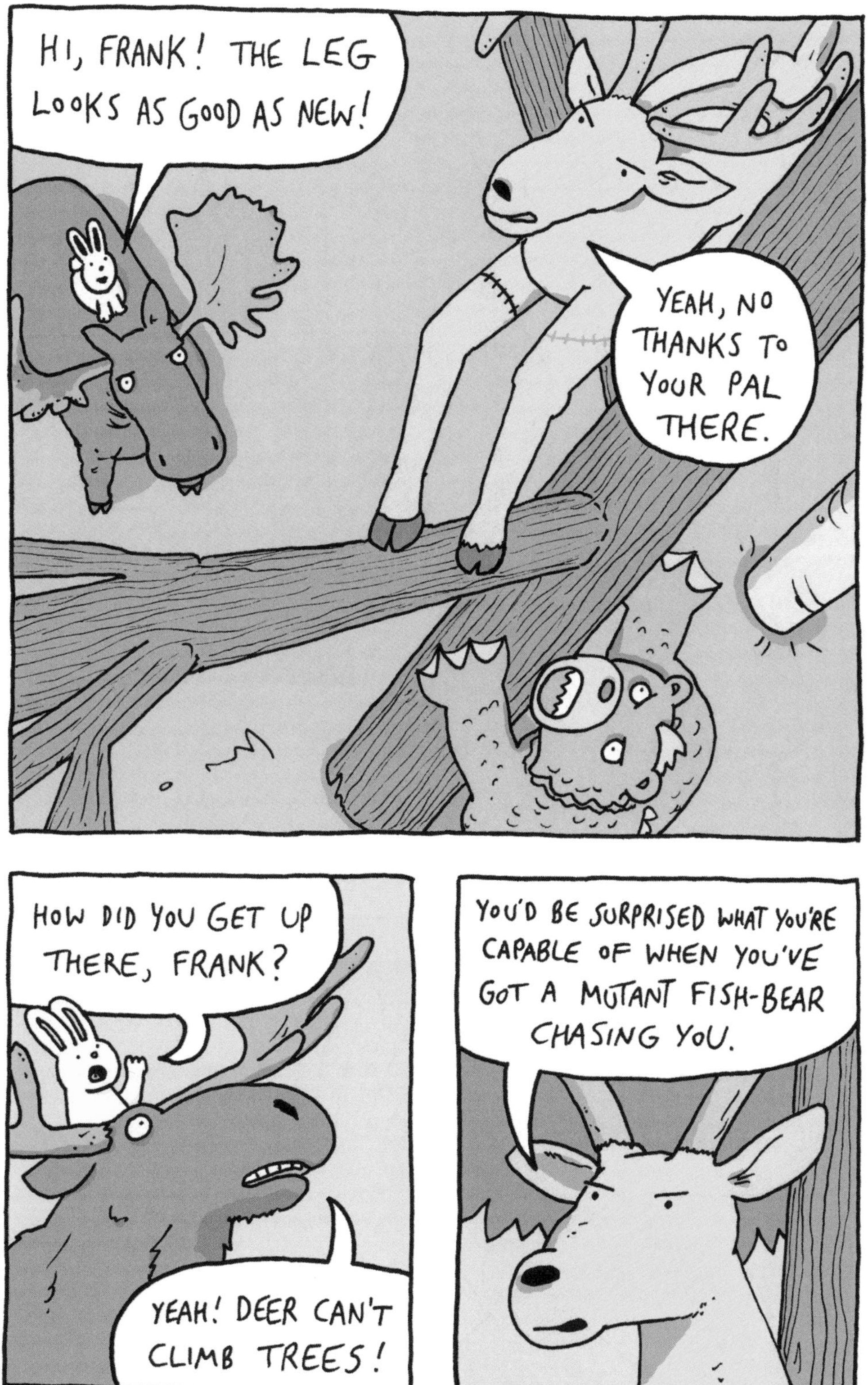
HI, FRANK! THE LEG LOOKS AS GOOD AS NEW!
YEAH, NO THANKS TO YOUR PAL THERE.
HOW DID YOU GET UP THERE, FRANK?
YEAH! DEER CAN'T CLIMB TREES!
YOU'D BE SURPRISED WHAT YOU'RE CAPABLE OF WHEN YOU'VE GOT A MUTANT FISH-BEAR CHASING YOU.

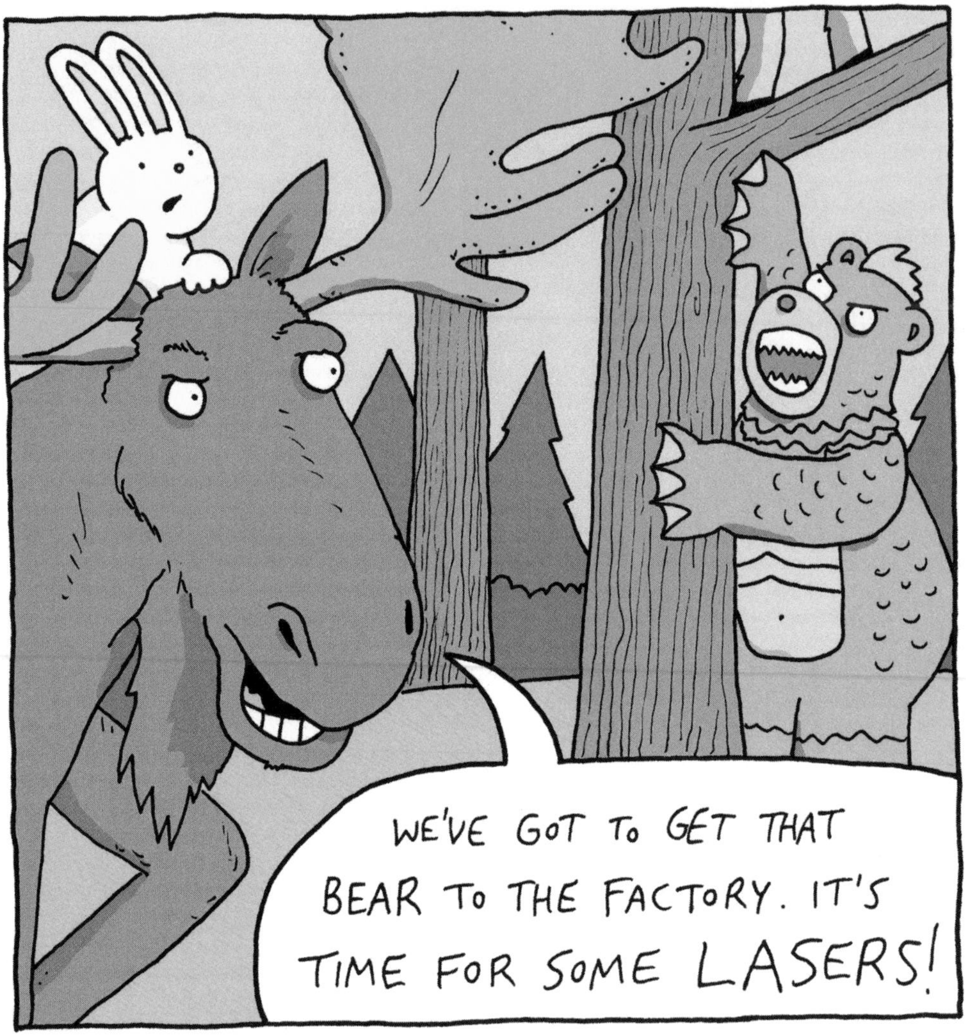
WE'VE GOT TO GET THAT BEAR TO THE FACTORY. IT'S TIME FOR SOME LASERS!

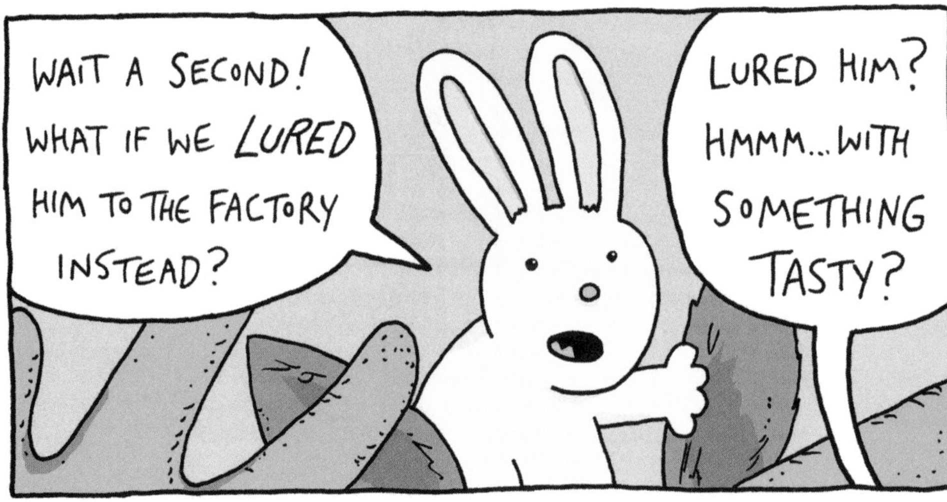
WAIT A SECOND! WHAT IF WE LURED HIM TO THE FACTORY INSTEAD?
LURED HIM? HMMM... WITH SOMETHING TASTY?

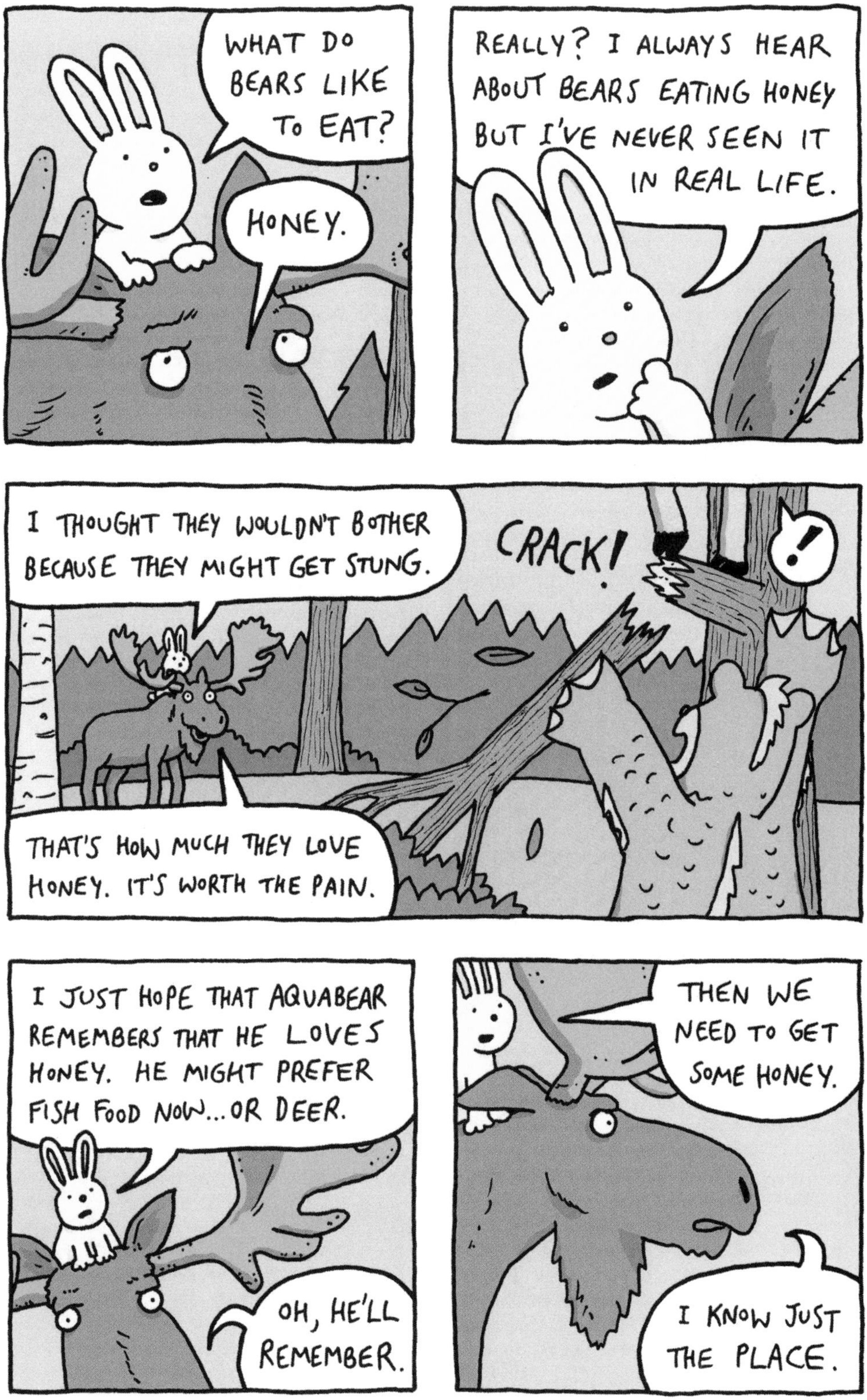
WHAT DO BEARS LIKE TO EAT?
HONEY.
REALLY? I ALWAYS HEAR ABOUT BEARS EATING HONEY BUT I'VE NEVER SEEN IT IN REAL LIFE.
I THOUGHT THEY WOULDN'T BOTHER BECAUSE THEY MIGHT GET STUNG.
CRACK!
!
THAT'S HOW MUCH THEY LOVE HONEY. IT'S WORTH THE PAIN.
I JUST HOPE THAT AQUABEAR REMEMBERS THAT HE LOVES HONEY. HE MIGHT PREFER FISH FOOD NOW...OR DEER.
OH, HE'LL REMEMBER.
THEN WE NEED TO GET SOME HONEY.
I KNOW JUST THE PLACE.

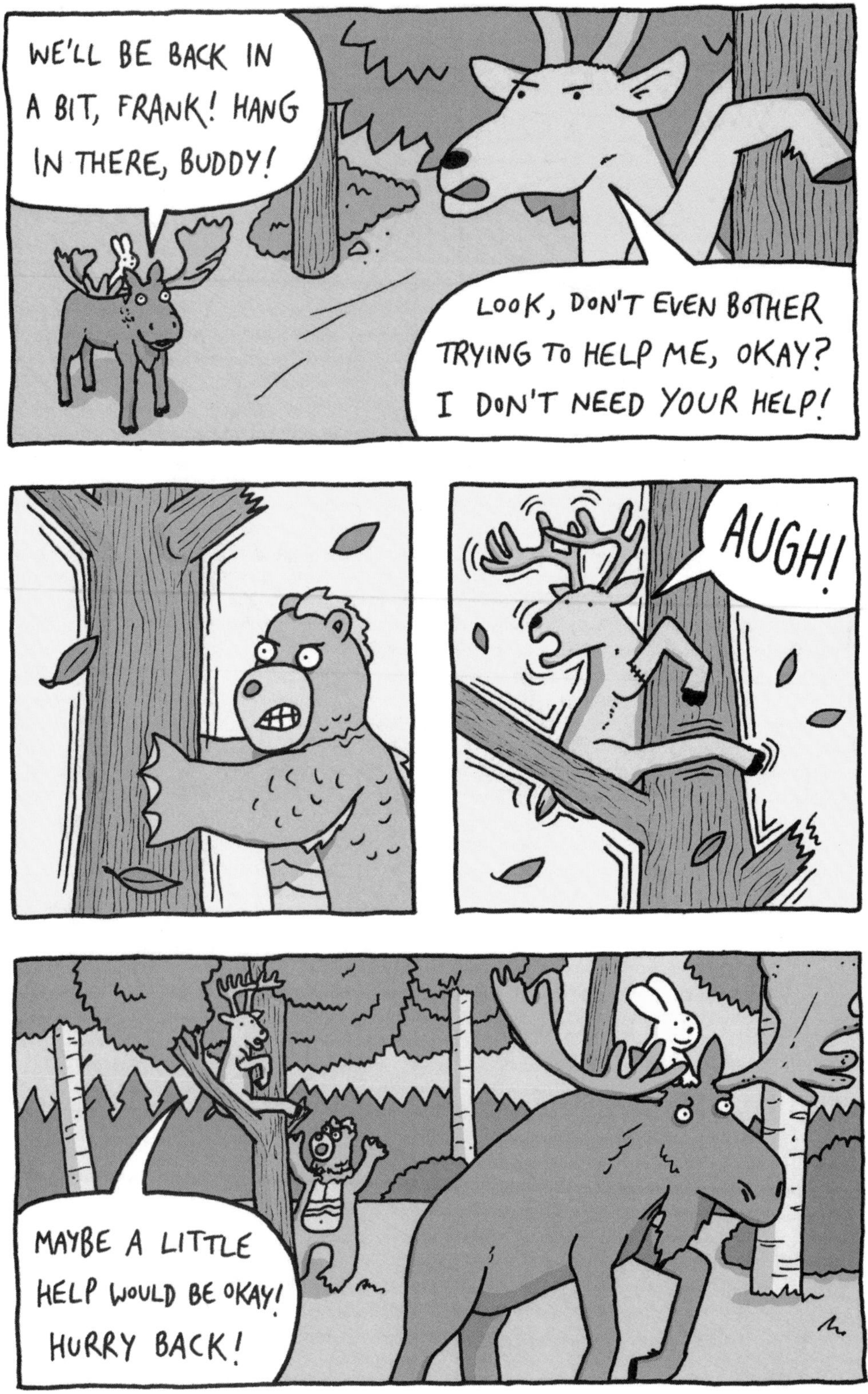
WE'LL BE BACK IN A BIT, FRANK! HANG IN THERE, BUDDY!
LOOK, DON'T EVEN BOTHER TRYING TO HELP ME, OKAY? I DON'T NEED YOUR HELP!
AUGH!
MAYBE A LITTLE HELP WOULD BE OKAY! HURRY BACK!

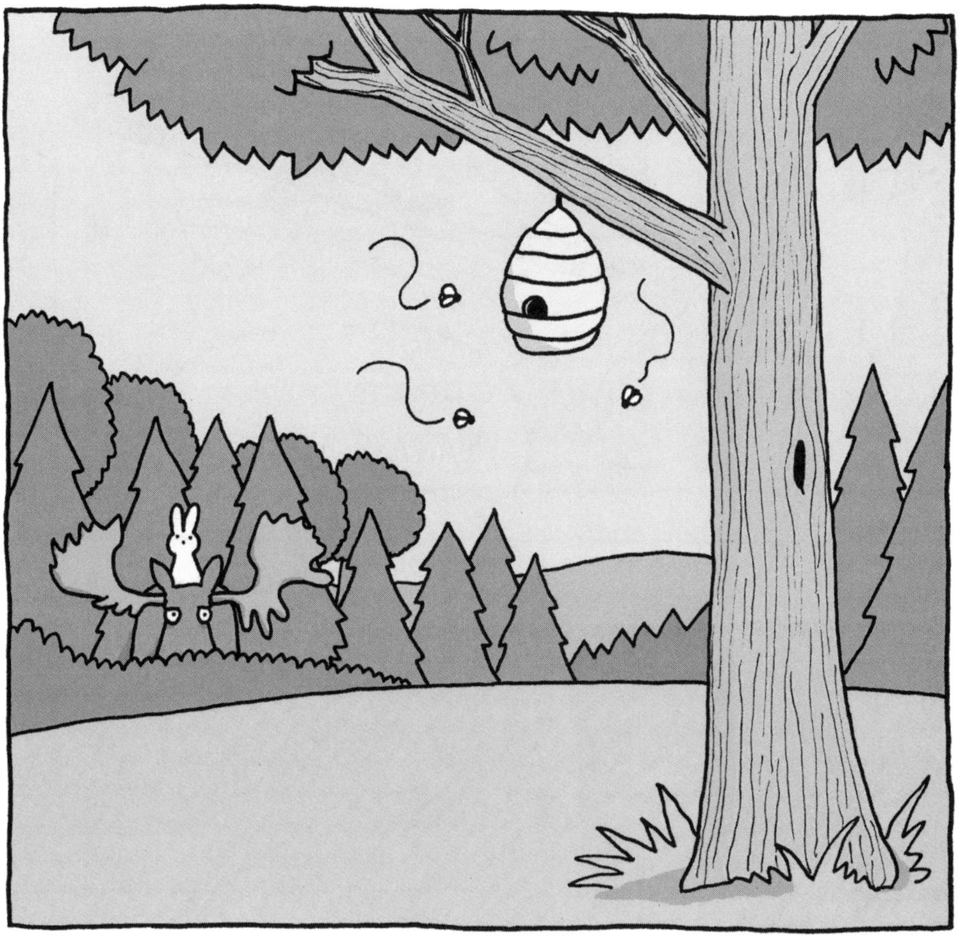

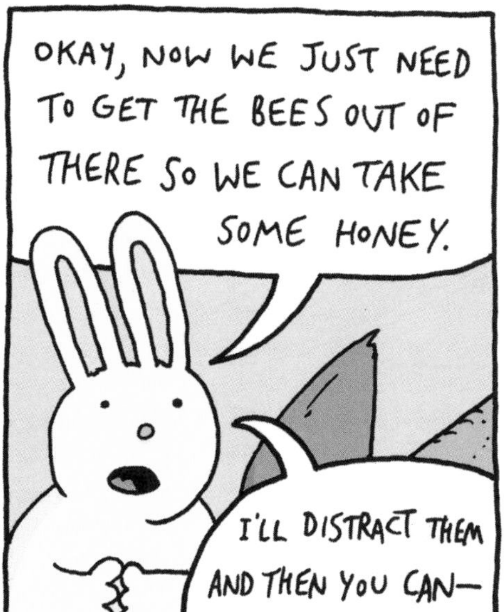
OKAY, NOW WE JUST NEED TO GET THE BEES OUT OF THERE SO WE CAN TAKE SOME HONEY.
I'LL DISTRACT THEM AND THEN YOU CAN—

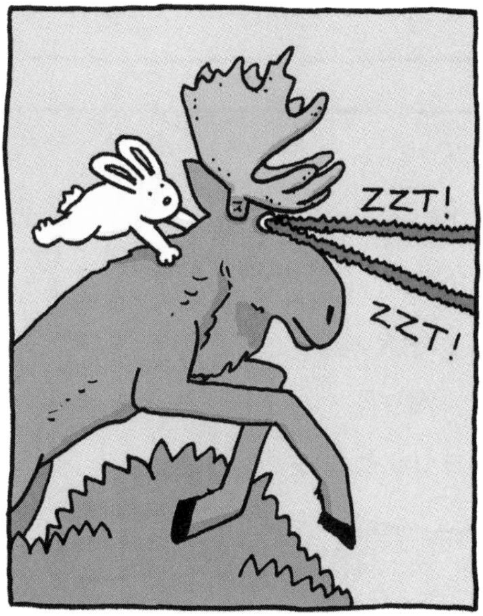
ZZT!
ZZT!

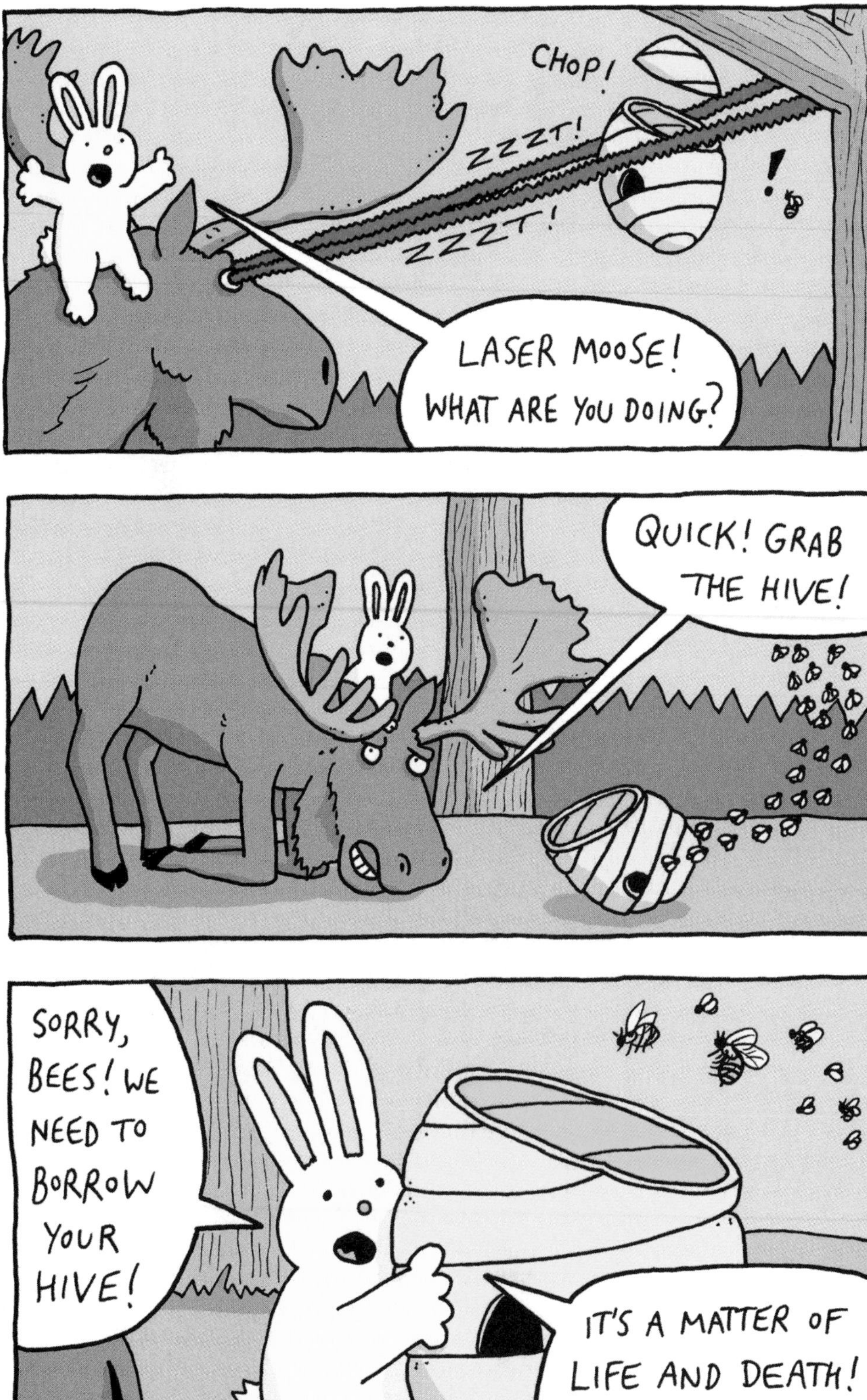
CHOP!
ZZZT!
ZZZT!
!
LASER MOOSE! WHAT ARE YOU DOING?
QUICK! GRAB THE HIVE!
SORRY, BEES! WE NEED TO BORROW YOUR HIVE!
IT'S A MATTER OF LIFE AND DEATH!

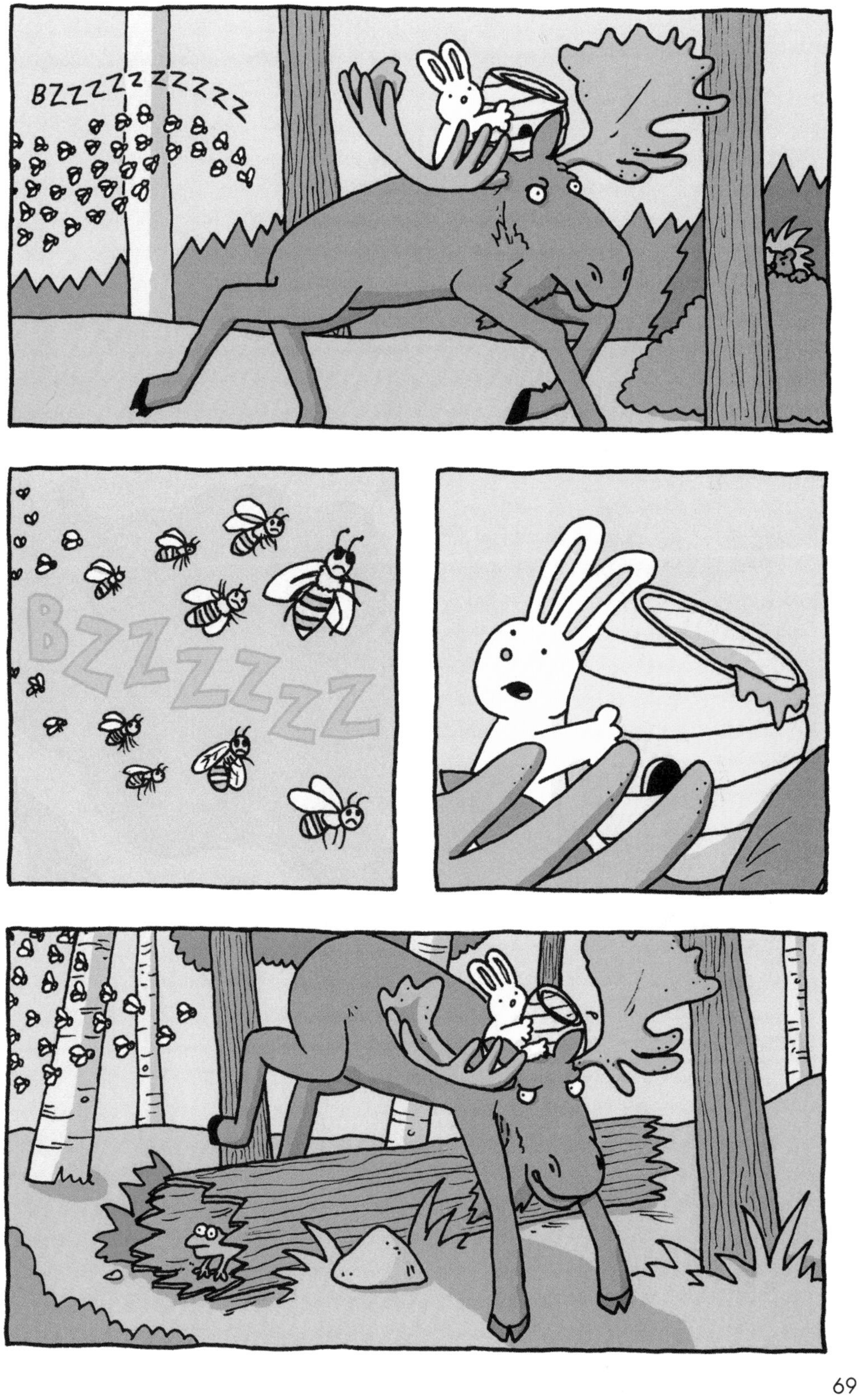
BZZZZZZZZZZ
BZZZZZZ

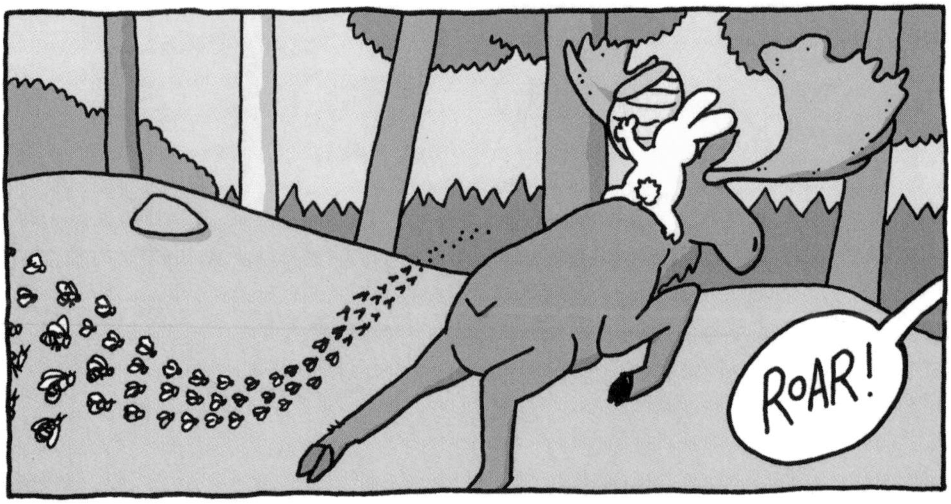
ROAR!

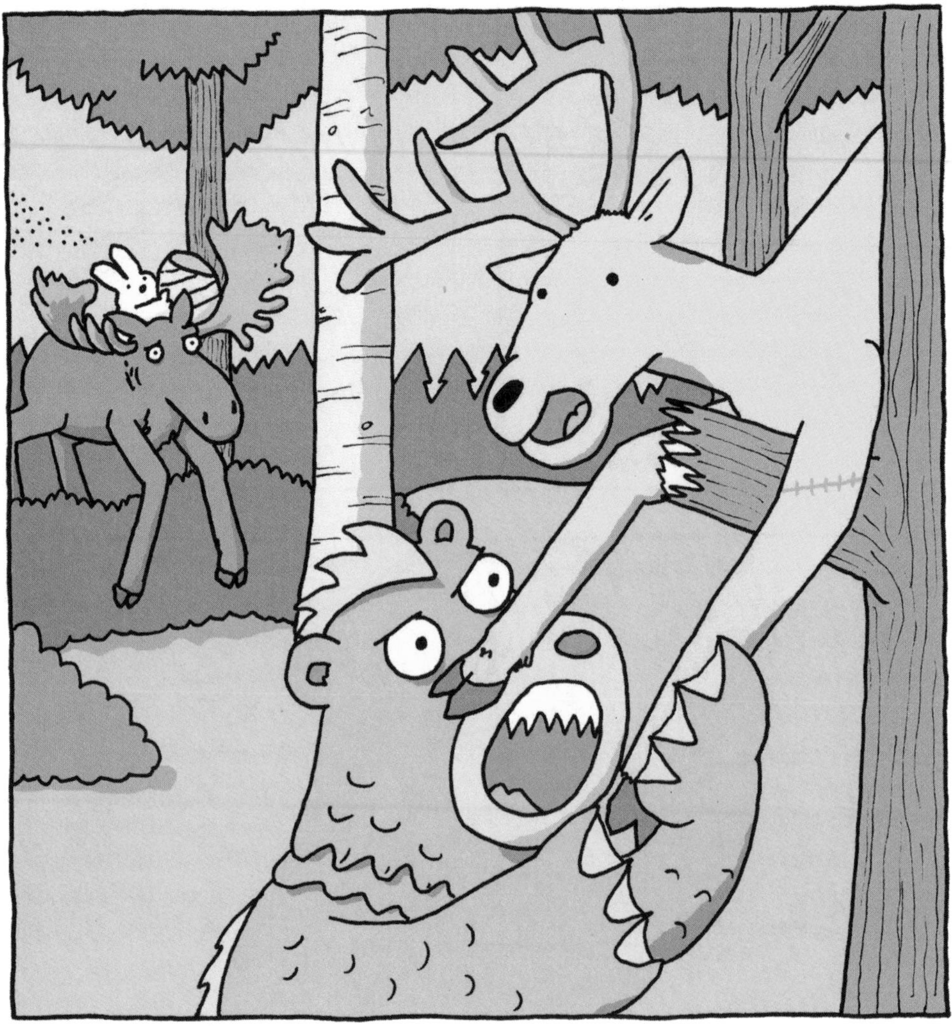

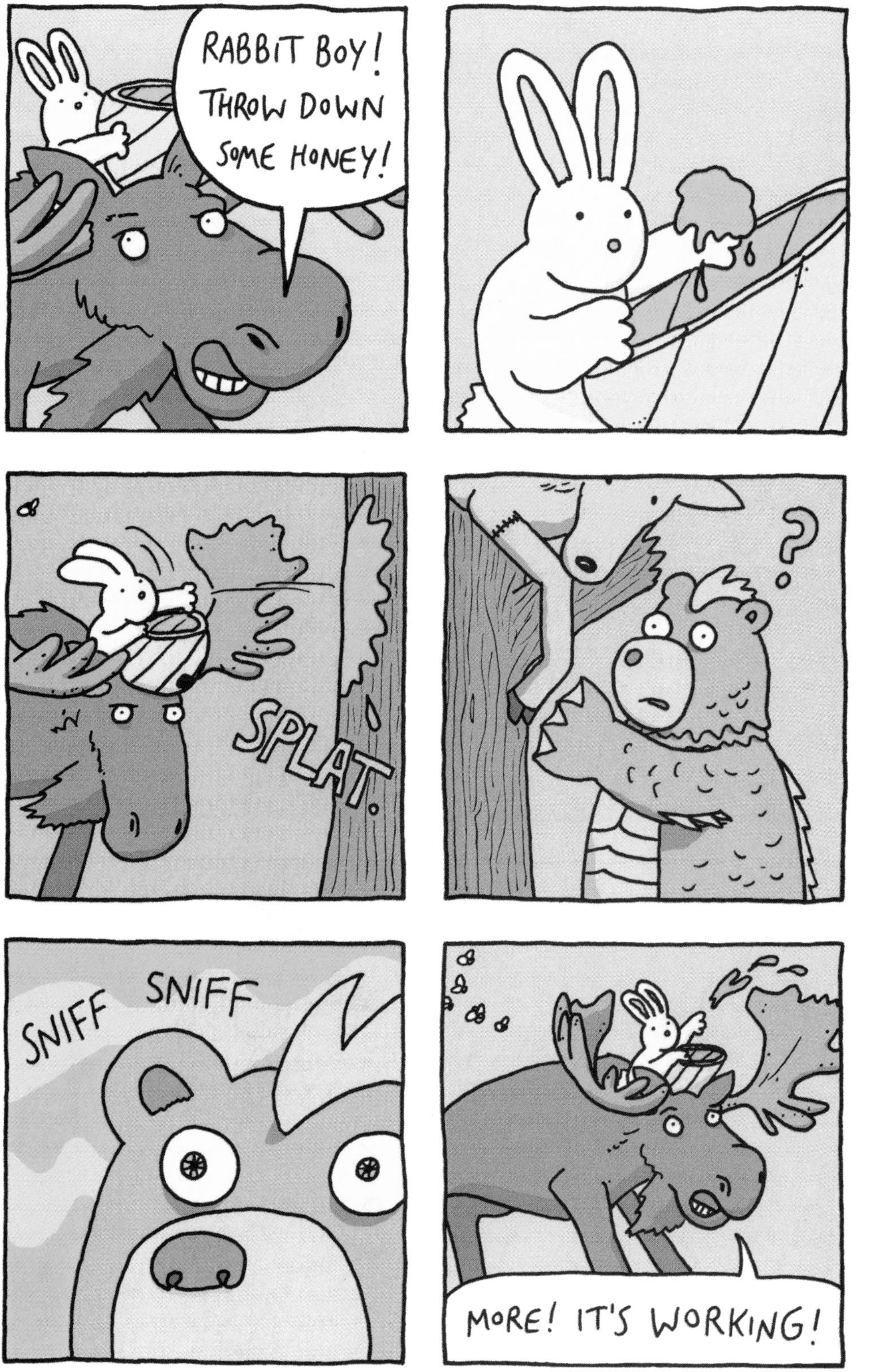
RABBIT BOY! THROW DOWN SOME HONEY!
SPLAT
SNIFF
SNIFF
MORE! IT'S WORKING!

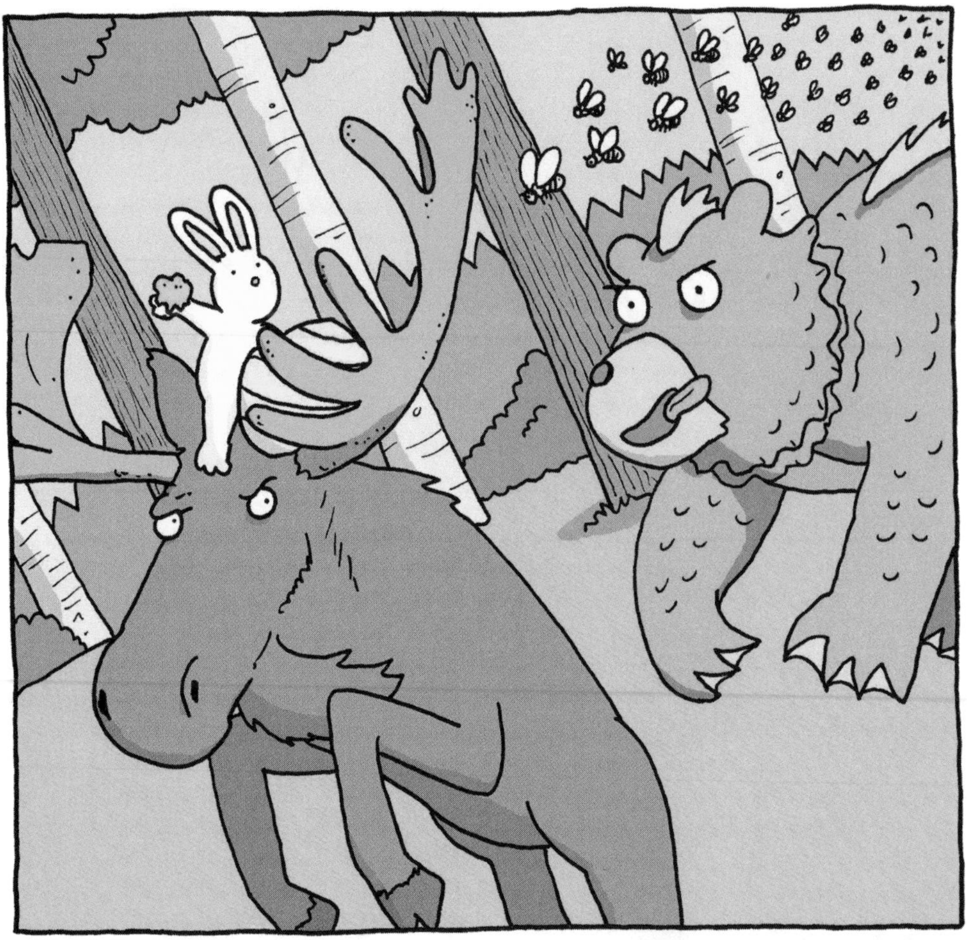

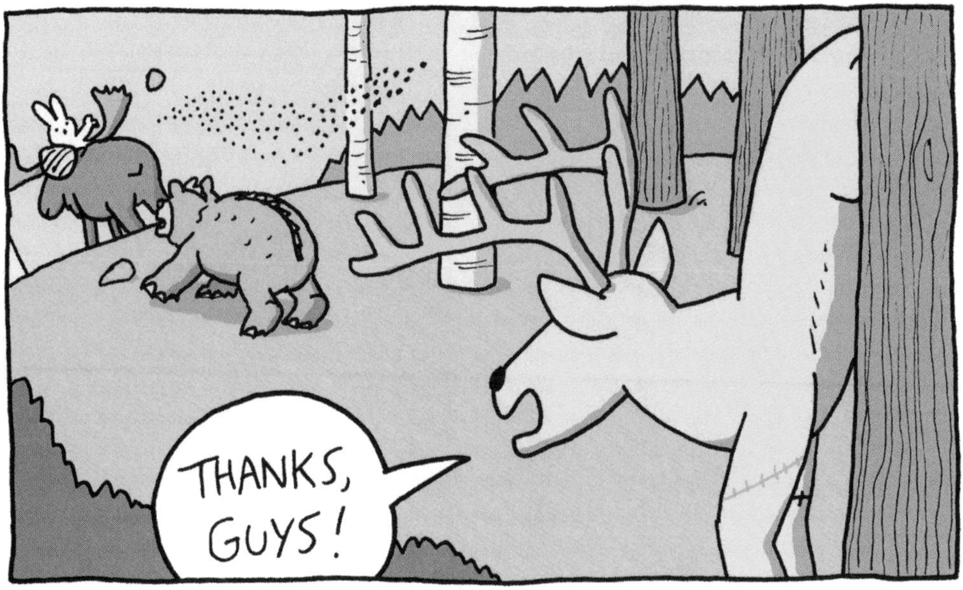
THANKS, GUYS!

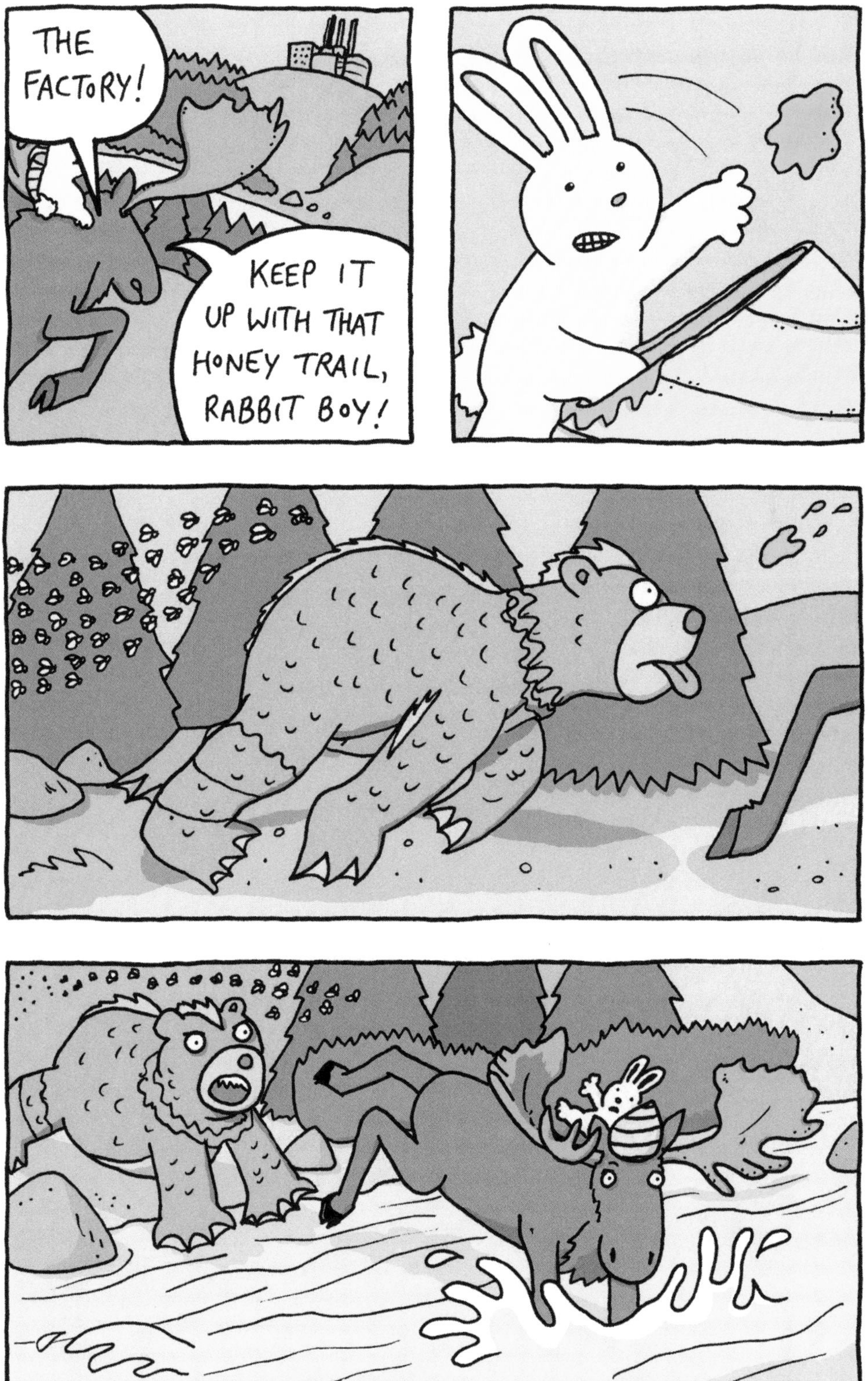
THE FACTORY!
KEEP IT UP WITH THAT HONEY TRAIL, RABBIT BOY!

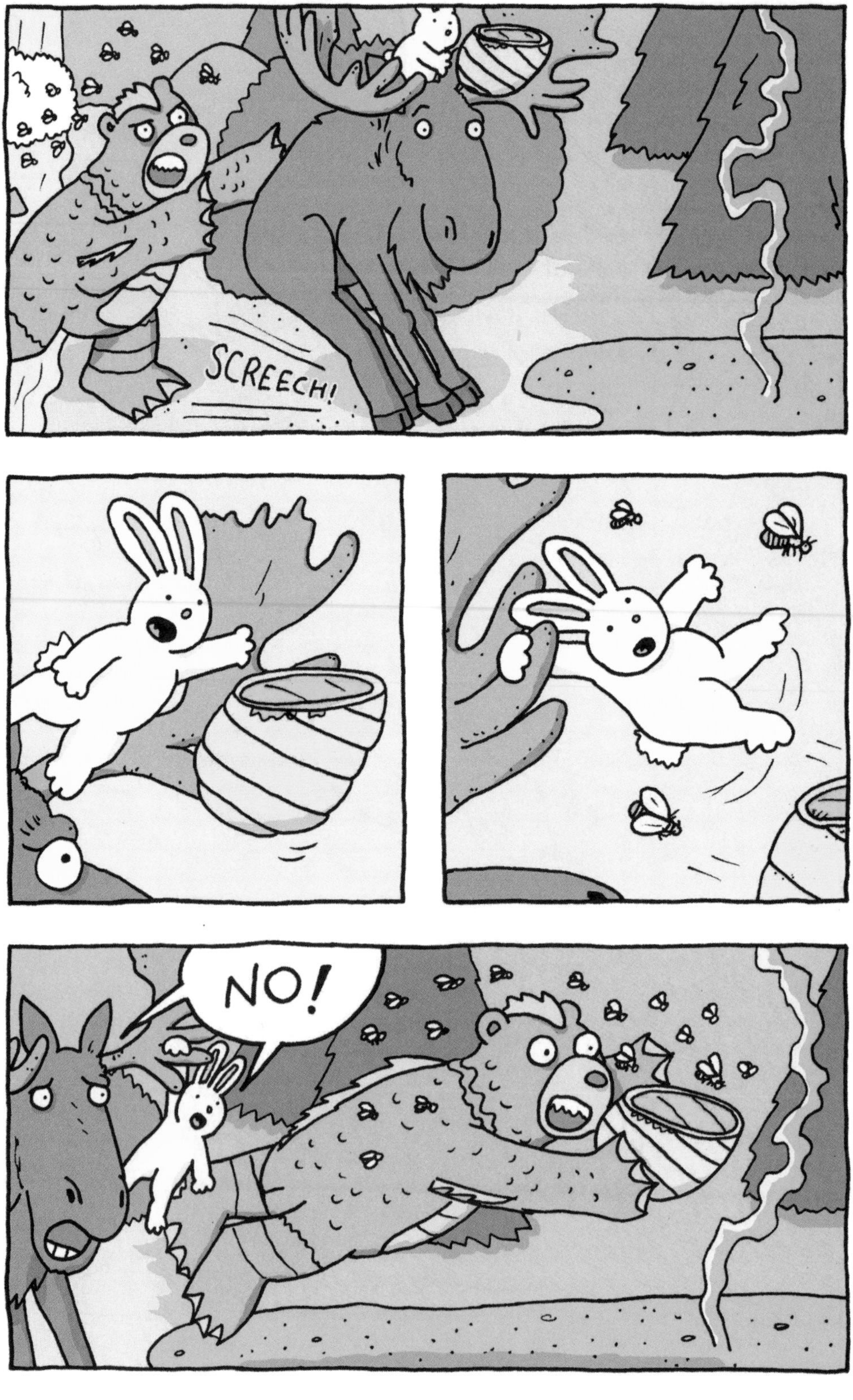
SCREECH!
NO!

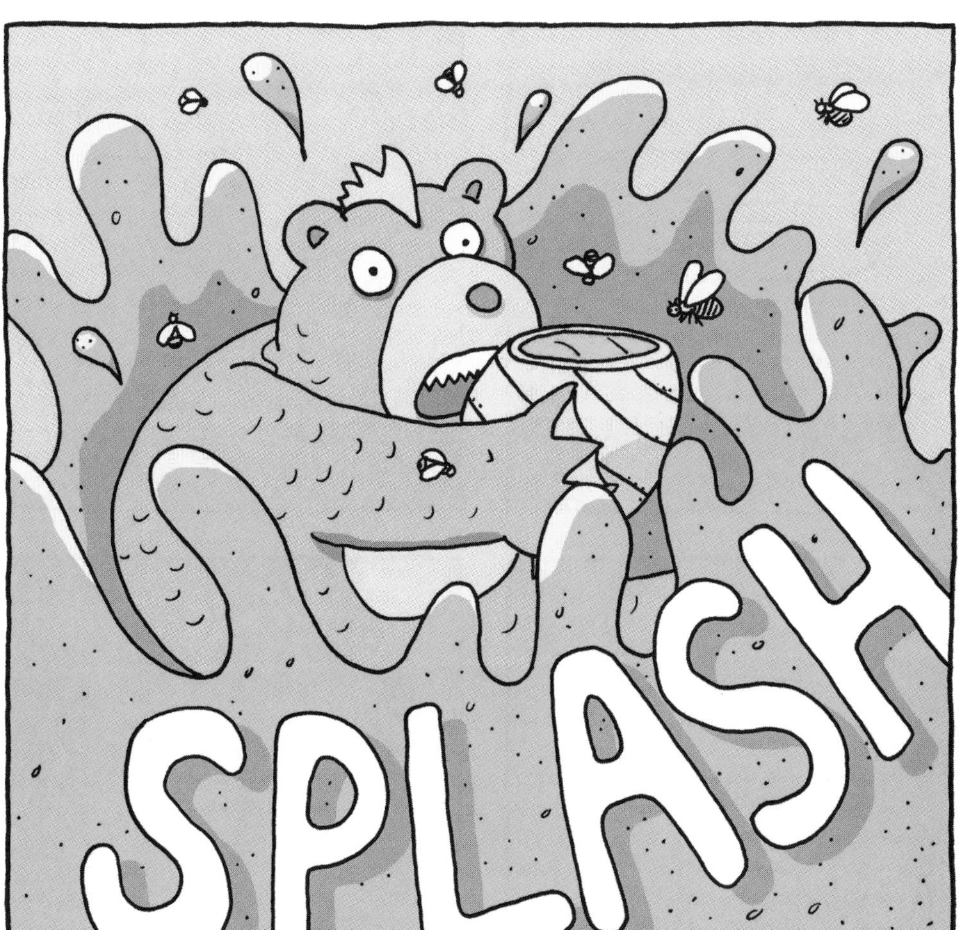
SPLASH

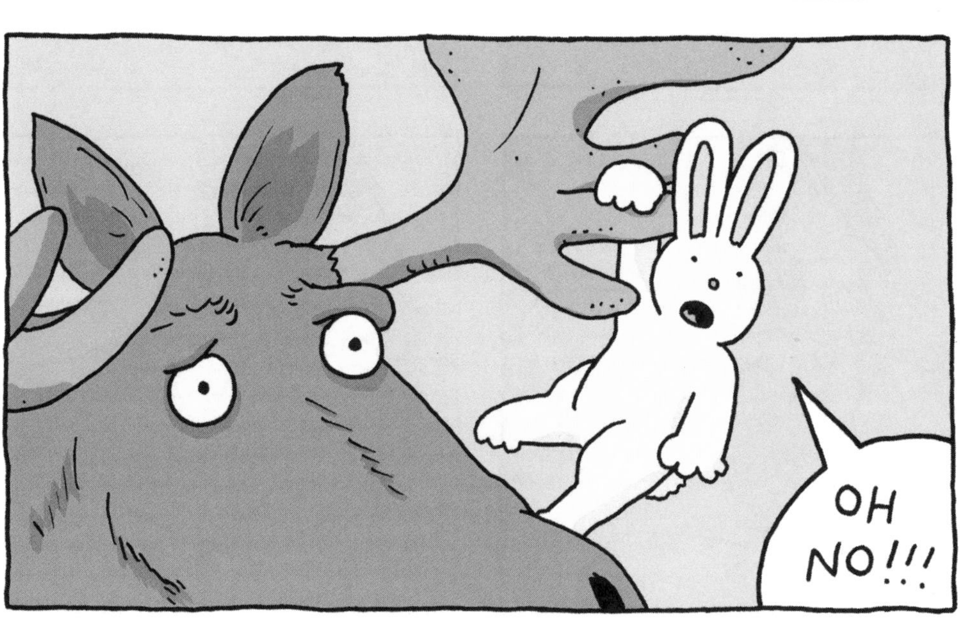
OH
NO!!!

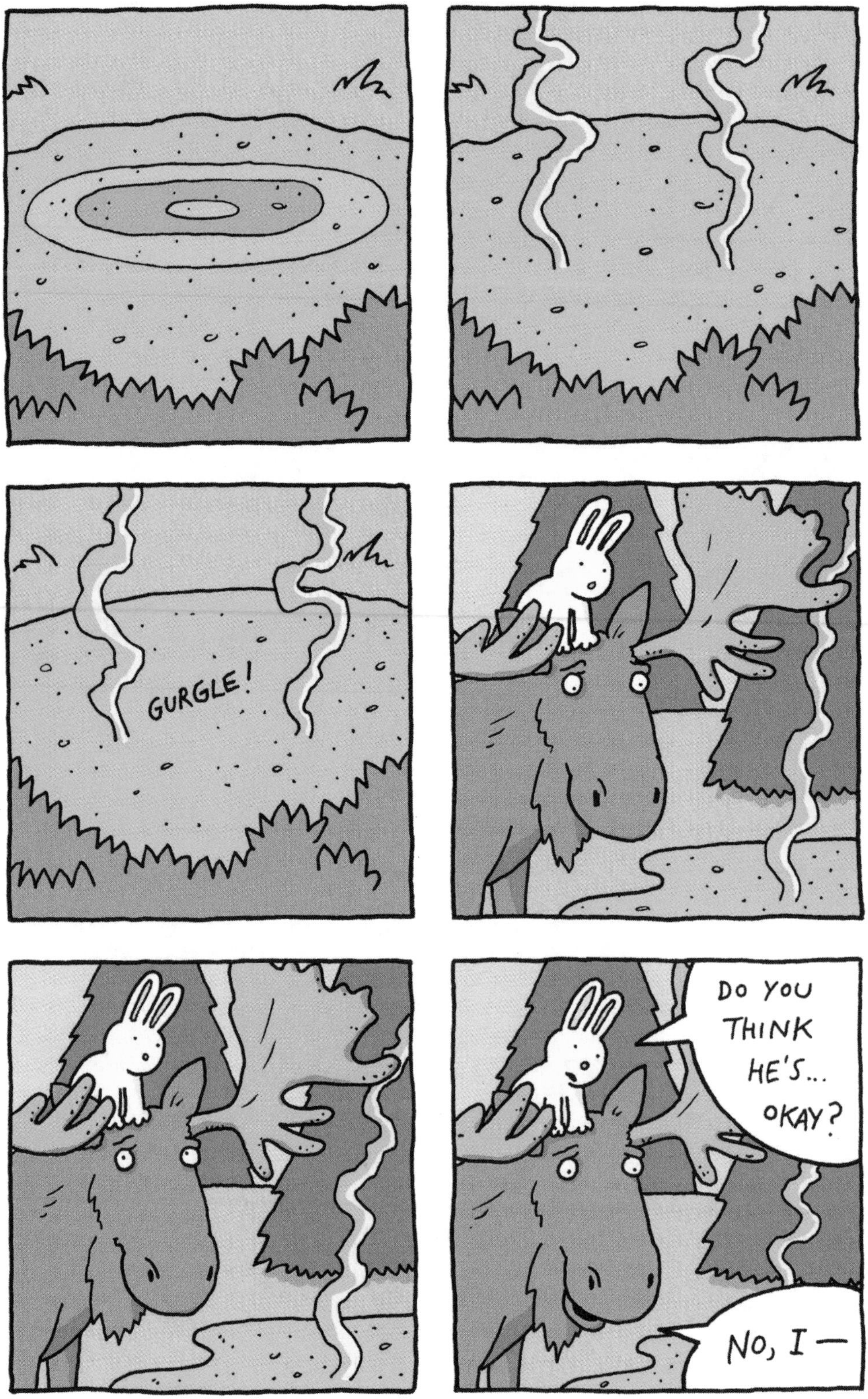
GURGLE!
DO YOU THINK HE'S... OKAY?
NO, I—

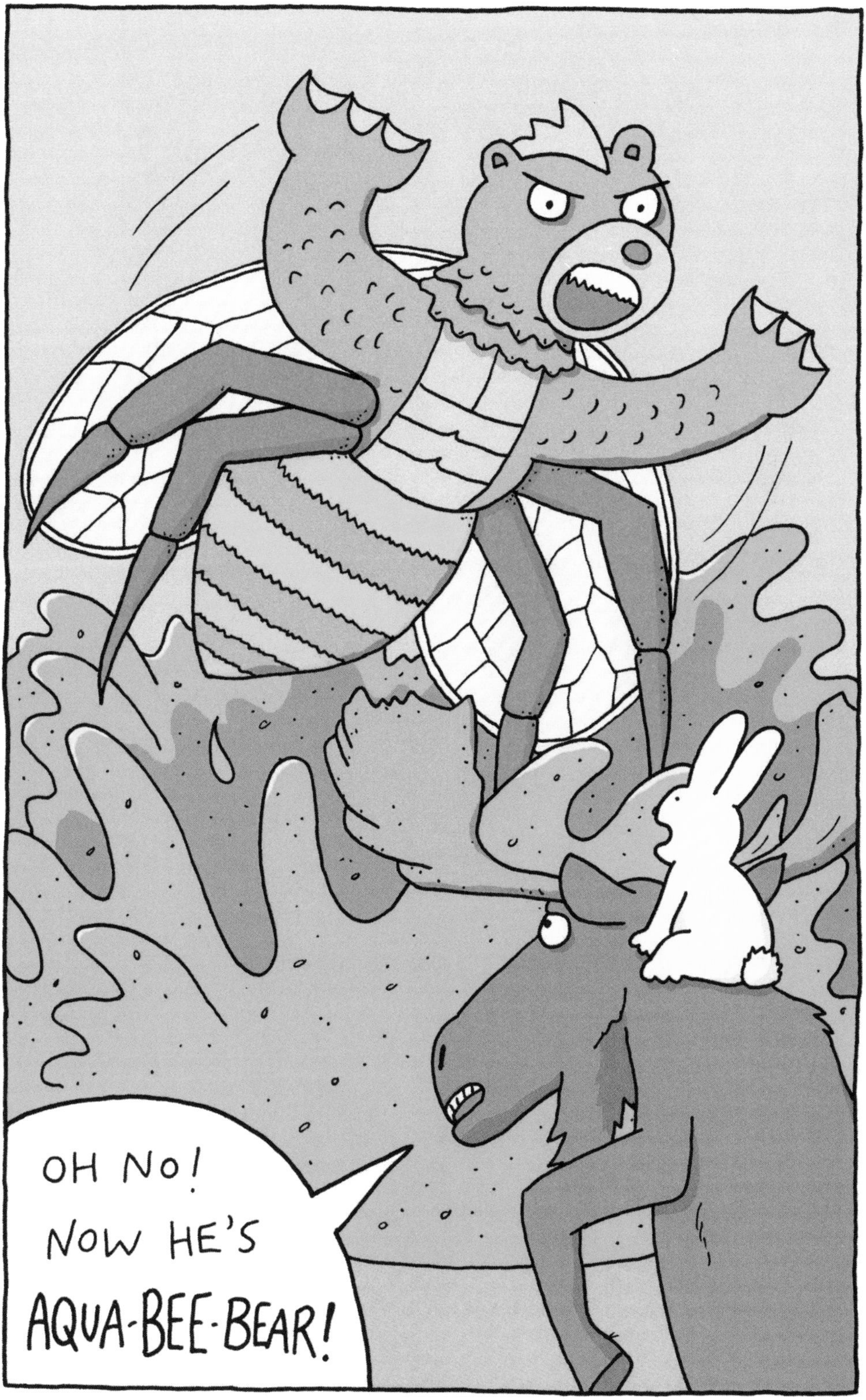
OH NO! NOW HE'S AQUA-BEE-BEAR!

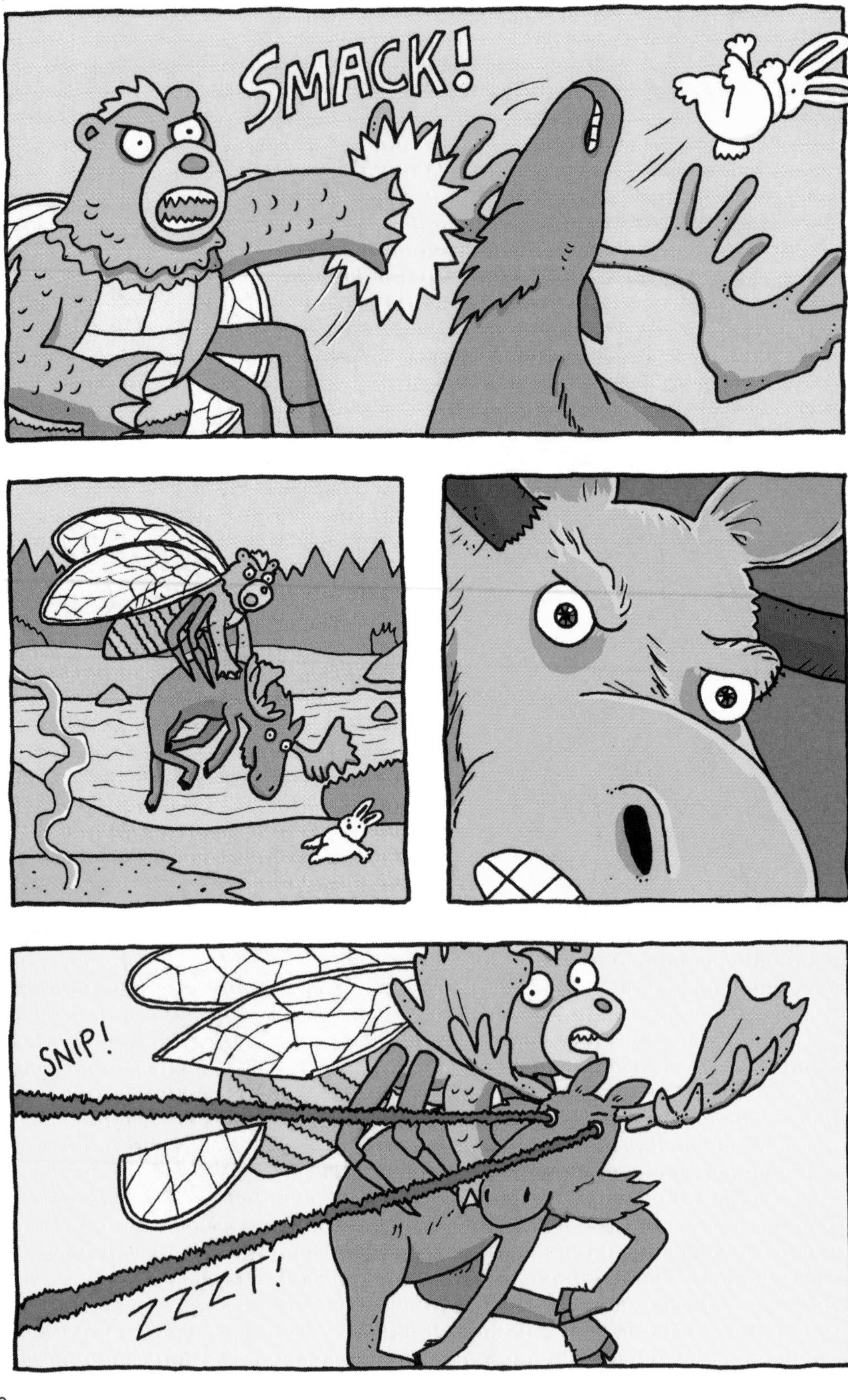
SMACK!
SNIP!
ZZZT!

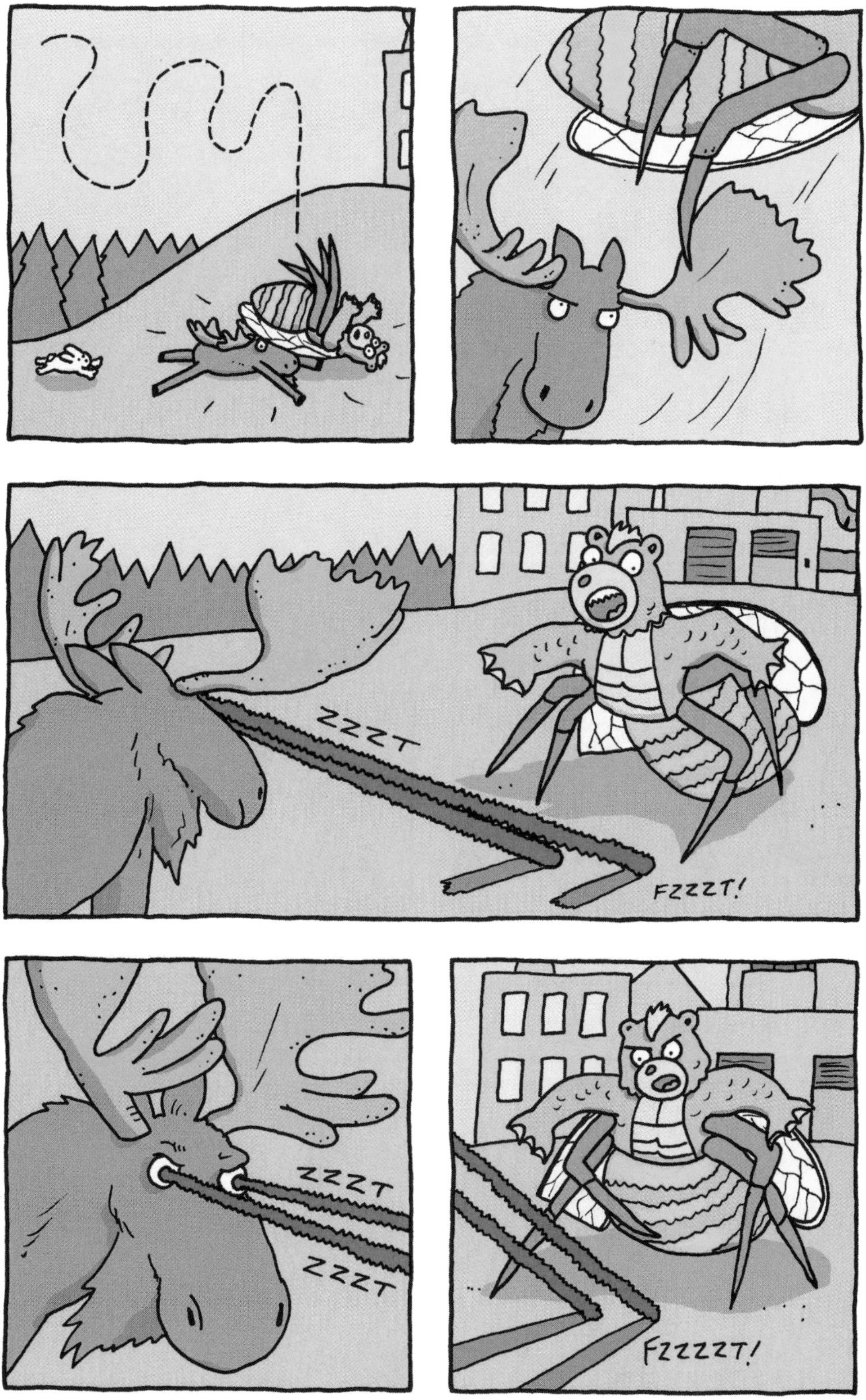
ZZZT
FZZZT!
ZZZT
ZZZT
FZZZZT!

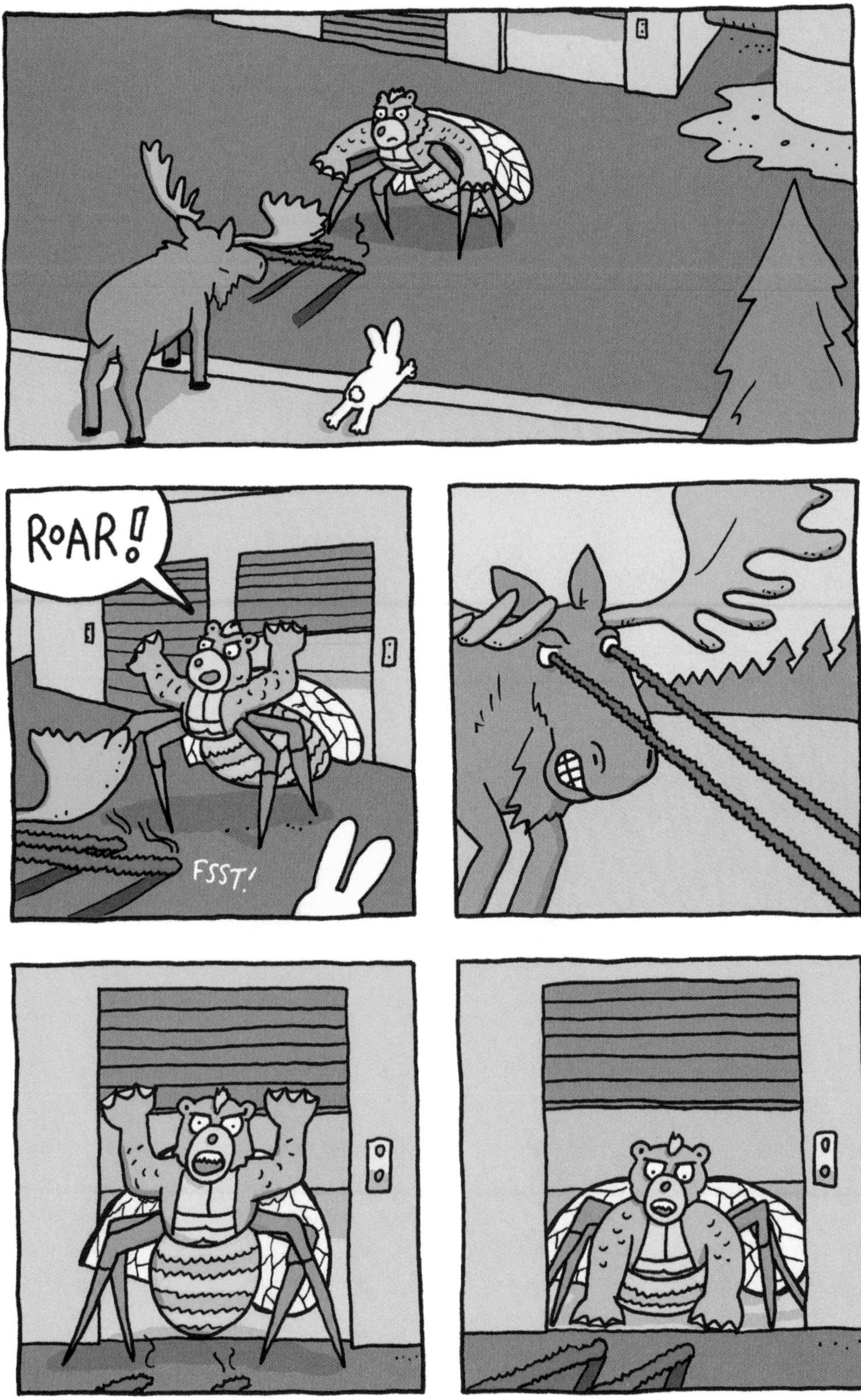
ROAR!!
FSST!

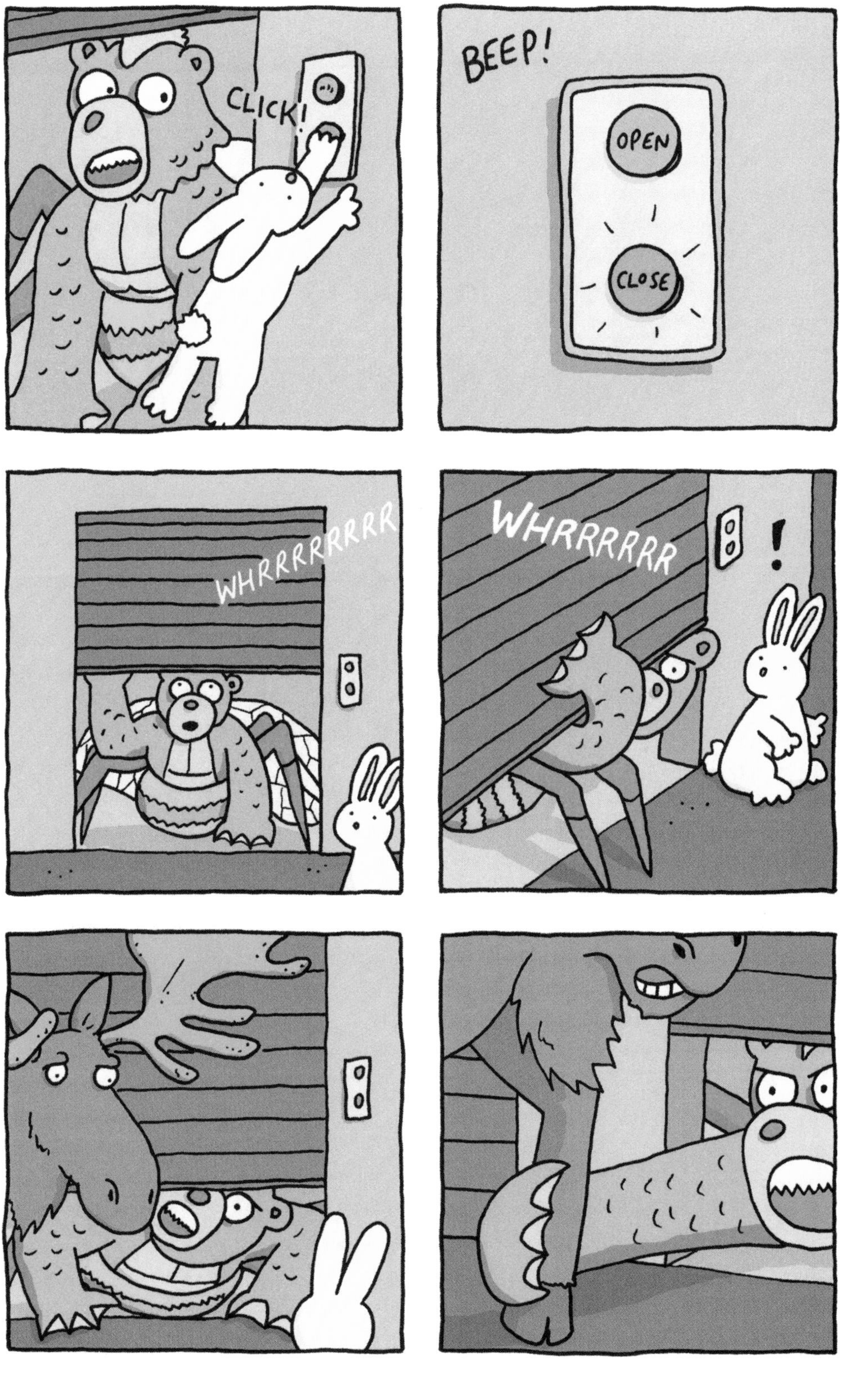
CLICK!
BEEP!
OPEN
CLOSE
WHRRRRRRRR
WHRRRRRRR
!

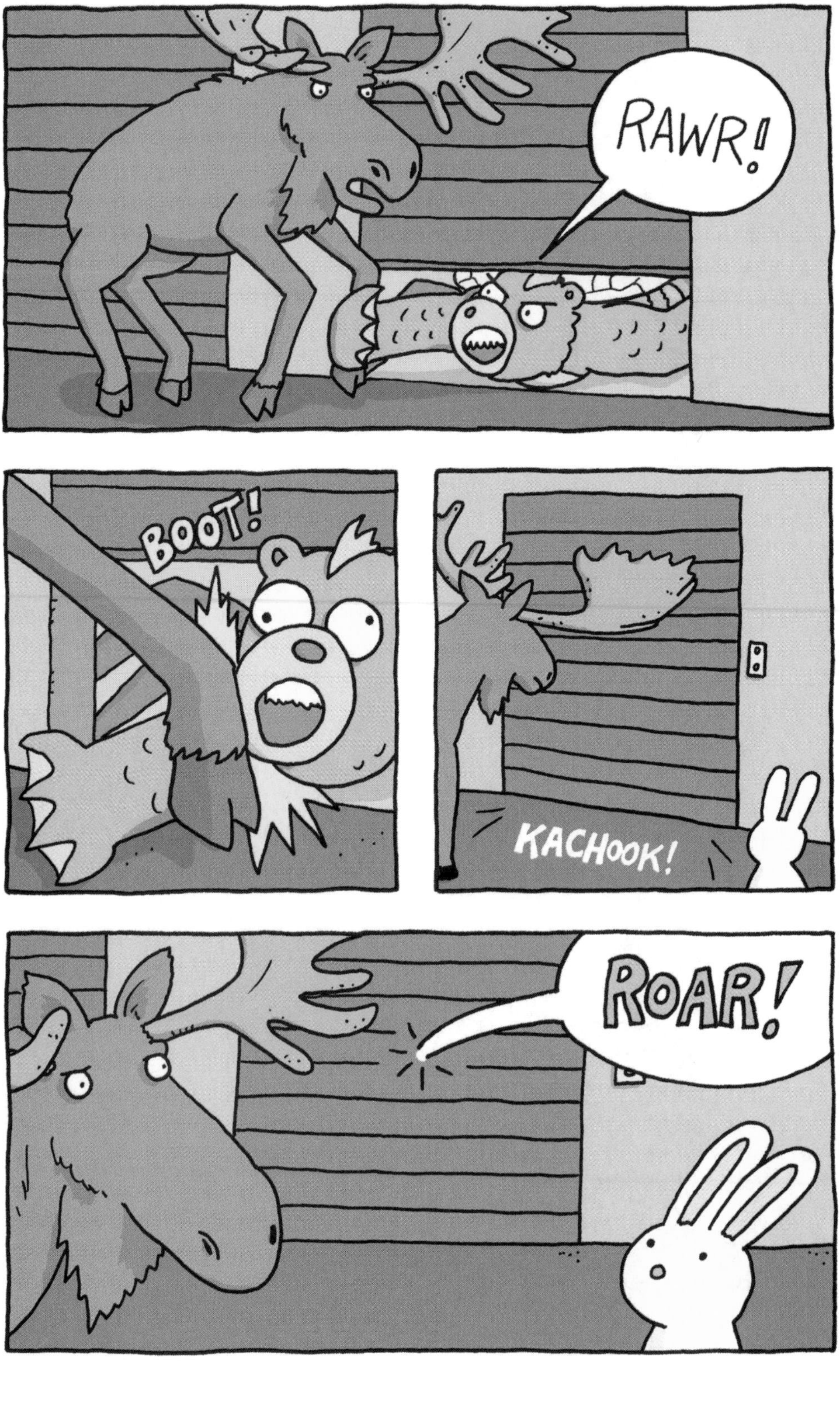
RAWR!
BOOT!
KACHOOK!
ROAR!

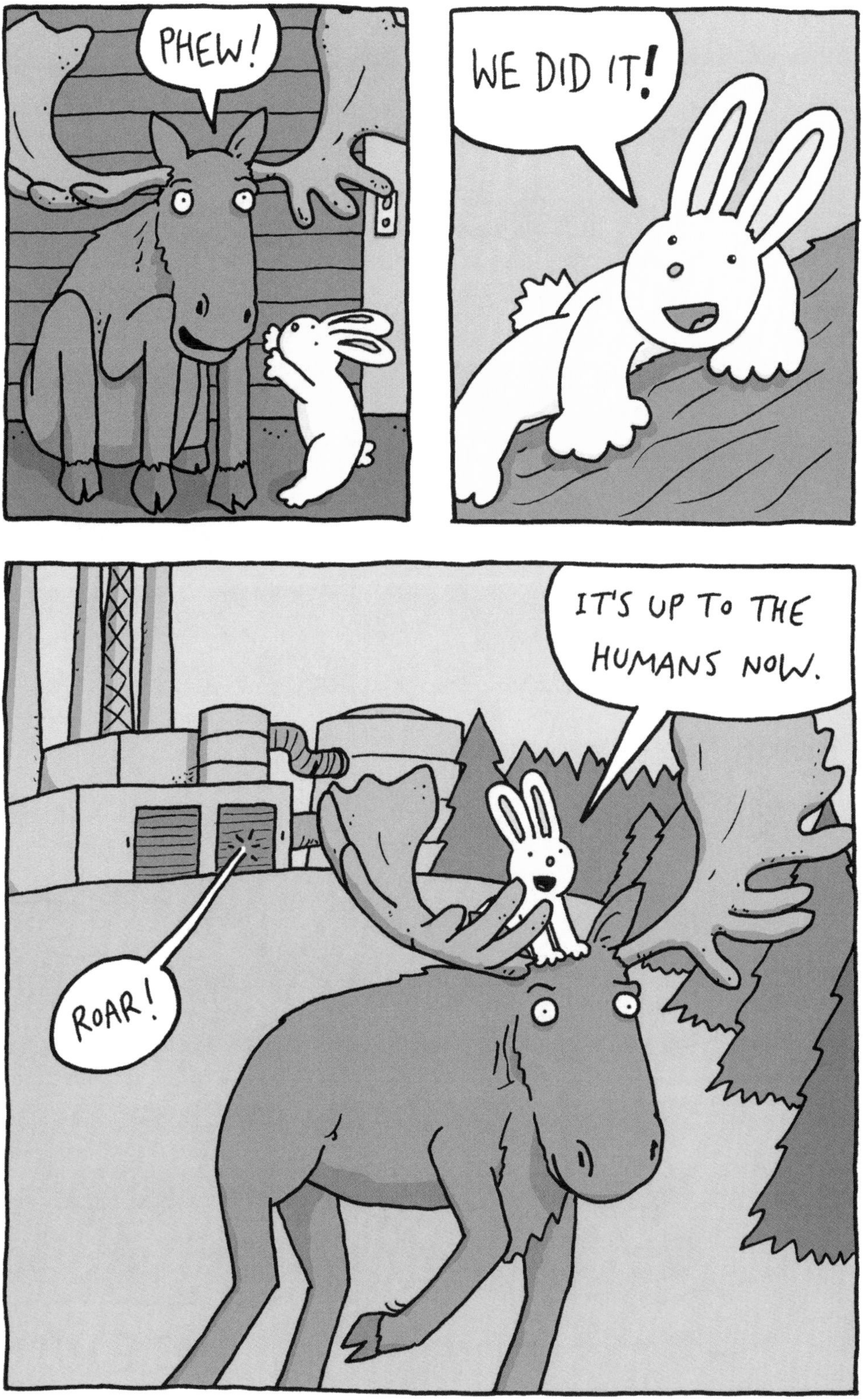
PHEW!
WE DID IT!
IT'S UP TO THE HUMANS NOW.
ROAR!

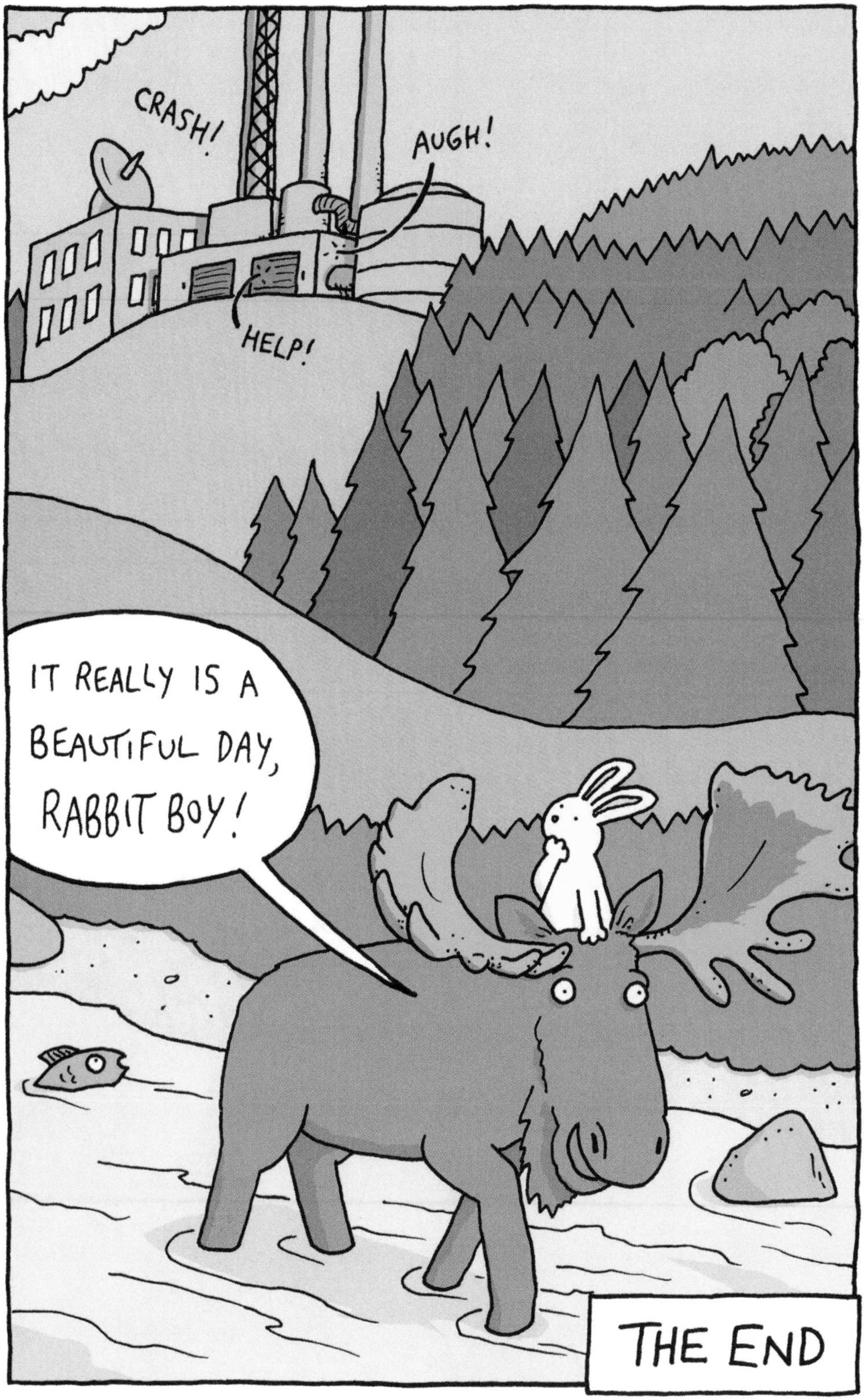
CRASH!
AUGH!
HELP!
IT REALLY IS A BEAUTIFUL DAY, RABBIT BOY!
THE END

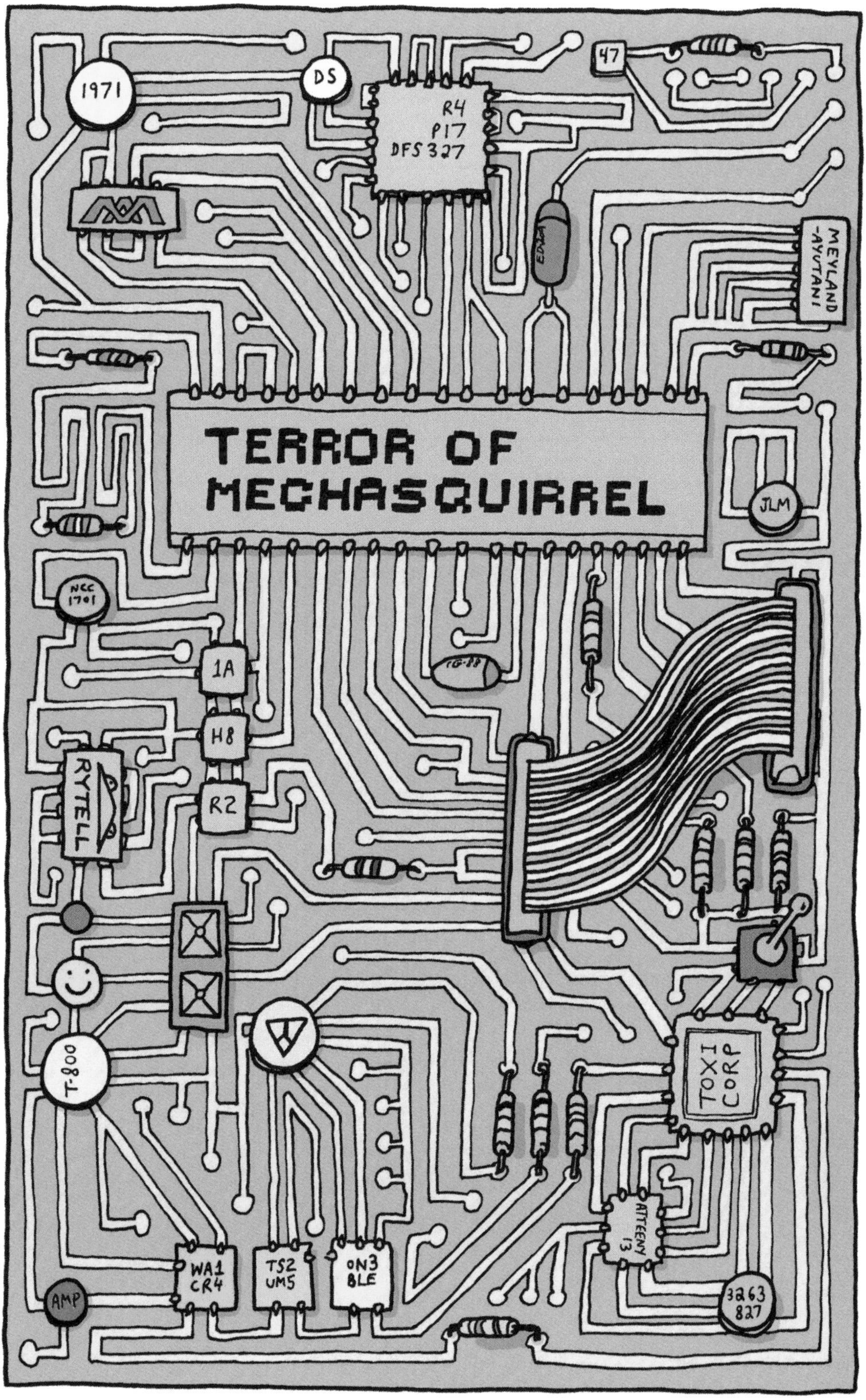

TERROR OF MECHASQUIRREL
1971
DS
R4 P17 DFS327
47
MEYLAND -AYUTANI
JLM
NCC 1701
1A
H8
R2
RYTELL
T-800
TOXI CORP
ATTEENY 13
WA1 CR4
TS2 UM5
ON3 BLE
AMP
3263 827

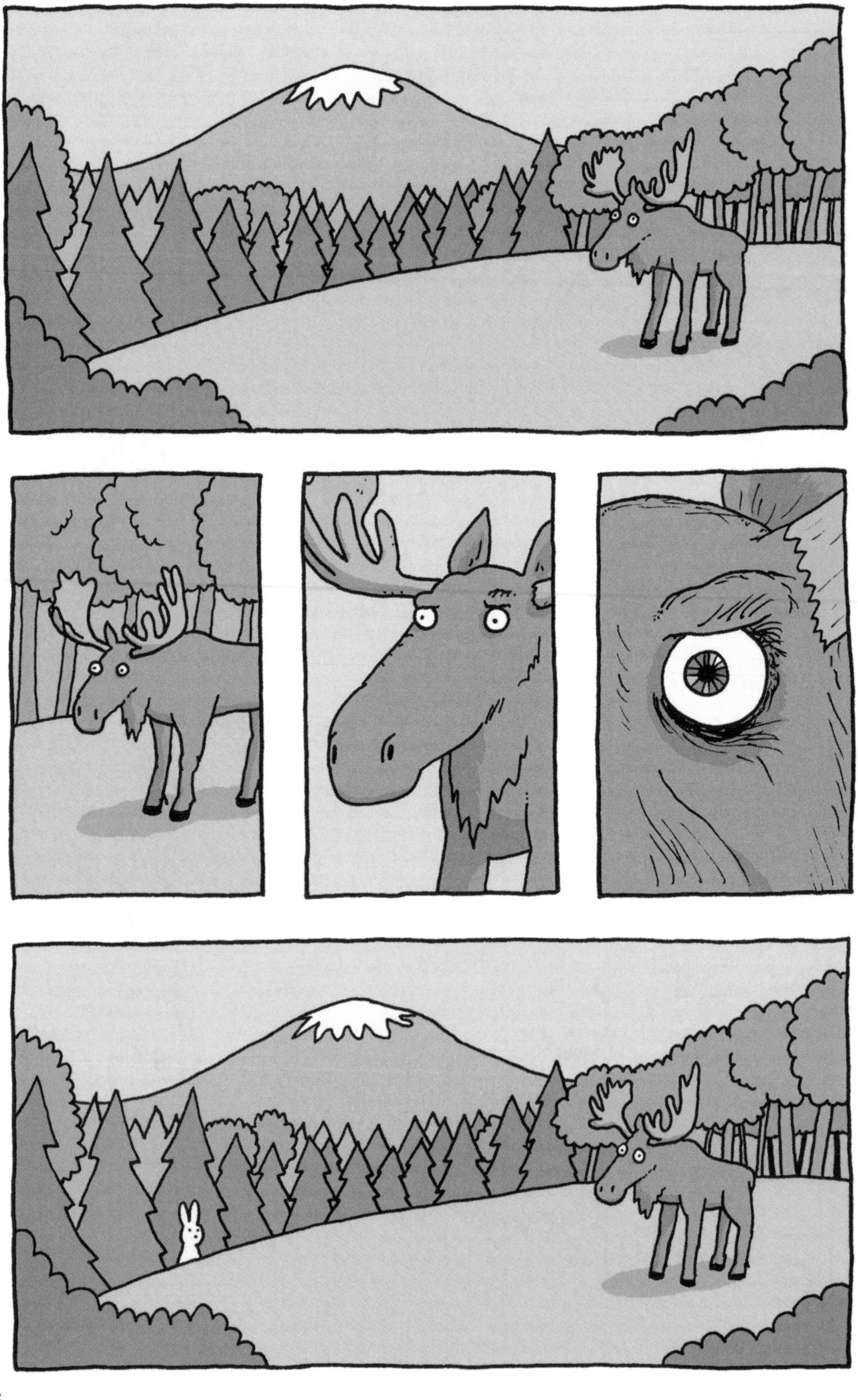

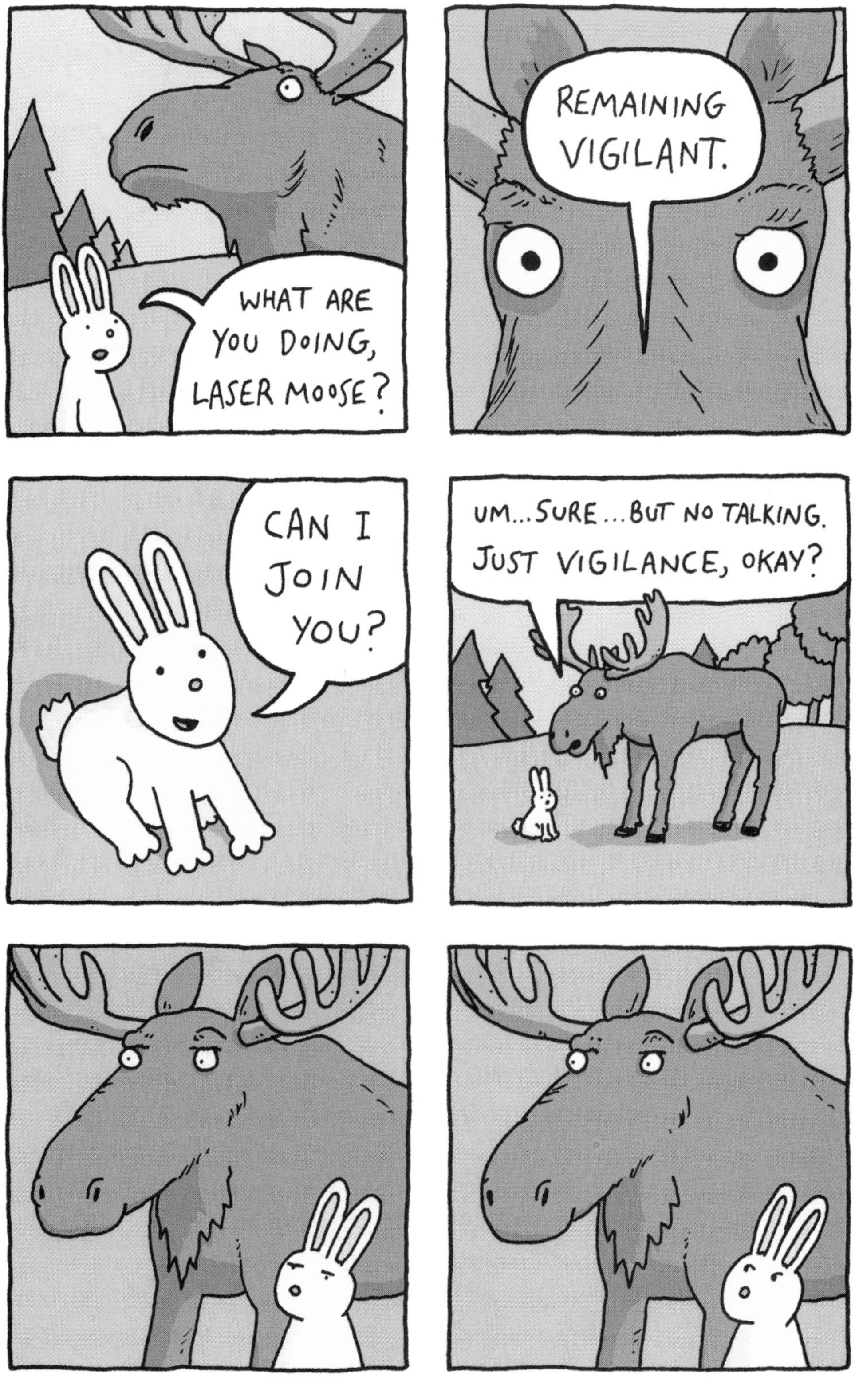
WHAT ARE YOU DOING, LASER MOOSE?
REMAINING VIGILANT.
CAN I JOIN YOU?
UM... SURE... BUT NO TALKING. JUST VIGILANCE, OKAY?

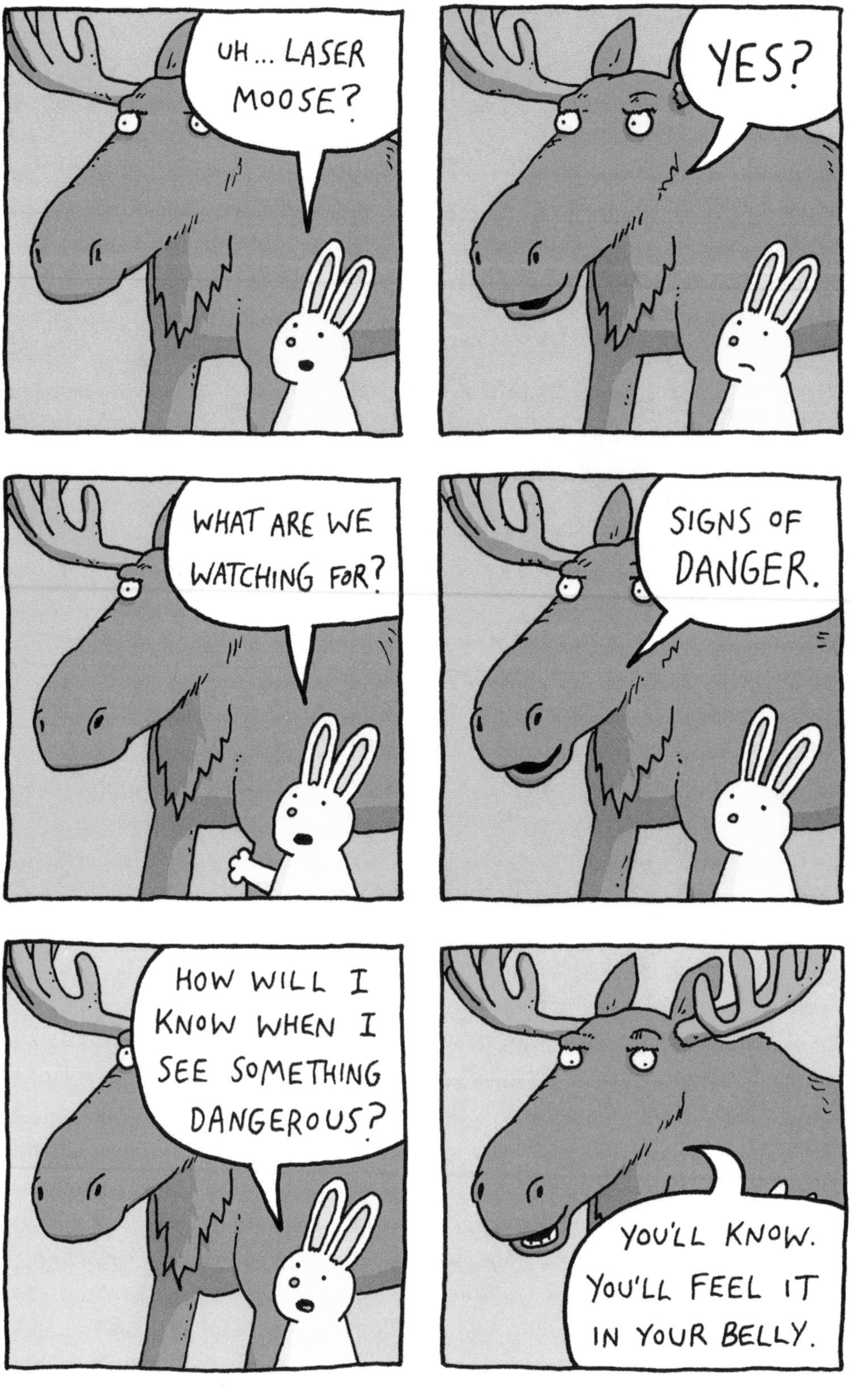
UH... LASER MOOSE?
YES?
WHAT ARE WE WATCHING FOR?
SIGNS OF DANGER.
HOW WILL I KNOW WHEN I SEE SOMETHING DANGEROUS?
YOU'LL KNOW. YOU'LL FEEL IT IN YOUR BELLY.

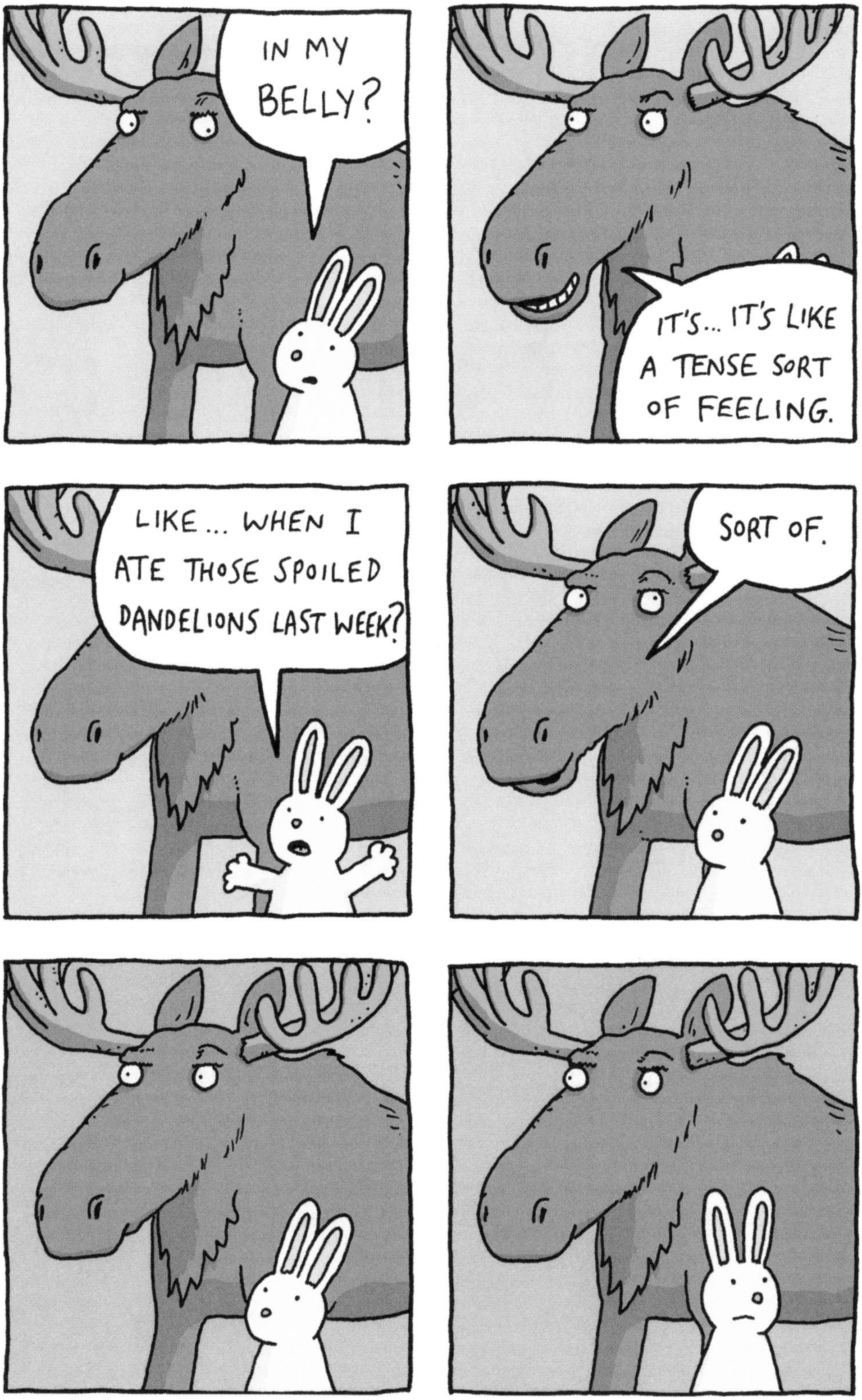
IN MY BELLY?
IT'S... IT'S LIKE A TENSE SORT OF FEELING.
LIKE... WHEN I ATE THOSE SPOILED DANDELIONS LAST WEEK?
SORT OF.

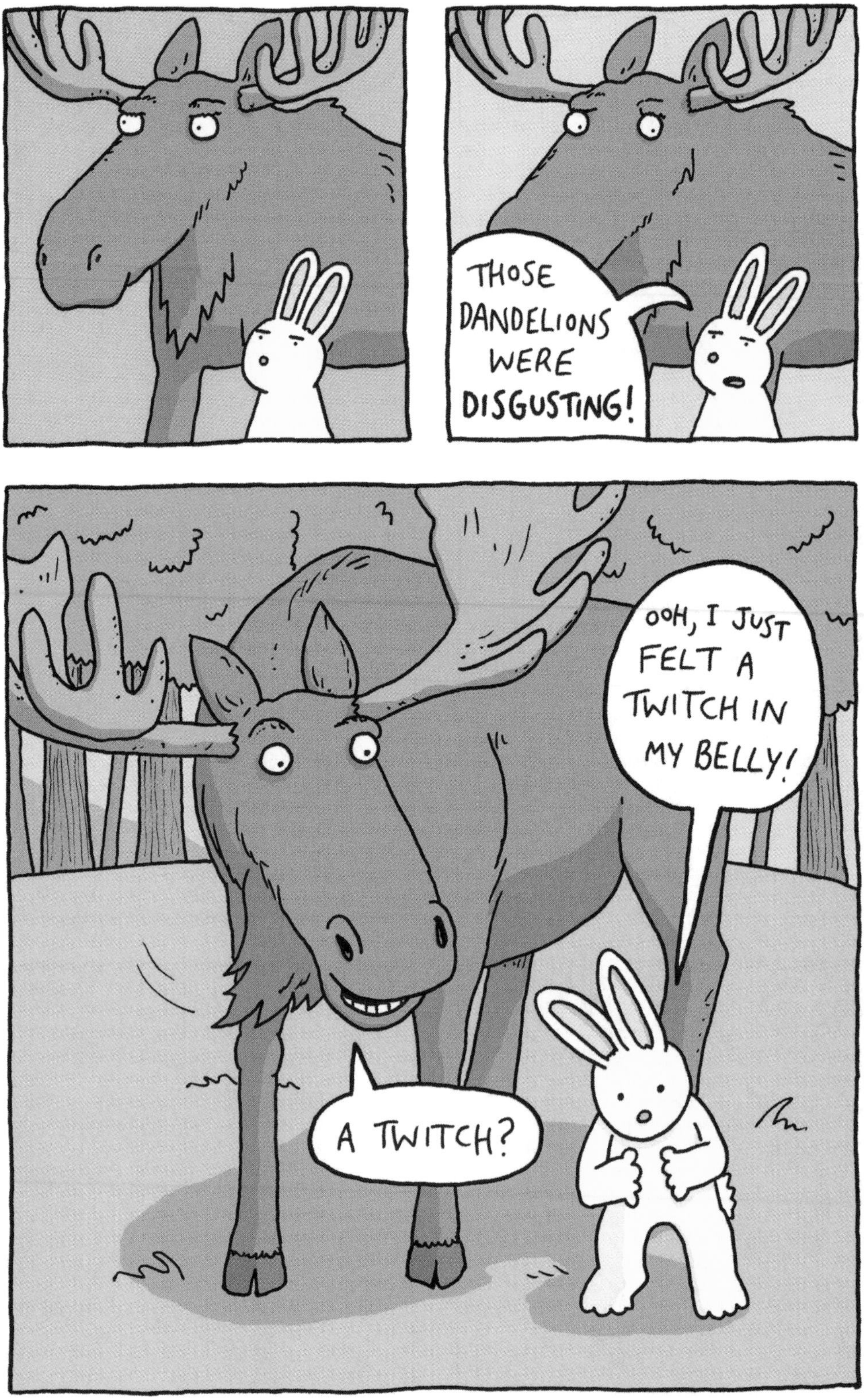
THOSE DANDELIONS WERE DISGUSTING!
OOH, I JUST FELT A TWITCH IN MY BELLY!
A TWITCH?

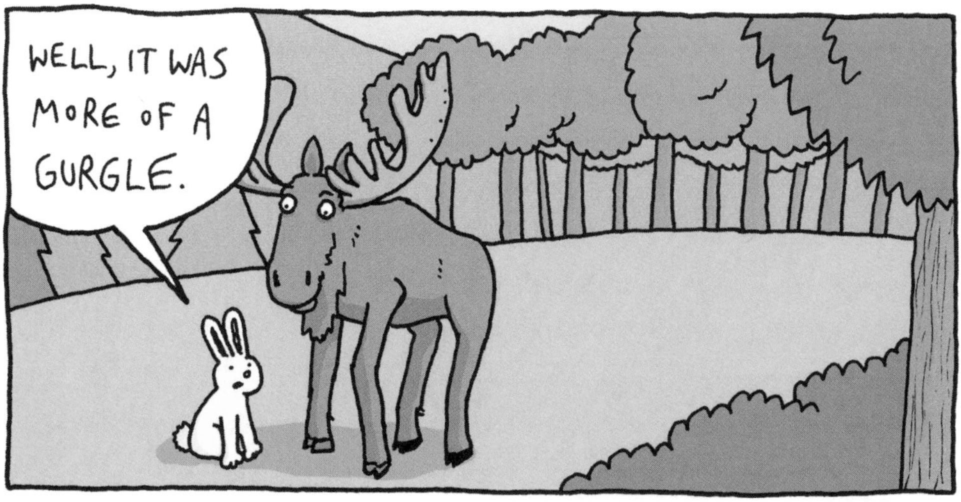
WELL, IT WAS MORE OF A GURGLE.

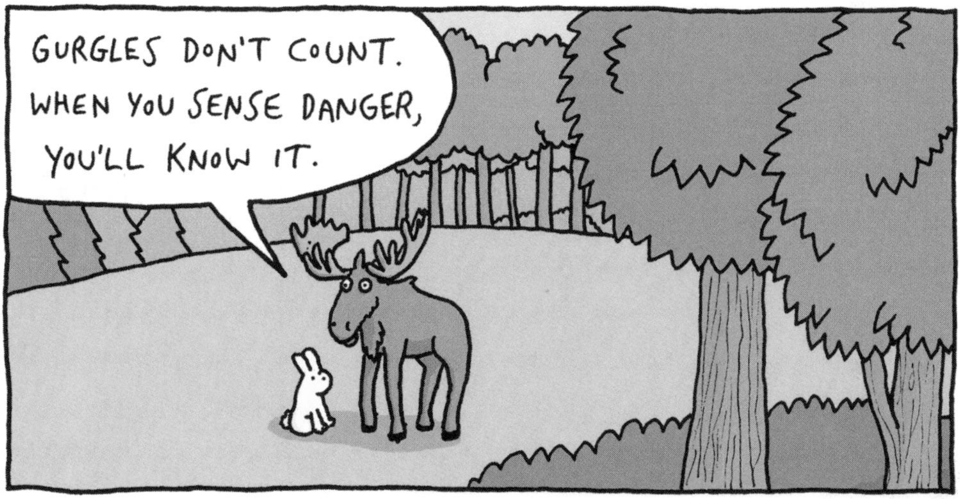
GURGLES DON'T COUNT. WHEN YOU SENSE DANGER, YOU'LL KNOW IT.

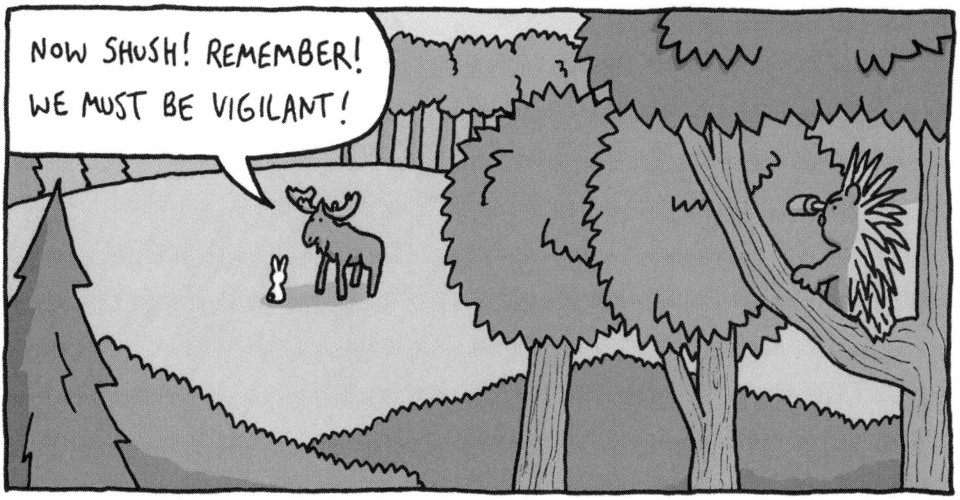
NOW SHUSH! REMEMBER! WE MUST BE VIGILANT!

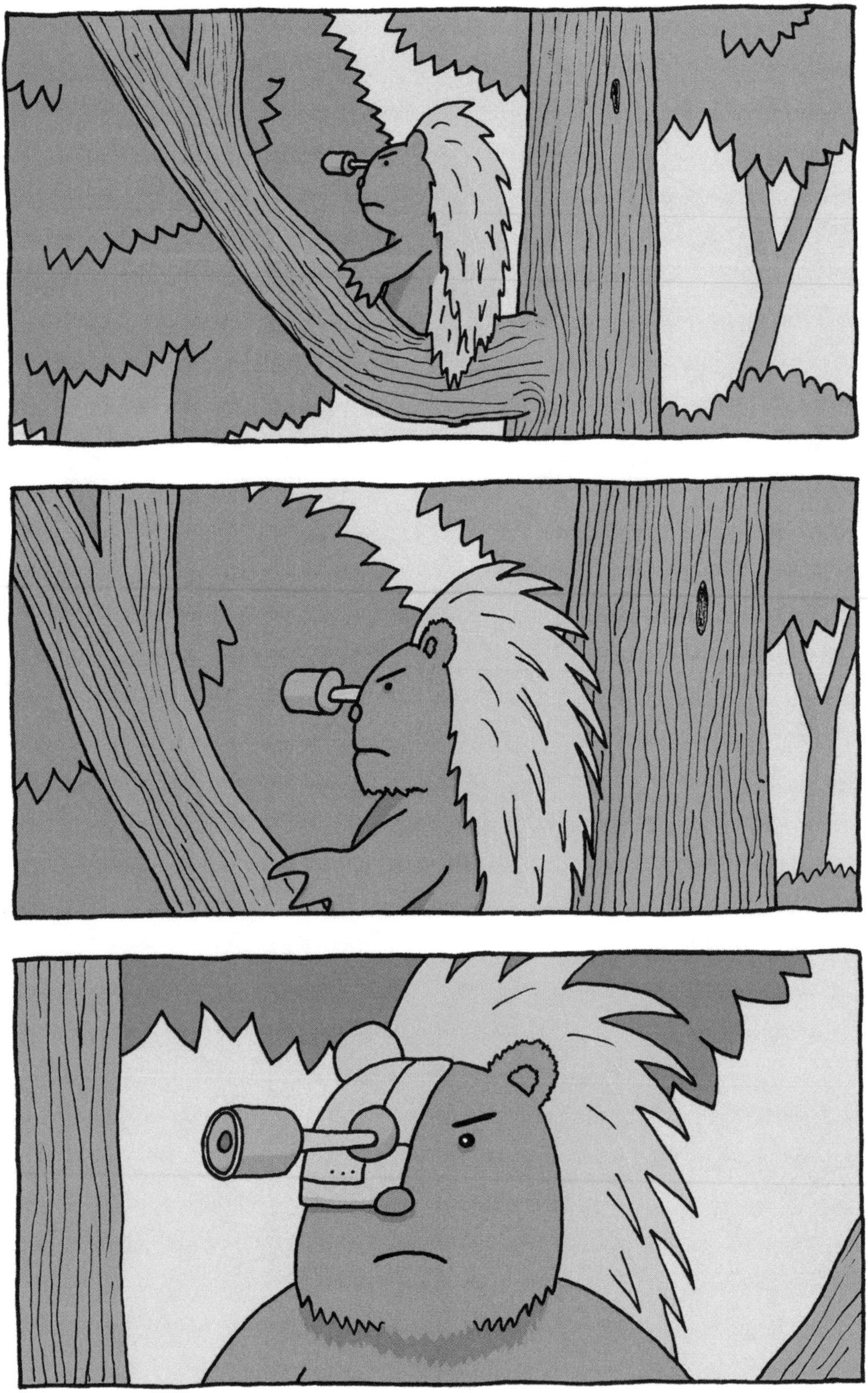

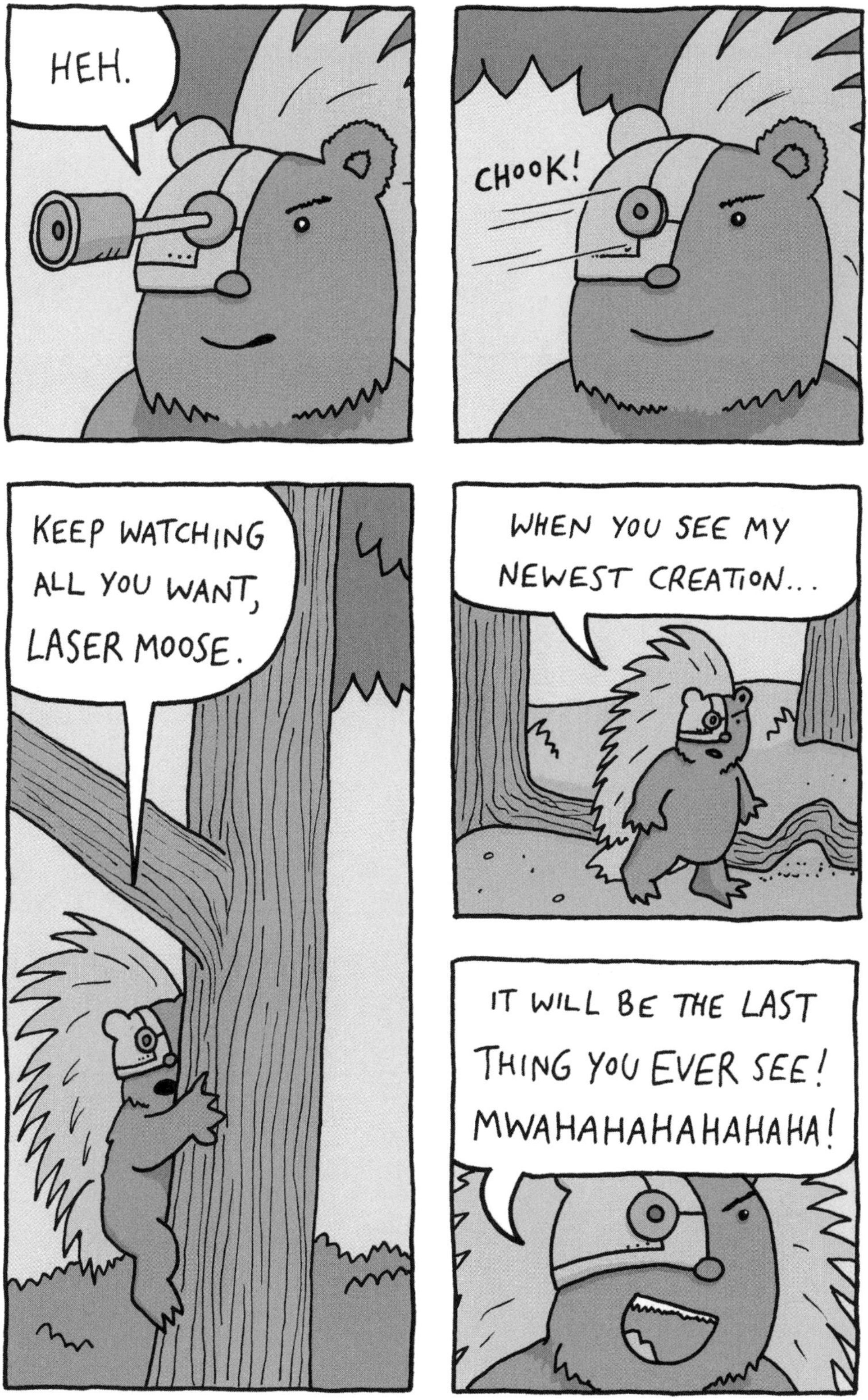
HEH.
CHOOK!
KEEP WATCHING ALL YOU WANT, LASER MOOSE.
WHEN YOU SEE MY NEWEST CREATION...
IT WILL BE THE LAST THING YOU EVER SEE! MWAHAHAHAHAHAHA!

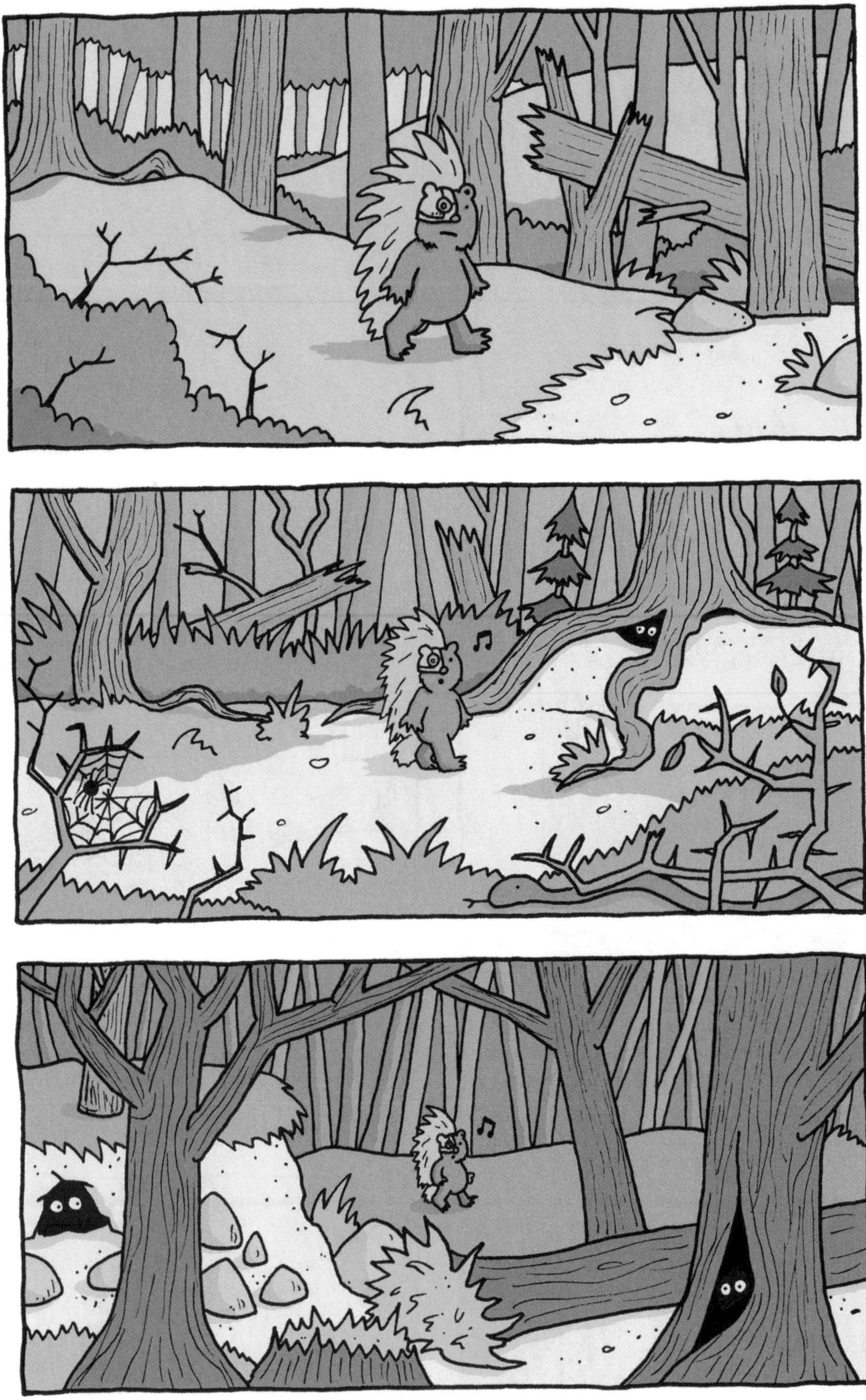

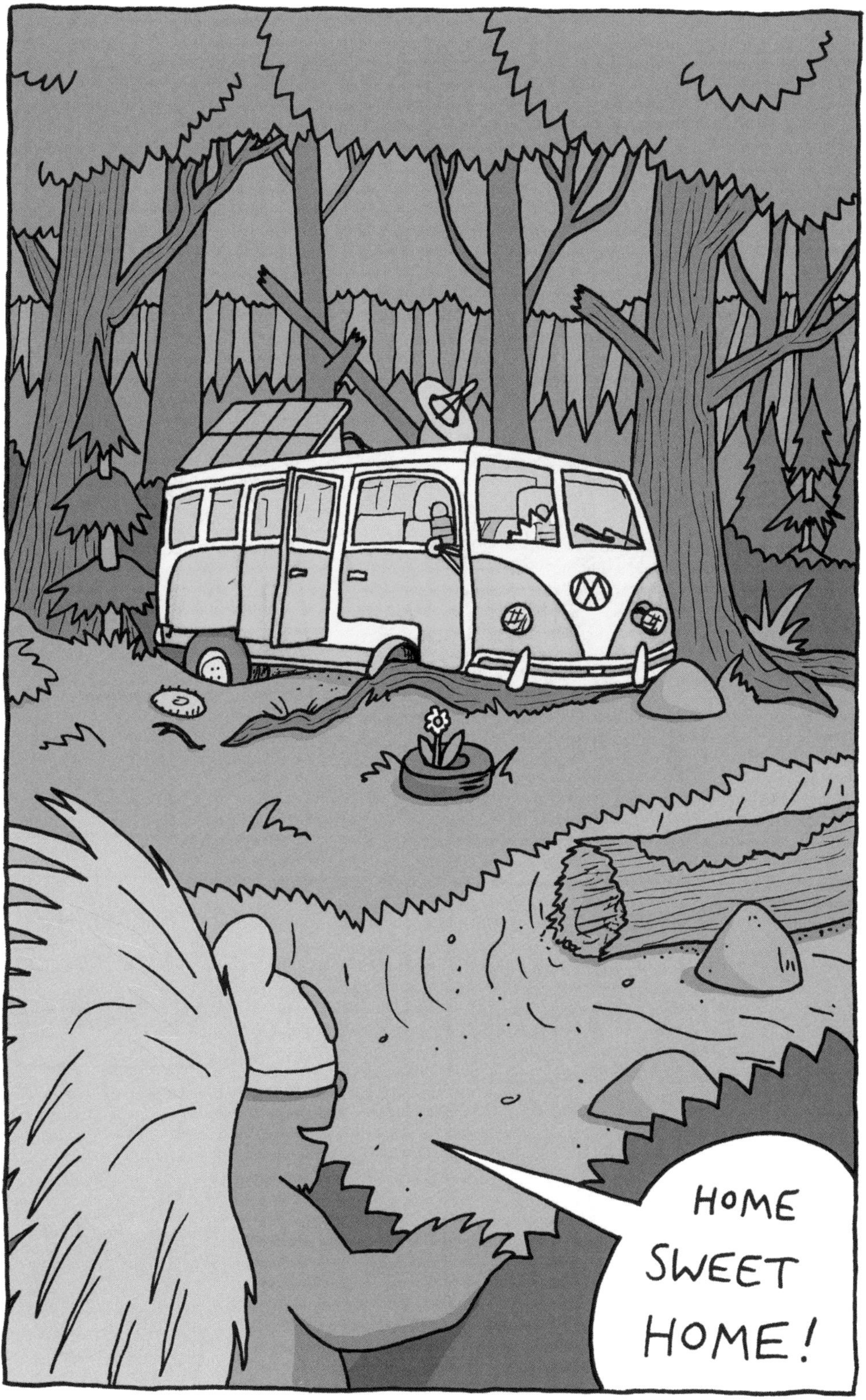
HOME SWEET HOME!

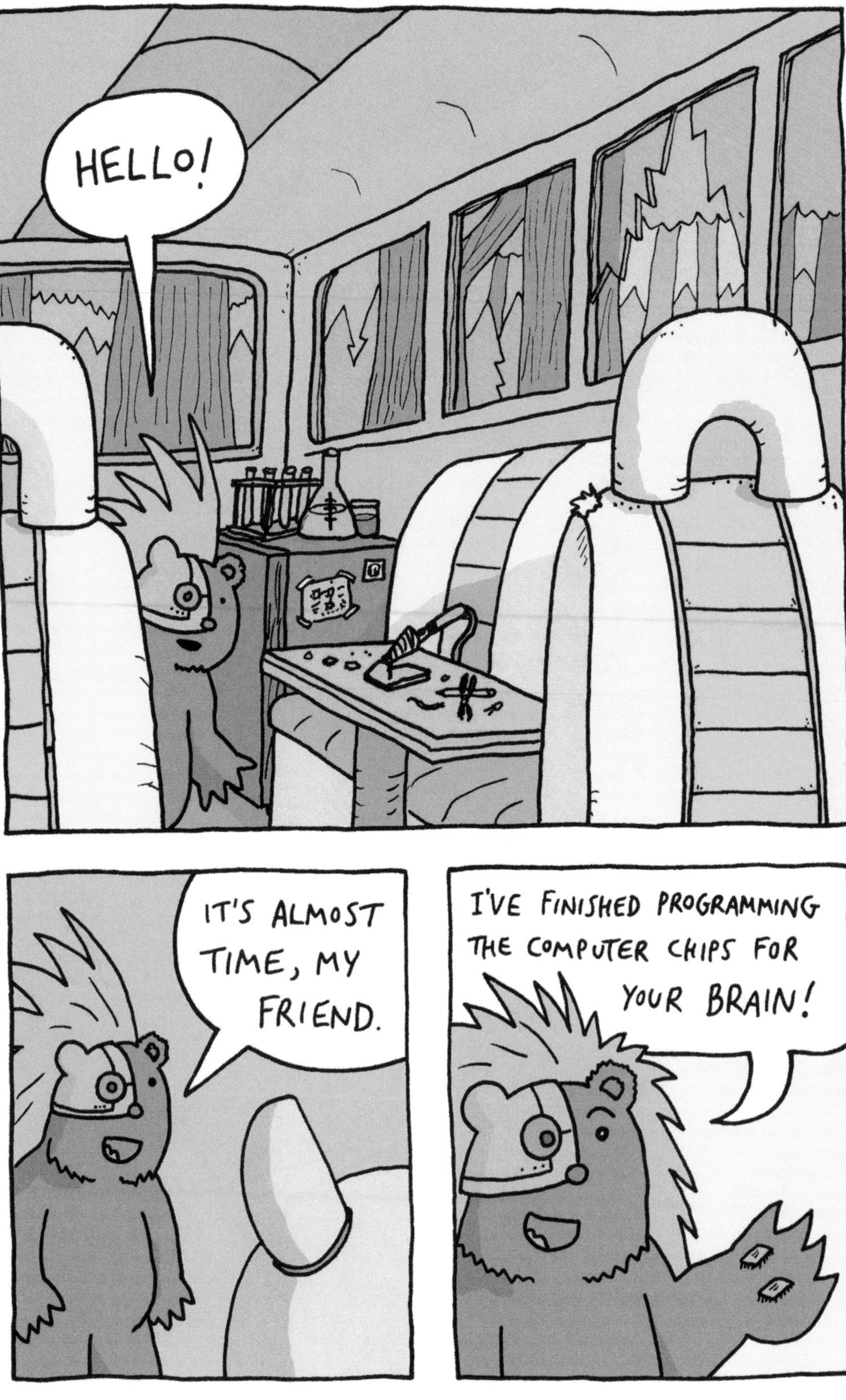
HELLO!
IT'S ALMOST TIME, MY FRIEND.
I'VE FINISHED PROGRAMMING THE COMPUTER CHIPS FOR YOUR BRAIN!

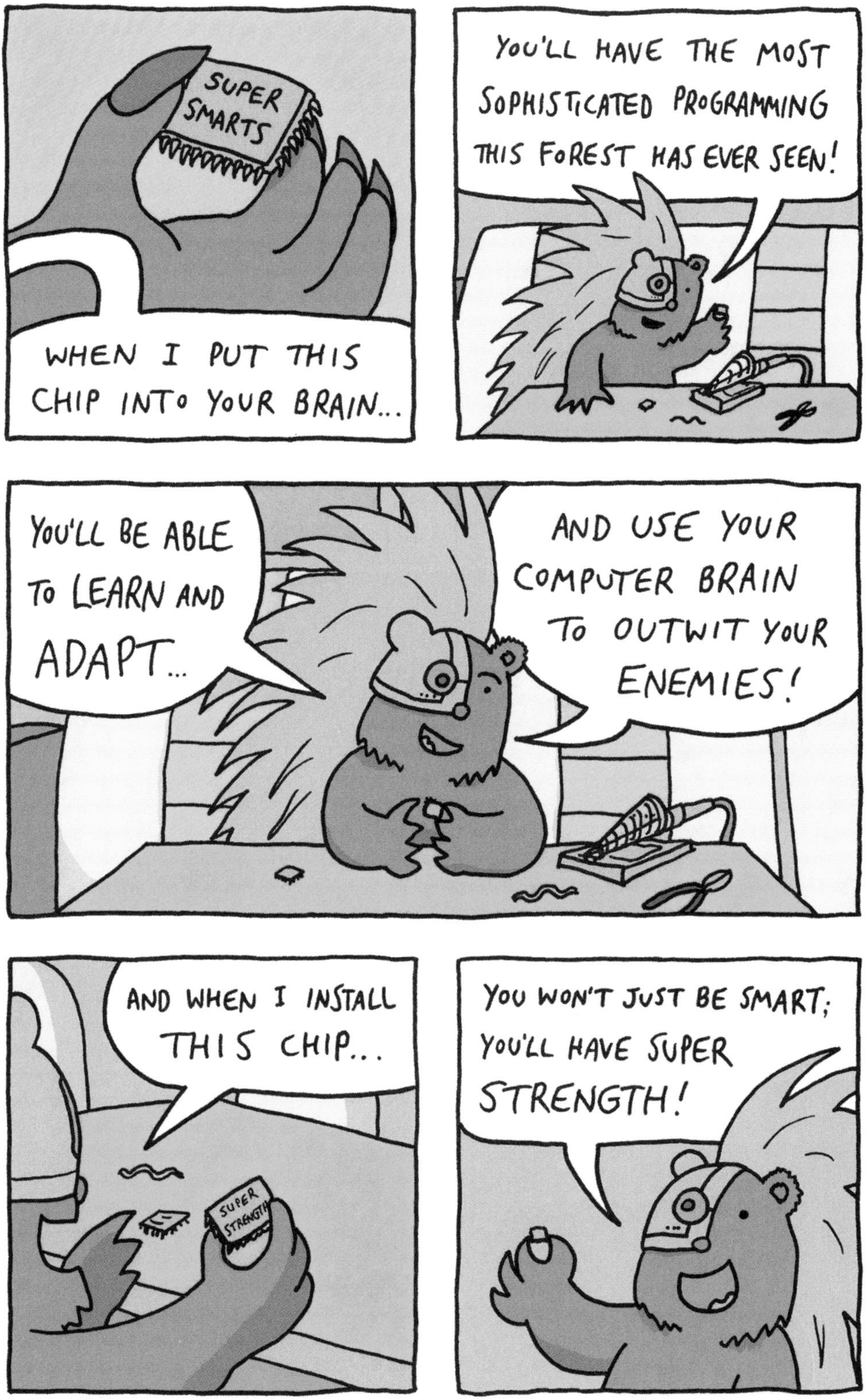
SUPER SMARTS
WHEN I PUT THIS CHIP INTO YOUR BRAIN...
YOU'LL HAVE THE MOST SOPHISTICATED PROGRAMMING THIS FOREST HAS EVER SEEN!
YOU'LL BE ABLE TO LEARN AND ADAPT...
AND USE YOUR COMPUTER BRAIN TO OUTWIT YOUR ENEMIES!
AND WHEN I INSTALL THIS CHIP...
SUPER STRENGTH
YOU WON'T JUST BE SMART; YOU'LL HAVE SUPER STRENGTH!

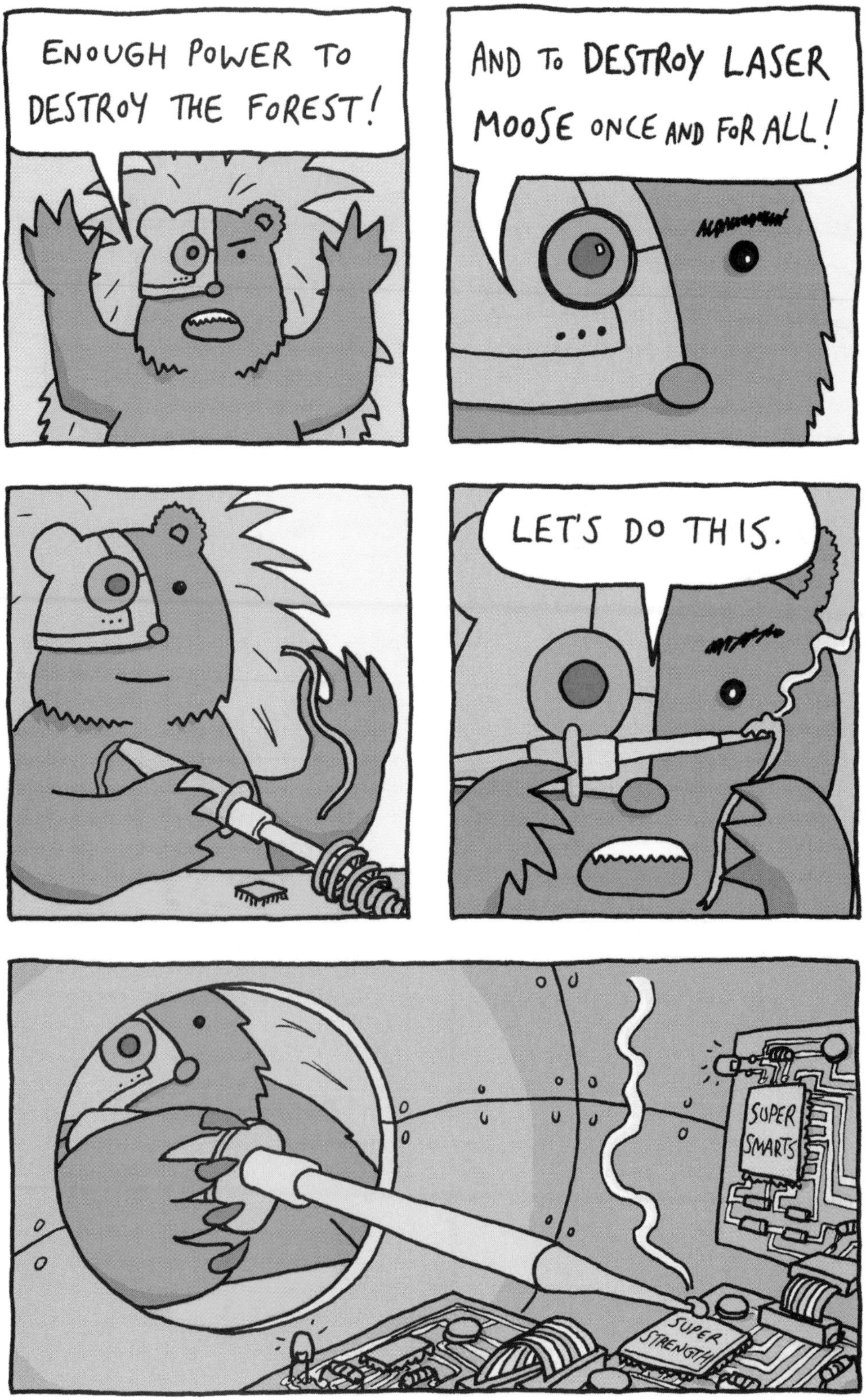
ENOUGH POWER TO DESTROY THE FOREST!
AND TO DESTROY LASER MOOSE ONCE AND FOR ALL!
LET'S DO THIS.
SUPER SMARTS
SUPER STRENGTH

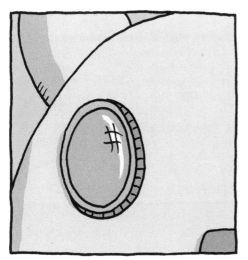
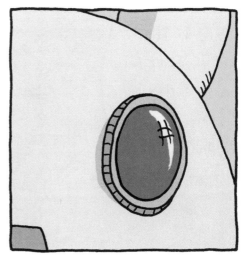

THERE. ALL FINISHED! HOW DO YOU FEEL, MECHASQUIRREL?

CHIPPITA-CHIP!

IT'S TIME. LET'S GO!

CHIRPY-DERP!

SYSTEM BOOT COMPLETE.
CHIPPITA-CHIP!
CHIRPY-DERP!
NEW OBJECTIVE: DESTROY LASER MOOSE.

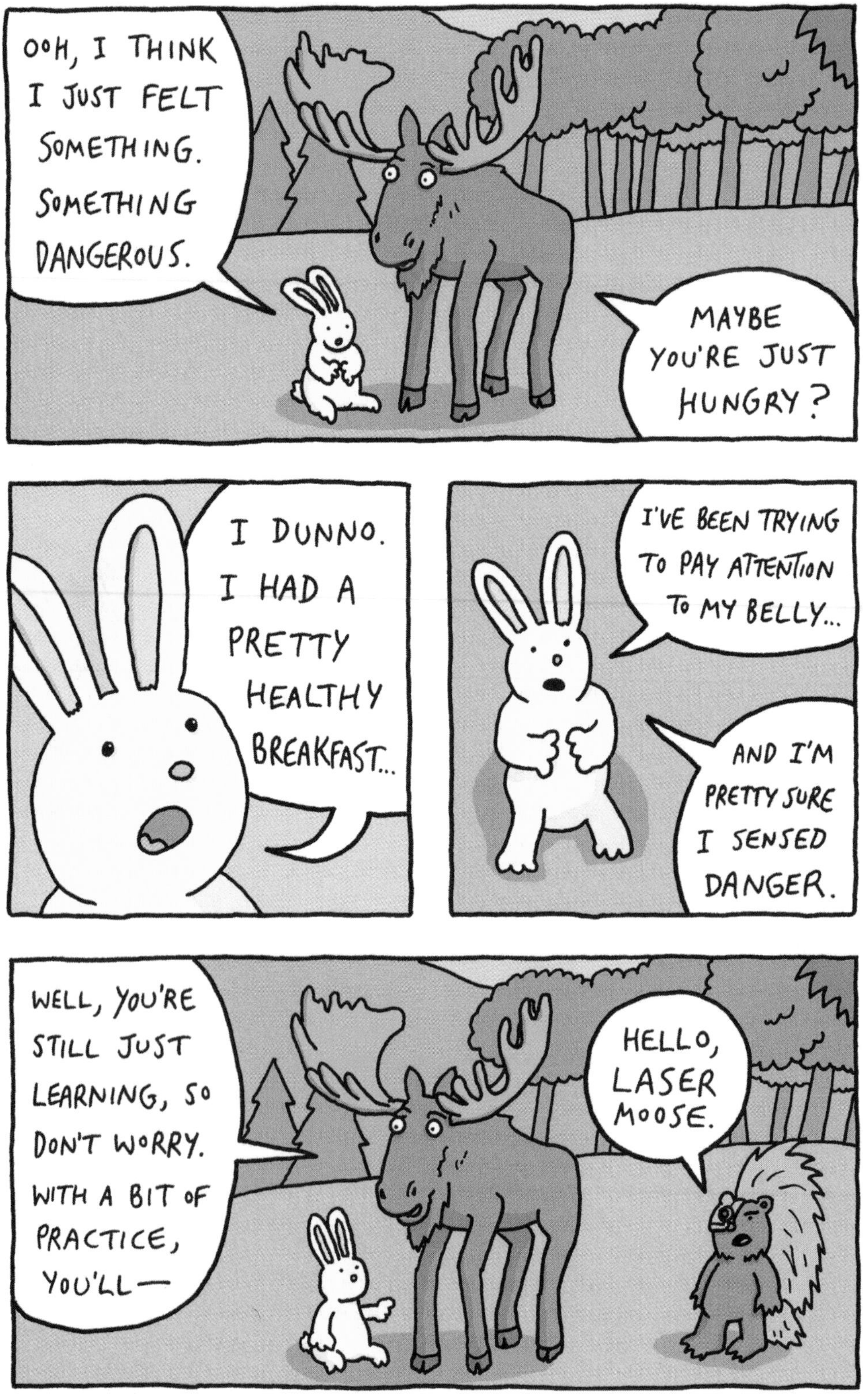
OOH, I THINK I JUST FELT SOMETHING. SOMETHING DANGEROUS.
MAYBE YOU'RE JUST HUNGRY?
I DUNNO. I HAD A PRETTY HEALTHY BREAKFAST...
I'VE BEEN TRYING TO PAY ATTENTION TO MY BELLY...
AND I'M PRETTY SURE I SENSED DANGER.
WELL, YOU'RE STILL JUST LEARNING, SO DON'T WORRY. WITH A BIT OF PRACTICE, YOU'LL—
HELLO, LASER MOOSE.

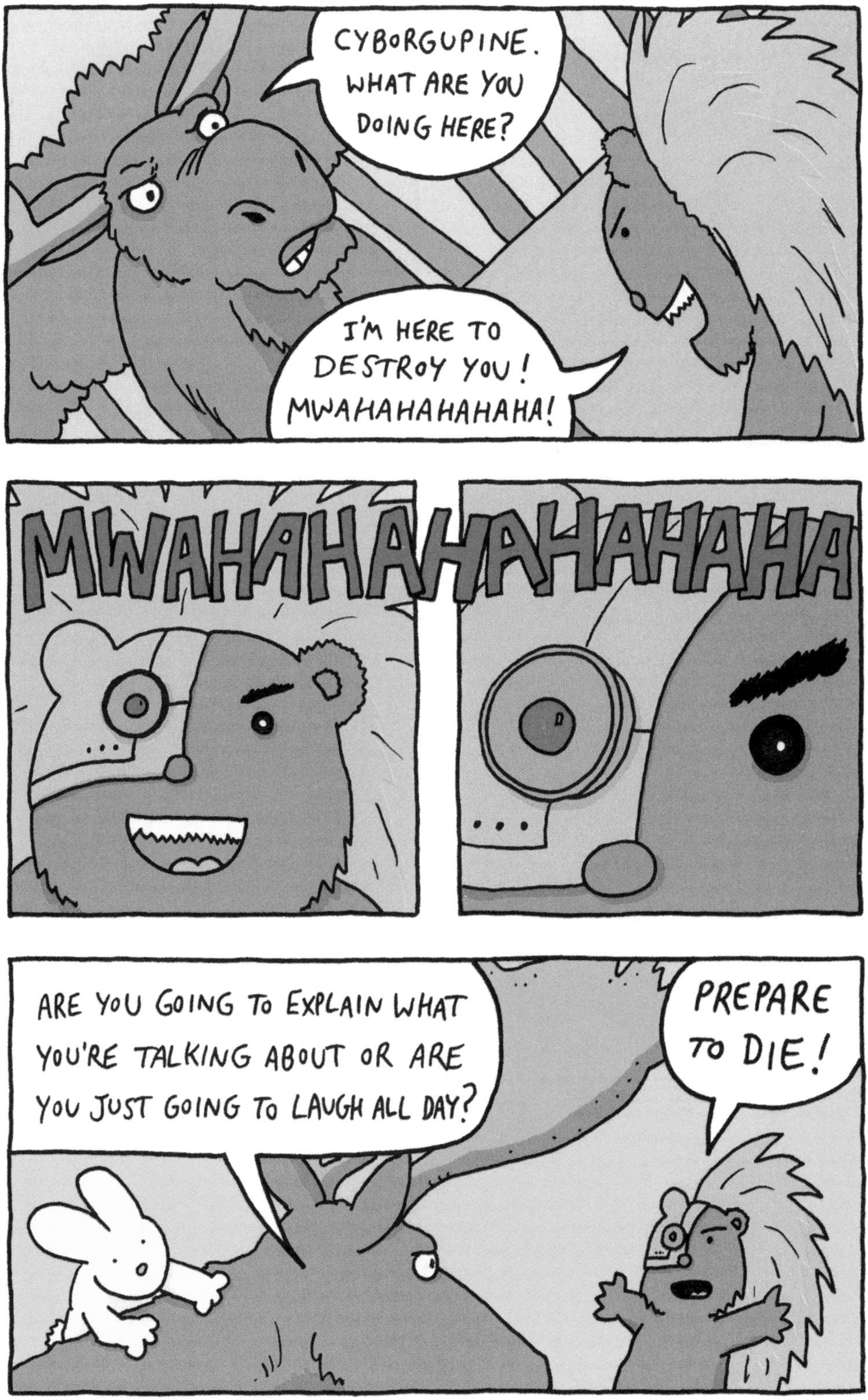
CYBORGUPINE. WHAT ARE YOU DOING HERE?
I'M HERE TO DESTROY YOU! MWAHAHAHAHAHA!
MWAHAHAHAHAHAHAHA
ARE YOU GOING TO EXPLAIN WHAT YOU'RE TALKING ABOUT OR ARE YOU JUST GOING TO LAUGH ALL DAY?
PREPARE TO DIE!

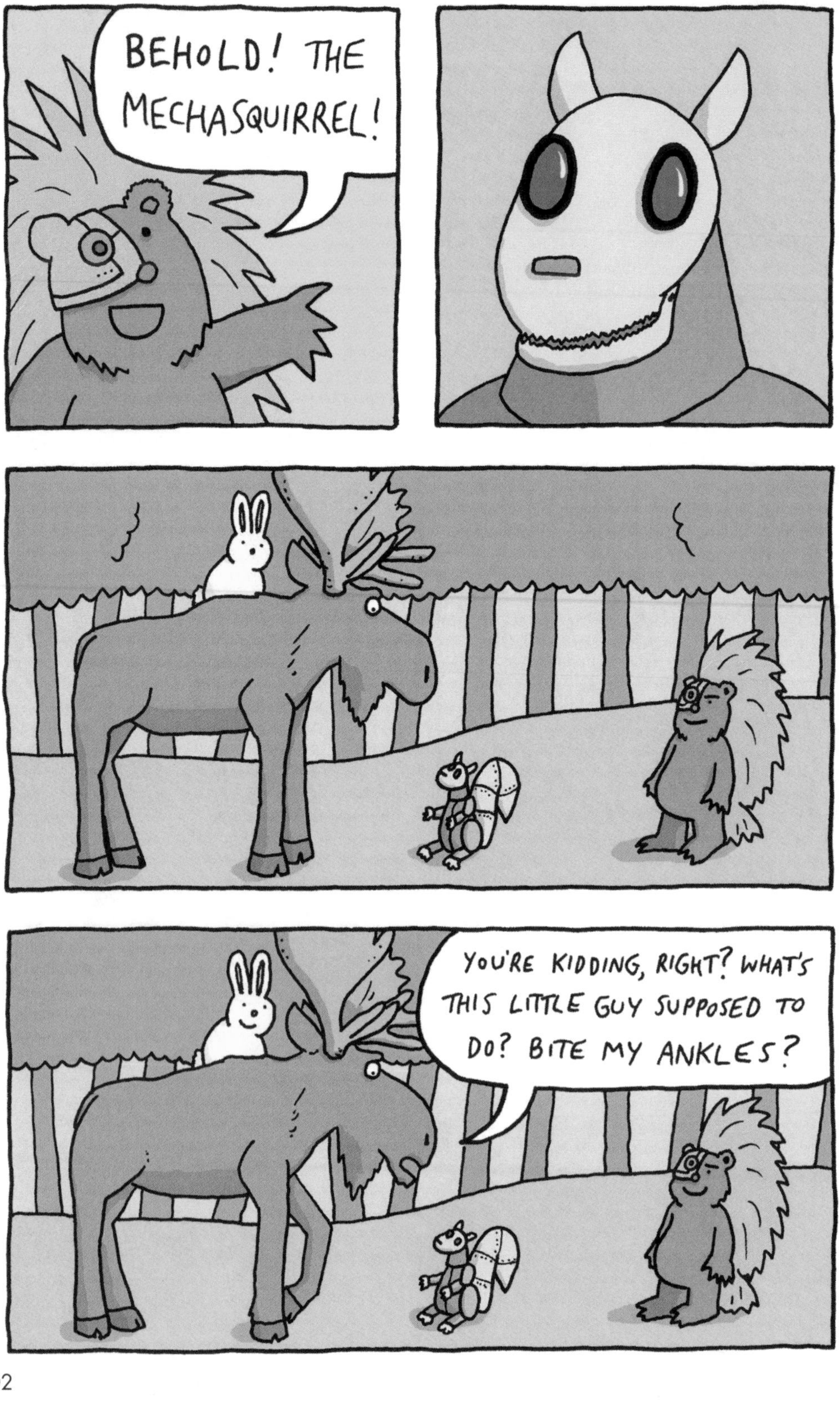
BEHOLD! THE MECHASQUIRREL!
YOU'RE KIDDING, RIGHT? WHAT'S THIS LITTLE GUY SUPPOSED TO DO? BITE MY ANKLES?

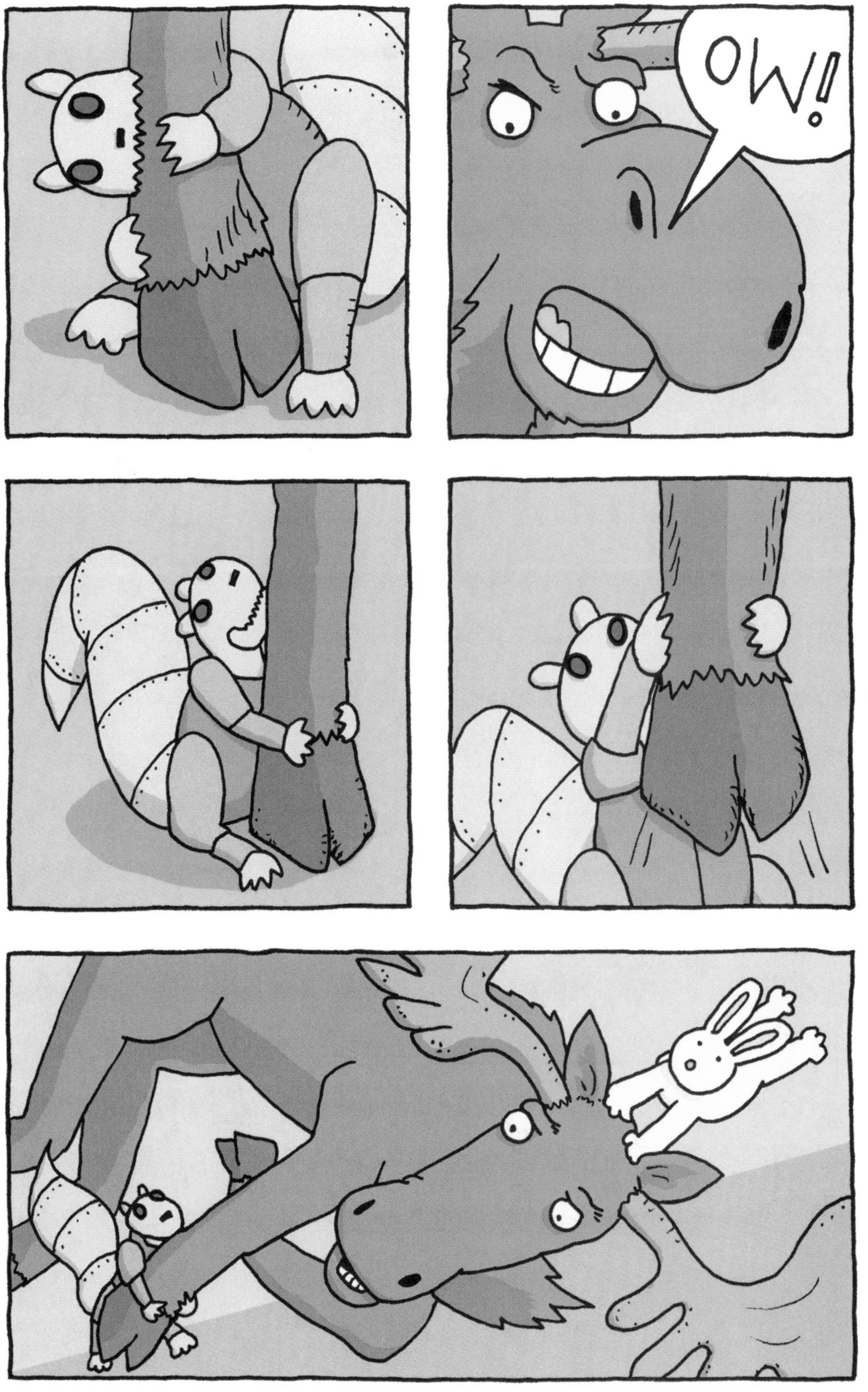
OW!

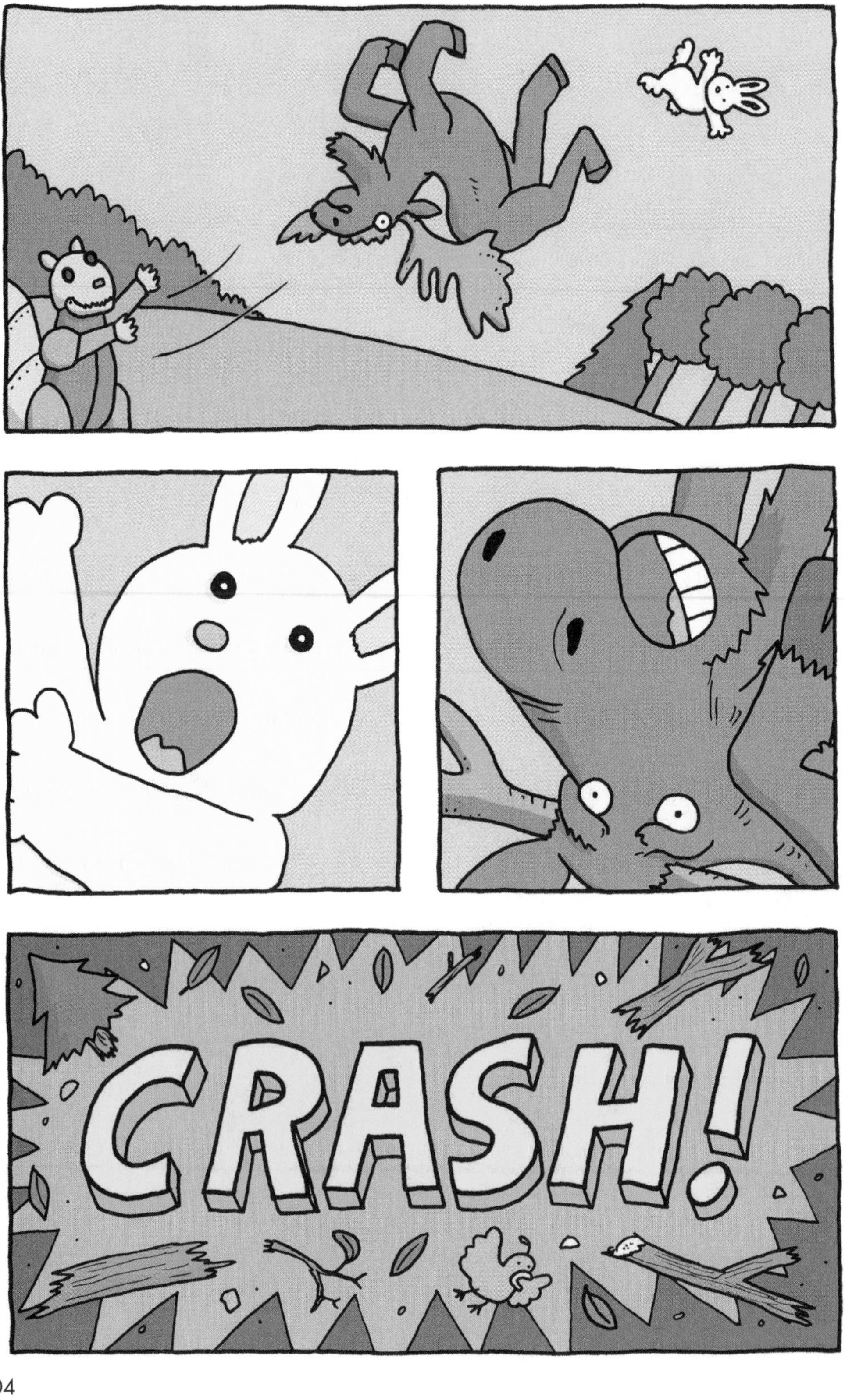
CRASH!

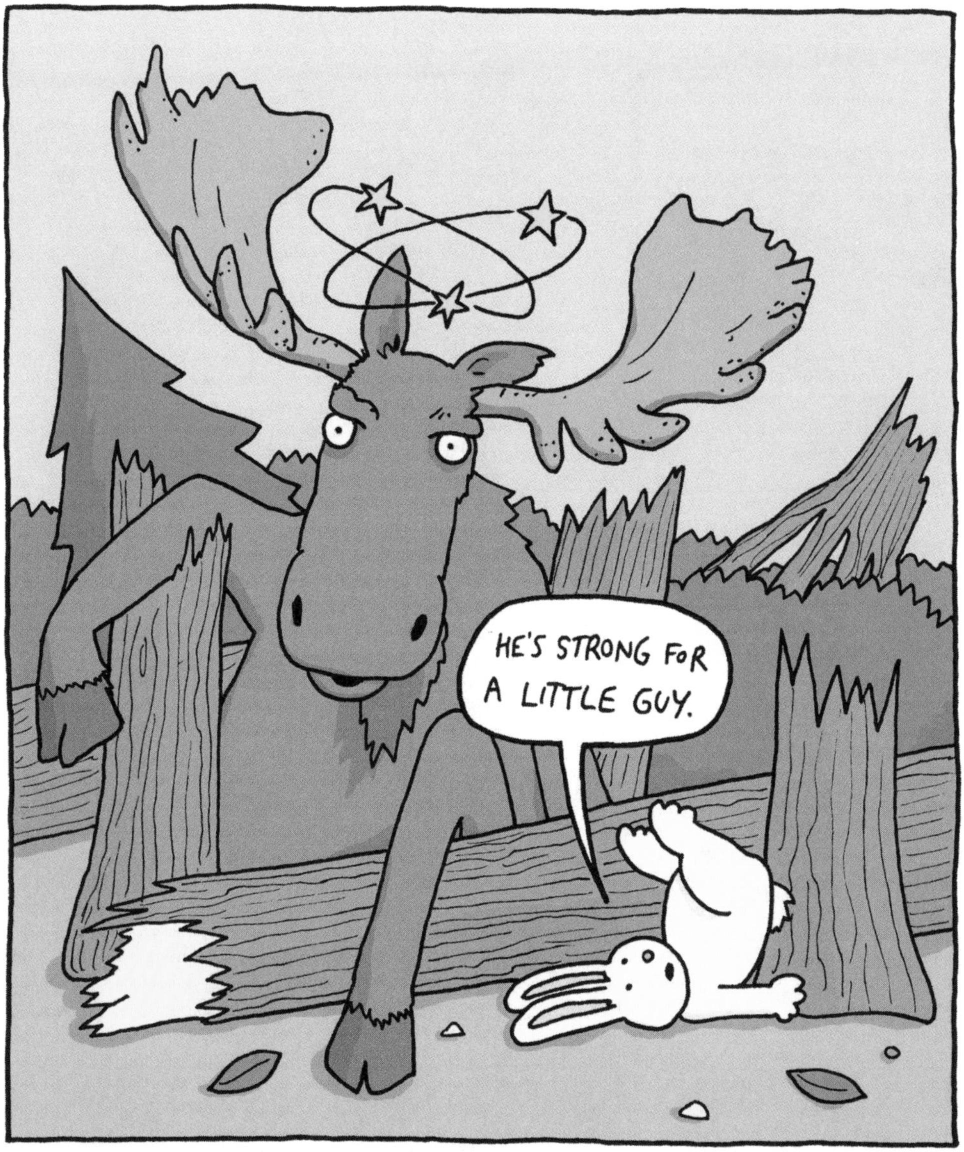
HE'S STRONG FOR A LITTLE GUY.

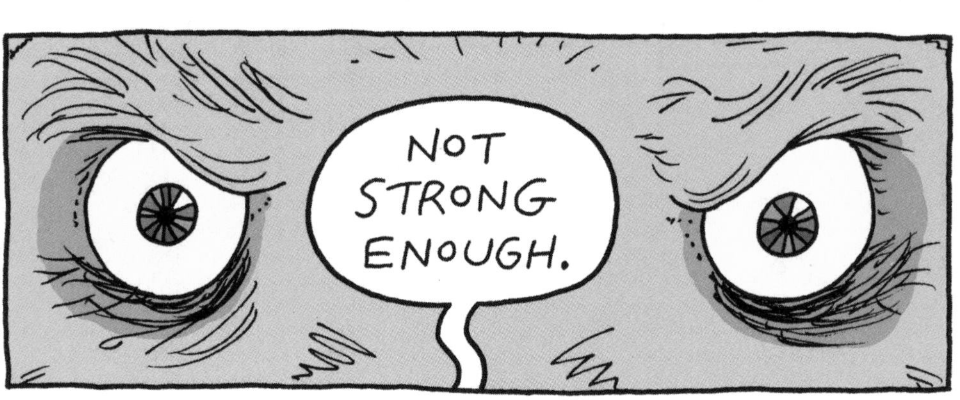
NOT STRONG ENOUGH.

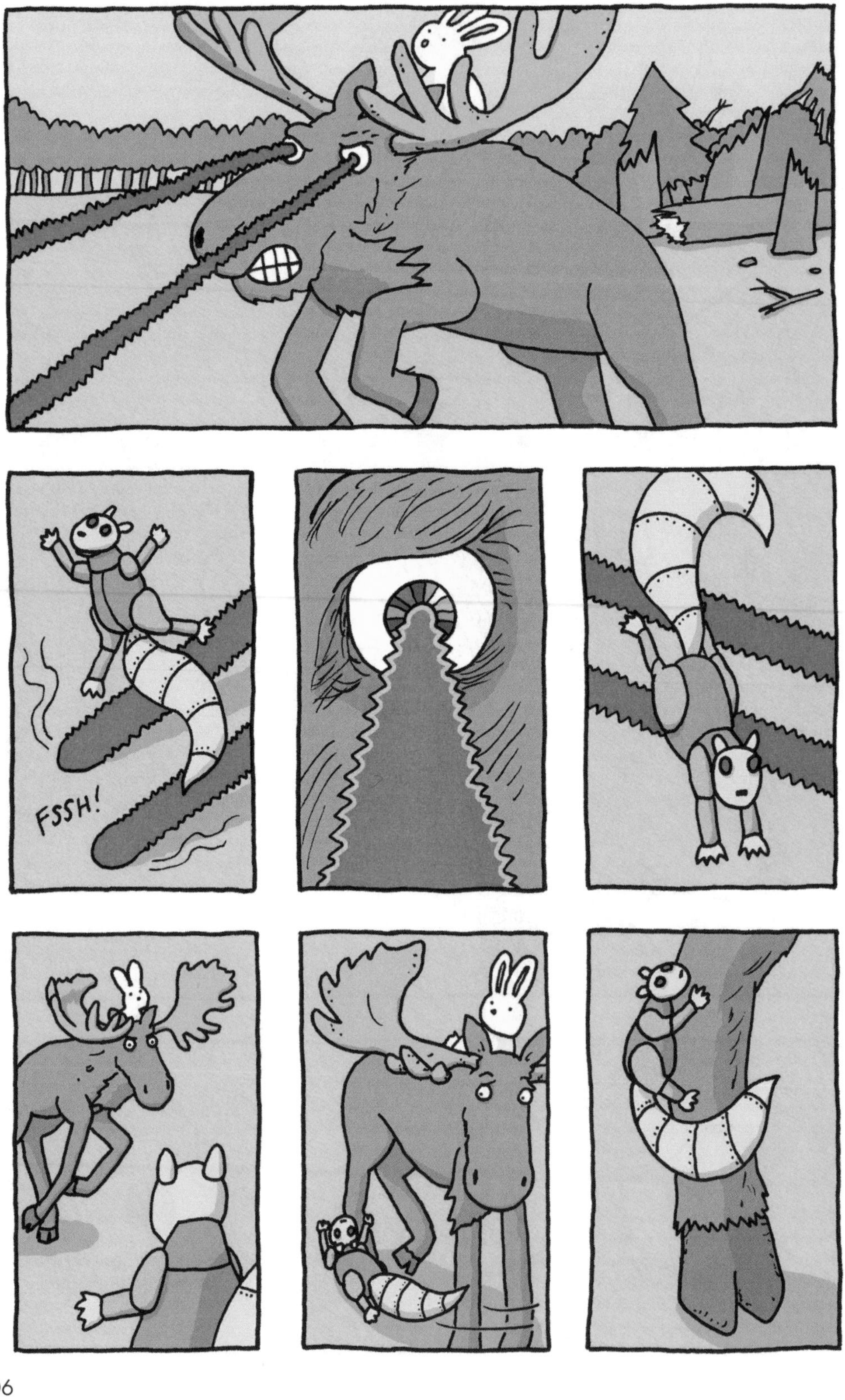
FSSH!

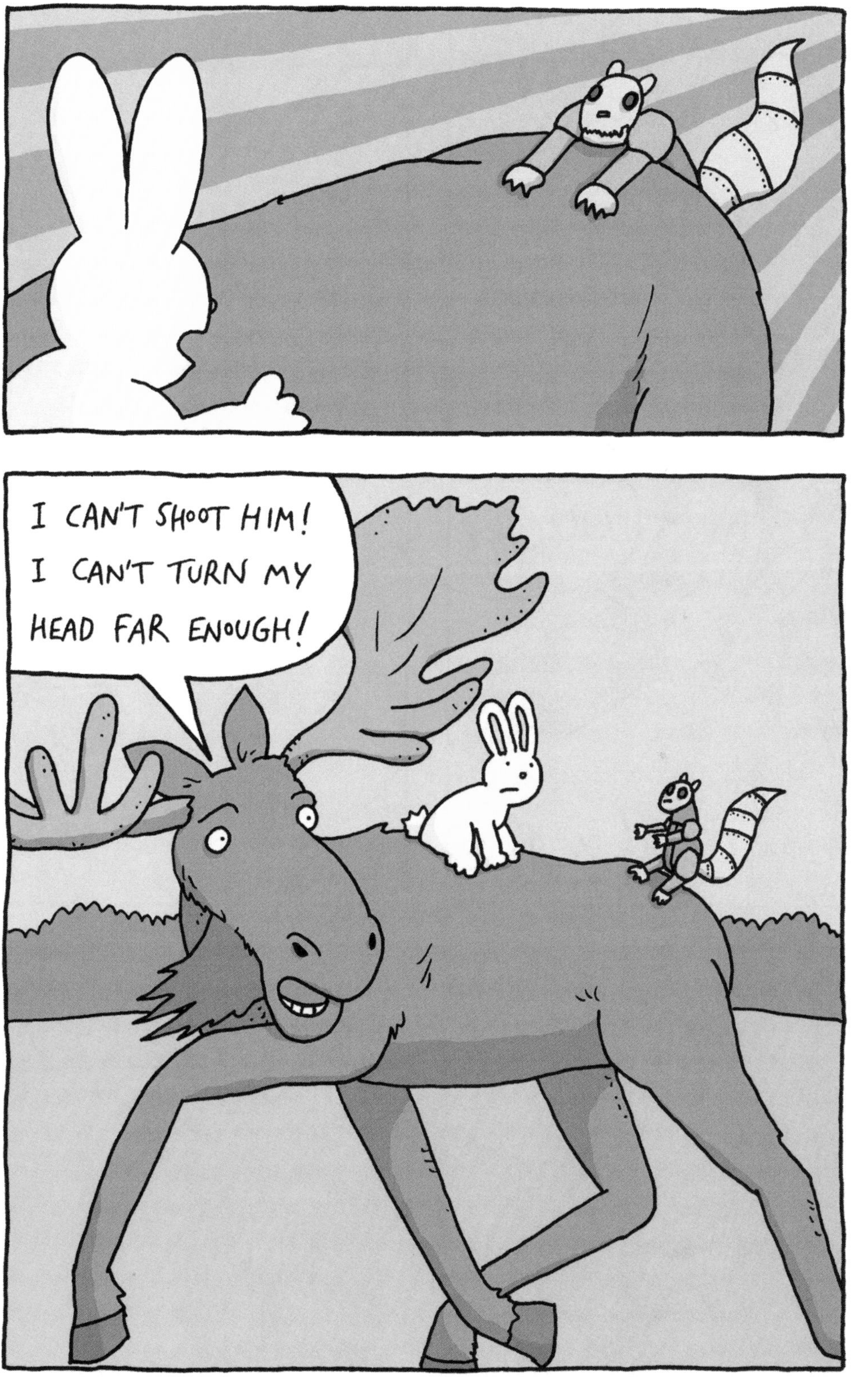
I CAN'T SHOOT HIM! I CAN'T TURN MY HEAD FAR ENOUGH!

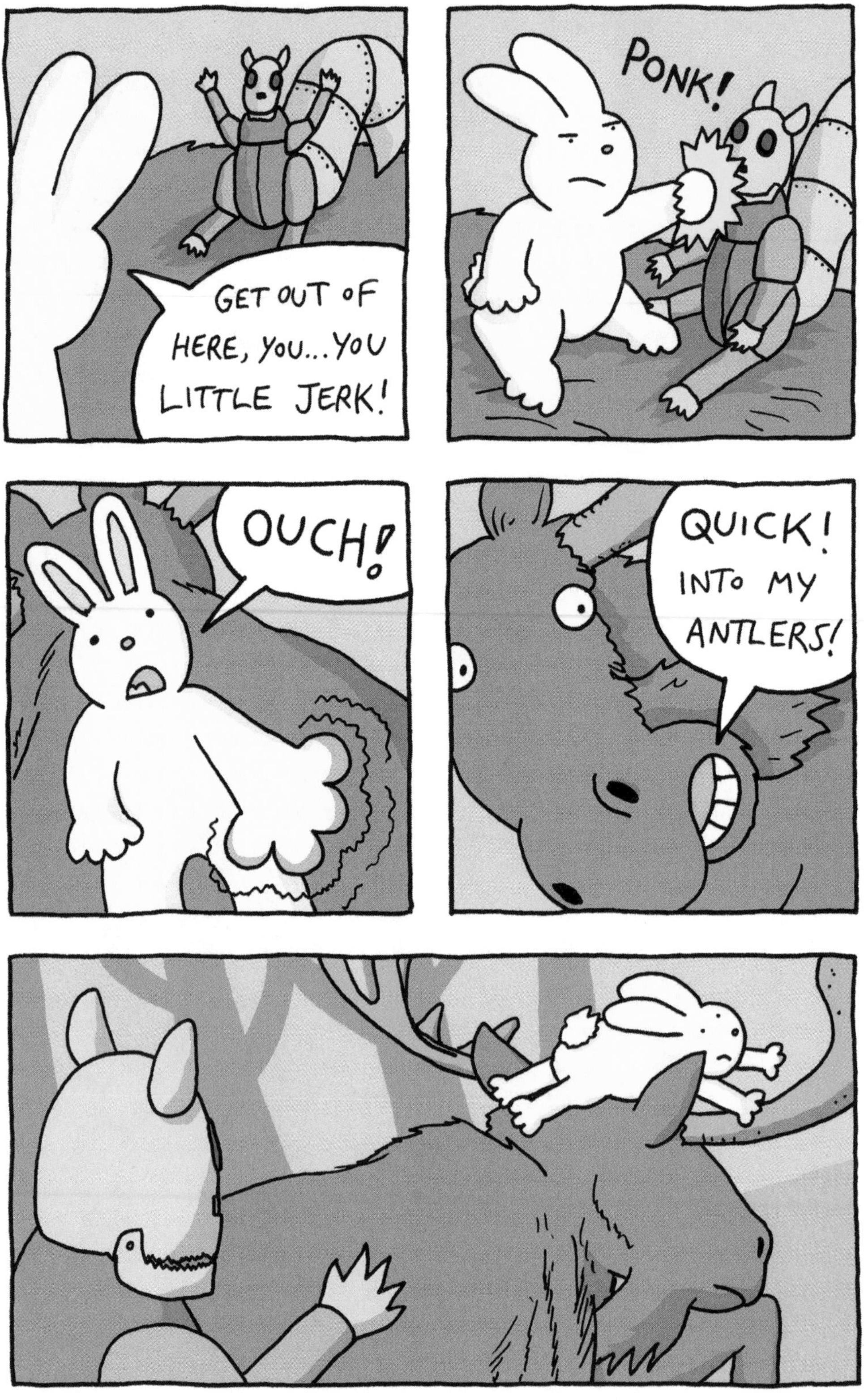
GET OUT OF HERE, YOU... YOU LITTLE JERK!
PONK!
OUCH!
QUICK! INTO MY ANTLERS!

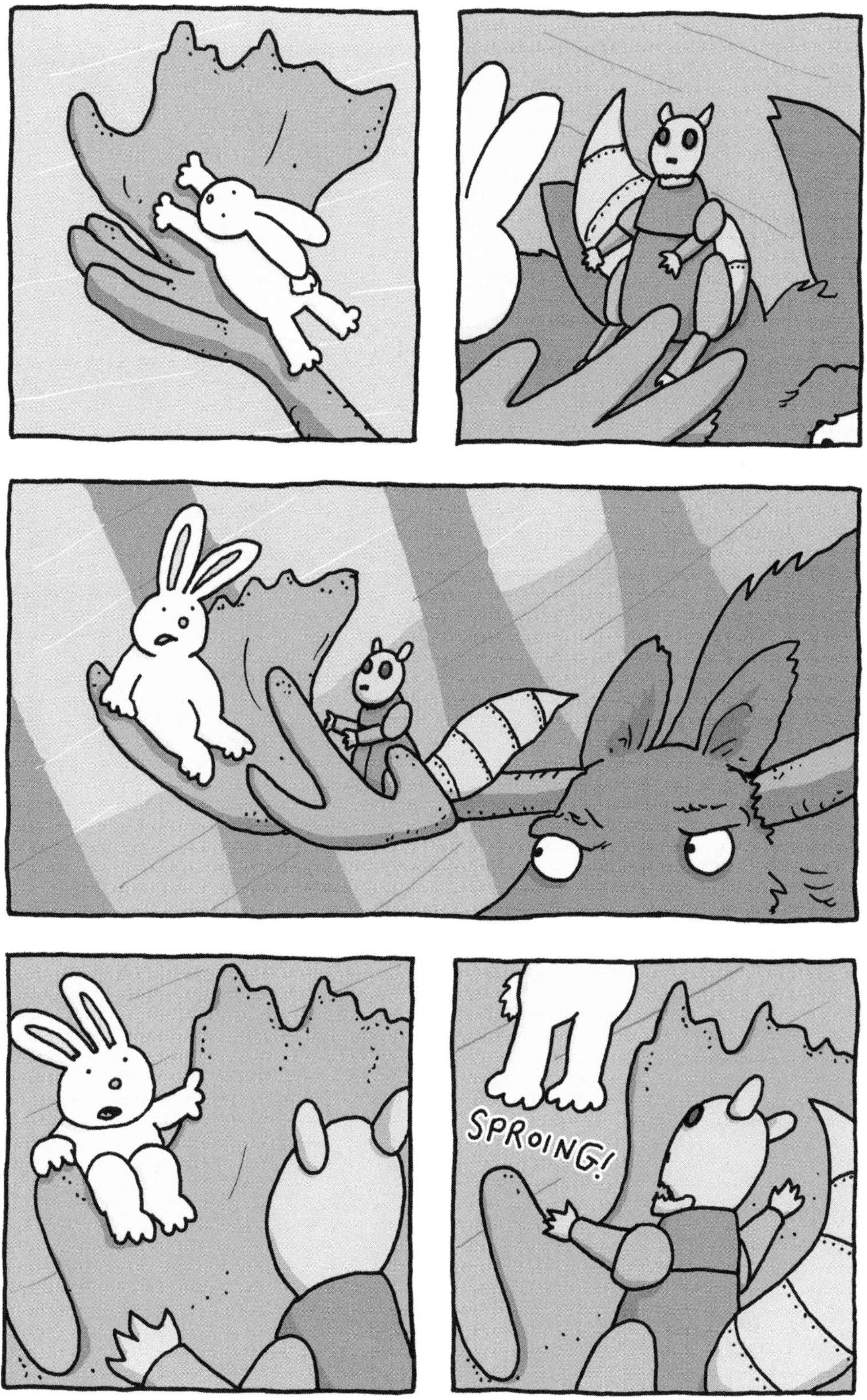
SPROING!

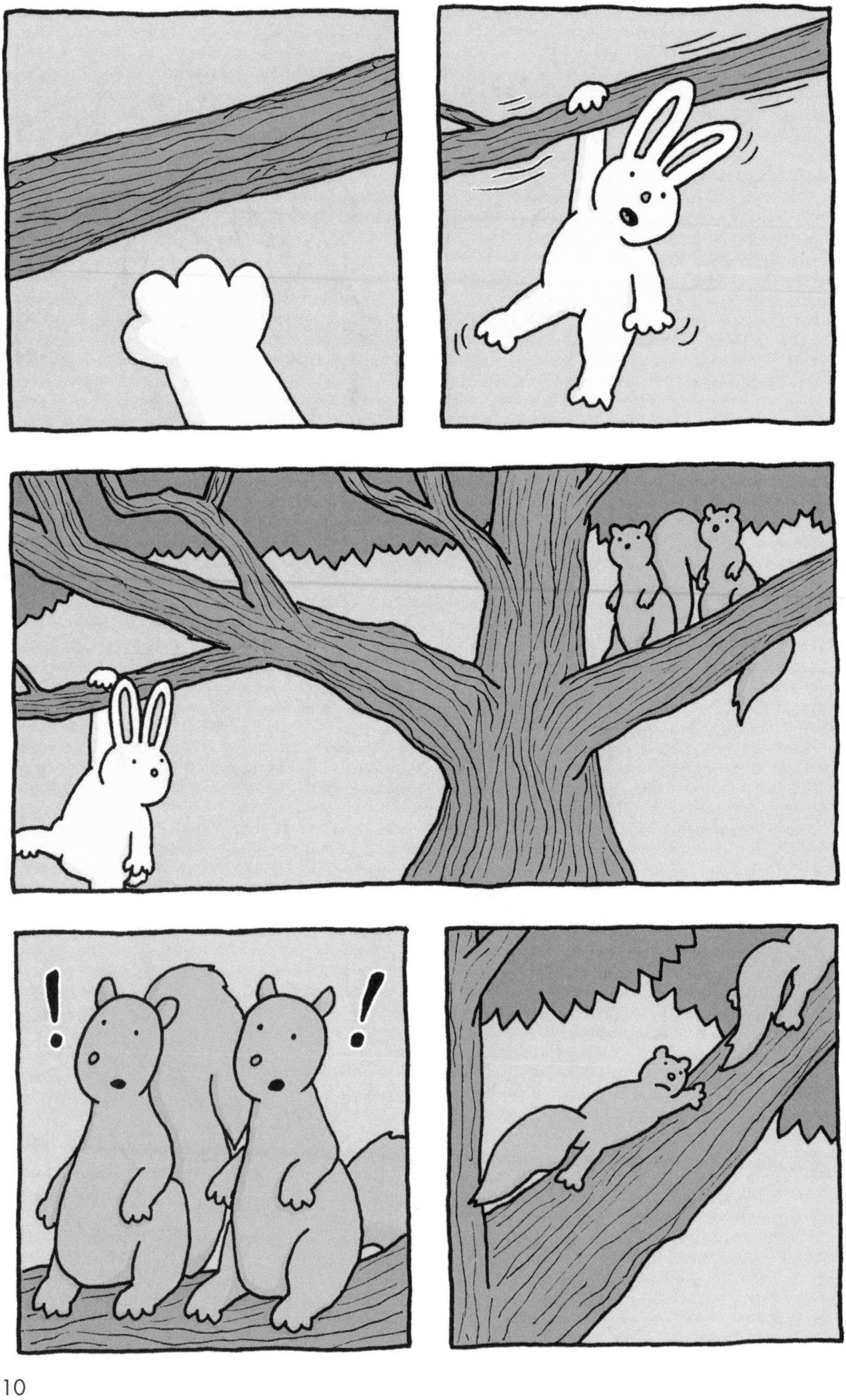
!
!

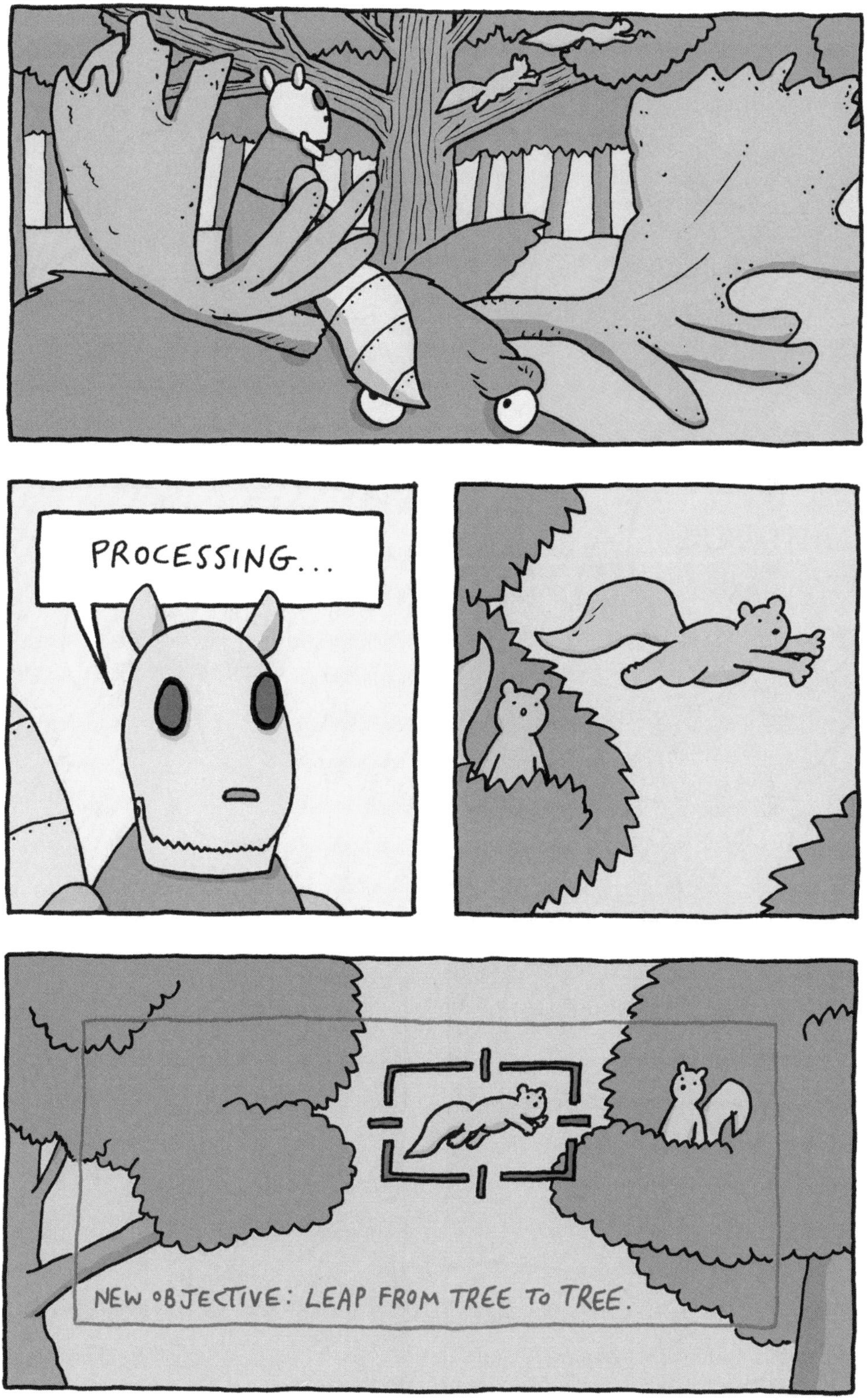
PROCESSING...
NEW OBJECTIVE: LEAP FROM TREE TO TREE.

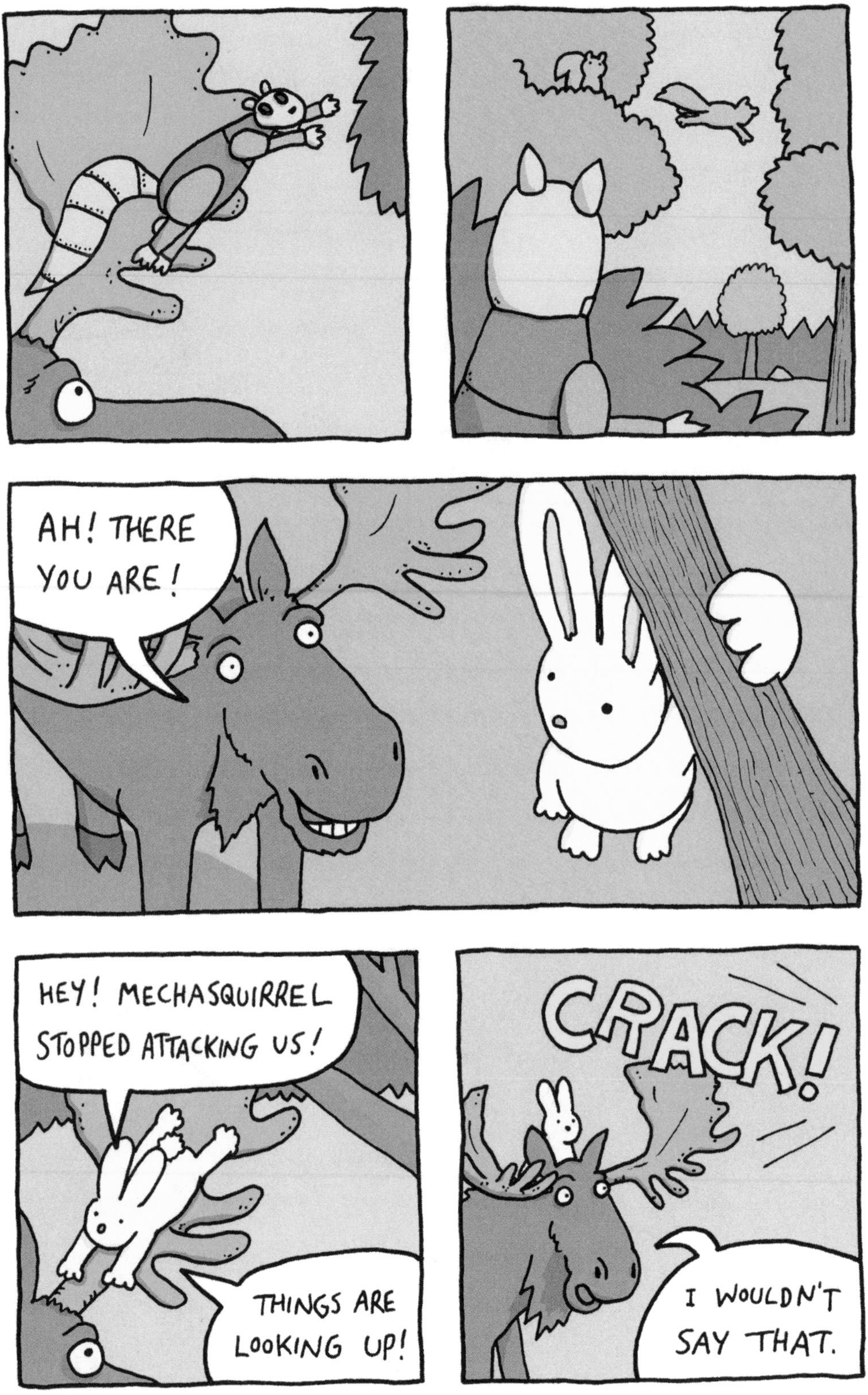
AH! THERE YOU ARE!
HEY! MECHASQUIRREL STOPPED ATTACKING US!
THINGS ARE LOOKING UP!
CRACK!
I WOULDN'T SAY THAT.

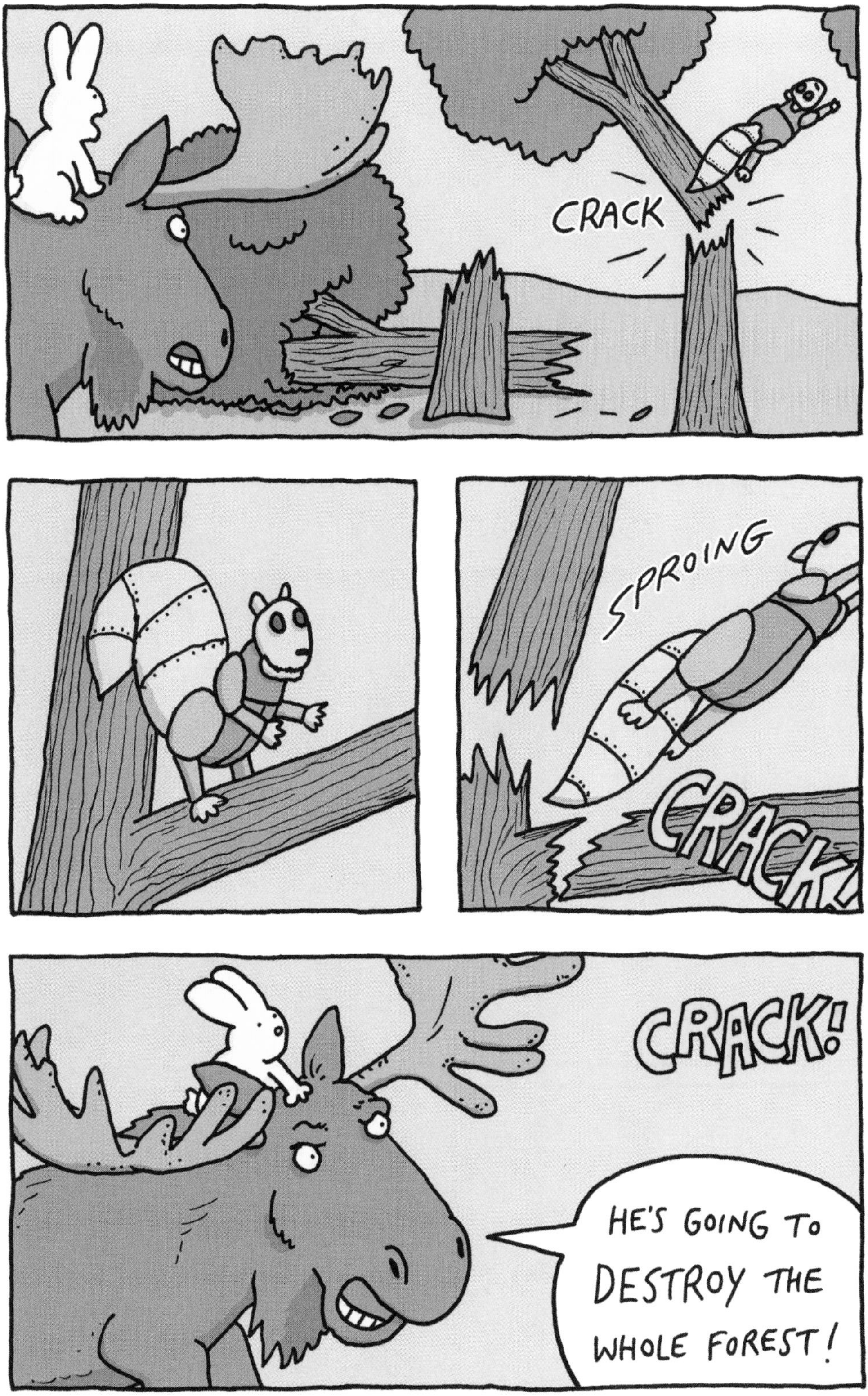
CRACK
SPROING
CRACK!
CRACK!
HE'S GOING TO DESTROY THE WHOLE FOREST!

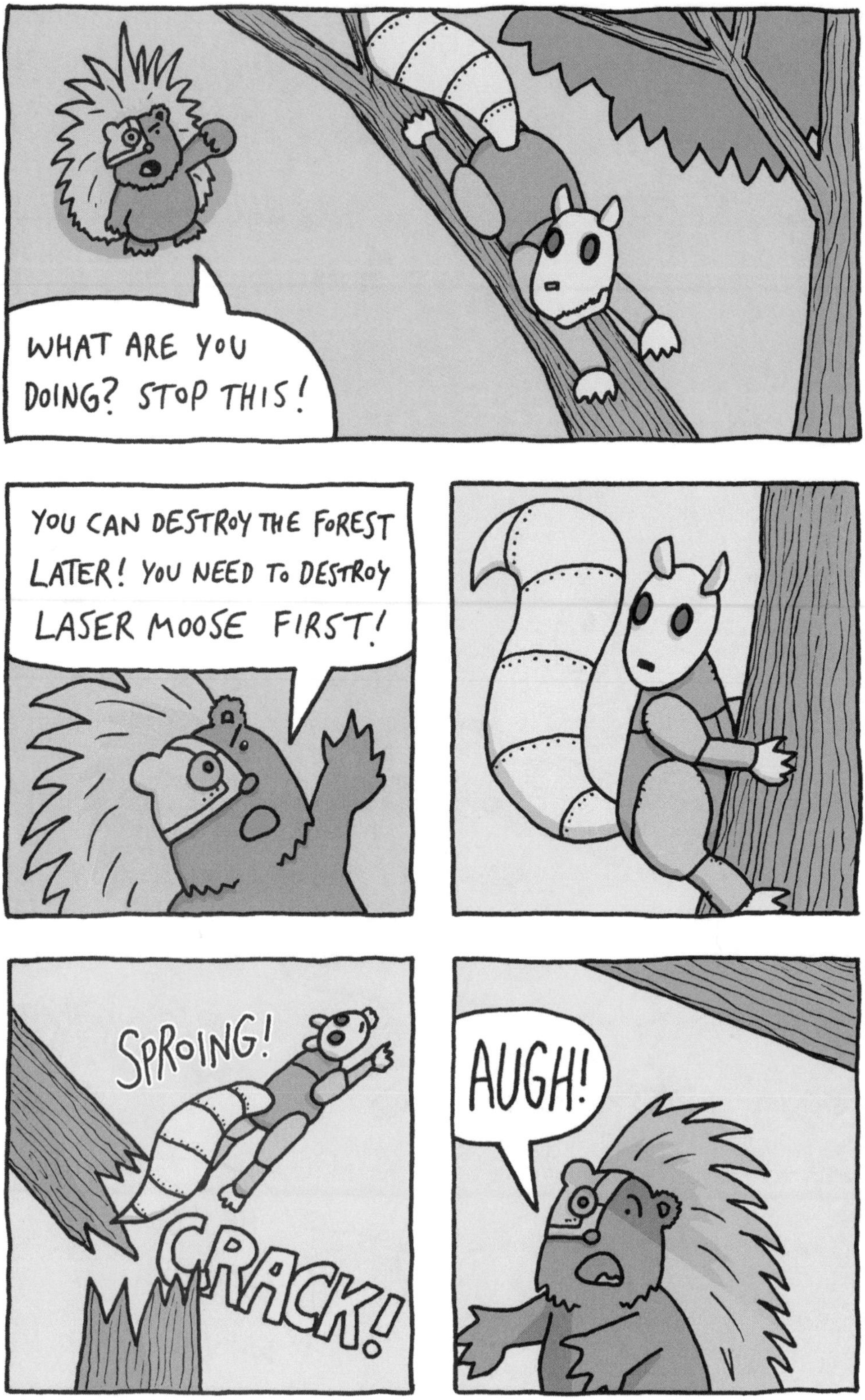

WHAT ARE YOU DOING? STOP THIS!
YOU CAN DESTROY THE FOREST LATER! YOU NEED TO DESTROY LASER MOOSE FIRST!
SPROING!
CRACK!
AUGH!

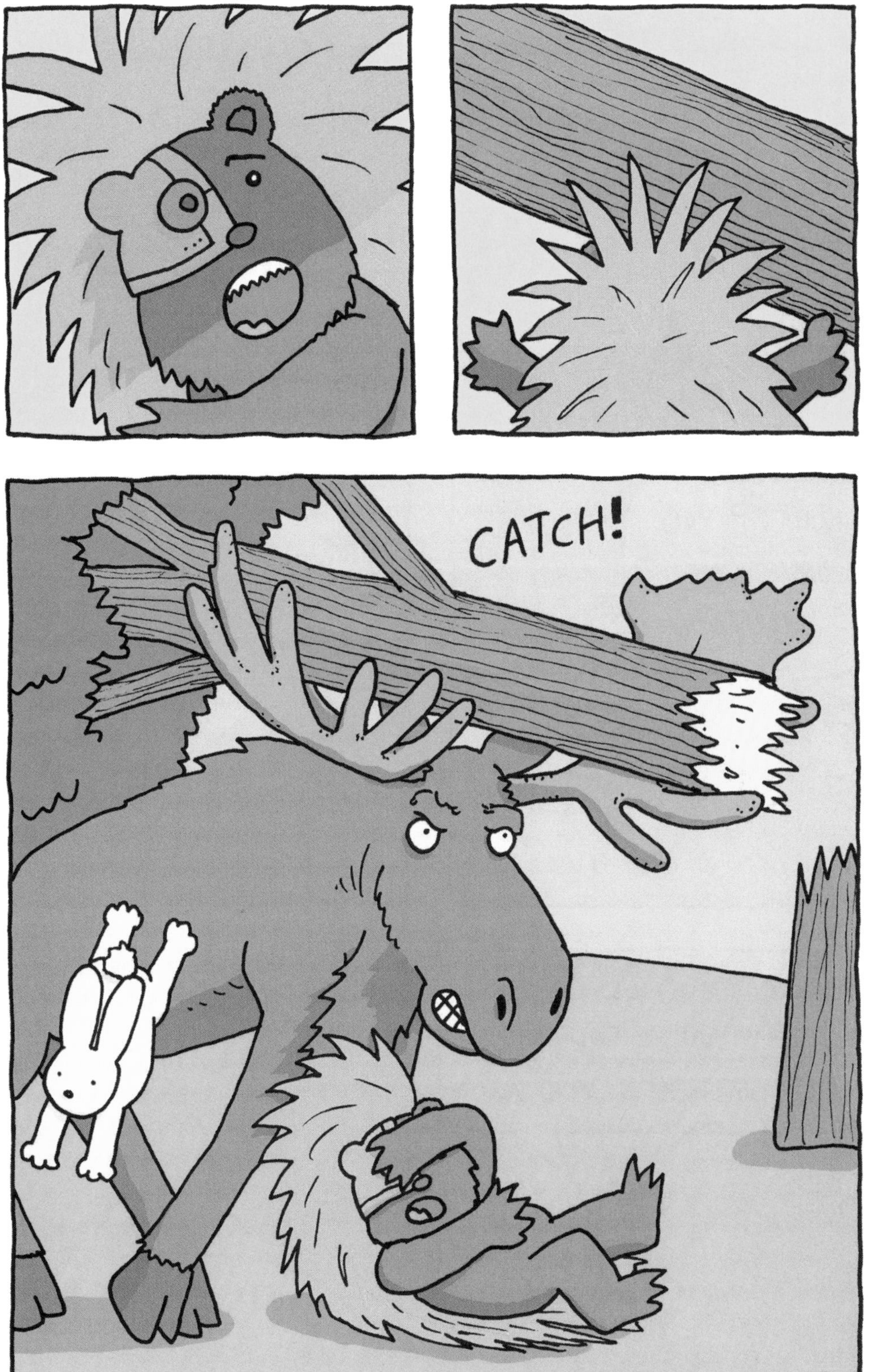
CATCH!

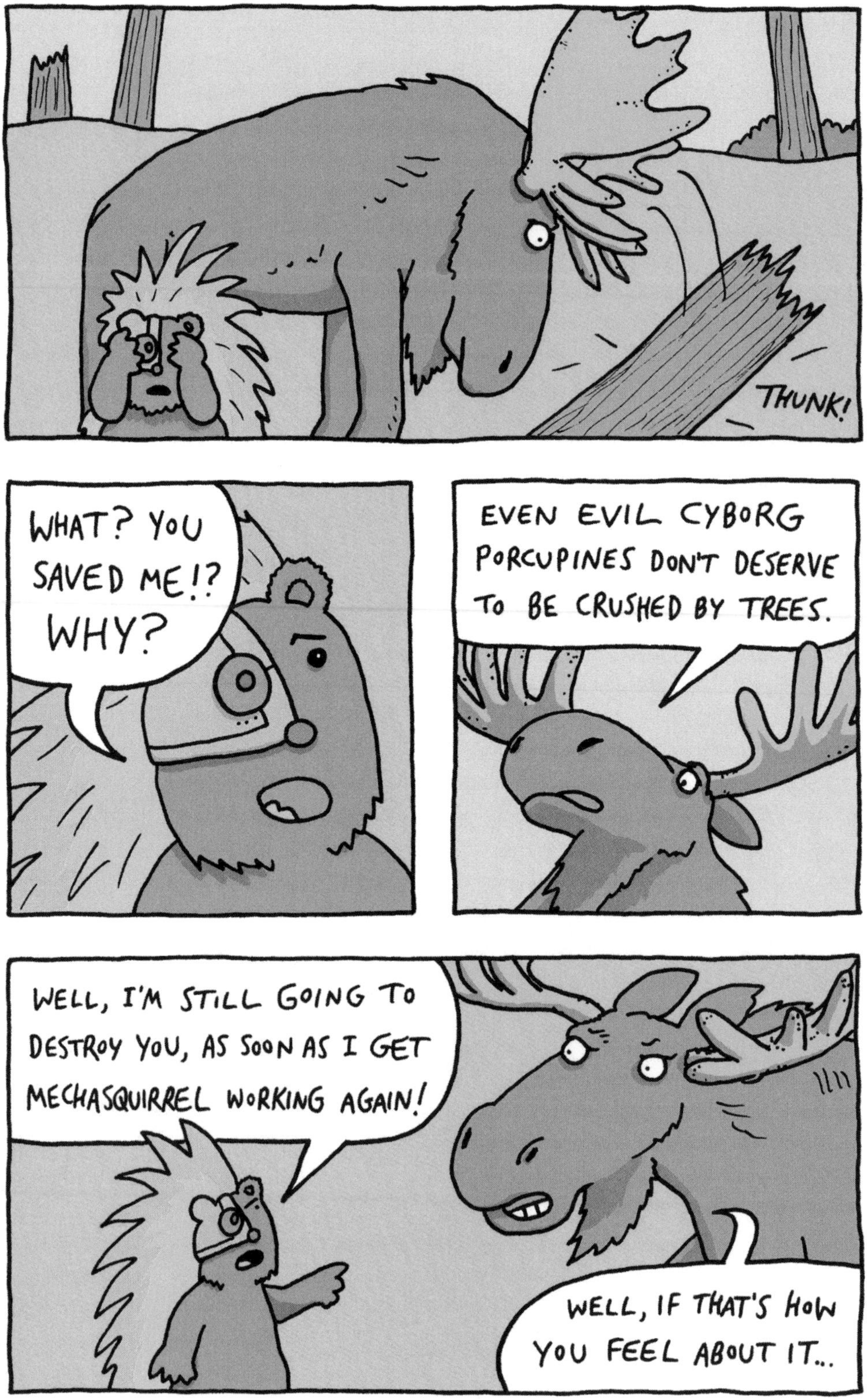
THUNK!
WHAT? YOU SAVED ME!? WHY?
EVEN EVIL CYBORG PORCUPINES DON'T DESERVE TO BE CRUSHED BY TREES.
WELL, I'M STILL GOING TO DESTROY YOU, AS SOON AS I GET MECHASQUIRREL WORKING AGAIN!
WELL, IF THAT'S HOW YOU FEEL ABOUT IT...

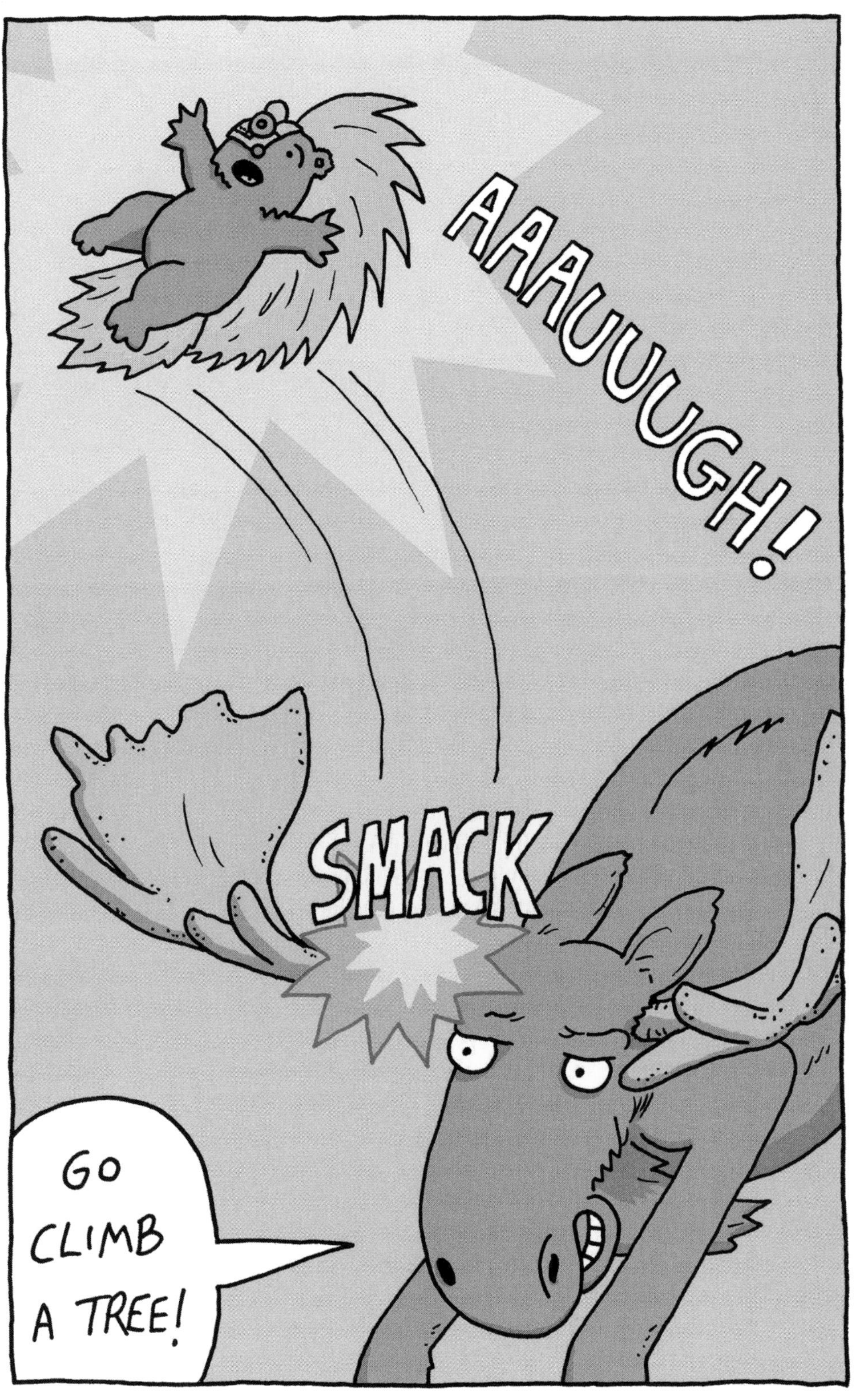
AAAAUUUGH!
SMACK
GO CLIMB A TREE!

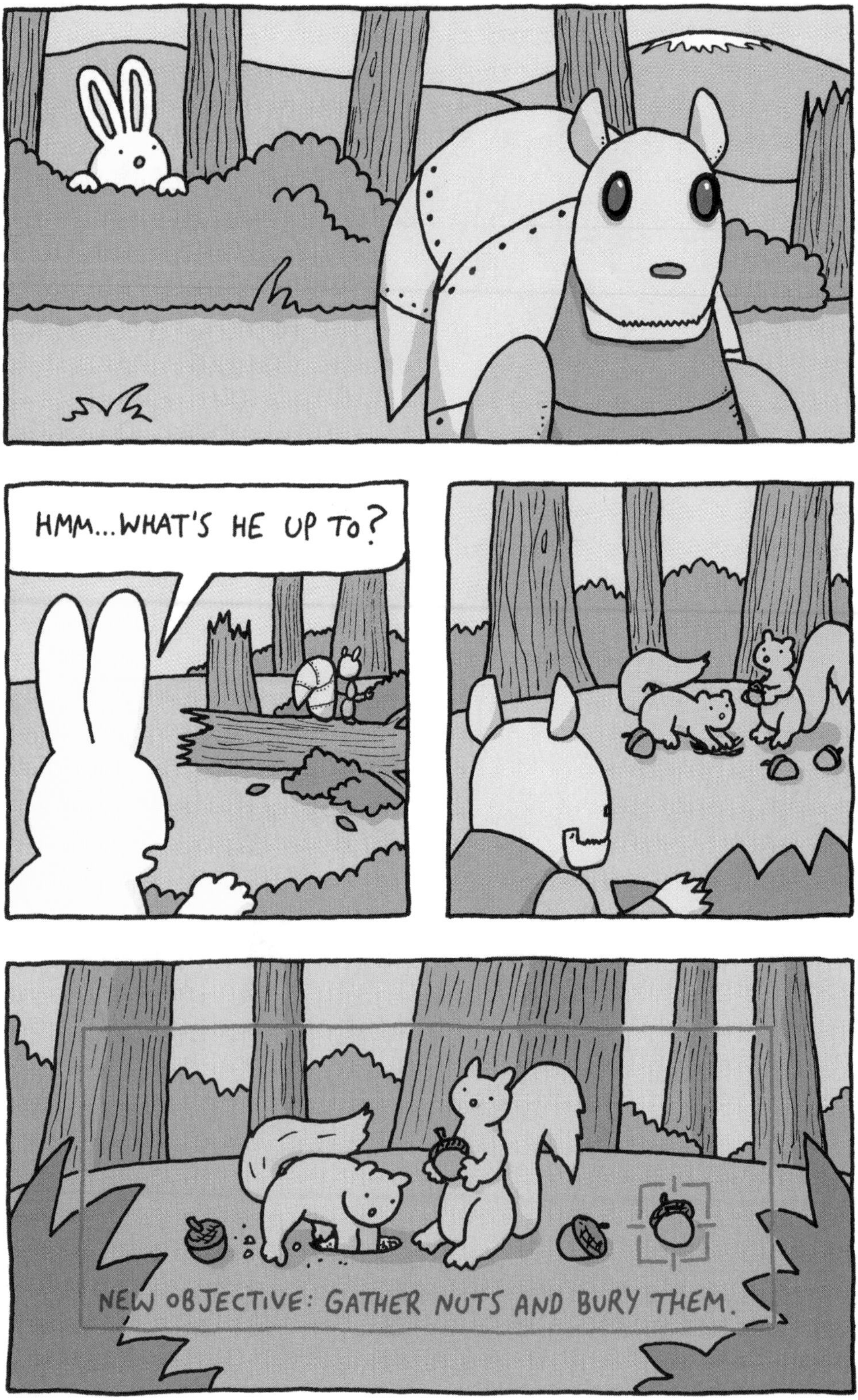
HMM...WHAT'S HE UP TO?
NEW OBJECTIVE: GATHER NUTS AND BURY THEM.

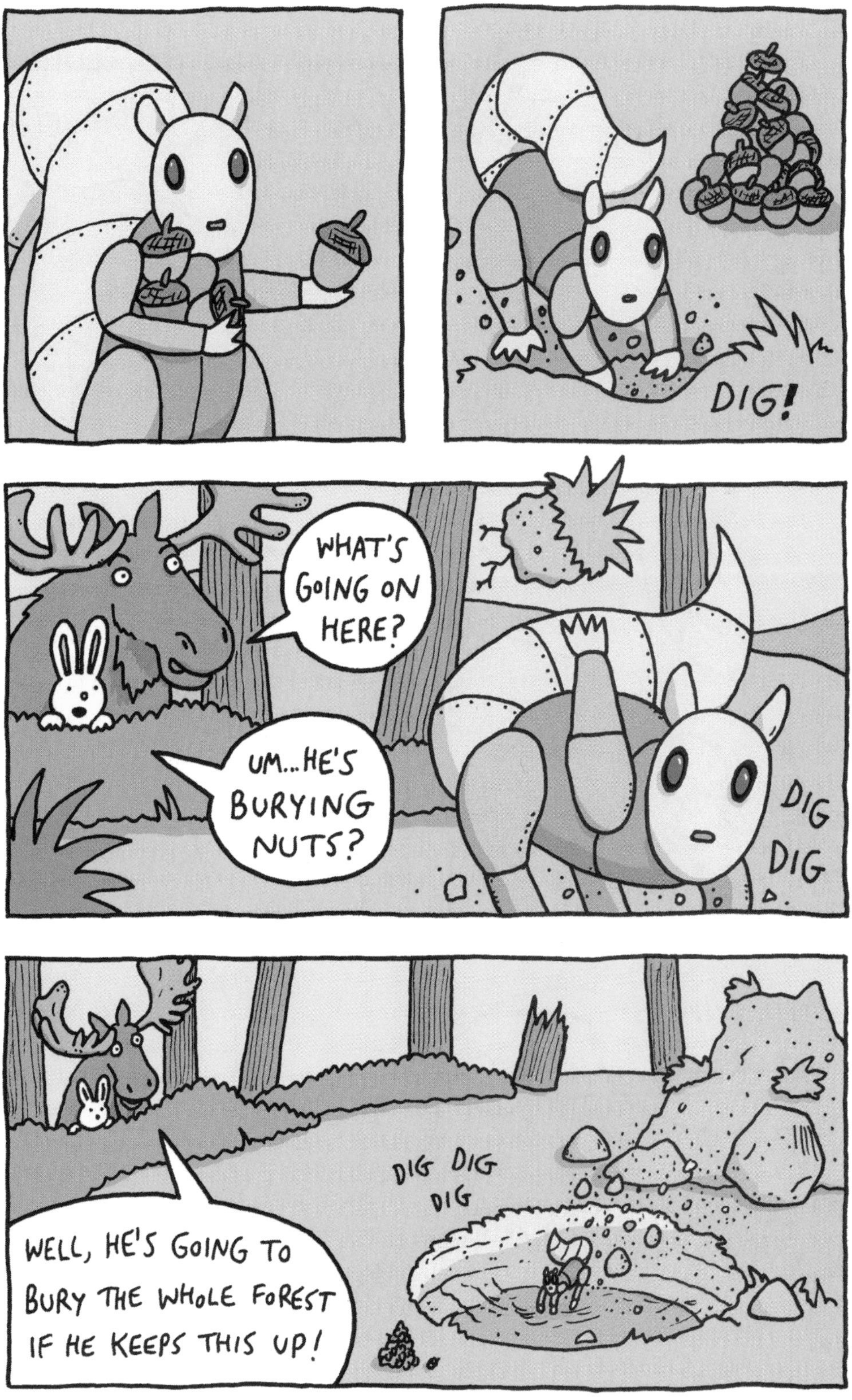
DIG!
WHAT'S GOING ON HERE?
UM...HE'S BURYING NUTS?
DIG DIG
DIG DIG DIG
WELL, HE'S GOING TO BURY THE WHOLE FOREST IF HE KEEPS THIS UP!

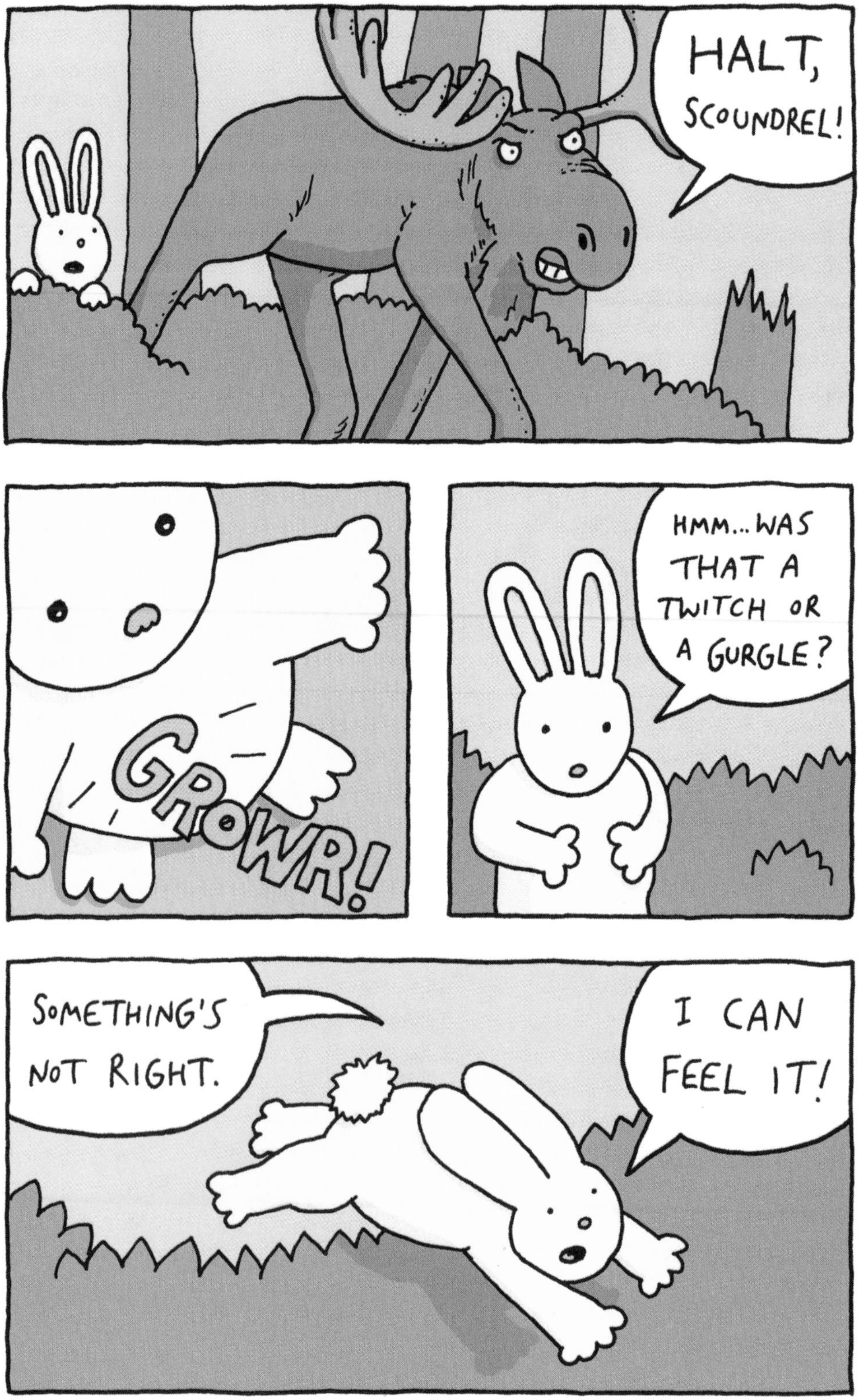
HALT, SCOUNDREL!
GROWR!
HMM... WAS THAT A TWITCH OR A GURGLE?
SOMETHING'S NOT RIGHT.
I CAN FEEL IT!

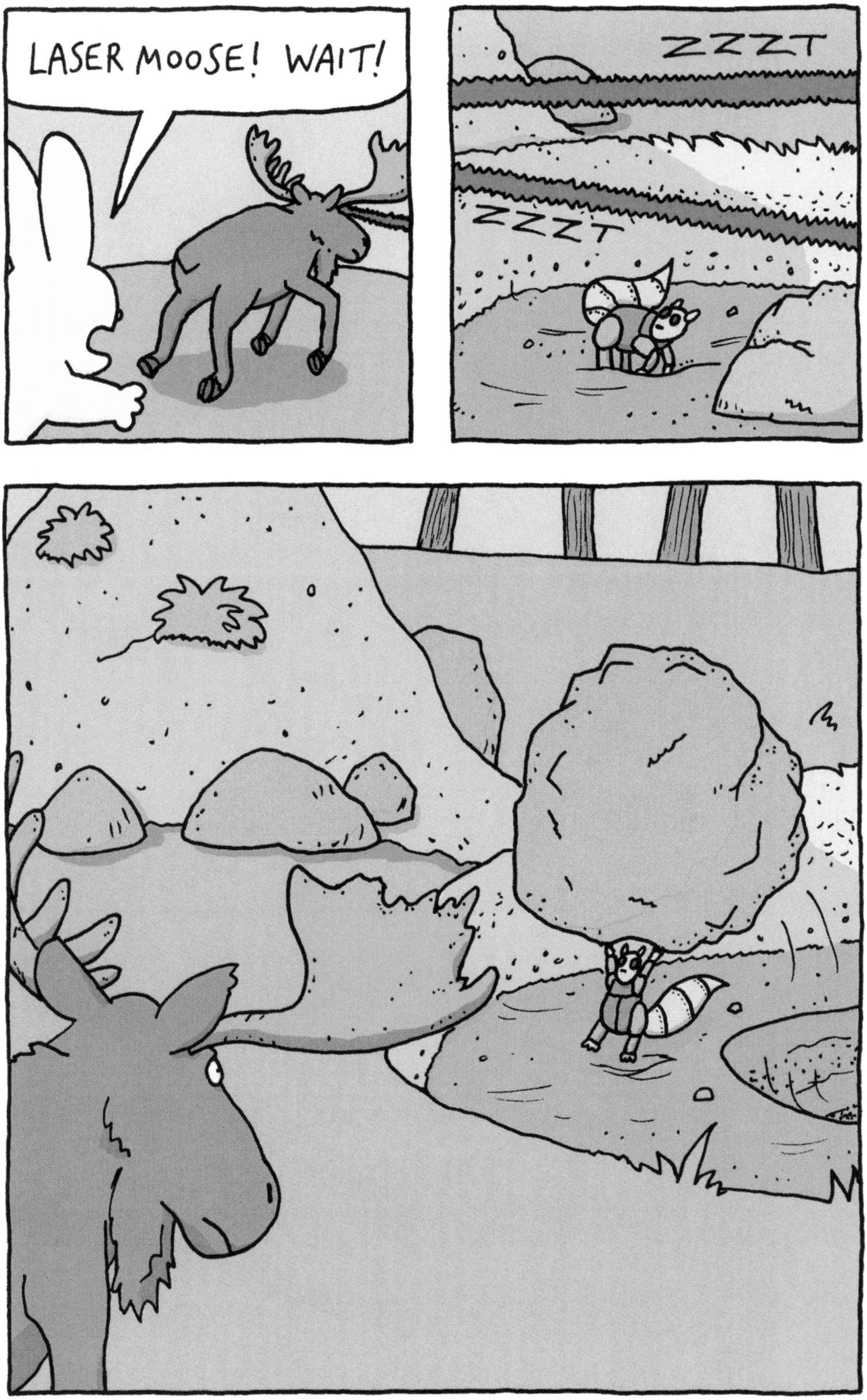
LASER MOOSE! WAIT!
ZZZT
ZZZT

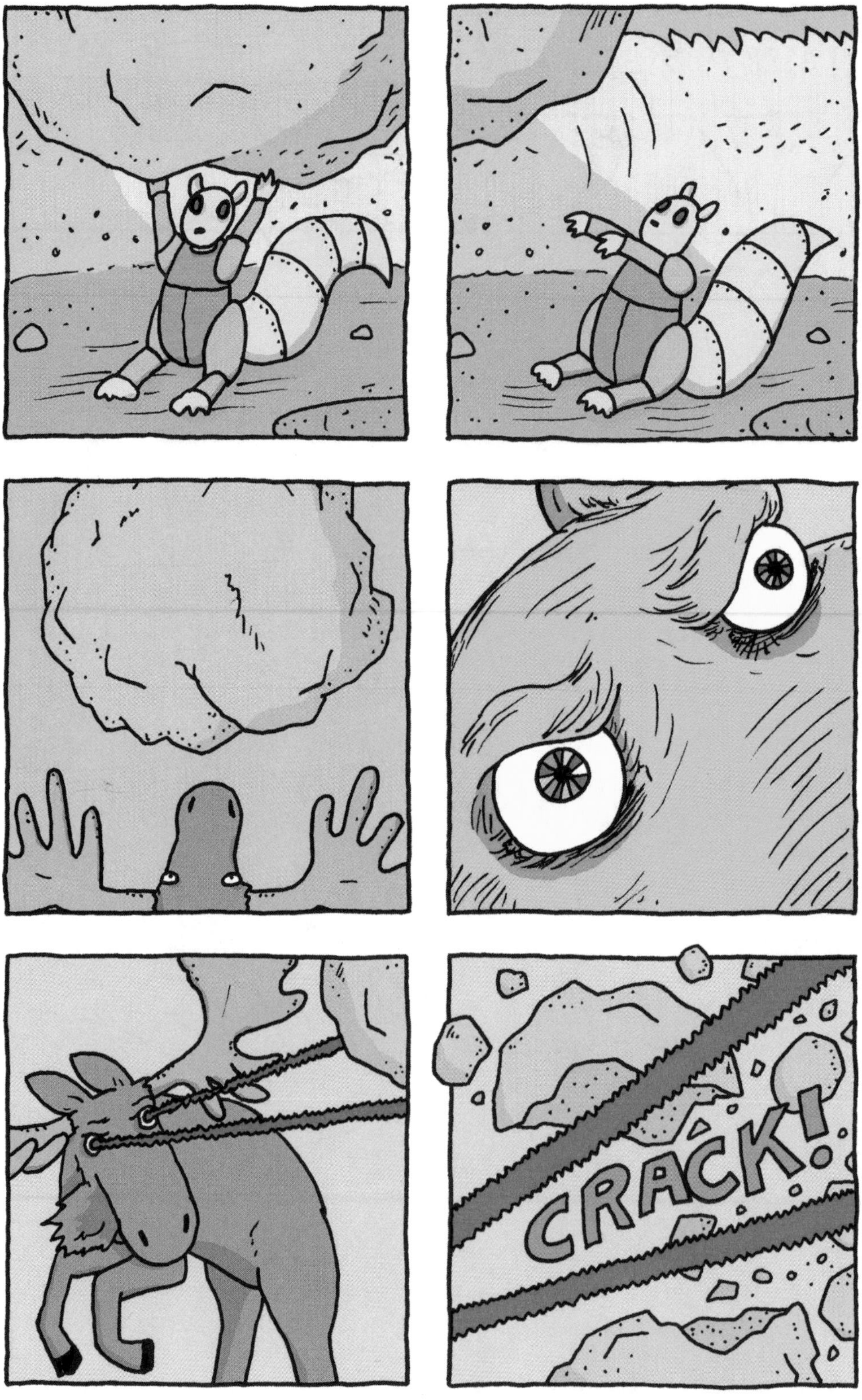
CRACK!

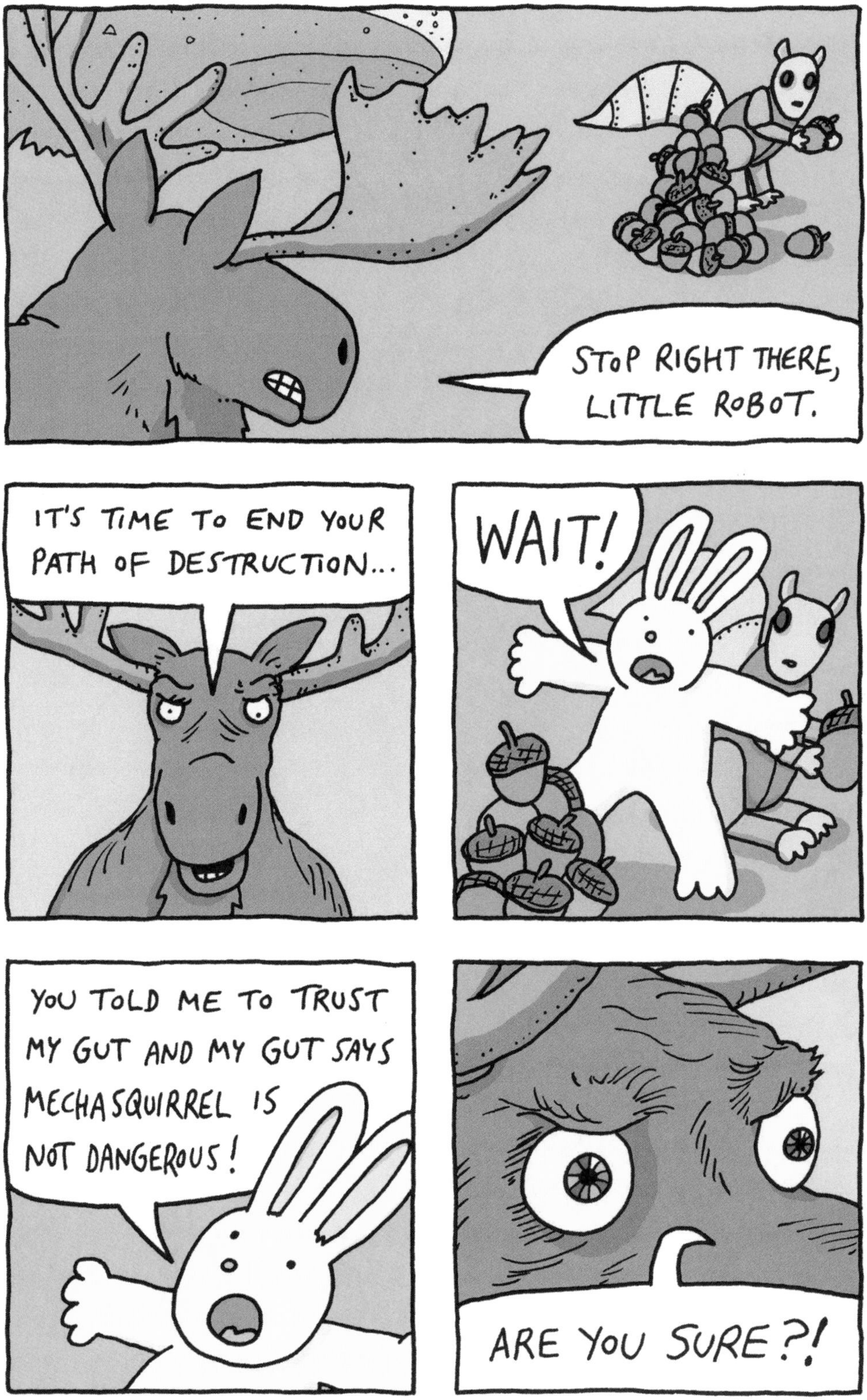
STOP RIGHT THERE, LITTLE ROBOT.
IT'S TIME TO END YOUR PATH OF DESTRUCTION...
WAIT!
YOU TOLD ME TO TRUST MY GUT AND MY GUT SAYS MECHASQUIRREL IS NOT DANGEROUS!
ARE YOU SURE?!

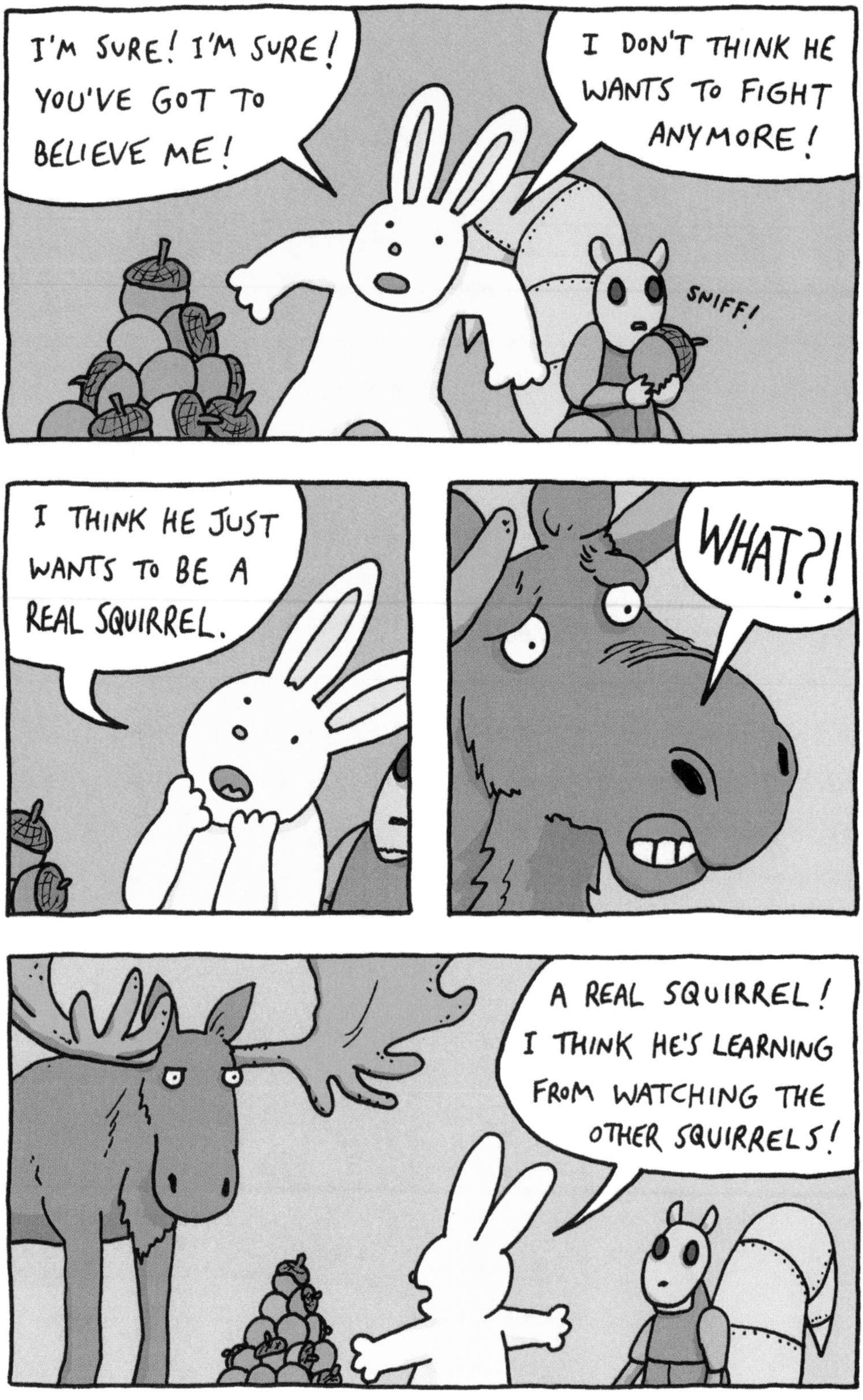
I'M SURE! I'M SURE! YOU'VE GOT TO BELIEVE ME!
I DON'T THINK HE WANTS TO FIGHT ANYMORE!
SNIFF!
I THINK HE JUST WANTS TO BE A REAL SQUIRREL.
WHAT?!
A REAL SQUIRREL! I THINK HE'S LEARNING FROM WATCHING THE OTHER SQUIRRELS!

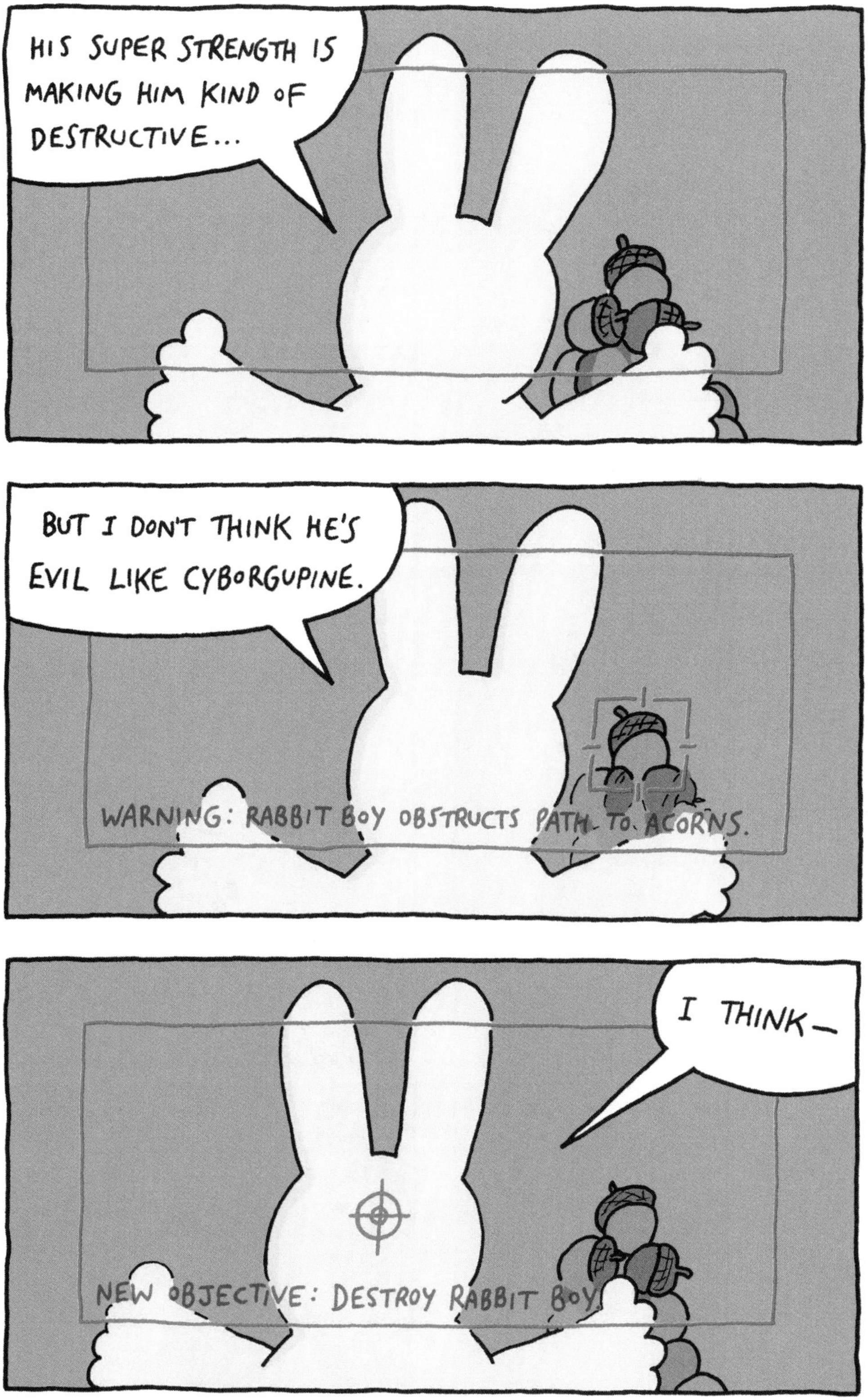
HIS SUPER STRENGTH IS MAKING HIM KIND OF DESTRUCTIVE...
BUT I DON'T THINK HE'S EVIL LIKE CYBORGUPINE.
WARNING: RABBIT BOY OBSTRUCTS PATH TO ACORNS.
I THINK—
NEW OBJECTIVE: DESTROY RABBIT BOY.

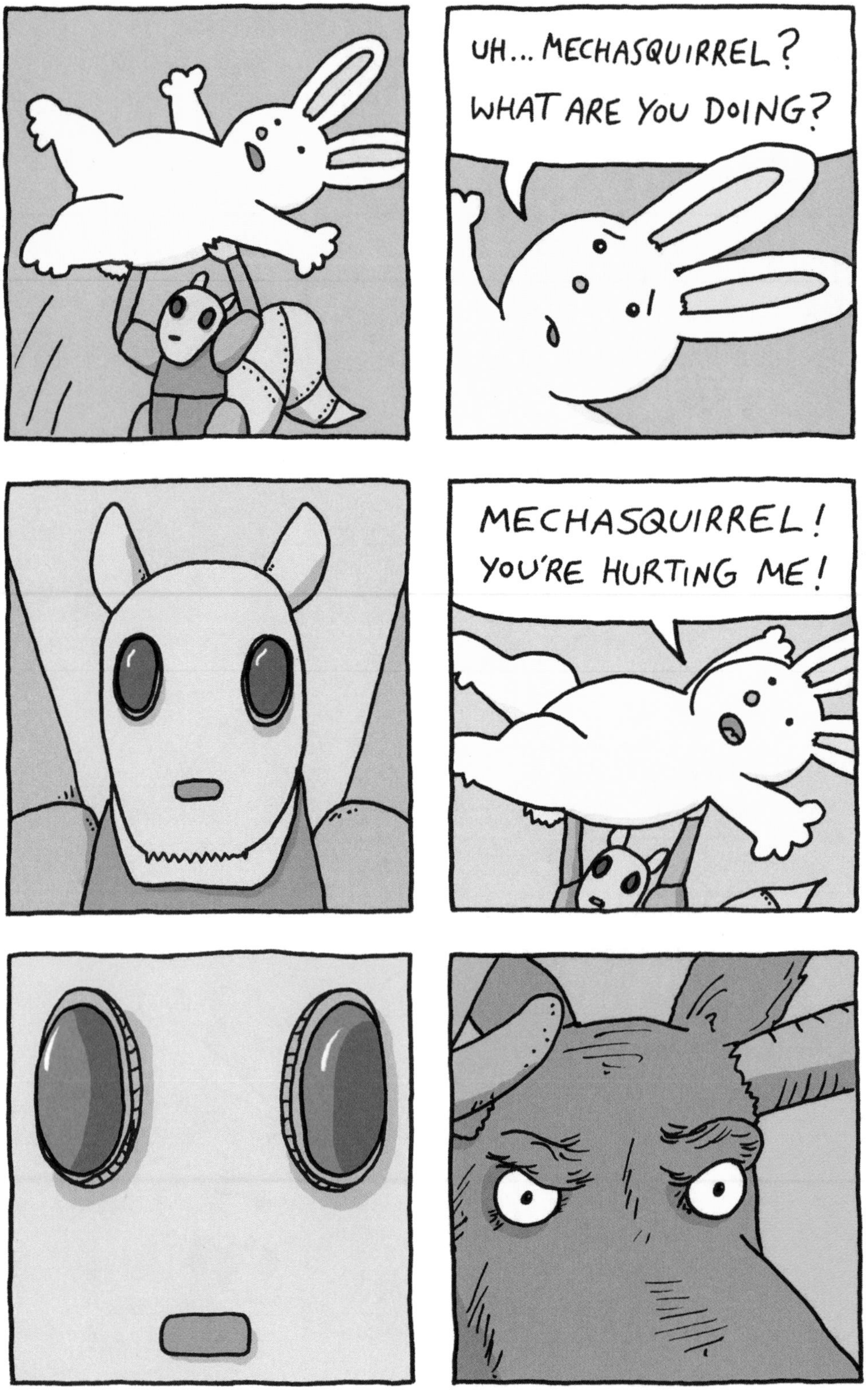
UH... MECHASQUIRREL? WHAT ARE YOU DOING?
MECHASQUIRREL! YOU'RE HURTING ME!

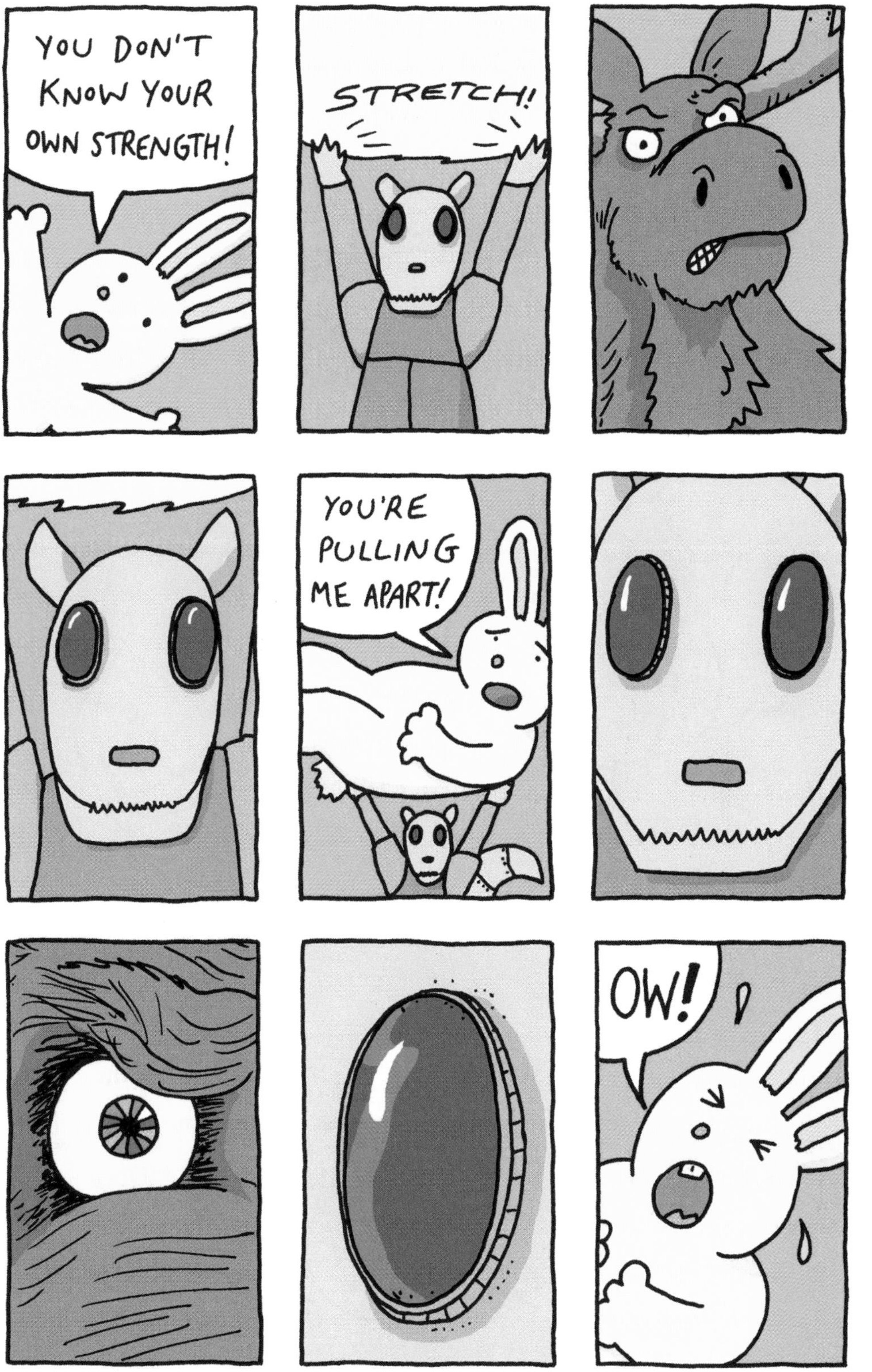
YOU DON'T KNOW YOUR OWN STRENGTH!
STRETCH!
YOU'RE PULLING ME APART!
OW!

ZZZT
ZZZT
CHOP!

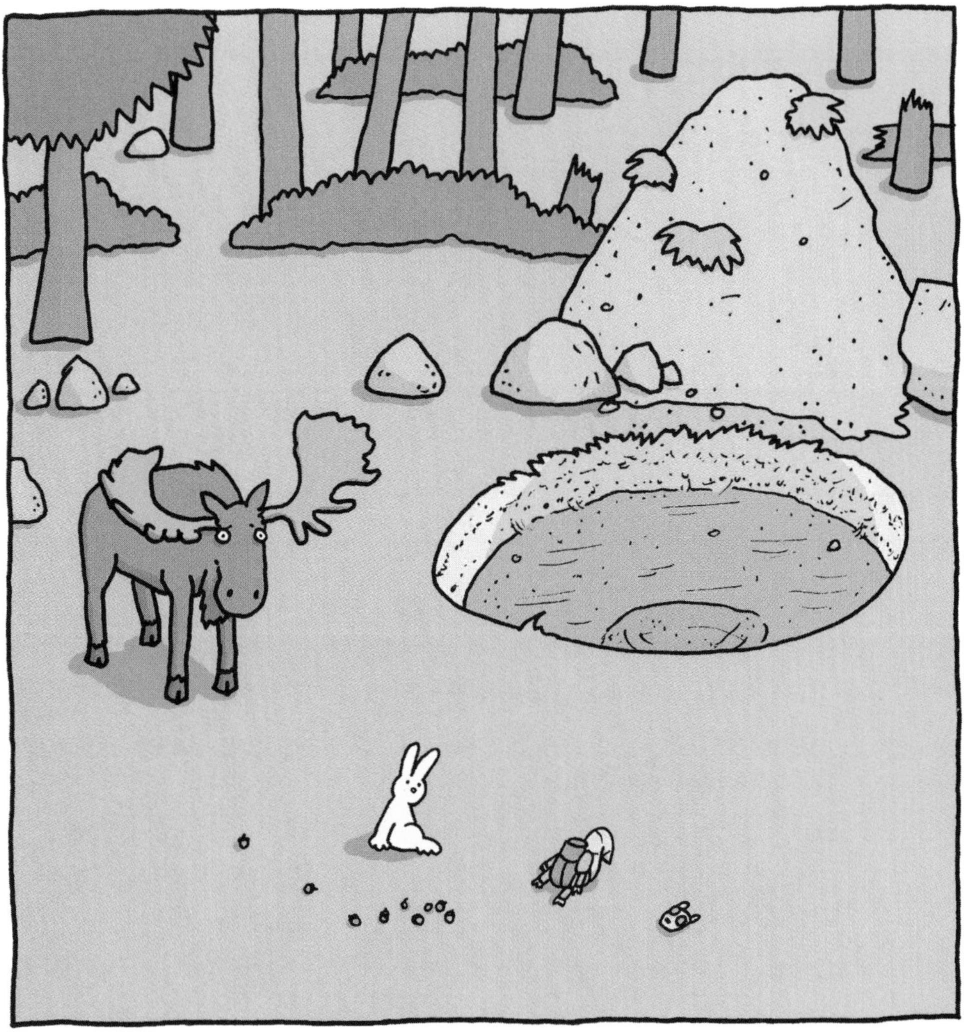

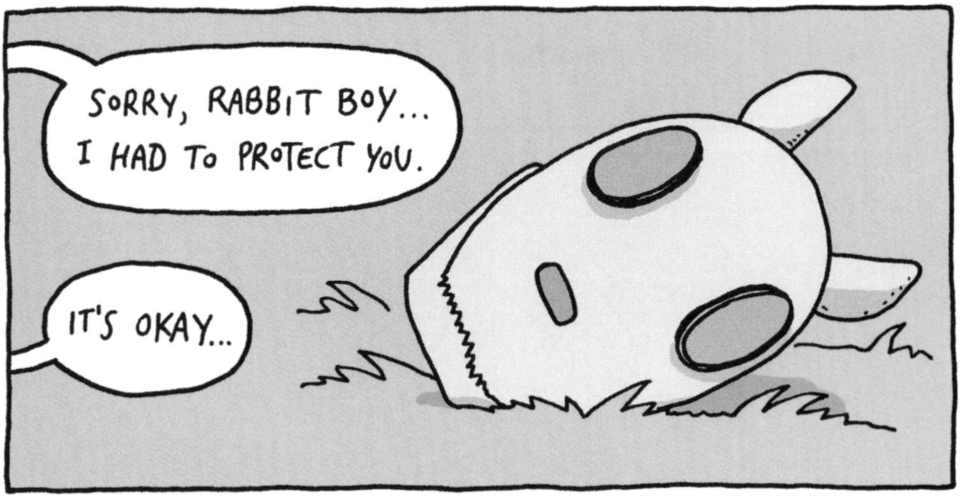
SORRY, RABBIT BOY... I HAD TO PROTECT YOU.
IT'S OKAY...

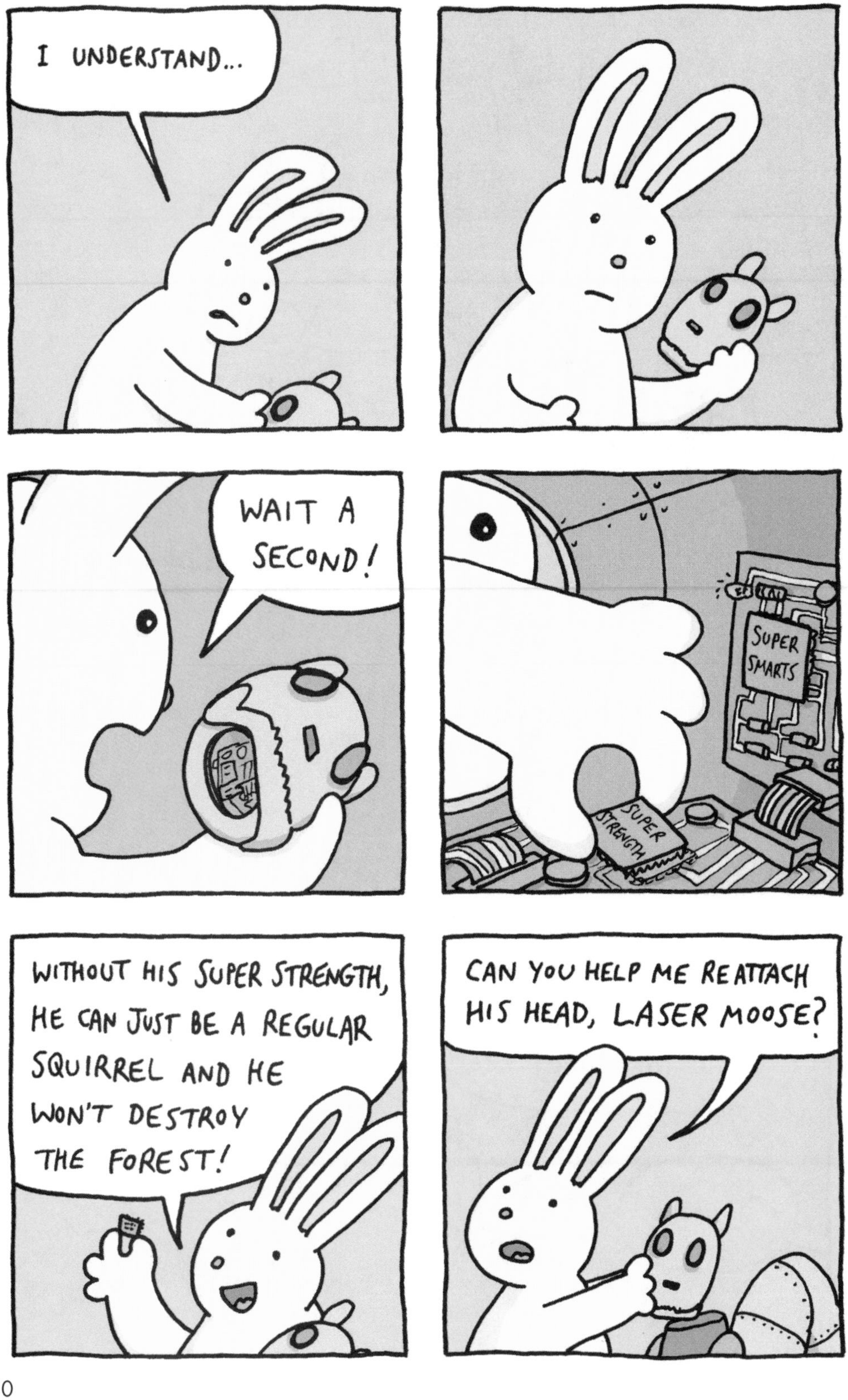
I UNDERSTAND...
WAIT A SECOND!
SUPER SMARTS
SUPER STRENGTH
WITHOUT HIS SUPER STRENGTH, HE CAN JUST BE A REGULAR SQUIRREL AND HE WON'T DESTROY THE FOREST!
CAN YOU HELP ME REATTACH HIS HEAD, LASER MOOSE?

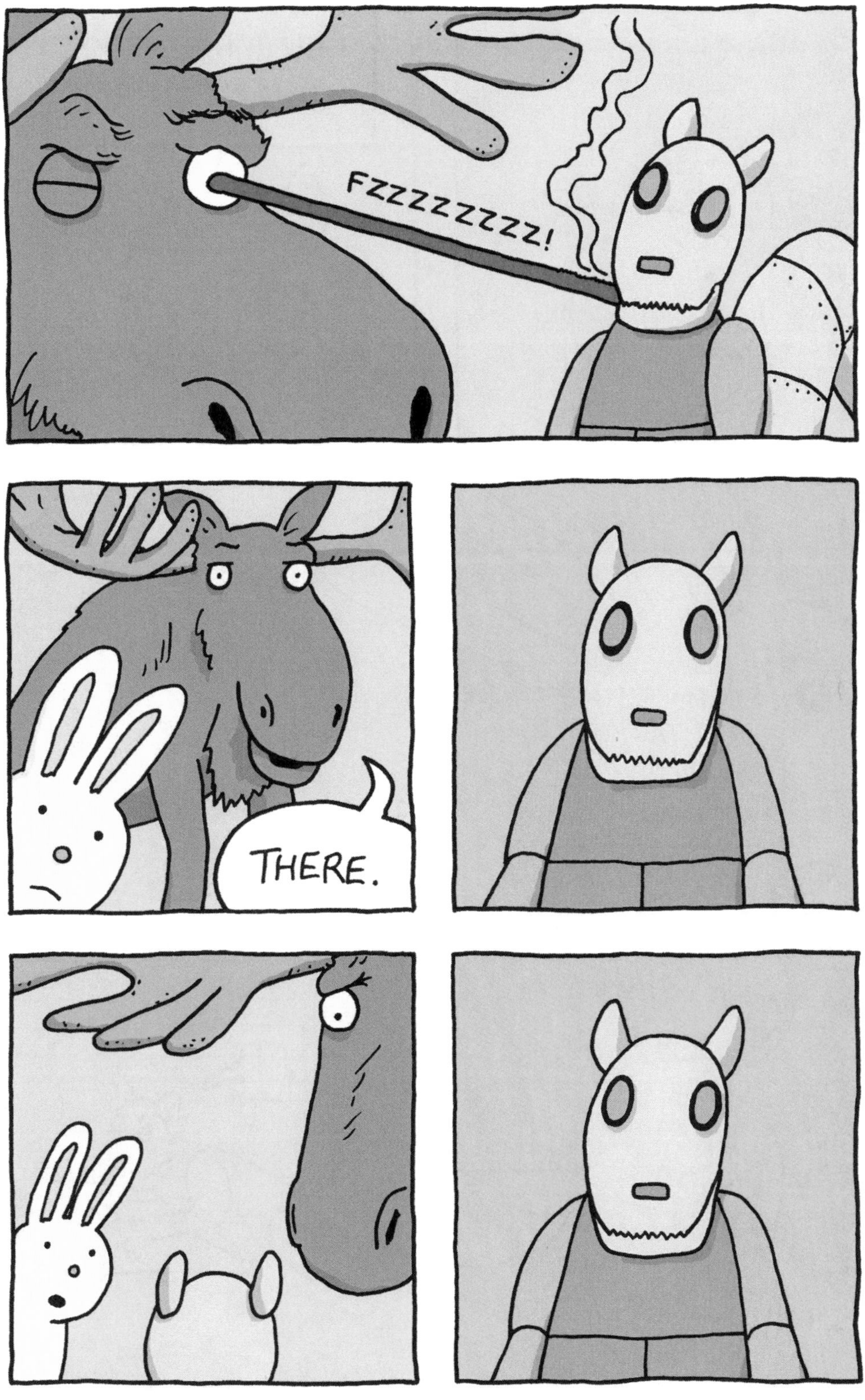
FZZZZZZZZZ!
THERE.

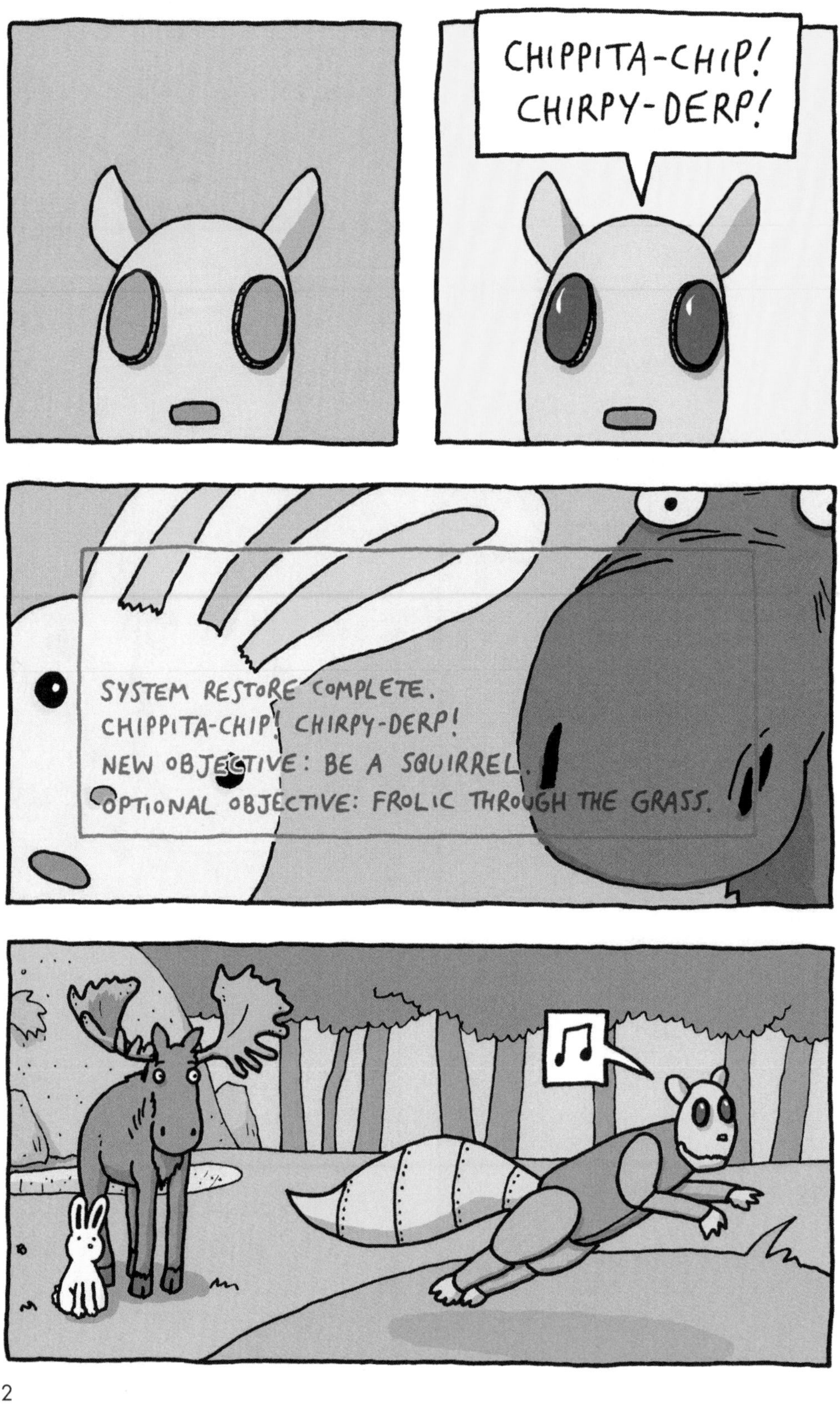
CHIPPITA-CHIP! CHIRPY-DERP!
SYSTEM RESTORE COMPLETE.
CHIPPITA-CHIP! CHIRPY-DERP!
NEW OBJECTIVE: BE A SQUIRREL.
OPTIONAL OBJECTIVE: FROLIC THROUGH THE GRASS.

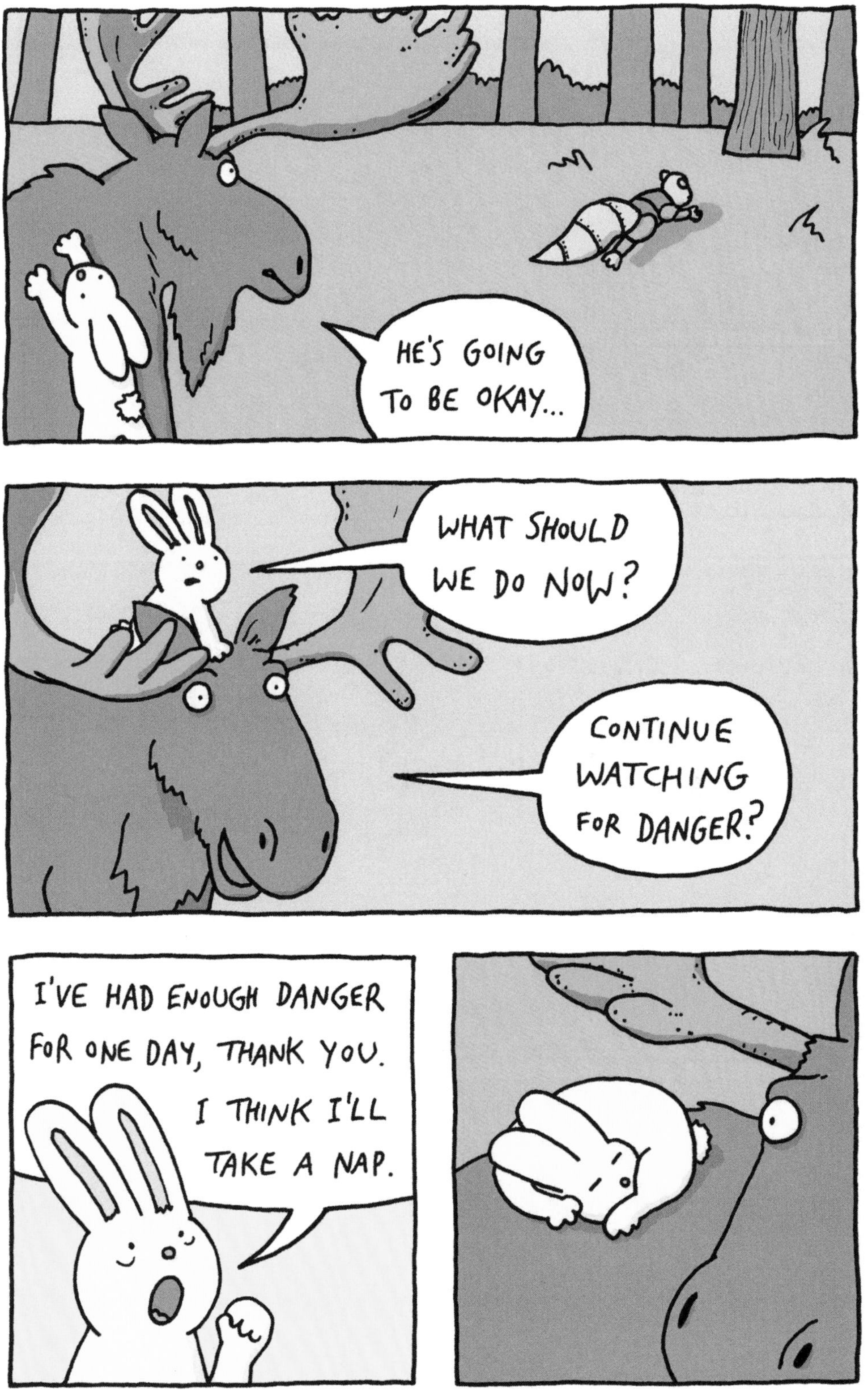
HE'S GOING TO BE OKAY...
WHAT SHOULD WE DO NOW?
CONTINUE WATCHING FOR DANGER?
I'VE HAD ENOUGH DANGER FOR ONE DAY, THANK YOU.
I THINK I'LL TAKE A NAP.

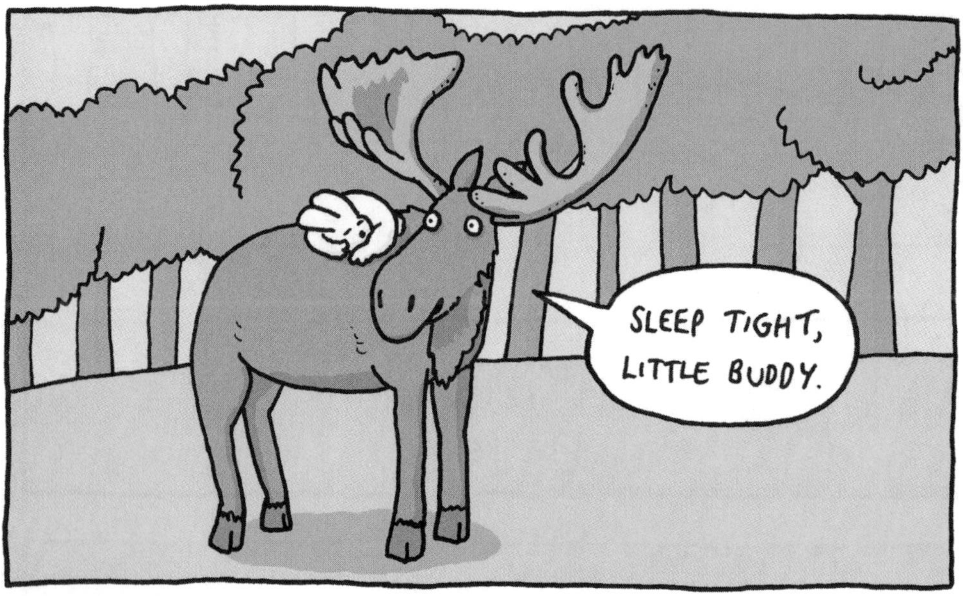
SLEEP TIGHT,
LITTLE BUDDY.

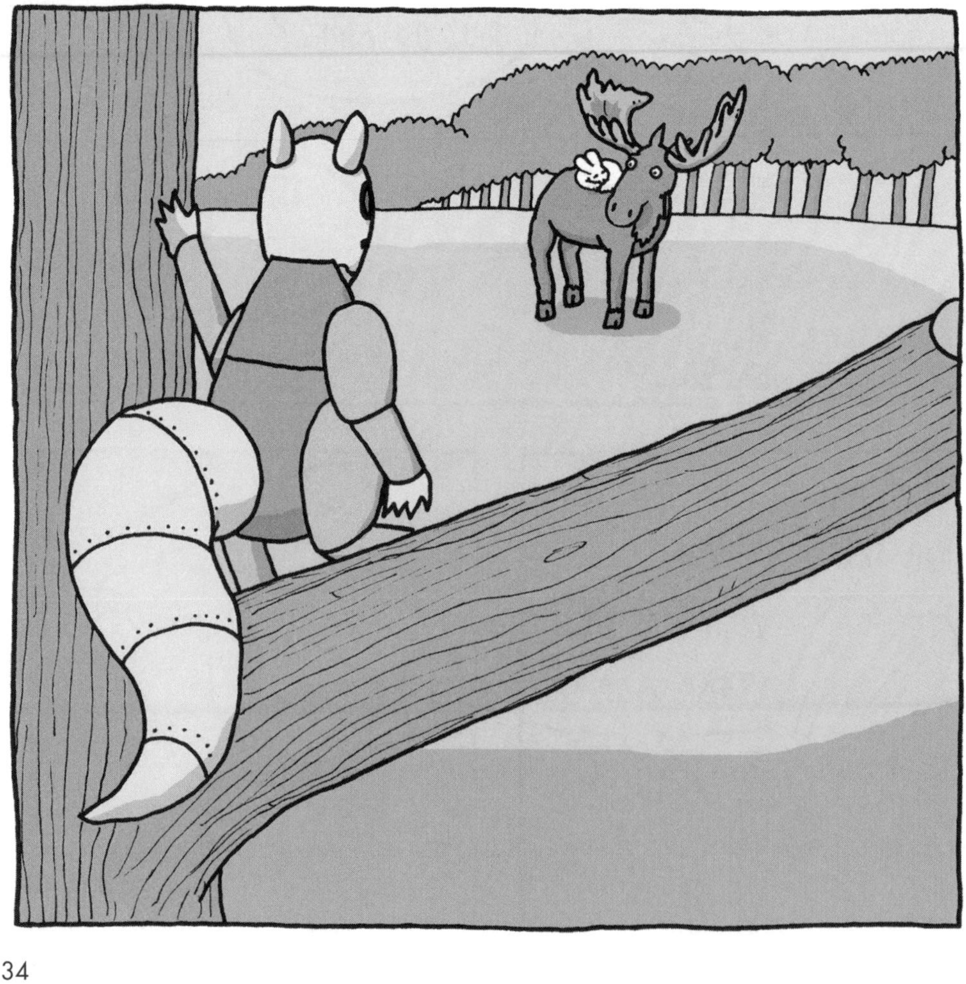

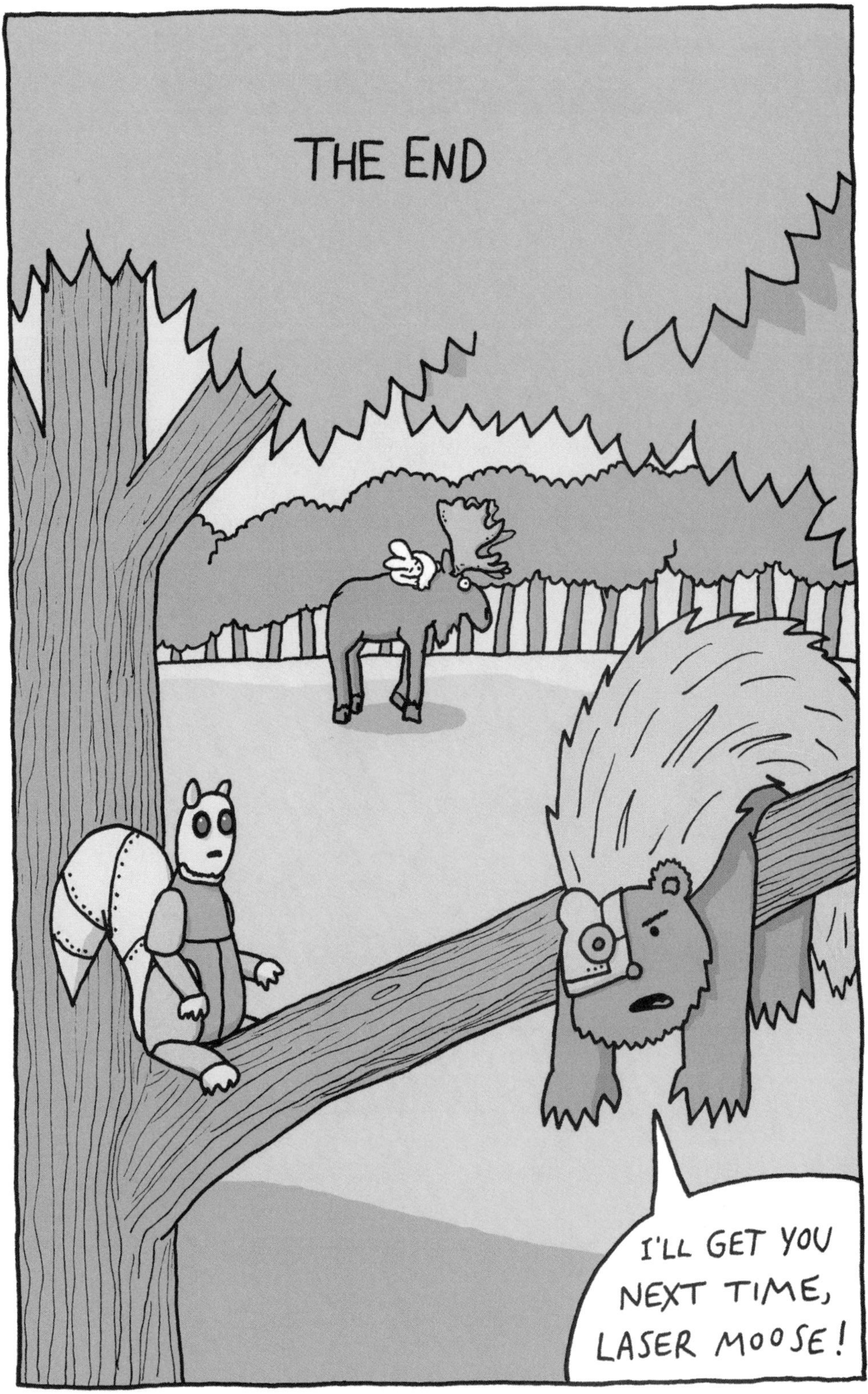
THE END
I'LL GET YOU NEXT TIME, LASER MOOSE!

MORE TO EXPLORE! Learn About LASERS!

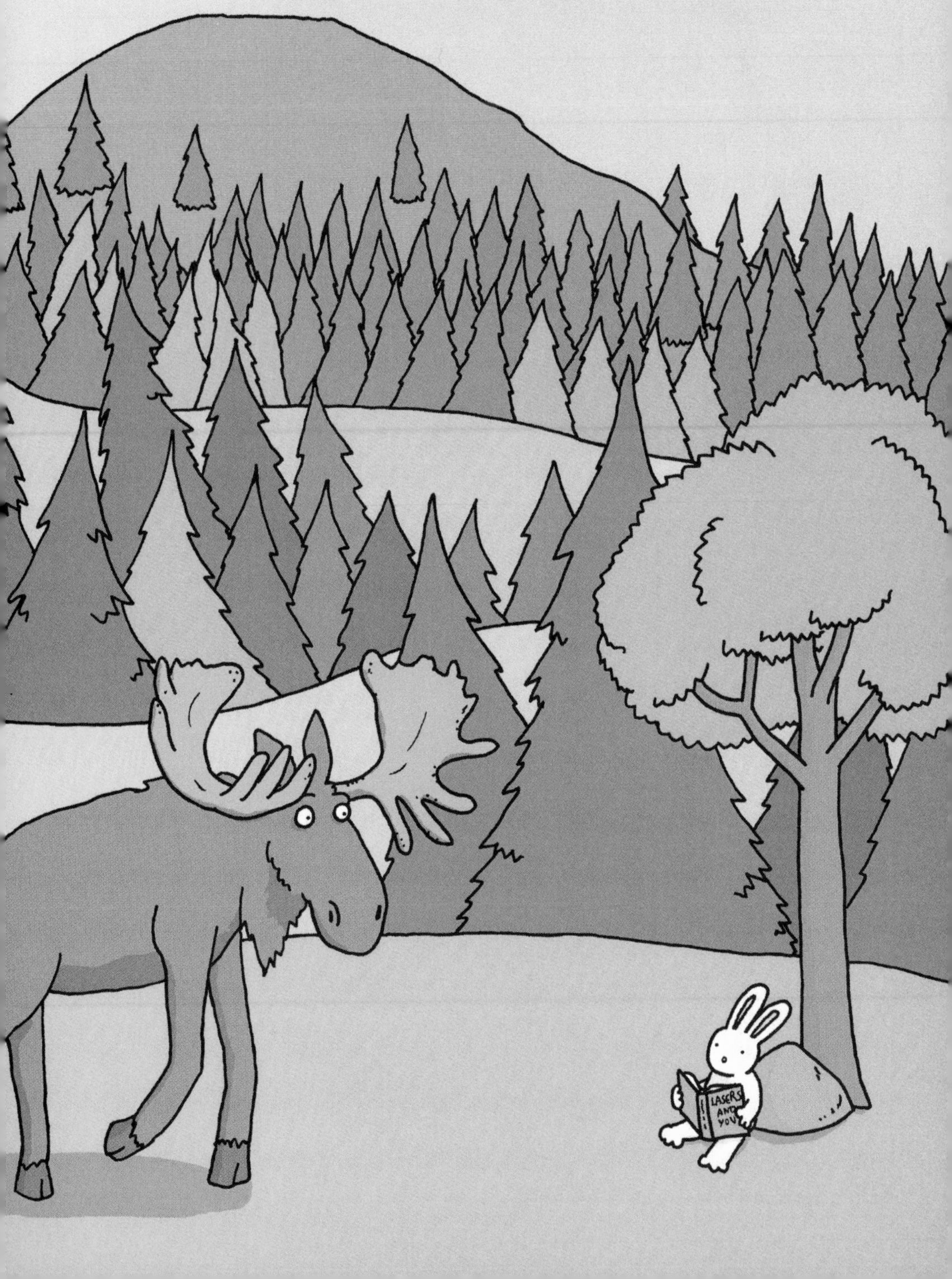
LASERS AND YOU

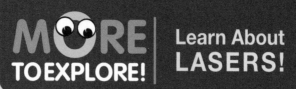

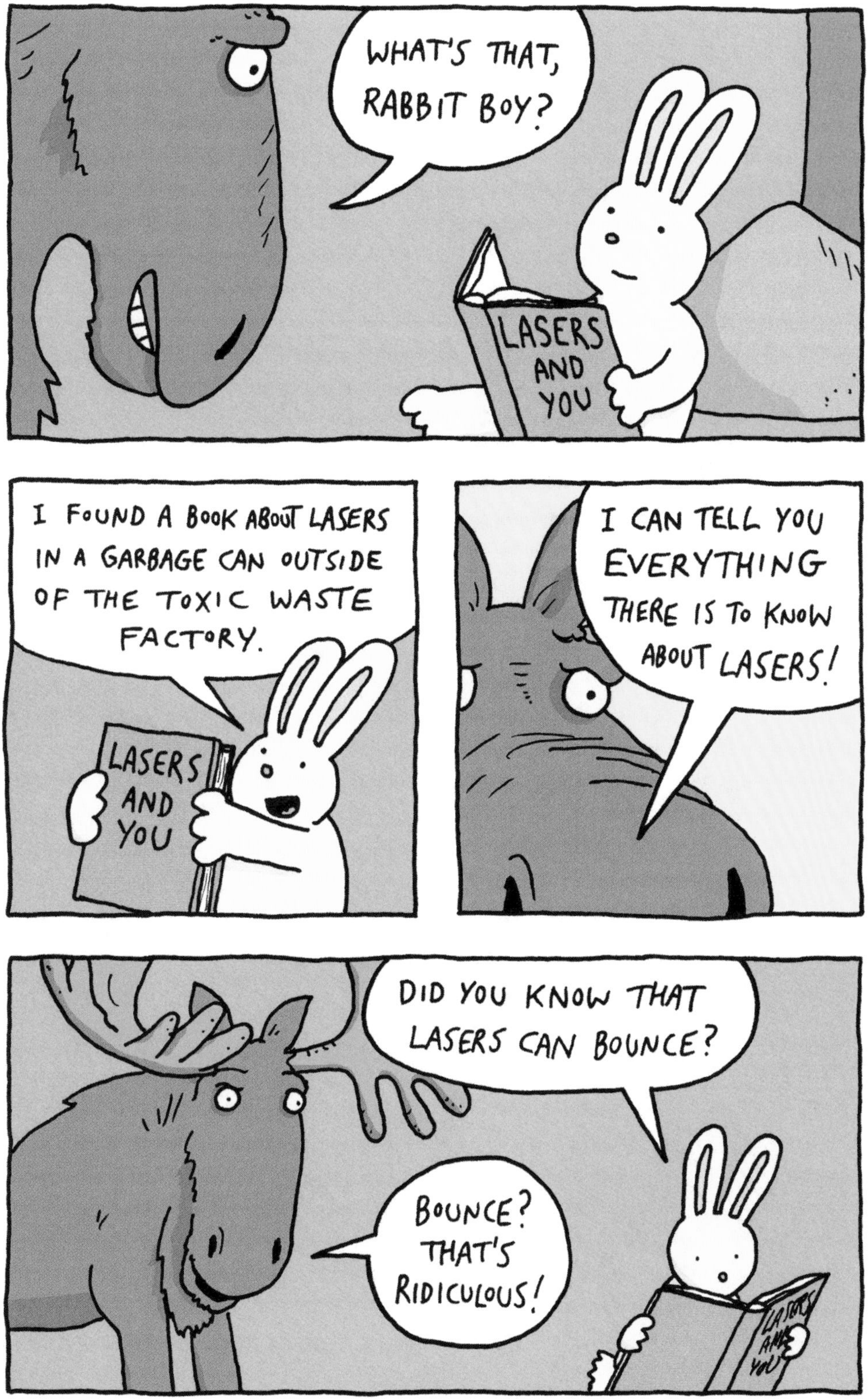
WHAT'S THAT, RABBIT BOY?
LASERS AND YOU
I FOUND A BOOK ABOUT LASERS IN A GARBAGE CAN OUTSIDE OF THE TOXIC WASTE FACTORY.
LASERS AND YOU
I CAN TELL YOU EVERYTHING THERE IS TO KNOW ABOUT LASERS!
DID YOU KNOW THAT LASERS CAN BOUNCE?
BOUNCE? THAT'S RIDICULOUS!

WELL, THEY DON'T BOUNCE, EXACTLY. THEY CAN BE REFLECTED, USING MIRRORS...

REFLECTED?

WHEN A LASER HITS A MIRROR, THIS ANGLE HERE IS CALLED "THE ANGLE OF INCIDENCE"...

THE ANGLE OF INCIDENCE

MIRROR

AND THEN IT REFLECTS OFF OF THE MIRROR AT THE SAME ANGLE, CALLED "THE ANGLE OF REFLECTION".

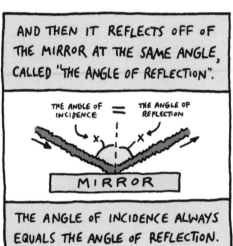

THE ANGLE OF INCIDENCE   =   THE ANGLE OF REFLECTION

X   X

MIRROR

THE ANGLE OF INCIDENCE ALWAYS EQUALS THE ANGLE OF REFLECTION.

LET'S TRY IT!

WE DON'T HAVE A MIRROR.

BUT I KNOW WHERE TO FIND ONE!

THERE'S A MIRROR ATTACHED TO THE SIDE OF CYBORGUPINE'S SECRET HIDEOUT!
TRY IT! TRY IT!
ZZZT!

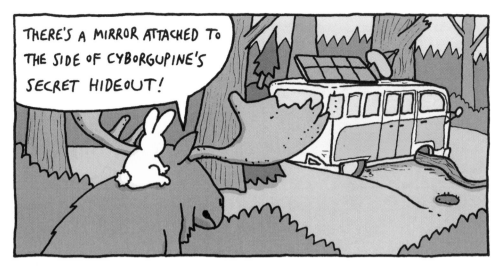

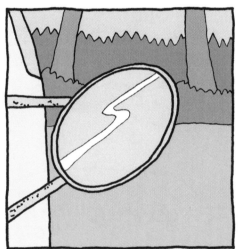

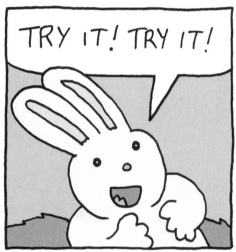

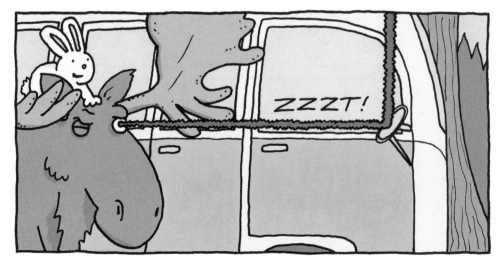

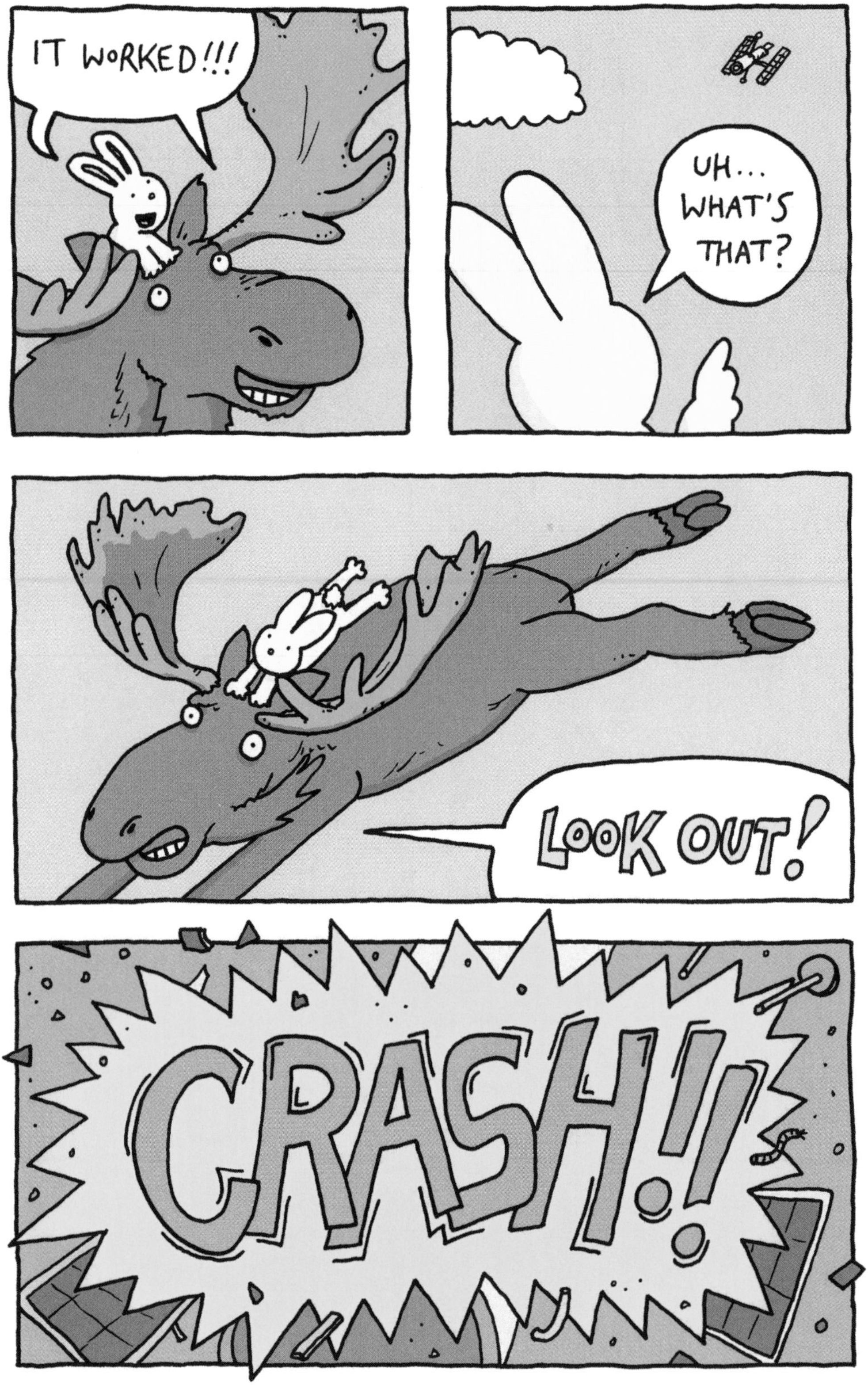
IT WORKED!!!
UH... WHAT'S THAT?
LOOK OUT!
CRASH!!

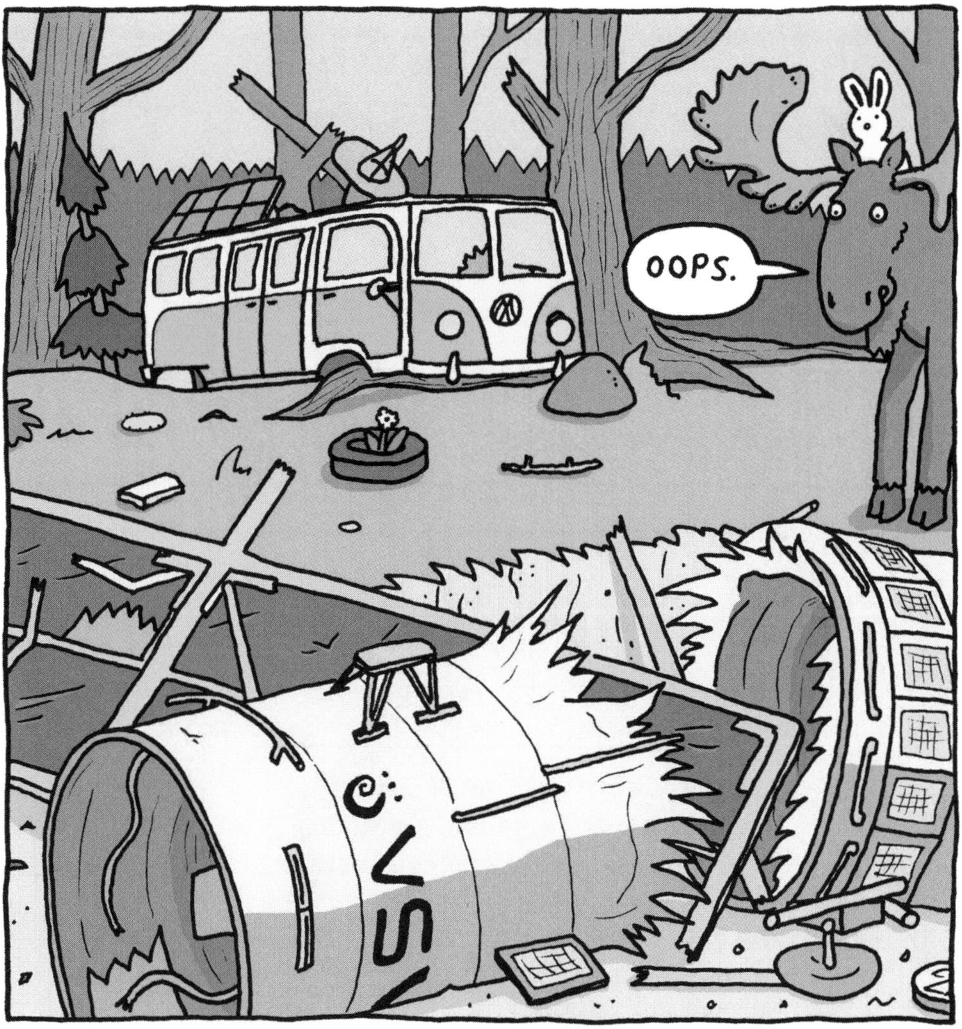
OOPS.

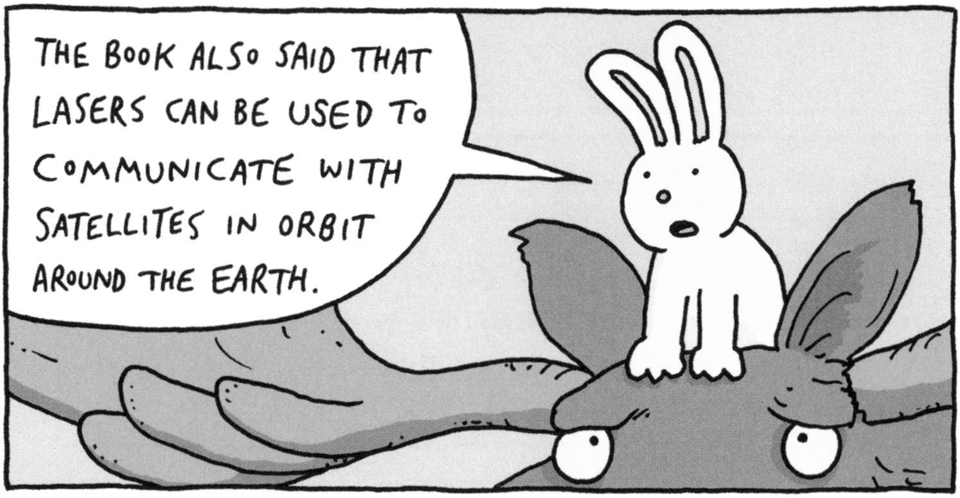
THE BOOK ALSO SAID THAT LASERS CAN BE USED TO COMMUNICATE WITH SATELLITES IN ORBIT AROUND THE EARTH.

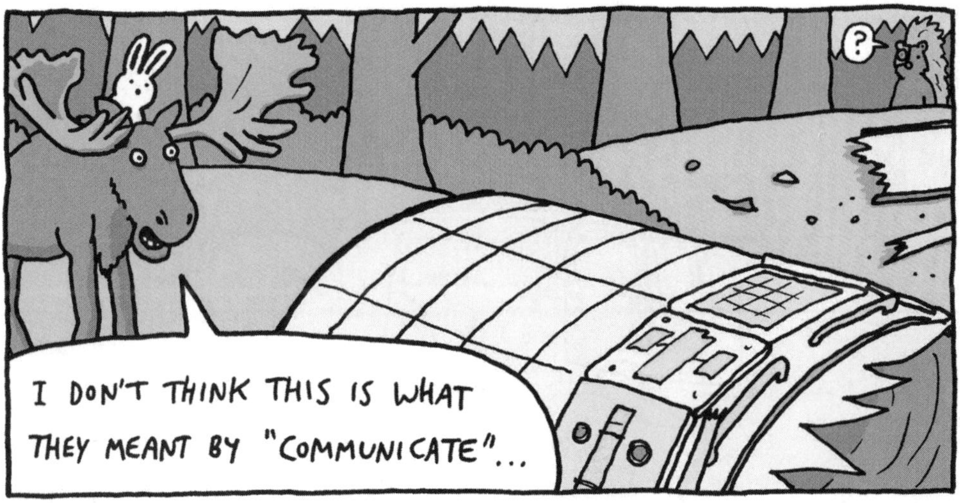
?
I DON'T THINK THIS IS WHAT THEY MEANT BY "COMMUNICATE"...

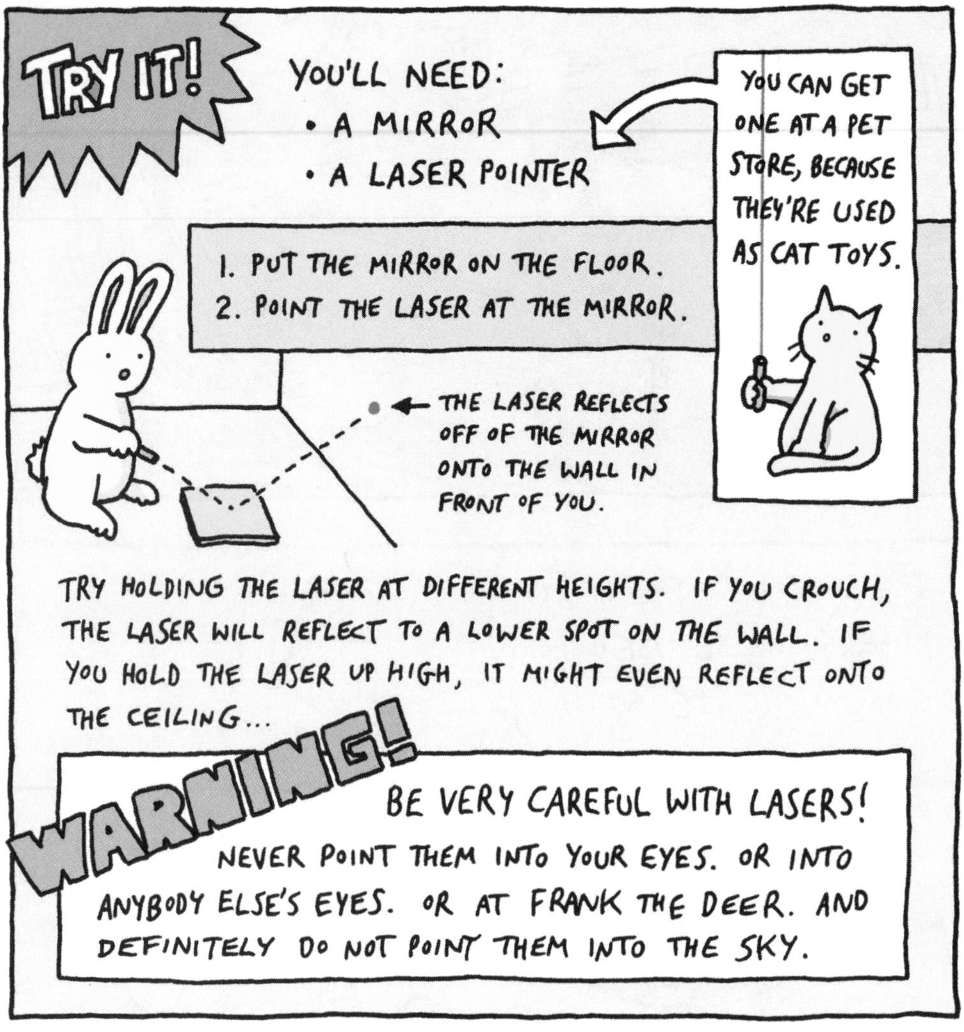
TRY IT!
YOU'LL NEED:
• A MIRROR
• A LASER POINTER
YOU CAN GET ONE AT A PET STORE, BECAUSE THEY'RE USED AS CAT TOYS.
1. PUT THE MIRROR ON THE FLOOR.
2. POINT THE LASER AT THE MIRROR.
THE LASER REFLECTS OFF OF THE MIRROR ONTO THE WALL IN FRONT OF YOU.
TRY HOLDING THE LASER AT DIFFERENT HEIGHTS. IF YOU CROUCH, THE LASER WILL REFLECT TO A LOWER SPOT ON THE WALL. IF YOU HOLD THE LASER UP HIGH, IT MIGHT EVEN REFLECT ONTO THE CEILING...
WARNING!
BE VERY CAREFUL WITH LASERS!
NEVER POINT THEM INTO YOUR EYES. OR INTO ANYBODY ELSE'S EYES. OR AT FRANK THE DEER. AND DEFINITELY DO NOT POINT THEM INTO THE SKY.

Andrews McMeel Publishing
a division of Andrews McMeel Universal
1130 Walnut Street, Kansas City, Missouri 64106

www.andrewsmcmeel.com
www.lasermooseandrabbitboy.com

18 19 20 21 22 RR2 10 9 8 7 6 5 4

ISBN: 978-1-4494-7094-4

Library of Congress Control Number: 2015959219

Made by:
LSC Communications US, LLC
Address and place of production:
1009 Sloan Street
Crawfordsville, IN 47933
4th Printing – 4/9/18

Editor: Jean Z. Lucas
Designer: Julie Barnes
Art Director: Julie Barnes
Color Assistance: J.L. Martin
Production Manager: Chuck Harper
Production Editor: Grace Bornhoft
Demand Planner: Sue Eikos

ATTENTION: SCHOOLS AND BUSINESSES
Andrews McMeel books are available at quantity discounts with bulk
purchase for educational, business, or sales promotional use. For information,
please e-mail the Andrews McMeel Publishing Special Sales Department:
specialsales@amuniversal.com.

Check out these and other books at
ampkids.com

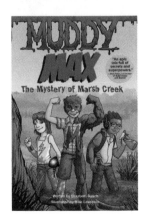

Also available:
Teaching and activity guides for each title.
AMP! Comics for Kids books make reading FUN!